Praise for
*Boo Who*

"Two weddings that might or might not take place, a gown four sizes too small, plans for one of the brides-to-be to become the new Martha Stewart, a town on the verge of bankruptcy—and just what's up with those owls? Rene Gutteridge has done it again! Just as she did in *Boo,* Rene takes the quirky, yet quite likeable, characters of Skary, Indiana, adds some even quirkier plot twists, tosses in some pop culture references, and mixes it all together for a fun read. *Boo Who* is definitely a good thing."

—NANCY KENNEDY, author of *Move Over, Victoria—
I Know the Real Secret* and *When He Doesn't Believe*

"What a funny, happy, redemptive book. It was a joy to immerse myself in the town of Skary, Indiana, with its quirky, lovable, but very real people. I hope to make many more visits to Skary!"

—LINDA HALL, author of *Steal Away* and *Chat Room*

"*Boo Who* was a one-sitting read that kept me riveted with its stunning characterization. Rene Gutteridge's tightly-written novel wrapped humor, mystery, and romance into a sumptuous feast I couldn't put down."

—KRISTIN BILLERBECK, author of *What a Girl Wants*
and *She's Out of Control*

# BOO WHO

A NOVEL

# RENE GUTTERIDGE

WATERBROOK
PRESS

Boo Who
Published by WaterBrook Press
2375 Telstar Drive, Suite 160
Colorado Springs, Colorado 80920
*A division of Random House, Inc.*

ISBN 1-57856-985-0

Published in association with the literary agency of Janet Kobobel Grant, Books & Such, 4788 Carissa Avenue, Santa Rosa, CA 95405.

Library of Congress Cataloging-in-Publication Data

Gutteridge, Rene.
    Boo who / Rene Gutteridge.
       p. cm.
    ISBN 1-57856-985-0
    1. Horror tales—Authorship—Fiction. 2. City and town life—Fiction. 3. Indiana—Fiction. I. Title.
       PS3557.U887B664 2003
       813'.6—dc22

                                                          2004008997

Printed in the United States of America
2004—First Edition

10 9 8 7 6 5 4 3 2 1

FOR CHERI

*a true joy and encouragement in my life*

## CHAPTER 1

"STEP BACK." Tension made Garth Twyne's tone harsh and his stomach sour. Everyone in the room kept a watchful eye on his shaking hand as it wielded the knife.

The two sheriff's deputies flanking him, each with one hand on his holster, glanced at each other nervously, then obeyed. Garth noticed a trickle of sweat rolling down Deputy Kinard's temple. It glistened its way down his puffy cheek and under the fat rolls of his chin. Garth pulled at his hair and looked at the knife he was holding. Barely holding. His limbs shook as badly as if he were on a date. And now he had a sudden urge to go to the bathroom. What timing.

"Why don't you set that knife down," Deputy Bledsoe said.

"Why don't you shut your trap!" Garth barked.

Both deputies gasped then swallowed down the air.

"Look, let's just all settle down here," Kinard said.

Hyperventilation declared its warning in the center of Garth's lungs. This was not a good sign. He'd performed a lot of different operations under a lot of different kinds of stress, but this was just absurd.

"Can't you two put your guns somewhere else?" he growled. "What are you going to do, shoot me?"

Bledsoe snorted. "We're just following the sheriff's orders, Garth. Besides, they're not even loaded."

Garth shot a skeptical glance to Kinard, who shrugged and said, "It's Skary, Indiana, for crying out loud. The only thing we'd need a bullet for is to kill a snake."

"I know a few of those," Bledsoe chuckled. His smile faded when he glanced at Garth and then the very real knife he was holding. "Anyway, what's the problem here?"

"The problem," Garth seethed, "is that this is a delicate procedure, and it's a little freaky having two men with guns breathing down my back."

"And add the fact that you'll probably be thrown in jail if you botch this thing again."

It was true, he'd botched it years before and then let the sheriff believe his cat was neutered, hence creating the cat crisis in town. No thanks to old Missy Peeple, who had exposed the scandal, he now was having to reperform the operation. At gunpoint.

"Quiet, Bledsoe," Kinard said. "Garth, just do what you need to do. We're just here to, um, supervise…make sure it's done right."

Garth gripped the knife, clenched his teeth, and swallowed. By the sheet-white expressions on their faces, he knew Bledsoe and Kinard probably didn't have the stomach to handle this. Skary's bravest, huh? They should step into his shoes for a day.

Kinard let out a gentle sigh. "That cat is a legend."

"A feline's feline," Bledsoe said with a salute. "A real lady's man. I could probably use some pointers from that guy. I haven't had a date in a year."

"All right," Garth sighed. "Let's just get this over with."

"Just remember, you kill this cat and you'll have to face the sheriff," Bledsoe said. "That cat is like a child to him."

All three men glanced down at the cat slumbering peacefully on the cold, metal table. This was a hard sight for any man to witness. Garth was about to make his first incision when Bledsoe stepped away from the table and toward the only window in the room, opened slightly to relieve the humidity that had suddenly formed when these two men first announced they'd be joining Garth for the operation. Outside the day was gray and sputtering a mix of snow and rain. It was as if the earth mourned for its most notorious cat.

"I can't watch," Bledsoe whispered.

Garth tried to concentrate on the task at hand. The knife still shook, but he wasn't about to delay any longer. He remembered quite well when, not long ago, this cat looked dead to the world, then suddenly came alive without a moment's warning. And this time the feline hadn't gone under without a fight, either. He'd scratched the daylights out of the vet twice. Thief knew his time carousing in the streets of Skary, Indiana, was about to be over.

"You've had a good life," Garth murmured. He hated cats. Always had. Besides an aggravating allergy to them that brought hives to his skin and water to his eyes, they were snobs. All of them. Always thought they were better than everyone else. Tails high in the air. Noses turned up. Eyes that always looked as though they were bored to tears at the thought of spending another second around you. Yet needy. So stinkin' needy. But as much as he hated cats, he couldn't help feeling a bit of remorse for this poor fool, who had single-handedly populated the town with his off-spring. Thief had even inspired a book by their town's celebrity horror writer, Wolfe Boone. If only Garth's life could be so exciting.

He glanced over his shoulder. Kinard had turned away, too, and was staring at the table of instruments that glinted in the room's fluorescent lights. A satisfied smirk formed on Garth's face, and finally his hand stopped shaking.

He looked back once more, and now both men peered out the window. He began the operation.

After a few moments, Bledsoe said. "Hmm."

"What?" Kinard asked.

"Look. There. In this tree next to the window."

"What? I don't see anything."

"See? Near the top. It's an owl."

"An owl? Oh, I do see it," Kinard said. "You know, I can't remember ever seeing an owl in these parts."

"Come on, give us a little hoot. Come on! Come on, little owl," said Bledsoe.

"Bledsoe, you sound like a moron," Kinard said. He turned back toward the vet. "Garth, how's it going over there?"

"You want to come and look?"

"No. No, um. Just keep it up, whatever you're doing."

Garth rolled his eyes as Bledsoe continued to call to the owl as if it were a one-year-old. "Hewwo, wittle owl. Hewwo. Gimme a hoot. C'mon. Gimme a hoot."

This continued for several more agonizing seconds until finally Garth stopped what he was doing and said, "Bledsoe! Knock it off! Owls only hoot at night or early morning."

"Oh." Bledsoe turned back around and observed the owl. The room was silent for several minutes, allowing for the concentration Garth needed to get it right this time. At last he set his instruments down, wiped his forehead, and was about to pronounce the operation a success when the silence was undone by a single sound, coming from outside the window.

*"Whooo."*

## CHAPTER 2

"WOLFE! TOP OF THE MORNING to you!" Wolfe smiled as Oliver Stepa-phanolopolis greeted him with a larger-than-life hug, followed by a good country slap on the arm, then checked his watch. "Right on time, my friend. That's what I like in my employees!"

Wolfe looked around. By "employees," he thought Oliver must mean Virginia, the receptionist, accountant, secretary, and backup car salesman who usually sat in a back office somewhere unless she was needed out on the "showroom floor," which Oliver had explained cur-rently was the first twenty feet of concrete out in front of the building. He hoped someday soon to build a real one, if business kept up.

In the far corner of the small reception area was a three-foot-high Christmas tree, lights dangling haphazardly from its sorry-looking branches. A Rudolph the Red-Nosed Reindeer clock with a blinking nose hung on a nearby wall, and underneath it on a small table rested a porcelain Nativity set. It appeared Joseph was missing an arm.

Oliver, grinning from ear to ear, now offered a solid and pudgy hand for him to shake, which Wolfe did. "Well," Oliver said as he looked out the front window of the building, "looks like we have a break in our usual stream of customers, so let's go back to my office, and I'll get you acquainted with the world of used car sales."

Wolfe followed him down a small, smoky hallway, which was strange because Oliver didn't smoke and Virginia was on the other side of the building. His office was a perfect box, but with a window, though the view was of the scrap yard across the street. Wolfe was amused that the stereotypical used-car salesman clutter was nowhere to be seen. Instead, the office was quite neat. On the walls hung cheap framed prints of various sports cars, and a strange-looking silk tree leaned into one corner instead of standing straight up, but overall the office was pleasing to the senses. Wolfe even thought he smelled a hint of vanilla.

Oliver offered him the vinyl seat on the other side of his desk, and then sat down across from him, scooting some neatly stacked folders to the left and pulling out a notebook.

"Now, Wolfe," he began, "I just want to make sure this is what you want. I mean, this is going to be quite a different kind of day than you're used to. I imagine your mornings start with a lazy cup of coffee and a half an hour in front of your window thinking out some creepy new story line. Things can get rather hectic here. Especially during car-buying season."

"When's car-buying season?"

"Well, anytime people's cars start breaking down."

"Oh." Wolfe had been energetic about the idea of finding a new career. But ideas and reality, as he was well aware from his former profession, can be worlds apart. It had been a good "idea" to work selling cars. However, dread—the very kind he loved to build into the plots of his books—now stalked him as fiercely as one of his famous villains.

Oliver prattled on. "So anyway, I have to say I was a little shocked when you answered the ad for a salesman position here."

It had only been a little over a month since Wolfe had been found facedown in the snowy forest near his home, on the brink of death. And just over four weeks since he'd asked Ainsley Marie Parker to marry him, the best day of his whole life.

Since then he'd tried day after day to write something. Nothing would come. Not even a poem. And then one snowy evening, when Ainsley had drifted off into a light slumber on the couch in front of the fireplace, Wolfe had an unbelievable urge to be ordinary, common, an average Joe. He'd lived years being a celebrity, giving interviews, collecting awards, attending writers' conferences and book signings. But he'd also lived years being alone. Now he felt a part of a community, he had friends, and people looked at him like he was one of them. He wanted that feeling to continue, and although he didn't need the income, he knew the best way to be normal was to do what everyone else did…get a normal job.

"I'm nervous," Wolfe admitted, shifting his attention to Oliver's eager face.

Oliver nodded. "I can show you the ropes, my friend. I've always wanted to mentor another salesman, but I never had a big enough business to hire anyone but me and Virginia."

"Are you sure I'm the salesman type?"

"We don't hire sharks here," Oliver said. "And we're no clip joint."

"Clip joint?"

"That's a dealership that has a reputation for overcharging. Good example is Ron's Car Lot, about fifteen miles east of County Line. Sure, we hammer the customers some—"

"Hammer?"

"It means put pressure on a customer to buy a vehicle. But it's always done in good taste."

"Okay."

"And we're a reputable car dealership. I won't lie. We've got some Tin Lizzies out there. What dealership doesn't? But we'd never sell a sled or even put it on the lot. And I've had some customers trade in some crop-dusters complete with a set of baldinis. But just one look and you know that we've got a lot full of cream puffs ready to bring in the long green." Oliver smiled.

"I have no idea what you just said."

"It takes a while." Oliver stood and went to the wall nearest Wolfe. A large white poster board hung by string around a tack. "It's a secret language."

"A secret language?"

"All car salesmen must learn it. It's how we communicate with one another." Oliver flipped over the poster, and handwritten in black marker was a list titled *The Secret Code Language*. Wolfe scanned the vocabulary list.

*Tin Lizzie—a very old vehicle*
*sled—a slow, cumbersome, and worthless vehicle*
*baldinis—bald tires*
*crop-duster—a car that blows smoke out the tailpipe*
*cream puff—a used car in excellent condition*
*long green—money*

The list went on and on. Wolfe felt his eyes grow wide. Oliver patted him on the shoulder. "Don't be afraid," he said. "It takes a while to learn these. That'll be your homework over the holidays. I want you to go home, memorize the list, and come back after Christmas able to say one whole sentence using five of these words."

Wolfe shook his head. "When do we learn the secret handshake?"

"Don't jump ahead, buddy. You've got quite enough to learn for now."

"Oh! Oh! Oh oh oh!"

The haughty and thin saleswoman, whose features all ended at some sort of sharp angle, gasped and stepped back a few inches. "What?"

"This one," Melb Cornforth said, stroking the silk, rubbing the lace between her fingers. "This one."

The saleswoman's left eyebrow popped up in question, creating a perfect triangle above her small eye. "Um…"

"It's just gorgeous. I'd look like a princess in this one." Tears welled in Melb's eyes. A princess. That's what she had become since Oliver had proposed to her. She whirled toward the mirror, holding the white dress in front of her. The sleeves poofed as if baby cherubim were holding up the material just for her. The gown flowed like a river, reflecting the light of what was sure to be a thousand candles lining the moonlit path she would walk down in her glass slippers. Oliver would be at the end of that path, hair slicked back on the sides, just the way she liked it. She glanced at the dress again in the mirror. Her wedding was going to be perfect.

And then she saw it, dangling from the arm of the dress, twirling in the draft of the room. The price tag. Her face flushed with anxiety. She had a budget. She knew the number in her head. She'd said it out loud five times before she left, making an oath to herself as she placed her checkbook next to her Bible. She. Would. Not. Go. O. Ver. Buh. Dget.

But. This. Was. The. Per. Fect. Gown.

No! Budget. No! Budget.

No budget. No budget. No budget.

She flung the dress away from her the way a Southern belle might push away a suitor. It landed in a heap on the ground. The saleswoman gasped and ran to the dress's aid. Scowling, she looked up at Melb and lifted the gown off the ground. Then Melb saw it. The price, doubly underlined: $3,000. She burst into tears.

"What's wrong?" the saleswoman asked, her tone curt with annoyance. "First you throw this dress on the ground and now you're crying?"

But she couldn't stop crying. This was the dress she wanted. This was what she'd dreamed of walking down the aisle, the sidewalk, the beach, the hotel lobby in for her whole life. But she could not afford three thousand dollars. Oliver had outlined their budget—*theirs* because now they were a couple soon to be on the same budget together—and stressed the absolute discipline required to withstand the temptation of spending more than allotted.

A hand tapped her back. "There, there."

Melb glanced at herself in the mirror. Black mascara caked her cheeks in perfectly even stripes from her eyes down to the corners of her mouth.

"Maybe he's not the one for you."

Melb cut her eyes sideways at the woman.

"It's just that you don't seem very happy about getting married."

"I'm ecstatic," she said, tears bubbling from the rims of her eyes. "It's just, that, well, this dress is everything I ever dreamed of. But…I can't afford three thousand dollars."

The woman's edgy expression softened as she glanced down at the dress. "Didn't you get it off that rack in the corner?" Melb nodded. "Well," the woman said, "that's our clearance rack."

She stopped in midsniffle. "Clearance, you say?"

The woman smiled for the first time since Melb had stepped into her uppity little dress shop. "Seventy-five percent off."

Melb was trying to do the numbers in her head, but couldn't quite carry the one and remember where to add the zero.

"How does $750 sound?" the woman asked.

"I'll take it!" she exclaimed, squeezing the dress with all her might. Every part of this dress was puffy, from the sleeves to the waist to the bow on the back.

The woman nodded. "That dress must've been waiting for just the right customer."

"Really? Why do you say that?"

"We've had it in the store since 1989."

"Well your *mama* has *arrived!*" Melb shouted, and then did a little dance like those she'd seen Pentecostals do. She'd always wanted to dance in church like that and shout to the Lord. But instead she was raised to believe that dancing was bad and that complete silence in church was preferred over shouting.

"And here's the veil," she said, handing Melb a headband. Melb put it on and looked into the mirror.

Her first impression was that she looked an awful lot like John McEnroe in his early tennis days when sweatbands were all the rage. But then her eyes caught the tulle flowing down her back like the hair of Rapunzel. She was a princess.

"Perfect."

The woman said, "Let me show you the dressing room where you can try it on."

"No need. Destiny brought this dress to me."

"But…it's a size ten."

"I'm going to shed a few pounds before the wedding, don't worry."

"But—"

"And I know these kinds of dresses always run big anyway," Melb said with a wink. The woman didn't wink back.

"But—"

"And I've got a girdle."

The woman said nothing more, but by the somber expression on her face, she knew the woman had her doubts. Yet Melb had no doubts whatsoever. After all, the dress had been waiting for her since 1989.

The woman cordially handed her the receipt and asked, "When is your wedding?"

"Valentine's Day. Isn't that just perfect?"

"Best wishes." The saleswoman handed her a sleek gray dress bag and nodded in dismissal.

Melb swung the dress over her shoulder and sauntered out of the store with unspeakable joy, practically prancing with each step. The perfect dress.

And only $550 over budget. Oliver would understand.

## CHAPTER 3

"ORDER! ORDER, PEOPLE!"

A dozen people stood in the community center, shivering beneath their coats because nobody knew how to turn the heat on. They now glanced in the speaker's direction as if they had just noticed she was behind the podium.

"Come now, we don't have rabies. Let's scoot together a little bit."

The small crowd glanced at one another and scooted a few chairs inward, still looking sparse among all the shiny silver chairs that lined the community center conference room in perfectly neat rows.

Missy Peeple would not allow herself to feel it, but inside she knew disappointment threatened like a bad case of heartburn. This was by far the smallest crowd ever to attend a meeting she called. No thanks to the Thanksgiving Scandal, as it was now known, she'd lost credibility within the town that she'd loved so much. When she passed townspeople on the street, they scowled at her now instead of nodding with the respect to which she had been accustomed.

Still, she would not be deterred. She had a vision for this town. She knew it would work. In fact, she'd bet her whole life savings on it just a little over two weeks ago. It had cost her nearly everything she owned, but she knew it would work. It had to.

The glum faces that stared back at her needed inspiration, and she was here to give it to them. She made herself stand tall, pushing her back straight as she held onto her cane.

"I've called this meeting today," she began, "to give you hope. As I'm sure all of you have noticed, our town has changed. Thanks to Wolfe

Boone, who has decided he no longer feels responsible for what happens to our beloved town, we will no longer be known as we were before. But do not fear!" She raised her hand over her head and pointed a knobby index finger skyward. A few people looked up, thinking she was pointing at something. "We will be known! Skary, Indiana, will not be a nothing town with nobody people. We will not sink back into obscurity. Do you hear me? We will continue to be famous. I will see to that."

"How?" came a voice near the back.

"I have already made a way. Because, my friends, I am smart and determined. And I always have a plan." She smiled and blinked slowly like the town matron that she was.

"Well, if we're not known for Boo, who will we be known for?" asked another voice.

"First of all, let's kill the pet names, shall we? Wolfe Boone no longer cares about this town, and saying his name with affection, like he means something to us, is just a sad reminder of what he's done. Secondly, you ask, what shall we be known for? Well, that is my surprise. That is why I am here. To make this very special announcement. From this day forth, Skary, Indiana's claim to fame will come from…drumroll, please…"

The crowd exchanged glances, and then two or three people timidly beat their hands against their knees.

"*Cats!*" Missy closed her eyes, anticipating cheers from the crowd. Instead she heard at least one hiccup and then mumbling. She opened her eyes to find the crowd looking at one another. "I said…*cats!*" But still, enthusiasm came only in the form of sporadic hiccuping.

Then someone said, "I don't get it."

"What's not to get?" she asked, her eyes narrowing on a younger man who looked like a farmer.

"I don't get how cats tie into the name Skary. I mean, it worked with Boo…Wolfe, I mean…because he wrote scary novels and it was this great play-on-words thing. But why would anybody come to Indiana to see a town full of cats?"

"*Because,*" she said wistfully, "we offer them incentive. We have a theme. All our stores cater to the cat lover. I've got more ideas than I could possibly share today, but I'm telling you this could work. We've got more cats in this town than we know what to do with. Why not use it to our advantage?"

But the crowd sat silent, staring at her as if she'd lost her mind. For the first time in all her life, Missy Peeple felt inferior. But only for a fleeting moment. Then she said, "Well, let's have a show of hands of who thinks this would be a good direction to take for our little town?"

One person raised his hand, and Missy saw he was their resident homeless person, Mac something-or-other, who tended to hang around Skary near the holidays because he knew people were generous when they felt guilty for just having spent two hundred dollars on Christmas lights for their home.

"Meeting adjourned," Missy spat, hobbled down from the platform, and exited through a side door. Outside the day was bright. The eve of Christmas Eve. The streets bustled with last-minute shoppers, darting in and out of stores at a steady pace. Nobody noticed her. They were too busy with their own pathetic lives.

Missy passed by Sbooky's, now only Booky's. The *S* had been taken down four days after Thanksgiving, but you could still see where it had once been. The Haunted Mansion restaurant was now known only as The Mansion. The little town that had rested in the comfort of its fame now sat on the brink of extinction. Every Christmas before, these streets had been filled with tourists. Now only townspeople.

Their faces even seemed cheery. Why did everyone get cheery around Christmas? What was there to cheer about? Annoying lights. Carolers who couldn't carry a tune. Kids wiping their snotty noses while they whined about what kinds of toys they wanted even though they had more things to do than the prime minister of England.

A jovial woman offered a smile as she passed Missy, apparently not recognizing her as the center of the Thanksgiving Scandal. Missy offered a frightful frown back and kept moving. She just wanted to get home.

Finally, five blocks later, she made it, her limbs tingling and shaky. She stopped to grumble about her neighbor's lights. The blinking kind.

Why must someone put blinking lights on their house if they must put them on at all? For two whole weeks she must endure the whole night's sky blinking while she was trying to sleep.

And to top off the annoyance, Mr. Turner had a Christmas tree in his front window whose lights also blinked, but out of unison with his house lights. For Missy Peeple it represented exactly what Christmas was…a mad, chaotic mess of electrically fed cheer.

She turned to walk up her porch steps and into her house. Once inside, she threw her coat aside and found her favorite quilt, tucking it over her legs and underneath her as she sat down to rest in her rocking chair.

So the town had not caught her vision for trapping tourists by way of cats. But they soon would. Already she had taken necessary steps to insure it would happen.

She's used her life savings to place a full-sized ad in two national newspapers that Skary, Indiana, was the most famous cat town in the world.

She couldn't wait to see the droves of people who would soon be crowding the streets.

"Come in!" Ainsley beamed, embracing Wolfe before he could even get in her doorway. She kissed him and then pulled at his coat playfully.

"My little elf," he joked, looking around the house. "The decorations look terrific."

Ainsley grinned. She'd been working on them all day, putting the finishing touches on the house before Christmas arrived. She couldn't believe she was going to get to spend Christmas as the soon-to-be wife of this extraordinary man. Every day she knew him she grew more and more in love, which she didn't think was possible. "Let me take your coat," she said, sliding it off his broad shoulders.

He followed her into the kitchen where she was getting ready to put three small legs of lamb into the oven for dinner. As he slid onto a bar stool at the kitchen counter, she asked, "So how was your first day of work?"

He laughed. "Interesting."

Her mood shifted. "Wolfe, are you sure this is what you should be doing? Writing is in your blood. It's all you've ever known. Do you think you can turn the switch off just like that? It's not like you have to work, you know."

"True." He sighed. "But for now I'm seeing what God has for me. I know there's something if I can just find it, you know?"

She squeezed his hand and smiled. "Well, did you learn how to sell a car today?"

"Learned there's a secret language. I have homework. And tomorrow I learn the secret handshake."

She giggled. "Well, leave it to Oliver to come up with a secret handshake. Oh, I talked to Melb today! She said she found the most amazing wedding dress."

"That's good," he said. "Have they set a date yet?"

"Valentine's Day."

"That's a week before ours, isn't it?"

"Yeah, and she felt bad about that, but I told her not to worry. She'd always wanted to get married on Valentine's Day. It'll be fine. By the way, I finally composed a list of everything we still need to do before the wedding." She reached under the counter and pulled out her notebook. Wolfe's eyes grew large. She laughed and said, "Don't worry. The list is only the back three pages of this thing. This is my wedding folder. I've been putting it together since I was ten years old. It has all my dreams in it. But you can't look, because it also has the wedding dress I'm making."

"Oh...," he said, though she knew he was secretly relieved he didn't have to look through it. She patted him on the hand and started to prepare the salad. In her thoughts, she noted everything she was going to need to do tomorrow in order to get ready for Christmas. But her mind traveled back and forth between her priority of Christmas dinner and her wedding day. She had a lot to do in just a few weeks, though she'd already done so much since Thanksgiving. The day after Wolfe asked her to marry him, she'd decided on a color scheme and designed her invitations. She was right on schedule.

"So what can I do to help with the wedding plans?" he asked.

"Pick a best man and two groomsmen."

"A best man and groomsmen," he repeated, scratching his head. "Do I have to?"

"Of course. You have to have three men standing up there, or it will look unbalanced."

"Can you hire these people?"

She laughed and shook her head. "Sweetheart, this isn't hard. You can use my brother, of course. And then how about Oliver and Alfred?"

Wolfe sighed. "Alfred. I wonder what that guy's up to. I haven't heard from him since he got fired. I don't even know if he's talking to me."

"Well, he'll have to talk to you if we ask him to be in our wedding." She sliced up a carrot. "And knowing Alfred, I'm sure he's bouncing back just fine."

Alfred Tennison slouched in the ratty vinyl chair at Gate 46 at La Guardia. It seemed to take energy to breathe these days. While dragging his carry-on behind him through the massive airport (it really should just be called a city and have its own zip code), Alfred had seen five different people reading Wolfe Boone novels. In the same ball of emotion he found anger, despair, grief, and pride, all coiled together. Nobody here knew who he was. But once upon a time he was somebody big. Somebody with power. A brilliant editor. This world had not seen the last of Alfred Edgar Tennison. He had the capability to bounce back. And already, he knew how he was going to do it.

A voice announced it was time to board the plane, and a crowd of people stood up, vying for a position in line, which was absurd since the seats were assigned. Sadly, there was no first class on this plane. Even sadder, he couldn't afford it anyway.

A small woman stood beside him. She was dressed from head to toe in holiday garb. Alfred glanced twice at her and saw that her earrings were flashing like a Christmas tree and across her chest was a string of gold tinsel. *How do you wash that?* he wondered. And then prayed she wouldn't be his seatmate.

She smiled at him as he was noticing that the ends of her shoes sported Rudolph the Red-Nosed Reindeer noses. "You going home for the holidays?" she asked him a squeaky drawl. When he didn't answer, she simply continued. "I'm from Indiana, but moved to New York to live with my sister who got cancer of the thyroid. But it's always nice to return home. What parts are you from?"

Alfred shifted his eyes back to the line that dawdled along, everyone staring at the woman with three kids being frisked to the side while security went through her two diaper bags. "I'm not from Indiana."

"Oh, you'll love it. It's a lovely place. Are you planning on spending the holidays there?"

Alfred sighed. The truth of the matter was that he hardly thought about the holidays. He wasn't big on celebrating the holidays of religions he didn't practice, in particular the religion that had pretty much turned his career into a train wreck. He rubbed his eyes and ignored the woman, who huffed her way forward, something from her garb jingling like a sleighbell. "Merry Christmas to you too, you jerk," she muttered.

He rolled his eyes. He couldn't help being a scrooge. He had nothing to celebrate anyway. All he had was an insane idea. One crazy idea that had dawned in his mind at precisely 3:47 a.m. on a Tuesday morning when he was just about to pop another sleeping pill.

Trudging forward onto the plane, oblivious to the streams of holiday smiles on the flight attendants' tired faces, Alfred found his seat next to a guy who looked as if he needed a bed.

He hoped all the holiday cheer he was sure to find in Skary, Indiana, would translate into sympathy for him and a willingness to at least hear his idea.

He was just going to have to make sure Wolfe was nowhere around Ainsley when he told her his idea.

## CHAPTER 4

SHERIFF PARKER TRIED to keep his eyes on the road, but his attention continued to drift to Thief, who lay morbidly still in the passenger's seat, wrapped in a warm blanket. Garth said the anesthesia would keep him groggy into the evening. Thief's eyes blinked, but not in the lazy way that Sheriff Parker was used to. Instead, he stared dully, lifelessly. The sheriff stroked his head and tried to concentrate on just getting home. The air was icy, and the roads could be slick as evening approached.

"It's okay, boy. You just rest," he said to the cat. But Thief hardly acknowledged him. Instead he rested his chin on his paws and did nothing but stare forward.

Once home, he took great care removing the cat from the car. He swaddled him and was carrying him to the front door when he heard a strange noise.

"*Whoo. Whoo.*"

Looking high into the Eastern Red Cedar that sat at the corner of their house, he saw an amazing thing. An owl. As far as he could remember, he had never seen an owl in Skary.

"*Whoo. Whoo. Whooo.*"

"Who to you, too." The sheriff noticed the owl was looking at Thief, and he pulled the blanket over the cat. He'd heard some owls ate unattended cats, and the way Thief was feeling, he would be easy prey. "Get outta here!" he yelled at the owl, but it sat there oblivious to his threat.

Inside, Ainsley jumped up and greeted him, looking at Thief. "Dad! How'd the operation go?"

"According to Garth, it went fine. But Thief seems different."

"How so?" Wolfe asked as they came into the kitchen.

"Just…different. Garth says it's the anesthesia."

"He probably just wants to sleep it off, Dad," Ainsley said. "Why don't you put him in his bed, and we'll check on him later. Dinner's almost ready."

He nodded and took the cat upstairs to his deluxe canopy bed that sat right next to his own. He even brought his food and water bowl up from the kitchen and placed it right next to Thief. But Thief hardly raised his head. And wouldn't look at the sheriff.

Kneeling beside the cat, he said, "You'll feel better in the morning." He gave the cat one long stroke, from the top of his head to the tip of his tail, and then left. Thief's eyes were shut, and his once perky tail lay like limp rope across the bed.

Melb paced the length of her bedroom, biting at her nails and then scraping the skin off her bottom lip with her front teeth. Oliver would be arriving at her home any minute, and she was going to have to break the news to him that she'd gone slightly over budget on her dress. But surely he would see the brilliance of how much money she'd actually saved. The trick came in convincing him without showing him this glorious, three thousand dollar dress that she'd yet to try on.

Lying across her bed, the whole dress seemed swollen with anticipation of draping itself over her body. Catching a glimpse of herself in her full-length mirror, she sucked in her tummy and pulled her shoulders back. Four dress sizes. That's what she was going to have to lose to get in this gown.

Not going to be a problem.

Outside she heard a car door shut. Oliver! She quickly zipped the dress back into its case and hid it in her closet. She tossed her curls around on her head and made sure she had some lip gloss on before running to greet the man she loved. Peeking through the peephole, she could see him gathering his things out of his car.

She stared down at the small diamond ring on her finger. It was gorgeous. And she knew it had been a lot of money for Oliver. After only two weeks of dating, he'd asked her to marry him. They found out on one of only seven dates before the engagement, that both their parents had dated only two weeks before getting engaged. Exactly two weeks from the day that Oliver had professed his love for her at Thanksgiving dinner, he asked her to marry him. Her parents had been married thirty-four years. His, forty-one. All deceased now. They knew they had history on their side.

Right before Oliver reached for the doorbell, she opened the door and greeted him with a big, fat kiss on the lips. He stumbled backward but managed to hold on to her shoulders and return the kiss with enthusiasm.

"Hello, darlin'," he said in that low, sexy voice she knew he reserved for only her and a few select auto customers.

"How was work?" she asked. She knew she would never grow tired of asking the man of her dreams that question.

Inside, he explained it was Wolfe's first day. "He was on time, but I hope he's the right man for the job."

"You don't think he is?"

"Well, I'm a little worried about his work ethic."

"Why is that?"

He shrugged, munching on the dregs of a bag of Lay's chips sitting open on the counter. She had meant to throw that in the trash when she got home, but it must've slipped her mind.

"Oh, you know. He was a writer. I'm not sure they understand eight-to-five. I just don't know if he has the ability to work hard."

She leaned on the counter, eying the bag of chips but trying to keep her concentration on Oliver. "Honey, I think the man knows how to work hard. He was a best-selling novelist."

"I know. But can a man who lives in a fantasy world every day really learn to dig his heels in and push himself? I mean, this is hard work. It takes a lot of concentration, a lot of endurance. And my goodness, you have to be able to handle rejection. What does Wolfe know of those things? Plus—and this is going to be a hard lesson for him to learn—you can't just work when inspiration hits you. Whenever a customer comes in, you have to be at your very best, inspiration or not."

She patted him on the arm. "He has a good teacher." She winked.

Oliver grinned at her. "Well, I think he's going to be a good student. He seems willing to learn. Anyway, enough about me. How was your day?"

Her skin tingled with fear and anticipation. "I did some wedding shopping today."

"Me too! And boy, did I find the deal of the century."

She cocked an eyebrow. She couldn't imagine his being better than hers. "Really?"

"Yeah. You know how when we planned our budget for the wedding we'd both agreed we wanted a limo to take us from the wedding back to our house, right?"

She nodded.

"Guess what I found?" he continued after she couldn't answer. "*A horse-drawn carriage!*" he shouted with a joy usually reserved for fourth-quarter touchdowns. She grew excited too. This was going to be perfect for her situation: He would tell her how he couldn't resist a horse-drawn carriage, and though it cost a little more, it would be totally worth it.

She couldn't contain her enthusiastic grin, which melted as he announced, "And I saved us a hundred bucks!"

"What?"

"Can you believe it?" His features radiated with pride. "My dear Melb, we are going to have the most beautiful wedding any budget has ever seen." He took her hand. "I'm telling you, this wedding is going to be wonderful. I know you won't be disappointed." He rubbed his hands together eagerly. "So? What's your big news? What'd you buy for the wedding?"

She smiled weakly. "It's a surprise."

He laughed. "Okay. I love surprises." Then he said, "And hey, you have been practicing spelling what will soon be your new last name, right?"

She nodded, figuring now was not the time to "surprise" him again and tell him she'd not yet been able to spell Stepaphanolopolis without the index cards.

She grabbed a new bag of chips.

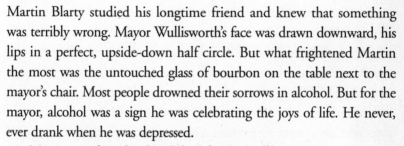

Martin Blarty studied his longtime friend and knew that something was terribly wrong. Mayor Wullisworth's face was drawn downward, his lips in a perfect, upside-down half circle. But what frightened Martin the most was the untouched glass of bourbon on the table next to the mayor's chair. Most people drowned their sorrows in alcohol. But for the mayor, alcohol was a sign he was celebrating the joys of life. He never, ever drank when he was depressed.

Martin, on the other hand, had finished off his glass.

"Sir, I think you're overreacting a bit."

The mayor's dull eyes lit with anger directed at Martin. "You've got to be kidding me. Haven't you looked at the numbers, Martin? Don't you realize what dire straits we are in?"

"I know. But I don't think you're to blame, and resigning as mayor would only hurt this town, not help it. We're in trouble, there's no doubt about that. But there's got to be another way."

The mayor rose, circling his wingback chair and standing before the raging fire that crackled and hollered up through the chimney. "I've seen this town go through ups and downs through the years, Martin. But this time is different. We're lost. We don't even know who we are anymore. Once we were a small town with a silly name. Then we became a small town with a famous resident. Then we became a famous town. And now…"

From behind him, Martin could see the mayor take out his hand-kerchief and wipe his eyes. He noticed how thin he had become, his pants hanging off him like a young boy in his brother's hand-me-downs.

"I can't sleep at night," the mayor said. "I don't know what to do."

Martin hugged his longtime friend. The mayor patted him affectionately, but then retired to his bedroom, asking Martin to show himself to the door. Listening to the bedroom door close, Martin shut his eyes and pinched the bridge of his nose, trying to come up with a solution.

Mayor Wullisworth was depressed, and Martin wasn't sure how to give him hope. He stood alone in the mayor's study, thinking he might finish off his friend's untouched bourbon, but decided against it. He needed to think clearly. Instead he stood solemnly, gazing at all the history books that lined the shelves of the study, his mind filing through options of how to solve this massive problem. How do you save a town on the brink of bankruptcy? If ever there was a hopeless situation, this was it.

And then something hit him. One word.

"History!" Martin cried. That was it! He would find out the town's history, see how it began, go back to the roots. Surely there was something there that could help him find this town's future.

The doorbell rang, and he left the study. No movement came from the hallway leading to the mayor's bedroom, and he knew the mayor wasn't expecting company. He went to the front door and decided to answer it so the mayor wouldn't be disturbed.

"Hello, Marty."

His chest constricted. Missy Peeple.

"Is the mayor home?"

"You have no business here, Miss Peeple," Martin said. "After the Thanksgiving Scandal, I think you of all people should know that."

He was about to shut the door when she said, "I know how to save this town."

Martin swallowed. He studied her wrinkled face, smiling and scowling at the same time. This woman was a foe, he knew that. But he also knew she would stop at nothing to save the town. Her fierce determination was what everyone feared the most about her.

"I'm sorry." He slammed the door shut. Then he heard the strangest thing. An owl. Hooting. He listened, and then the sound faded into the night.

## CHAPTER 5

REVEREND PECK TRIED to keep a warm smile steady on his face as he stood outside his church, shaking hands with the ten people who had showed up for the special Christmas Eve service. Even while he stood there, he could hear a town full of carolers, their vocal cords straining to climb the pear tree of all Christmas songs. What in the world were they doing singing about partridges on the Eve of Christ's birth? He'd read somewhere this particular song had a secret Christian meaning behind it, but nobody he knew could tell him what that secret was. The reverend shook his head as they moved to a new rendition of "Jingle Bells" sung to the tune of "O Holy Night."

His stomach turned.

Where was everybody? Didn't they understand what Christmas meant? Why weren't they at church?

Wolfe and Ainsley strolled out of the church, holding hands and laughing. When they saw the reverend, he could tell they sensed something was wrong. He didn't even try to hide it behind a smile.

"Are you okay?" Wolfe asked.

He shook his head. "I am losing this town," he said. "There was a change at Thanksgiving. The whole town. You remember. And now, look," he said, pointing down the street to the singers. "They'd rather be out singing about a one-horse open sleigh than listening to one of my sermons."

"Reverend," Ainsley said, taking his hand, "come to our house tonight. Have Christmas Eve dinner with us. Please. I insist."

"Thank you my dear," he said, "but I think I'd rather be alone."

Ainsley and Wolfe exchanged worried glances, but the reverend tried to smile. "I'm fine. I just need to figure some things out. Please, go on. And thanks...thanks for coming."

They both hugged him warmly and then went on their way. Reverend Peck lingered a few seconds longer, trying to understand what God wanted him to do. He went inside, hoping to find the offering basket half-full. Instead, there was a twenty. At least someone had given. He took it and knew that he at least had enough money to eat for the week. That was one less thing on his mind.

He decided to walk the streets of his town, hoping the good Lord would speak to him, give him some insight into how to help these people. He walked the gravel hill that led him into Main Street. Lights hung from every store window. And though the streets weren't crowded, people milled about here and there.

He could still hear the carolers.

Then he noticed something peculiar. In front of The Mansion, his favorite restaurant, a noisy crowd stood. As he approached, he noticed whole families standing around, giggling, conversing, and carrying on. The women wore their favorite Christmas sweaters. The men smoked their pipes and told tall tales. Something about the entire scene warmed his heart and disturbed him all at the same time.

After several minutes of observing this, he decided to find out what all the commotion was about. Why the big crowd?

He approached the Jamesons, a young, bright family. He'd met the father, who sold tires, and the mother, who stayed at home with their children, a few weeks back when Wolfe had been lost in the snow. Mr. Jameson had come to volunteer his time.

"Hi there," Reverend Peck said, offering a hand to Mr. Jameson, who immediately recognized him.

"Hello, Reverend!" he said. His wife smiled and shook his hand too as they exchanged pleasantries.

"What's all this about?" The reverend gestured toward the crowd.

"You haven't heard?"

"Heard what?"

"Chef Bob is offering a special Christmas Eve dinner to the first hundred people who arrive. It's some fancy ham dish. Everyone rushed here to try to get a spot. Cost twenty bucks a plate!"

"A fancy ham dish."

Mr. Jameson laughed. "Yeah! And I don't even like ham! But I figured it had to be something special if he was only serving a hundred people." He shrugged. "So I figured I'd bring the family down to see if we can get in. It's looking iffy. We arrived late, I guess."

"Late?"

"Yeah. There's been people camped out here since lunch so they could get in! We've just been here since around five."

"Honey, look," his wife said. "Carolers! Isn't that wonderful?" The family turned to admire a dozen cheery faces bobbing their heads along to "Frosty the Snowman."

The reverend said to Mr. Jameson, "You know, I had a Christmas Eve service tonight."

The man's face registered surprise and guilt. "Oh. No. I hadn't heard." He cleared his throat. "We would have o'course been there if we'd known. Right, honey?"

"Honey" was still gleefully swaying to the carolers and had tuned the men out.

"Yes, well, maybe next year." He shook Mr. Jameson's hand and headed home.

A fancy ham dish beat out the message of baby Jesus. How could he compete with fancy ham? What was fancy ham, anyway? Part of him thought he might hang around the restaurant and see if he could get in. But sorrow drew him into the isolation of his home.

As he arrived at the parsonage, his breath freezing in front of him with each labored step he took, he stopped.

"Whoo."

The reverend looked around. Had someone spoken to him? "Hello? Is someone out there?"

"Whoo. Whoo."

He looked up and almost laughed. An owl! He'd never seen an owl in these parts. It was huge! The Great Horned Owl cocked his head and regarded him.

"*Whoo. Whoo.*"

"Who gives a rip about church, you say?" He unlocked his door and went inside. He didn't have fancy ham, but he thought he had a can of Spam in the cupboard.

Dr. Hass had watched from a distance, across the street, as the sheriff's deputies declared his home foreclosed. Standing in the Los Angeles monsoon, he had cringed as they chained the front driveway gate and stuck it with a bright orange sign announcing that very fact.

He had stood there soaking wet, despite his three hundred dollar, plaid-lined raincoat.

All he possessed consisted of two suitcases full of clothes, a trunk crammed with sentimental items, a box full of books, and about five thousand dollars in cash. Oh, and the raincoat.

What had his life come to? A puddle of an existence. As the two deputies had driven away, he'd gazed at what was once a magnificent Bel Air mansion, complete with a pool, eight bedrooms, four stories of glory, and plenty of envy power.

And that was just his home base. He'd also gained an amazing repu-tation, carefully cultivated over the years, which was now worthless. People he'd spent years socializing with pretended they did not know him. They'd once trusted him…never liked him…but trusted him. Now they scorned him.

With thunder tumbling across the sky and a downpour reminding him that if hope was about to raise its head not to bother, Dr. Hass had felt low but not defeated. Because on the day he discovered he would soon be homeless, he'd just finished reading *Who Moved My Cheese?* for the eighth time. Some people's heroes were presidents or athletes or sol-diers. But he had four heroes, and their names were Sniff, Scurry, Hem, and Haw. Two mice. Two littlepeople. Haw's motto was taped to the top of his mirror, just above his receding hairline: "You can believe that a change will harm you and resist it. Or you can believe that finding New Cheese will help you, and embrace the change. It all depends on what you choose to believe."

Well, this was his Big Cheese Moment. It hadn't looked like Cheese, standing on the sidewalk about to drown in a downpour. But this *was* Cheese. A big wedge of sharp cheddar.

He smiled to himself, then caught the driver of the taxi in which he now sat giving him a funny look.

"You getting out here?"

"In a moment," he said, remembering a quote from his Anger Management Daily Calendar of Quotes: *A temper tantrum makes you look like a spoiled three-year-old.* A month or so ago, he might've grabbed the cabby by his toupee and slapped him clear across the street. But today he held up a polite index finger. He'd come a long way. And he intended to go even further.

As he was packing one last suitcase two nights ago, he'd realized he had a passion. Not just a love. Not just a talent. But *a passion.* And what had made him famous and charismatic all these years would now make him even more successful and well known.

He had discovered a cure for his mother (quite by accident), and now he would conquer the cure for others. He'd be written about in medical journals for years. All he had to do was prove his theory.

Dr. Hass looked down at the paper he was holding with the full-page ad that he knew was getting ready to change his life.

"Skary, Indiana. Wonder how this place got its name?" he mused aloud, looking out the window at the house in which he was soon to reside.

"No idea. Minutes are ticking by here, buddy."

He handed over a large wad of cash and got out. The cabby helped him unload everything from the trunk, but only to the sidewalk outside the house. "Have a nice Christmas," he muttered just before zipping away in his cab.

The doctor was not into the festive spirit of the season, but his heart danced with the idea of a new beginning and a new town. New opportunities. Running from those out to get you always did provide for new opportunities.

"Home sweet home. Skary, Indiana." And then, with amusement, he noticed that the yellow color of his house and the angle at which the roof pointed upward looked amazingly like a big wedge of cheese.

Ainsley settled into Wolfe's arms. A bright and feisty fire crackled in front of them. "Is this music too cheesy?" She laughed. The Mannheim Steamroller CD she'd just put in was her favorite Christmas CD.

He smiled. "Well, I have to admit I haven't listened to Mannheim Steamroller at Christmas since I was in an elevator at Bloomingdale's."

"Cute," she said, punching him in the arm. She nestled into his chest. "This just brings back good memories for me."

He stroked her hair. "As long as we don't have to play them at our wedding."

She giggled and popped up. "I think I've picked the perfect music. I listened to music all last week. We've got a lot to do before the wedding, but I think we can get it done."

"All I care about is that you are there."

"Well, I want our day to be memorable. Down to every last detail."

His light tone shifted. "Honey, I just want to make sure you don't get your expectations too high. I mean, sometimes things go wrong at weddings."

"The key to keeping things from going wrong is in the planning. If you plan and prepare, it's much less likely that something will go wrong."

"I just don't want you to be disappointed, that's all."

They stared into the fire for a while, listening to the synthetic sounds of Steamroller. Then Wolfe said, "Have you thought any more about starting your catering business?"

"I just figured I'd think about it after the wedding. I'm already so busy as it is."

He tilted her chin his way. "I know I've told you this before, but Ainsley, you don't have to work. You certainly don't have to work at the restaurant. I have plenty of money to support both of us for the rest of our lives."

"But we're not married yet. When we're married, I'll consider it."

He grinned. "You have a stubborn streak, don't you?"

She shrugged. "Just idealistic, I guess. Besides, for the first time in years, the restaurant is starting to become what I remember it being. I wouldn't call it quaint, but it's getting there. At least we don't have eyeballs floating in the sodas anymore." She winked at him.

"Okay. But you understand, don't you, that you will never have to worry about money again?"

She swallowed. No, she did not understand that. She couldn't even comprehend it. It was a foreign concept to her.

The doorbell rang. "Are you expecting someone?" Wolfe asked.

"No." She sat up. Maybe her father had invited Garth over. The sheriff remained worried about Thief since his operation. All Thief wanted to do was sleep. She listened for her father to go to the door, but the house was quiet. Sighing, she left Wolfe's warm and comfortable arms and headed to the door.

Opening it, she nearly gasped.

"Hi Ainsley. Merry Christmas to you," said Alfred Tennison.

## CHAPTER 6

AINSLEY OPENED HER MOUTH to speak, but it was Wolfe's voice that filled the air.

"Alfred!"

She watched Alfred's expression morph from cordiality to surprise to worry.

"Wolfe. I, um, I didn't expect to see you."

Wolfe stood next to her and folded his arms. "Where else would I be on Christmas Eve but with my fiancée?"

"Of course, I'm sorry," Alfred said, shoving a gift into Ainsley's arms. "Well, may I come in?"

Wolfe and Ainsley exchanged glances, and though she really didn't want company tonight, she also knew it would be rude to turn away a guest on Christmas Eve.

"Sure," Ainsley smiled. But Wolfe was not smiling. They followed Alfred into the living area. He looked around as if he'd never been in the house before. Maybe it was just bringing back bad memories for him. The last time he was here, Wolfe had nearly died.

Ainsley headed to the kitchen to fix them all hot caramel apple cider. She could hear light chitchat, but when she returned to the living room, Wolfe said, "What brings you back to Skary, Al?" He gestured for him to sit in the leather chair near the fire. "And to see Ainsley?"

"Straight to business, eh?" Alfred asked. He looked at her. "Why don't you open that?"

"Oh…um…okay." She untied the satin ribbon from the gold

Williams-Sonoma box. Inside, there was a shiny silver ladle engraved with her name. She looked up at Alfred. "It's beautiful."

He smiled. "It's pure silver. I figured you could use it tomorrow for that wonderful gravy you make."

She nodded and looked at Wolfe, who was staring at Alfred. Alfred then said to him, "How's everything going? Are you writing?"

"I'm working at a car dealership."

A cocked eyebrow showed Alfred definitely did not approve. "That must be...stimulating."

"It's different."

"Why aren't you writing?"

He sighed, leaning back into the couch and grabbing his cider mug. "I don't know, Al. It's just not what I need to do right now. I've lived this extraordinary life, and it brought me to a place of complete emptiness. I can't write the kinds of things I used to write. I thought I'd try living an ordinary life and see what God does with that."

"God," Alfred sighed. "Cheers." He lifted up his mug to the heavens. "The most famous writer in the world selling used cars. God works in mysterious ways, eh?" His tone was flat.

"So why are you here?" Wolfe asked. "Bringing my fiancée gifts?"

"I really just wanted to talk with Ainsley alone," he said, the steam from his cider flushing his face. At least *something* was flushing his face.

"Which is exactly why you're going to explain why you've traveled all the way from New York to be here on Christmas Eve."

"There's nothing for me in New York anymore. They fired me, and nobody in their right mind would hire the editor whose fame comes from losing the most famous writer in the world to Jesus Christ."

"I'm not the most famous writer in the world, Alfred. And you know, you might think about what Jesus could do for you."

"He's done quite enough already, thank you."

"Well, stop stalling. What are you up to?"

Alfred shrugged. "I'm just trying to decide what to do with my life, you know? Well, of course you know. You're selling cars. That makes you happy. I, on the other hand, need something a little more stimulating."

"Such as?"

"You know, before I became an editor, I was an agent for ten years."

"Yes."

"Well, I think I have a talent for spotting talent. I can't see a major religious revival coming, but I can spot talent. That is one thing I know for sure."

Wolfe set down his mug. "Alfred, I've told you, I'm done writing for now."

"I'm not talking about you."

"Then why are you here?"

"I'm talking about Ainsley."

"Me?" she asked.

He smiled warmly at her. "Yes, my dear."

"What about her?" Wolfe asked, his arm suddenly in front of her like a mother shielding a child from a growling dog.

Alfred engaged her eyes. "Ainsley, as you know, Martha Stewart is on her way out of the Domestic Kingdom."

"Al!" Wolfe shouted.

She looked at Alfred. "What do you mean she's on her way out?"

"Because of the scandal," Alfred said.

"Al!"

"What scandal?" she asked, and suddenly Alfred was looking very flustered and Wolfe was looking very angry.

"You know, insider trading—"

"Alfred!"

"She doesn't know about the scandal?" Alfred said to Wolfe. "I thought she adored all things Martha!"

"What scandal?" she demanded.

Wolfe sighed, turning to her. "Honey, listen. It's nothing."

"I want to know what he's talking about!"

"How can she not know about this? It's been all over the papers," Alfred said.

"Alfred, shut your trap," Wolfe commanded. Alfred nervously swallowed a sip of cider.

"Wolfe, what is he talking about? Did Martha get sued by someone? I thought that would happen to her someday. People get jealous."

"It's a little more complicated than that," he said gently. "And tonight's really not the time to discuss it."

She felt herself growing angry. "Wolfe! I'm not a baby. I want to know what's going on. How could something be happening to Martha and you not tell me about it?"

His eyes reflected hurt and confusion. He glanced at Alfred, who could only sit there with the cider up to his lips.

"Sweetheart," he tried again, "let's not talk about it on Christmas Eve. There will be plenty of time to discuss this later."

She turned to Alfred. "Alfred, I demand you tell me what's going on right now. Why are you here, and what does this have to do with Martha?"

She watched his nervous eyes dart back and forth between herself and Wolfe. Finally he set down his mug and folded his hands together. "I'm betting my whole life's happiness that Martha's time in the spotlight is over. For good."

"What?" she gasped.

"Alfred!" Wolfe yelled, but she held up a stern finger.

"And I believe I'm sitting in the room with the person who is destined to replace her."

The town had settled into a silent Christmas Eve. Families were now gathered in their warm homes, carrying on traditions they'd grown bored with years ago, entertaining relatives they hated. The streets were quiet, except for the sound of two small feet dragging across the concrete of the sidewalk.

Missy Peeple walked north on Madson Street, her body rigidly cold, but her heart afire with purpose. The scrooge inside Missy wanted to take her hatpin and pop the inflatable manger scene that sat in front of house number 255. But it was Christmas Eve, after all. Good tidings and all that nonsense. So she kept walking. She needed to get to 347.

Madson Street glowed with its lights and its razzle dazzle. Every Christmas this street won for being the most garishly decorated, though the plaque read something like, "Brightest Star in Skary." It was a stupid contest anyway, mostly because there was one plaque and twenty-eight houses, which always caused "good cheer" to fly right out the window. Common sense tells you that you hand out candy canes, not a plaque, but she wasn't the mayor. Oh, what she could do in an elected office!

From here she could see Garth's house, unlit and looking like a black hole. It was the only dark spot on the street. At least she admired Garth for that. He never had gotten caught up in the Christmas nonsense.

Her legs ached. She couldn't walk the way she used to. In her day, she'd walked all over this town with no problem. Now all she could manage was a few blocks. Huffing her way to the top step of his house, she rang the doorbell, the only thing glowing on the outside of his home.

After a few moments, the door opened. Garth crossed his arms and scowled. "What do you want? It's Christmas after all. Isn't your season in late October?"

"I just wanted to come in for a bit."

He laughed. "Puh-lease. You coming in for a bit is like asking a cobra to…to…I don't know, stay for dinner. Anyway, the point is, no."

"Garth, you haven't even heard why I'm here."

"I don't need to hear anything." He lowered his voice. "You promised me Ainsley, and I ended up with—"

"Garth, babycakes. Who is it?"

Missy peeked around him. She could've sworn that sounded like Ginger, his not-so-bright assistant. "A close second," Missy winked.

"A close nothing. The love of my life is now with the love of her life. And you know what? This week my life took an all-time low turn, as I neutered an animal at gunpoint. So you'll have to excuse the trust issues here, you cranky bag of…of…"

"Charm?"

"Yeah. Right. Charm. You've charmed your way into being Skary, Indiana's most hated resident."

Missy Peeple swallowed, her eyes moistening just a tad. His frozen features made her realize that even he thought that sounded harsh. She mastered her emotions and looked him in the eyes.

"Our town is in trouble, Garth."

"So what? I'm just the vet. With the number of animals running around this place, I'll have work until the day I die."

"But don't you care what will happen to it?"

"I cared about one thing and one thing only. And now she's tying the knot to Wonder Writer. I'll never have another chance with her."

"Never say never, dear Garth."

And then the door slammed in her face. She regloved her hands and tightened her scarf around her neck. It took her twenty minutes to walk back home, and before she got there, she stopped by the community center to see what time Christmas lunch would be served.

She hated turkeys. The way the translucent skin around their necks hung like it was barely attached reminded her of her own fading beauty, neck skin and all. But she would eat the turkey anyway, because, after all, the head was chopped off.

Unlocking her front door, she realized that she'd been a little too credulous in her belief that the town would rally around her plan. Apparently she was the villain now. Well, so be it. They hated her. Soon they'd be indebted to her because, as she imagined it, within the next month this town would be filled with a new breed of people.

After a good five-minute cry, Ainsley recovered from the shock of hearing about Martha Stewart's woes and tried to focus. But in the meantime, Wolfe had chewed poor Alfred up one side and down the other, all the while Alfred tried to explain he couldn't imagine there was a person on earth who didn't know about Martha.

# THE BIGGEST THING
## TO HAPPEN
### TO SKARY, INDIANA.

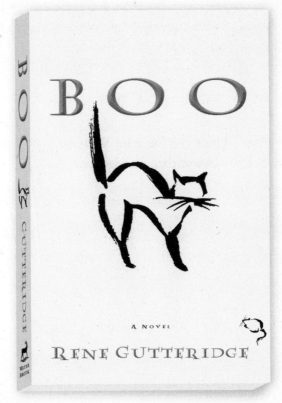

When best-selling horror novelist Wolfe "Boo" Boone gives up the genre, his neighbors in Skary, Indiana, plot to change his mind.

**Available in bookstores everywhere.**

It was true, she didn't know. She'd heard a few rumors here and there but had dismissed them as tabloid. She never read the newspaper or listened to the news. The world was too horrible for her. She liked the quiet naiveté of Skary.

The kingdom's walls had now been knocked down.

After hearing Wolfe shout for the better part of five minutes, she stood and touched his arm. "Wolfe, it's okay. Alfred didn't mean anything by it."

Relief flooded Alfred's unsettled features. He smiled timidly at her, then shifted his attention to Wolfe. Wolfe gave him a sharp look and turned to her. "Are you okay?"

"I'm fine." She smiled. "I guess I saw the signs and ignored it. It's just so shocking."

"I'm sorry you had to hear this on Christmas Eve," he sighed. "I was going to tell you, but I wasn't sure when. Anyway, innocent until proven guilty, right?"

Both of them turned as Alfred let out a laugh. His smile faded and he cleared his throat.

"Anyway, enough of this nonsense. Alfred, you need to go. You've caused quite enough trouble for one night."

"Wait," she said. "He hasn't told us why he's here."

"Sweetheart, things can wait."

"Actually, the time is now," Alfred said. "There is urgency."

"Urgency for what?" Wolfe demanded.

"May I?" Alfred asked, gesturing toward the seat he'd previously warmed.

"Sure" and "No" came out at the same time, and Ainsley and Wolfe exchanged glances. Wolfe shrugged and said, "It's your home."

She rubbed his arm, trying to cool the tension that had heated the room. "It's okay, honey. Let's just hear him out."

Ainsley and Wolfe sat together on the couch. "So. Alfred," she said, "why are you here?"

Alfred cleared his throat and cracked his knuckles before saying, "Ainsley, I see something in you. Something very special. You have this

innocence about you, this likableness that sets people at ease. And you're as attractive as a bowl full of worms to a bird."

"Okay…let's just leave the metaphors to me, shall we?" Wolfe piped in.

"Sorry. Anyway, what I'm trying to say here is that America needs a new domestic sweetheart, Ainsley. There are millions of women who are devastated right now. Granted, there are millions more who are cheering. But nevertheless, America needs someone to show them how to cook apple pie and how to stuff a turkey and how to make lemonade without a packet. Do you see where I'm going with this?"

Her jaw had dropped. "Are you saying you think I could be the next Martha Stewart?"

"I know you could."

"Hold on just a minute," Wolfe said. "Is this a joke?"

"Why would I be joking? I used to be an agent, Wolfe. I know talent when I see it. And I also know opportunity."

"This is absurd!" Wolfe said.

She crossed her arms. "What's so absurd about it?"

Wolfe looked perplexed by her question, but to her, there wasn't anything at all absurd about it. She was capable. She'd watched the woman as long as she could remember. She knew every move, every nuance, everything about her. Why couldn't she step into her shoes?

"Ainsley," Wolfe tried, "I think this is a little silly."

She couldn't help but scowl. "What's so silly about it?"

Wolfe cupped her shoulder. "Sweetheart, we need to talk about this. I mean, we've got the wedding to plan—"

"I can do both."

"She can do both," Alfred repeated with a smile.

"But…but…"

"But what, Wolfe? You've been begging me to start a catering business. That is exactly how Martha Stewart started. This could be really big for me. Alfred believes in me, and he doesn't have anything better to do with his time, right, Alfred?"

Alfred agreed with a shrug.

"So what's the problem here?"

A sigh caused Wolfe to slump into the couch as he stared at his feet. Then he said, "Ainsley, I've walked the road of fame. It's not all it's cracked up to be. I'd even say it's a curse."

"But I have you, and Dad, and others to keep me grounded. Besides, who says I'll be famous?"

He took her hands. "You just don't know what it's like to go everywhere and be recognized. There's never any peace, never any obscurity. You have to watch yourself at all times, make sure you're not doing anything stupid. And it's so much pressure. Do you know what it feels like to disappoint a million people?"

"Do you know what it feels like to disappoint one?" she said, more angrily than she wanted. Wolfe's expression told her he was wounded. "I'm sorry. I didn't mean that."

"I just don't want you to get hurt."

"I can take care of myself," she said, squeezing his hand. "And now I have you to take care of me too."

"So it's a go?" Alfred asked.

"Alfred, give us a couple of days, will you?" she said, aware of Wolfe's growing frustration. "It's Christmas, and we shouldn't be focused on such things."

"Oh. Yeah. Right." Alfred stood, sliding on his gloves. "Okay. I will call you in a couple of days."

She shook his hand. "Thank you, Alfred. I appreciate your confidence in my abilities."

"You're welcome."

"Have a Merry Christmas."

"Um…yeah…"

She stopped him as he pulled on his coat. "Alfred, what are you doing for Christmas? Where are you staying?"

"Oh, just up at the motel they ripped off from Wolfe's *The Gleaming*. Previously called The Wonderlook, but now I think they're calling it 'wonder-if-we're-booked'." Alfred was the only one laughing at his joke.

"But what are you doing tomorrow?" she asked.

"He's fine, he's fine," Wolfe said, trying to usher Alfred to the door. "Alfred hates Christmas, right?"

"Right."

"Wrong! Nobody I know hates Christmas. Alfred Tennison, you must join us for Christmas lunch tomorrow."

She did not miss Wolfe's obvious eye roll, but how could she let the poor man spend Christmas alone? "I insist," she added.

"Oh, no, that's okay. I know that is family time for you," Alfred said, looking at Wolfe.

"Yes. Family time. Now run along."

"Wolfe, tell him he has to stay. We'll have plenty of food."

Wolfe shot her a look, but minding his manners as she knew he would, he said, though rather meekly, "Yes. We insist."

Alfred grinned. "Well, my goodness, how could I miss out on an opportunity to spend Christmas with the most famous caterer in all of Indiana?"

With a groan, he guided Alfred to the door. Ainsley stood behind him, her arms entangled with his.

"Good night, Alfred. See you tomorrow," Wolfe said. "And listen, no talking catering or business or anything else tomorrow, okay? I won't even discuss my writing."

Alfred smiled. "You are sooo yesterday. Take a look at Skary's new claim to fame. She's the gorgeous blonde standing behind you."

## CHAPTER 7

WOLFE PULLED THE WARM COVERS over his body, trying to get a few more minutes of sleep. His eyes were heavy with the remnants of the hefty conversation with Ainsley last night after Alfred left. He didn't get home until after 2:00 a.m.

But sleep eluded him. It was, after all, Christmas morning. Wolfe stretched his arms over his head and smiled, imagining that in just a few years, a little boy, or maybe a girl, would be tugging at his pajamas whispering that Santa Claus had come. "Get up, Daddy!" He would touch Ainsley's arm, who would lazily roll over into his shoulder and cup their little one's face.

But for now, he would have to settle for Goose and Bunny, his German shepherds, who stood next to his bed whimpering out their bladder pain.

"Okay, okay," he said to them. "Give me just a minute." He pulled on some warm pants and a sweater and then went downstairs to put on some boots. He thought about making himself a cup of coffee first, but by the way his dogs' ears were urgently perked, he realized he'd better take them for their morning walk now. And there was no just letting them out the back door. He'd failed to walk them yesterday. Today he was not getting off the hook.

Outside, he was delighted to see it had snowed. He thought after his last experience with snow he might not ever want to see it again, but he couldn't deny the beauty of a white blanket covering the landscape.

Goose and Bunny were enjoying their usual romp outside their normal boundaries as they walked the quiet streets of Skary. He couldn't

stop smiling at the thought of spending Christmas Day with Ainsley. He'd always liked the holidays, but since his parents died, he'd spent them alone, usually going over picture albums. He liked listening to Christmas music, and a couple of years had actually fixed himself a simple traditional dinner.

But this year... This year was going to be magical. Ainsley's home replicated the North Pole with all its lavish decorations. One day soon, she would do the same thing to his home. *Their* home. The smile widened on his face.

God had blessed him more than he could ever imagine. And the wedding wasn't even here yet.

Wolfe decided on his way home to stop by Reverend Peck's parsonage. He knew the reverend rose early. He softly knocked on the door, and after a few seconds the reverend answered, beaming at the unexpected company. Wolfe ordered Goose and Bunny home and then accepted the reverend's invitation to come in.

"Merry Christmas, Wolfe!" The reverend embraced him enthusiastically, but Wolfe noticed he looked very tired and had dark purple circles under his eyes.

"Reverend Peck, are you all right? You look tired."

The reverend smiled as they sat at the small breakfast table near a large bay window that was filtering in the morning light. "I am tired. I was up all night."

"Sick?"

"No, not sick. Inspired."

"Really?"

"I know how to fix my church," Reverend Peck said, a twinkle in his eye. "I know how to get people to come."

"How?"

"Can't tell you. I'm still working on the plan. But it hit me last night. It all came rushing to me like a giant wave."

Wolfe nodded, his curiosity piqued. "Well, I can't wait to see what happens."

"Coffee?" the reverend asked.

"No, thanks. But Reverend, may I ask where you will be spending Christmas this year?"

"Here," he smiled. "Now don't go feeling sorry for me. Every year I get invited somewhere. But this year I thought I'd spend it with the Lord. Quietly."

"You're sure?" Wolfe asked. "You know Ainsley will be very upset if she knows you're here by yourself."

"Don't tell her," the reverend said. He grinned, and Wolfe couldn't remember the last time he'd seen the reverend this enthusiastic. He couldn't help but wonder what the grand plan was. "But maybe you can drop by a plate of leftovers later."

"I'll make sure I do that," Wolfe said, standing and shaking his hand. "Have a merry Christmas, Reverend."

"It will be a Christmas I'll never forget."

"See?" her father said, worry carving deep creases into his brow. "Nothing."

Ainsley and her father stood over Thief, who was flopped across the sheriff's bed in his typical lazy way. Ainsley wasn't sure what exactly her father was referring to. Cats by nature were lazy, and why Thief lying on the bed was any need for concern, she didn't understand. But her father had been complaining that Thief hadn't been himself since the surgery.

"It's only been a couple of days," she said, patting her father's shoulder. "Give him time."

The sheriff glanced at her. "It is a traumatic operation, I guess."

"Sure," she said. "He'll be back to his old self soon."

He stroked the cat's body tenderly. "I just hope he's okay."

"It's Christmas morning, Daddy. Don't worry about it today, okay?"

They left the room together. "Let's go downstairs. I have a present for you."

Her heart leapt the same way it had when she was a little girl. She loved this time of morning, when they'd go downstairs, drink gourmet

coffee, open presents, and eat the special Christmas pastry she would bake. She galloped downstairs and to the tree.

It sparkled in the morning light. She'd chosen silver to be her theme this year, and it was gorgeous. With just a bit of gold thrown in, their whole tree seemed to glow with heavenly snow.

"Here," her father said, handing her a small box, wrapped with the clumsiness of a male. She smiled. Her dad had never figured out how to make crisp corners or use invisible tape. She carefully unwrapped it. Inside there was a beautiful floral journal. She looked up at him. "A journal. You know how I love journals! I can record all my thoughts about the wedding."

He grinned. "Open it up."

Ainsley carefully picked up the journal, opened it, and gasped. Her mother's handwriting filled the pages. She looked at her dad.

"I've been waiting to give this to you until you were to be married. This was your mother's journal that she kept while we were engaged, all the way up to our wedding day."

Tears blurred her vision, and she embraced her father, holding him tightly. After a few moments, he combed the hair out of her face and said, "Are you okay?"

She nodded but couldn't speak. As excited as she was about getting married, she also knew it meant leaving her father, something she'd wanted to do for years but now realized was going to be harder than she'd realized. Imagining him alone in this old house tore her heart to shreds.

"Daddy," she cried, "this is so perfect. I can't wait to read it."

"I hope it brings you some guidance as you plan your own wedding."

She sniffled away her tears and then handed her father his present. Without regarding the silk bow or silver wrapping, he tore it open. She couldn't help but smile. Luckily, she wrapped packages like that for her own satisfaction.

"A cookbook?" her father asked with a laugh.

"Not just any cookbook. *The Male Species Guide to Cooking Anything.*"

The sheriff smiled. "I guess it's time for me to learn the kitchen," he sighed. "I know I'll get tired of making myself cold cereal after a while."

"I love you, Dad," she said, hugging him. "I'd better get to the kitchen myself. I have a big feast to prepare. By the way, Alfred Tennison will be joining us."

"Wolfe's editor?"

"Ex-editor. And I know, I know, Christmas is family time, but Alfred didn't have anywhere to go for Christmas, and he's practically family to Wolfe."

"That's fine, sweetheart," he said. "You know what's best."

Just as she was headed for the kitchen, the doorbell rang. She checked her watch. She didn't expect Wolfe this early but would be glad to see him no matter what the time.

Opening the door, she found Melb there heaving out sobs while trying to explain something that Ainsley couldn't understand. She pulled her inside the house.

"Melb, calm down. Calm down. Please. Take a deep breath. Are you okay?" She couldn't remember ever seeing anybody this upset.

Melb's whole face was red and splotchy, her eyes bloodshot. "Oh, Ainsley," she finally managed, "it's all so terrible."

"What happened?"

"Oliver!"

Ainsley guided her into the living room, shooing her curious dad back into the kitchen. Taking her coat, she sat them both onto the couch. "Did you two have a fight?"

"Not really," Melb said. "Oliver doesn't know I'm upset."

"Why are you upset?"

"I just…I just don't know if I can marry a man who is so frugal with his money. I mean, the man is saving us hundreds of dollars on this wedding."

"That's a bad thing?"

Melb eyed her. "I don't expect you to understand. You don't have to worry about money."

"Melb," she said, "please, tell me what this is about. I don't under-stand why you're upset."

Melb shook her head. "Oliver is brilliant with money. He set up this account and this budget for us to plan our wedding."

"That's a good thing."

"I guess. But I found this beautiful dress, Ainsley. My dream dress. But I went $550 over budget."

"Oh. Well, Oliver will understand."

"I thought he might. But then he told me he saved a bunch of money *and* was able to get us a horse-drawn carriage. And then I found out he also saved us four hundred dollars on our honeymoon."

"Where are you going?"

"To the Bass Pro Shop up in Cincinnati."

Ainsley was about to say something but decided to each his own.

"Anyway, he got some great deal on hotel rates there." Melb sniffled. "He's going to kill me!"

"Over a dress?"

"That's not all. I also received the invitations in the mail."

"How exciting!"

"Except I spelled Oliver's last name wrong! I left out a couple of *o*'s and a *p*, I think." Melb melted into sobs again. "I'm going to have to pay for them to be reprinted!"

"Melb, Melb," she said, patting her shoulder. "It's going to be okay."

She shook her head. "No. He's going to think I'm some crazy woman who doesn't know how to live on a budget." She glanced at Ainsley. "And I am some crazy woman who doesn't know how to live on a budget. I've never lived by a budget my whole life, Ainsley. I don't know how!"

Ainsley squeezed her hand, not sure what to say, except, "Melb, I do know your best bet is to be honest with Oliver."

"I don't know," Melb sighed, swiping at her tears. "Besides that, I have to lose four dress sizes by Valentine's Day. Maybe I'm overly emo-tional because I've been depriving myself of sugar lately."

"Listen, everything is going to be okay. I know planning a wedding is stressful—"

"You're not stressed out."

"That's not true. I have a lot to do before the big day."

"Your wedding is going to be perfect."

"So is *yours*," Ainsley said, squaring Melb's shoulders directly to her. "Melb, you are marrying the most awesome guy in the world!"

A small smile erased Melb's panic-stricken features. "I know." The smile wilted. "I don't know if I can live up to him."

"He's just as lucky to have you. You are caring, tender, passionate. The guy is crazy about you, Melb. Don't forget that."

"Okay." She stood, but instead of heading to the front door, she went to the kitchen. Luckily, Sheriff Parker had disappeared upstairs to get dressed. "I smell some sort of pastry with cream cheese."

Ainsley pointed to the oven. "Breakfast."

"I'd love some. But just a small serving."

Martin Blarty awoke to the feeling of being attacked by birds. He screamed and flailed his arms until he realized it wasn't birds, just massive amounts of paper on top of him. He'd fallen asleep the night before, doing research about the town while listening to an owl hooting outside his window. That made for a terrifying dream this morning, and now a mess of papers in a pile next to the couch.

Martin's back ached, and his eyes were practically glued shut, but he rose anyway. It was Christmas morning, and he always spent it with Mayor Wullisworth. This year Oliver and Melb would join them too. Just the thought of spending Christmas with his closest friends caused the sleepiness to fade. After a quick shower, Martin dressed, even put cologne on, and then went to the living room to gather presents for everyone.

*The vase in the corner will do nicely for Melb,* he thought, and took it, packaging it carefully with bubble wrap before putting it in a box and wrapping it up. For Oliver, he decided on the nice Oriental print of a large fish his great Aunt June had given him three birthdays ago. Oliver

always said he wanted to travel the world. For the mayor, he decided on a biography of Rudolph Giuliani. Martin had read it three times and figured it might inspire the mayor that he could be a good leader through tough times.

There. Christmas shopping done. He hated waiting until the last minute, but it had been a busy winter.

Then he went to the refrigerator to get his green bean casserole. He knew the mayor would be fixing his world-famous fried turkey, which everyone always anticipated. This was Martin's first year to do green beans. Usually he brought the rolls. But Oliver said Melb was fond of bread, so Martin decided to be generous and let Melb be in charge of that.

Surprisingly, the green bean casserole was not hard to make. The recipe on the side of the green bean can said to add some sort of cream-of soup. At the store, he'd decided on clam chowder. That was his favorite soup anyhow, and who in the world would like cream of celery? Those green stringy stalks were hard enough to eat with peanut butter. The recipe had also called for fried onions on the top, so he was fairly sure he could get away with onion rings from Big Bess's Burger Joint. He'd laid them on top in a very precise way, a pattern resembling the Olympic rings.

After putting everything in his car, he drove over to the mayor's house, humming along to gleeful Christmas tunes on the radio. On his way over, he thought about his research on the town of Skary last night. It perplexed him how little information there was. He'd spent the evening at the town hall, trying to come up with some sort of history, but there wasn't much to go on. Where had all the papers gone? Entire folders lay empty in the filing drawers. But a layer of dust on everything indicated these folders hadn't seen the light of day in years.

He forced the thoughts out of his mind. This was Christmas. There would be time to worry about Skary on another day.

Pulling into the mayor's driveway, he loaded his arms with presents and the casserole and went to the door. When there was no answer to his first ring, he pressed the doorbell again. Again no answer. And he

was growing colder by the minute. Maybe the mayor was in the shower, though legend had it he showered only on Tuesdays.

He decided to go around to the other side of the house. Maybe he could see in through a window. Tromping through the snow, he went to the back porch and gasped. He didn't have to look through a window to find the mayor. There he was, sitting in his pajamas and smoking a pipe on a snow-covered lawn chair. His skin was tinted blue.

"Mayor!" Martin cried, rushing to him. The mayor turned, regarding him with a wave of his pipe.

"Martin! Top of the morning to you!"

"What are you doing out here?"

"Enjoying a beautiful and sunny summer morning."

Martin stood there, shivering beneath his wool coat. "Excuse me?"

"Would you like to join me?"

"Mayor, it is thirty degrees out here. There's snow everywhere. It's…it's Christmas morning."

But the mayor did not seem to hear him. Instead he puffed his pipe and hummed a tune about summer rains. His lips were purple. Martin's own lips, he was sure, had drained of color.

"Come on, why don't we come inside?" he suggested, taking the mayor by the arm and pulling him to his feet.

"I suppose it is time for me to get dressed," the mayor said. "I have a full day of work ahead of me."

Martin slid the glass door open and guided the mayor inside. He quickly poured him a cup of coffee and insisted he drink it immediately. After a few moments, color returned to the mayor's face.

"Sir, it's Christmas morning," Martin said. "It's not summertime."

"Can't you hear the birds whistling? The grass is so green! The sky so blue! It's going to be a terrific day in the town of Skary, Indiana!"

Martin gulped down a ball of fear.

## CHAPTER 8

AINSLEY SCURRIED ABOUT the house, trying to decide exactly how to set the table. She knew Alfred would be joining them, and that Butch, her ever-mysterious covert brother, was planning on being there too. Melb was loitering around the kitchen—surely she would spend Christmas with Oliver! But she didn't look as though she was leaving anytime soon.

Chewing on a fingernail, she decided to go ahead with place settings for six. That was safe. She didn't want to put the extra leaf in the table; it would ruin the decorations she'd fashioned for the smaller version of the table. But six could easily sit around the gleaming hardwood. Worriedly, she glanced into the kitchen at Melb, who was staring into the oven at the turkey.

"Melb, isn't Oliver going to be worried about you?"

"I can't face him yet," she said. "I don't know how I'm going to tell him about being over budget."

"Look," Ainsley said, "don't do it today. Christmas is never a good day to break news to people. Get through the holidays, and then sit down and talk with him. He'll understand."

"When's this turkey going to be done?"

Ainsley sighed. "Another couple of hours."

A knock interrupted Melb's next question, which Ainsley thought was going to be about the pumpkin pie. Hoping it was Wolfe, she couldn't help but show surprise at what stood in her doorway. It was Martin Blarty, dressed in a sweater seemingly made of cologne, and the mayor, in his pajamas.

"Is your father home?" Martin asked, his eyes intense with worry.

She ushered the two in and called for her father, who was upstairs with a ball of yarn trying to induce excitement out of Thief. When the sheriff came down, Martin greeted him at the end of the stairs.

"He's lost his mind," Martin whispered loud enough for everyone to hear.

His statement was met by skeptical looks until the mayor walked to the window, looked outside, and said, "It looks like a balmy afternoon, folks. At least in the seventies, wouldn't you say?"

"It's morning," Melb blurted out. Indeed it was. And with the heavy snow that fell last night, no one could imagine what the mayor was talking about.

"He thinks it's summer," Martin said. "I found him outside on his lawn chair smoking a pipe in his pajamas."

"My goodness," Ainsley gasped, holding her hand over her mouth. But the mayor seemed completely oblivious to all the concern. "Dad, what should we do?" she pleaded in a low whisper. Everyone but the mayor had gathered around the sheriff.

"There aren't going to be any doctors available today," the sheriff sighed. "We could take him to the emergency room at the county hospital, but knowing the mayor like I do, he would kill me if I made a fuss over him like that."

"He's having a nervous breakdown," Martin said. "He's been depressed lately, over the town, but I never imagined it would come to this."

"Let's just watch him today," the sheriff said, studying the mayor as he stood almost catatonic at the window. "Keep an eye on him. If he doesn't improve soon, we'll take him to the hospital."

Sorrow filled Martin's eyes as he looked at the mayor. "I can't believe this has happened. I should've seen this coming."

"Martin, nobody could see something like this coming. He'll be okay. The mayor is a resilient man."

"I know," Martin nodded. He looked at Melb and the sheriff. "Can we please just keep this a secret? I don't want the mayor humiliated."

Everyone agreed. Then the sheriff said, "Martin, why don't you two stay here for Christmas dinner? I know the mayor always cooks a turkey for you all."

"Fried turkey," Martin sighed. "And I brought green bean casserole. Melb was going to bring the rolls. I think Oliver was fixing a pie."

"We have plenty," said the sheriff, giving a nod toward Ainsley. "She always fixes like we're feeding an army."

Ainsley managed a polite smile. Where was everyone going to sit? And where in the world was Wolfe?

Wolfe stood on his front porch watching the oldest woman he knew shiver as though she were cloaked in snow. The poor circulation probably accounted for her pale complexion too, because though it was cold, Missy Peeple was bundled like a mummy. It was going to be hard to speak with her out here for fear she might freeze to death in midsentence. Yet the memories were fresh from the last time he'd invited her into his house. She'd ended up at the hospital, and he nearly ended up in jail.

"Miss Peeple," he said sternly, "I'm not sure I want to talk to you. It seems everything that comes out of your mouth causes trouble. Besides, it's Christmas. Don't you have someplace to be?"

"No," she said emphatically. "I'm the only remaining member of my family."

*Great.* He sighed. *Lonely old lady needing attention on Christmas morning.* "Why are you here?"

"I wanted to have a frank discussion with you," she said through chattering teeth. Wolfe couldn't stand it any longer. He wasn't about to have this woman pass out twice at his house. He invited her in despite his renewed angst.

The warm fire drew her, and she stood there for a moment before unwrapping two scarves and unbuttoning her coat. From inside her coat, she removed a lavishly decorated gift.

"This is for you," she said.

Wolfe tried not to let his eyes roll. Accepting gifts from this woman was like taking money from the mob. Eventually it was going to catch up to you. "You brought me a gift?"

"Go ahead, open it," she urged.

With great trepidation, he opened the gift. Half expecting toy snakes to fly out, he would've been less surprised at that choice than what was actually inside the box. "You, um…you bought me a copy of my own book?"

"Not just any book, Mr. Boone. Your greatest book ever. *Black Cats.*"

"Okay…why?"

"Because I want you to know how much it has inspired me. This town can make a turn, Mr. Boone. But we need your help."

"Something about the word *we* makes me nervous, Miss Peeple. What have you got planned now?"

"Just to save this town. By making it known for its cats. Others have not seen my vision, but I thought you might, since you wrote a whole book about them."

Wolfe suppressed a chuckle. The woman was adamant. "I appreciate your fortitude, Miss Peeple. Obviously, no one cares more about this town than you. You've proved you will stop at nothing to save it. But we can't always be the savior."

This brought a ferocious scowl to the already severe features of Missy Peeple. "No one understands," she said. "I can save this town if given a chance. I know how to make it famous again. And all these crazy felines running around here can help us."

He shook his head. "I can only imagine what you've stirred up in that head of yours. I want no part of it. God Almighty knows what this town needs. He has Skary's best interest at heart. And I know He has a plan that doesn't include your mischief."

A small, satisfactory smile appeared on her face at his last word. Her nose lifted high in the air as if the way she stood beckoned to be noticed. It did not. She was wobbly and weak, and if she hadn't had a cane in her hand, it was not certain that she could make it across the room. Still,

there was a semblance of importance that did not go unnoticed by Wolfe and others.

The novelist in him could not deny he was curious about this woman, what made her tick. Perhaps the truth would be scarier than anything he'd ever written about!

"Merry Christmas," she said as she walked to the door. "Just know, my friend, that the key to saving this city is within the pages of your book."

Wolfe opened the door for her, but did not say anything. This woman had something up her sleeve, once again.

Back at home a half hour later, Missy Peeple stirred her hot cocoa as she gazed out her bedroom window, watching people of all ages swarm into Blinkland next door. What was it about Mr. Turner that was so appealing to all his relatives? He had lived next to her for thirty-something years. They'd never gotten along. He was fifteen years younger than she, but his hair was frosty white, which did little to explain away the "winter flakes" that always covered the shoulders of his dark sweaters. Though he was continuously smiling, it only accentuated the fact that his nose hairs hadn't seen clippers and his mouth hadn't seen a mint in a decade. Yet every Christmas, oodles of people came to see him.

Sighing, she closed her curtains. From the corner of her eye, she caught the small, framed picture of her dear sister, Sissy. They'd spent holidays together before she died, though they never put up a Christmas tree or lights, or even gave each other presents. But at least it was somebody.

She picked up the picture, but she stared into the eyes of distant memories. She thought it so odd how childhood memories could seem so near, yet the events of yesterday could've been a century ago. Old age did strange things to people. Luckily, she hadn't hit old age yet, unlike her neighbor, who was so needy he made everyone drop what they were doing to come visit him on one of the coldest days of the year. A little self-awareness might do the poor fellow some good.

Missy poked at her bun and set Sissy's picture down. She was never one to second-guess herself, but she had to admit, her visit to Wolfe Boone was extraordinarily risky. What it was about that man that made her take such risks still baffled her. *He* baffled her. It amazed her that a man could throw away years of work that had led him into what every person in their right mind wanted in life. And not only that, throw away the entire identity of a town without a second thought. That kind of lack of regard fascinated her, and there was a certain strength in it that she found tantalizing.

Perhaps that is what had led her up the steps of his house and into his living room. Maybe that is what made her risk everything to give him that book. Little did he realize what truly lay in the pages of that book. He didn't understand that inside was the key to saving the town.

It would be a last resort. There were other ways, and if people would listen to her, Skary would thrive again. But she was beginning to get that sinking feeling that nobody would listen to her anymore.

Thus, radical steps.

She just hoped it wouldn't come to that. Because if it did, life would never be the same for her again.

## CHAPTER 9

WOLFE WAS SURPRISED when he finally got to Ainsley's house and Oliver answered the door, a grim look on his face. "Things aren't good," he said, greeting Wolfe with a handshake.

"What's wrong?" Wolfe looked over the top of Oliver's bald head to find a crowd of people in the living room. "Why is everyone here?"

"It's a long story," Oliver sighed.

But he didn't have to wait long to find one thing out of place, besides all the people that were supposed to be at their own homes celebrating Christmas. Mayor Wullisworth stood in the middle of the room in his pajamas. And there was something odd about his face. It was bright and cheery. Mayor Wullisworth, by all previous impressions, never seemed to be the jovial type. Wolfe's eyes quickly scanned the room.

Garth! What was Garth doing here? The sheriff had Ainsley's former suitor in one corner, talking up something serious. Wolfe sighed. That man was the last person on earth he wanted to see, especially on Christmas.

Alfred stood in another corner, scanning the bookshelves and drinking an eggnog. Melb Cornforth was pacing nervously while holding a sliver of pie on a plate. Butch was checking his reflection in the hallway mirror. And Martin Blarty looked as though he'd just seen a ghost.

"Excuse me," Wolfe said, rushing past Oliver and going into the kitchen, hoping to find Ainsley. She was in there, but, as he could've guessed, the Christmas cheer that put color into her cheeks had drained away.

"Are you all right?" he asked, turning her shoulders to him.

She looked up into his eyes. "Where have you been?" Her chin quivered.

"I'll tell you later." Wolfe sighed. "I am so sorry I'm late. What is going on?"

She pulled him into the pantry. Tears brimmed on her bottom lashes. "This is a nightmare!" she cried. "All these people! I planned for three other people for Christmas dinner, and then four when Alfred showed up, and now I've got…I've got… How many people are out there?"

Wolfe pulled her near and held her tight. She cried into his chest, then looked up at him. He said, "You can do this. I know you can."

She sniffled. "I know. But it's just not what I planned."

"Is there going to be enough food? Should I run home and get something?"

She shook her head. "Ollie, Melb, and Martin all brought their dishes, and I do have a pretty big bird. I can easily make a few more side dishes."

"I'm afraid to ask, but what is going on out there?"

She wiped her tears. "Apparently Mayor Wullisworth is having some sort of meltdown. I don't know. And then Dad brought Garth over because Thief hasn't been acting himself lately. This just isn't how I pictured our first Christmas together."

"Sweetheart, as long as I'm with you, I don't care what else happens. Your house glitters and shines with all that is magical about Christmas. It's like something out of a magazine. But as long as you are in my arms, that's all I want."

She swallowed back more tears and smiled. "I know. Me too."

"And the more people that are here, the more there are to appreciate what hard work you've put into the house to make it look like heaven."

She laughed, then looked at him sheepishly. "Did you see the manger scene I set up over the fireplace? I made it glow by adding lights under the cotton material I laid out."

He squeezed her hand and led her out of the pantry. "I'll go look at it right now. Do you need any help in the kitchen?"

"No, I'm okay. I'm putting you in charge of crowd control though," she smiled. But her smile faded a little. "I swear, if one more person shows up for dinner, I'm going to—"

But before she could get the entire sentence out, Melb rushed up to them, her eyes wide with impending news.

"Set another place. Martin just went to get the reverend."

"Why?"

"Something about an exorcism."

Ainsley rushed passed Wolfe and into the living room. Her father was still speaking to Garth about Thief when she pulled him to the side.

"What is this about an exorcism?" she asked, hardly able to hide the tension in her voice.

The sheriff rubbed his chin, glancing down at her. "Hmmm. Had never thought of it before, but maybe that's what would get Thief back on his feet." This brought a wry smile to Garth's lips. It quickly faded as Ainsley shot him a look.

Suppressing her exasperation, she said, "I don't think it's for *Thief.*" She gestured toward the mayor, who was sniffing the Christmas tree as if it were a huge bouquet of daisies.

"Oh." The sheriff shrugged. "Well, whatever works."

"Dad! It is Christmas! I will *not* have an exorcism in this house on Christmas!"

"Lower your voice," the sheriff said as a few people glanced their way. "Honey, can't you see there is something wrong with the mayor?"

"I realize that," she scowled. "But we are supposed to be roasting chestnuts on an open fire, not casting demons into one."

The sheriff pulled her into a side hug. "I know how much Christmas means to you, and how you always want everything to go perfectly. You are so much like your mother. Tell you what. I'll speak to the reverend and make sure no exorcisms take place until after we eat."

She wanted to cry all over again, but her anger was crowding the tears out. Was the whole world going mad? She was just about to lose her temper when the reverend walked in with a somber expression that quieted the whole room. He looked at the mayor with a compassion that suddenly reminded her of the human being standing by the tree in his pajamas. She watched as the reverend patted the mayor on the back, then looked at the crowd as if the only thing that mattered in the world was this man.

Guilt now replaced anger, and she sighed, walking back into the kitchen. Melb was in there and said, "The flag popped up. Turkey's ready."

Ainsley pulled on her oven mitts. "Thanks."

Melb Cornforth stared at the giblet gravy, her hand hovering over the fancy silver ladle. She then stared down at her plate. She'd chosen white meat over dark and two rolls minus the butter, skipped the mashed potatoes, and gotten the green bean casserole instead, which looked very curious with onion rings on top and some kind of lumpy creamed concoction floating the beans. She also had a nice pile of pimentos, her favorite condiment, thanks to Ainsley being generous enough to let her raid the pantry. She'd cut a lot of calories, but the giblet gravy beckoned her.

"Sweetie pie, you okay there?" Oliver asked.

"I'm fine," she breathed. "I, um, I'm just deciding on the gravy."

"Oh."

Seconds ticked by, and she was suddenly aware that the line behind her was now waiting for the gravy. She bit her lip. She couldn't remember ever eating turkey without giblet gravy.

"Maybe just a little bit," she said.

"What?" Oliver asked.

"Nothing. Um, sorry. I'll just be getting some gravy." One ladle full. One. That's all. She dipped the ladle into the gravy, spread the sauce over as much as one ladlefull would cover, and moved on to the drinks.

In the living room, she sat down on the couch and put her plate on the coffee table. In the corner, she caught Thief lying on a blanket, watching her without interest. The last time she'd sat here, she thought that cat was dead and she was sniffing its fur. Bad memories. She decided to move over to the other couch by the fire. As she sat down, she remembered this was where she blew out the seams in an extra small T-shirt when she sneezed over the mayor's cologne. More bad memories.

Across the rug, there was a nice wingback chair. She moved over there and decided the haunting might cease because she'd never sat in this chair before. She stared at the plate in her hands, but all she could hear in her head was *four dress sizes* echoing over and over again.

She could do this. She was Melb Cornforth, for crying out loud. A strong woman, and soon to be married to Oliver S. What more motivation did she need? She glanced up, watching Oliver lick mashed potatoes off his wrist before spotting her across the living room and giving her a big grin. She smiled back, but her stomach grumbled its protest that she had forgone the mashed potatoes. Small portions. Chew food until it's liquid. Don't eat more than the size of your fist. Drink eight glasses of water. She smiled. This was doable.

~⟨⟩~

Wolfe had never played host in his life, but he thought he was getting the hang of it. He'd offered people drinks, brought others napkins, made sure everyone had a place to sit. He'd even refilled the gravy bowl after Melb Cornforth practically poured the whole thing on her plate after her third pass through the line. He didn't blame her. Ainsley made the best giblet gravy he'd ever tasted.

He scanned the crowd. Everyone looked happy, and it sort of reminded him of Thanksgiving, minus the sinister plots and not-so-dead cat. Not to mention his near-death experience. Even Alfred looked to be enjoying himself, and he was glad his old friend didn't have to spend the holidays alone. The mayor looked somewhat perplexed as to why he was eating turkey and stuffing in July, but he was eating nevertheless.

What bothered Wolfe, though, was knowing Ainsley was not having a good time. Though she was able to pull herself together enough to offer that winsome smile everyone came to expect, her eyes reflected disappointment. He knew he had to cheer her up.

His first plan was to remind her of her excellence as a hostess, not to mention her knack for decorating. In fact, he realized, he hadn't had a chance to admire the special manger she'd set up. After a quick glance around to make sure there were no dire needs, he decided he'd go look at the manger, then find Ainsley and tell her how wonderful it looked.

Over the fireplace, she'd fashioned an amazing setup. A large wooden manger, complete with details like hay and sackcloth, was the backdrop to the story the figurines told…the story of the day the earth's soul found its worth. Somehow she had used tiny Christmas lights to give the illusion of a majestic glow. In the middle of the manger, a small, bundled baby Jesus lay quietly asleep. Kneeling over him was a serene-looking Mary and a proud-looking Joseph. Between these two, a mighty and beautiful angel hovered, arms swept up in worship, wings spread. To their left, humble and lowly shepherds stood with their staffs in their hands, their animals in tow. Two were kneeling. One stood with his hand over his heart.

And to their right…to their right…nothing. Where were the Wise Men? Wolfe stood baffled. The space was completely empty, as if something had formerly been there, but was now gone. He peeked around the side of the manger, just to see if the Wise Men had somehow gotten distracted and needed to quickly wrap their gifts. But there was nothing. He rubbed his brow line, trying to decide what to do. If Ainsley had indeed forgotten to put the Wise Men out, she'd be horrified to realize that no one had told her. That was not the likely scenario, though. Biting his lip, Wolfe decided he'd better go tell her. She would want to know.

He found her in the kitchen, alone. The guests were happily munching away at Christmas dinner. Ainsley was putting another batch of rolls in the oven.

"Hey," Wolfe said.

She mustered a smile for him. "Hi."

"Aren't you going to eat?"

"I'm not hungry."

"Sweetheart, don't let this ruin your Christmas. Everyone is happy. I know this isn't what you wanted, but it's working out."

"I know," she said quietly, adjusting the temperature on the oven.

"Then what's wrong? You look so down."

She shook her head, staring at the tile beneath her shoes. "This is just very hard for me to take."

"What? The company?"

"No. Not the company."

"What then?"

She guided him to the doorway and pointed to the crowd in the living room. Everyone seemed fine. He shrugged, raising his eyebrow to indicate he wasn't sure what she was talking about.

"TV trays."

"TV trays?"

She nodded, her words choked. "People are eating off TV trays."

"And...?"

"And I never would've imagined the day people would eat off TV trays in my home. I didn't even know we had TV trays in this house. Dad said they were Aunt Gert's." She looked up at him. "I probably sound like a horrible snob. But to me, a dinner as special as Christmas needs to be shared at the table, with a linen tablecloth, candelabras, wineglasses, garlands fashioned with scented pine cones and silky red ribbon. Instead, I've got...TV trays. And a buffet line."

He squeezed her hands. "You've always had such high expectations for yourself. There is no way you could've predicted this many people would come for dinner. And the fact that you were able to feed a crowd with no notice is nothing short of miraculous. Everyone will be gone soon, and then we'll sit in front of the fire, just the two of us, and you can unwrap the gift I got you."

Through teary eyes, she smiled brightly at him. "I can't wait. I have a gift for you too!"

He stroked her cheek and then kissed her forehead. And also realized this was not a good time to mention the Wise Men. She retreated into the kitchen, and he gazed at the TV trays in the living room. Frankly, he'd always liked eating off them.

## CHAPTER 10

THE REVEREND STOOD near the mayor, who was sitting in a wingback chair reading a book about sailing he'd taken from the sheriff's library. He seemed oblivious to the fact that the entire room, huddled in several groups in various places in the living area, was staring at him. Their collective breath-holding nearly depleted the room of oxygen.

"Well?" the sheriff asked after a few moments. "What are you waiting for?"

The reverend cleared his throat. "I'm sorry. I'm, um…just a tad nervous. I've never done this before." He looked down at the paper sack he was carrying and carefully began pulling out a book.

"Is that your exorcism book?" Melb gasped, eyes wide.

"No, it's Wolfe's fourth book, *Spirits Within*."

"What?" Wolfe stepped forward, from behind Ainsley. "What'd you bring that for?"

"Don't you remember? You wrote an exorcism scene on page 266."

"And?"

"Well, it's the only thing I have to go by."

"But it's fiction," Wolfe said. "I made it up!"

The reverend shrugged. "Scared the daylights out of me, so I figure you must've gotten something right."

The room took a step back as the reverend took a step forward, opening the book to page 266. The mayor continued to read about sailing, still unaware that his head might start spinning any second.

After several minutes of unabated silence, the sheriff blurted, "Well, what are you waiting for? Permission from the demon?"

The reverend shook his head, his face dark with contemplation. "There's just something not right. I'm not quite sure…"

The crowd glanced around, and then Oliver suggested with a jab of his thumb over to the stereo, "Maybe we should kill the Christmas music."

Everyone heartily acknowledged with nods that "Jingle Bell Rock" was probably not setting the right mood for the exorcism, so Oliver turned off the music.

"Okay," the reverend said. "Let's just get this over with." He lifted Wolfe's book and started reading. "All right. Looks like we get him seated." He looked up. "Okay, good. Now, it says here that I'm supposed to lay my hands on him and say, 'Everyone step back. I'm not sure what's going to happen.'"

The whole room took a giant step backward, except Wolfe, who was standing there looking shocked, and Butch, who'd pulled out some sort of large military knife.

"And then my hands are supposed to tremble because I'm nervous." Everyone glanced at the reverend's hands. "Okay, we're right on track there."

Wolfe was about to say something, but the reverend continued. "Now, at this point, looks like the demon-possessed is going to struggle and spit on me. Can someone get me a towel?"

Melb ran for the kitchen.

"And I'm supposed to stand my ground, look him in the eye"—the reverend's voice rose with each word—"and say, I command you, demon, to leave this man *now!*"

Everyone gasped, waiting in anticipation, but the mayor just continued to read his sailing book. After a few anticlimactic moments, the sheriff asked, "Well? What's supposed to happen then?"

"According to the book, he's supposed to turn green, his skin starts to melt, and he talks in a weird voice…and, oh my, well… Let's just say he curses."

"Oooooh." The crowd studied the mayor, then suddenly, all eyes were on Wolfe, who could only shrug.

The sheriff said, "This obviously isn't working. Maybe you skipped a step."

"Or maybe he's not demon-possessed," Wolfe offered.

A few nods indicated that might be a possibility.

"Well, you're the expert," Butch said. "What's your assessment?"

"I'm not an expert," Wolfe said, "but I'd say we might be more effective if we joined around the mayor and prayed for him."

"Ohhhhh," said the crowd, and by the way everyone scurried toward the mayor, it was evident prayer was a much more comfortable solution than exorcism.

And so, for a few quiet moments, the group prayed for the mayor. Afterward, there was a peacefulness in the room that didn't come from the Christmas lights or the smell of turkey. Everyone smiled and hugged one another.

And then, from the doorway of the kitchen, Ainsley said in a cheerful voice, "Pie, anyone?"

"Come here," Wolfe said, beckoning Ainsley to the floor in front of the Christmas tree. As dusk lulled Christmas evening into a quiet slumber, and the entire house was filled with sparkling tree lights and golden-orange sunlight, she fell into his arms, exhausted.

"My goodness," she sighed. "It can't already be evening, can it?"

Wolfe smiled down at her. How beautiful she was! He couldn't wait to be her husband. He looked around and they were finally alone. Butch was passed out on a couch in the other room. Apparently in combat he could fight fatigue off for days at a time, but that's no match for what turkey can do to you. The sheriff was upstairs, concerning himself with a cat he thought was acting particularly weird because he wanted to lie around all day.

"Here," he said, handing her a present.

She clapped her hands together like a little girl. "I've been waiting

for this all day! This doesn't happen to be a clue to where you're taking me on our honeymoon?"

"Not a chance! You find that out after you say, 'I do.'"

After admiring his wrapping job, she pulled apart the bow and opened the package. She covered her mouth and gasped. "Wolfe!"

"Do you like them?"

She held up the diamond earrings, looking at him with tears in her eyes. "I don't suppose it's a coincidence that these are exactly like the ones my mother used to wear?"

"I had a designer in New York make them." He smiled. "I noticed your mother wearing them in that portrait you have of her on the mantel. Your dad let me take the picture to get it copied so I could send it to the designer."

"They're exquisite." She touched them with delicate fingers. "Thank you." She hugged him tightly, then kissed him. "I am so in love with you."

"Good thing, since we're getting hitched in two and a half months!"

She giggled. "Here. Open mine!"

Wolfe copied Ainsley by looking at the wrapping job, which included shiny gold paper, a huge satin bow, and trinkets hanging off the sides. She smiled at him, acknowledging that he'd taken the time to look at the package before ripping into it.

Then he ripped into it. *Mere Christianity!*" he exclaimed. "How did you know I've never read this book?"

"Because," she smiled, "every book you've ever read is on a bookshelf somewhere in your house. I know you'll like it. C. S. Lewis is one of my favorites."

"I'd been wanting to read this! Thank you," he said, wrapping his arms around her. "What do you say we just sit like this all weekend until I have to go back to work on Monday?"

She laughed. "It's strange to hear you talk like you have a regular Monday-through-Friday job."

"I know. I've only been to work one day, though, so I guess I can't judge it yet."

"Is Oliver okay to work with?"

"Yeah, as far as I can tell."

She shook her head. "I have to admit, I have a hard time picturing you selling cars."

"Maybe that's because I haven't sold one yet. I might be good at it, you know."

"Maybe." She smiled, and then they held each other and stared into the fire for a moment. But the silence was shattered by a frightened gasp from Ainsley. She sat up.

"Ainsley? What's the matter?" he asked.

Her mouth hung open as she pointed to the mantel. "Where are the Wise Men?"

Dr. Hass stepped out onto his front porch, which extended the entire length of his new home. He'd only seen pictures, so it was nice to see it in person now. He could eventually hang his sign from the porch using a pole so it stuck out, easily read. He smiled at the thought.

For him, Christmases were usually spent at lavish parties where women wore dresses that seemed to completely undermine the reason for the holiday, yet nobody complained. Now he stood alone in a small town with nobody to party with. He had to admit, the silence was soothing.

A cat leapt onto the porch, its tail strung high in the air. She rubbed against his arm as he leaned against the porch rail. "Good kitty," he said. "You look hungry." He started to dart inside for a saucer of milk but then remembered the sheer number of cats in town. He didn't want to send a message that he was a soft touch, always good for a free meal. The cat purred loudly and made an attempt to come inside, but Dr. Hass stuck his foot out as he opened the screen door. "Nope. Not today, kitty. Go find another home."

Inside, the house was not empty, thanks to the family who had decided to sell the furniture along with the house. His footsteps echoed

as he crossed the old wooden floors. He would buff those, make them nice and shiny. His suitcase and other things were still in the foyer. For a third time on this day, he wandered around the three bedrooms, the two bathrooms, and eventually ended up in his large office, where he knew he would be spending an exceptional amount of time. It was perfect. All the wood was dark walnut, with built-in bookshelves and a nice view of the backyard through a large picture window. From there, he could also see the garage apartment.

But as he stood in his office, one overwhelming thought canceled out all the excitement of his new life. How was he going to make a living? He'd never worried about it before. Since he was sixteen, he'd managed to make it on his own. But that was always in the big city.

He'd resigned himself to the fact he would no longer be living the grand lifestyle to which he was accustomed. He was okay with that. No more fancy cars, fancy pads, fancy women. But there was still the question of whether he would be able to make a living. That single question had driven him for years and years, far beyond its answer, which was yes. But the fear of not making money made him continue to make money and eventually become the man everyone liked to hate. He sighed, looking around the house once more, and decided to unpack his few belongings. The old life had chewed him up and spit him out. Now he hoped it had regurgitated him into a new life.

Standing in front of the beautiful bay window that gave him a good view of Skary, he reminded himself not to fall into the trap of believing he was going to have to take desperate measures. This was Skary, Indiana. Life was simple here. Things worked out as they should, when given enough time. The pace was slow.

Dr. Hass was turning over a new leaf. He'd said good-bye to his old self. But he knew old habits were hard to break.

"Who would take the Wise Men?" Ainsley's desperate cry had roused Butch off the couch and brought the sheriff downstairs in a hurry. They

all stood in front of the mantel, gazing at the place where the three Wise Men once stood.

"You're sure you set them out?" Butch asked, a quizzical eyebrow pointed toward his nonreceding hairline.

"Butch! Of course I set them out! Do you think I would forget the Wise Men?"

Apparently Butch was the only man in the room who did. He shrugged and then wandered around, looking for clues. Ainsley just stood there, perplexed. Nobody had any answers.

Wolfe rubbed her shoulders, but she didn't seem comforted. She turned to him. "I know those Wise Men were there this morning. Somebody took them during Christmas dinner. Who would do that?"

"Maybe it's intended to be a little joke," Wolfe said. "I'm sure they'll bring them back."

"Some joke." She sighed.

"Perhaps it was the mayor. He isn't in his right mind today," the sheriff said.

Ainsley moped into the kitchen, where she fixed herself and Wolfe cups of hot cocoa. Handing it to him after sprinkling slivers of chocolate on top, she shook her head. "Seems like every major holiday ends up with some crazy event occurring, some crisis."

"I guess it does kind of seem that way, doesn't it?" he said.

"What's the next holiday? Valentine's Day?"

"Yeah."

"Well thank goodness, there's already a major event scheduled."

"Melb and Oliver's wedding."

"Let's just pray that's enough for fate to leave that holiday alone."

## CHAPTER 11

MELB CORNFORTH WAS HURRYING along Fourth Street on her way to the deli, trying to convince herself if she took the long route and burned some calories, she might be able to eat a bearclaw and still lose weight.

It had been two weeks since Christmas, since she had discovered that not only did she have no willpower, but she actually had negative willpower. If the thought even entered her mind that she shouldn't eat something, her desire for that food tripled. Except reverse psychology didn't seem to work. She'd tried thinking of how much she didn't want to eat raw carrots. She still didn't want to eat raw carrots.

And the more she thought about not fitting into her wedding dress, the more stressed she became. And the more stressed she became, the more she ate. It didn't help that she still hadn't told Oliver she'd gone over budget. Secretly, she was hoping she might be able to save money some other places.

She'd spent the morning practicing how to spell Oliver's last name correctly, and then practicing her new signature. She once thought "Cornforth" was a long last name but now realized she had nothing on Oliver. For about fifteen minutes she wrote it over and over, and once she got the hang of where all the vowels went, she finally nailed it, even though she had to make up a little song about it. Oh, well. Whatever worked.

What wasn't working was her plan to lose four dress sizes. And that was exactly where her mind was when she found herself on top of a man in the middle of the sidewalk.

"*Oh! My!* I am so sorry!" Melb climbed off the man and stood to her feet. She watched as the man slowly stood up, and saw on his face the most horrible grimace. Her whole life flashed in front of her eyes, and she imagined she was about to be murdered in the middle of Fourth Street. She hoped they would find her body soon.

But then the man sneezed. Melb screamed. It's amazing how much a sneeze and a gunshot can sound alike. The man looked at her after wiping his nose. "Are you okay?"

Her whole body was trembling, but she managed a smile and a nod. "Again, I'm so sorry. I was in deep thought."

She looked at the old house in front of them, one she knew had been abandoned for over a year. "Do you live here?"

"Just moved here. Dr. Hass." The man extended a hand.

"Doctor?"

"But I'm not a medical doctor, I'm—"

"A *psychologist?!*" she gasped and then jumped up and down in excitement. "That's exactly what I need! Why didn't I think of it before?"

"Ma'am, listen, I—"

"You just moved here. I understand. You probably don't even have your office set up. But listen, I'm willing to pay high dollar for your services. Doctor, I am desperate."

The man stood there, looking flabbergasted. Melb decided to sweeten the deal. She pulled out a wad of cash from her purse. "Look, I'll pay you in cash right now. I need someone to talk to. I was going to use this as a down payment for a caterer for my wedding, but I think it will be better spent with you."

He looked down at the money in her hand and cupped her shoulder. "Tell me about your problem."

Reverend Peck could hardly contain his excitement. Since before Christmas, he had been working out his plan, and now he was just a few days

from completion. As far as he was concerned, this was divinely inspired. He'd thought of every detail. Now he just had to implement it.

As quickly as a man his age could work, he unbolted every pew from the floor.

"There. Perfect. Just the right amount of squeeze. Try it one more time."

Wolfe tried not to sigh with boredom as he shook Oliver's hand, *squeezing* it firmly but gently.

"Perfect!" Oliver said. "That's exactly how you want to greet every customer. That says you're not overbearing, but you're confident. Look 'em in the eye, too. Give 'em that killer grin. But remember, don't squeeze too tightly. That freaks people out. They think you know too much about 'em. They think you're out to sell them a car and nothing else."

"What else would you be out for?"

"You want to build trust with the customer, Wolfe. It's all about trust. Any of these people can drive fifteen miles down the road to Gordon MacNamera's place. They gotta believe that they are not the only customer who has been to your lot that day. Your handshake has to say, 'Glad you're here, but I'm not desperate.' And listen, don't hold out on the ladies. They like the firm handshake too. Nothing grosses a woman out like a limpy-noodle handshake."

"Okay."

"Now, once you've closed the deal—and not to discourage you, but it's going to be a while before I'll let you close a deal—then you firm up that handshake, and you place your other hand on top of theirs. It's the 'we've bonded for life' handshake, and they'll remember that the next time they need a car. All right, let's try that one."

Oliver held out his hand, but Wolfe shook his head. "You know, Oliver, maybe we could take a break. This is a…a lot of information to process."

Oliver slapped his head. "Of course, I'm sorry. I forget sometimes,

you know? It's as natural to me as breathing. But hey, don't get discouraged. You're doing great on the secret language. I'm real proud of you on that."

"Thanks."

"Tell you what. Why don't you take fifteen minutes, get some air? And then we'll go over some of the trade secrets I've been hinting about."

"Terrific."

Wolfe walked out of Oliver's office, his head pounding from all the effort it was taking him to pay attention. It had been two solid weeks of training. Oliver had yet to let him even talk to a customer, for fear he might make a mistake and blow the whole deal.

What deal Oliver was talking about, Wolfe wasn't sure. So far, in two weeks, Oliver had sold one car. And Wolfe had seen only a handful of other customers come on the lot. How did this man make a living?

He'd watched Oliver talk to the customers. He was quite good with his body language. They always seemed at ease. And he admired that Oliver took great care in how he approached the customers. Wolfe had been trained in everything from how to dress to look professional but not uppity, to the secret handshake.

And as fascinating as all this behind-the-scenes car selling was, Wolfe had to admit to himself he was feeling quite empty. But maybe it was because he'd been sidelined. As soon as Oliver let him get in the game, maybe things would look up.

He didn't miss writing, at least what he used to write. But what he did miss were those early morning hours when his mind would wander to the faraway places he created, where journeys began, characters were birthed, emotions within him and his new world merged. Now his mornings consisted of a quick cup of coffee and a straightening of his tie, which Oliver indicated was of utmost importance, since "a crooked tie could indicate a crooked tie owner." Or something to that effect.

But where emptiness lingered from his former craft, not so far away in his soul was the unbelievable joy he felt for Ainsley. Every day he grew to love her more, which amazed him, because every day he didn't think

it was possible to love someone more. Still, he couldn't help but wonder if this was what God had for his life.

"Wolfe!"

He turned around from where he'd been leaning on the front of the building. Ainsley was running up to him, her face shining with happiness.

"Hi!" He embraced and kissed her. "What are you doing here?"

She handed him a paper sack. "I baked up some blueberry muffins and thought I'd drop you by a couple, in case you got hungry later. I have a feeling you are not packing yourself a proper lunch."

"Bologna doesn't count?"

She made a grimace, and he laughed.

"You look good," Wolfe said, brushing her hair away from her face. "Are you on your way to work?"

"Actually," she said, her voice full of excitement, "I just quit work!"

"What? Really?"

She nodded. "I did. I can't believe it. It was very hard, but I did it."

He hugged her. "That's terrific news! Now you'll have all the time in the world to plan the wedding."

"Well…"

"What?"

"That will give me more time. But that's not why I quit. I've been meeting with Alfred this morning."

He tried not to let the irritation he felt become apparent in his features. He smiled. "Oh?"

"Wolfe, this is so exciting. I can't begin to tell you. Alfred has this entire plan for me. He's been really thinking this through. And honey, it's…it's everything I've ever wanted to be."

He swallowed down the words he wanted to say and tried to listen. "Tell me more."

"Well, he's got this idea that I will start small, just doing some small catering jobs around Skary and nearby towns. We'll get the local papers to give me some coverage on those things. He said as I gain more exposure, we'll need to come up with some big event for me to do, and he's

going to bring out a film crew and basically make it like my first show. I think he called it a pilot. Once we get that edited, he's going to show it to some TV execs, see if they like me. He's also got a photo shoot lined up for me. He's says it is as much about the look as the cook. He says I have this way about me where I seem nice but knowledgeable." She clasped her hands. "Isn't this exciting?"

"Honey, um, what about the wedding?"

"What about it? I'll have plenty of time for both. Now that I'm not working, I have all the time in the world. Oooo, which reminds me, I gotta run. Alfred wants me to stop by the local hardware store and see if they'd let me put on a bake sale outside while teaching the finer points of woodworking."

"You know woodworking?"

"Not really, but Alfred says Martha doesn't know everything either, but she has a lot of experts helping and teaching her, so then she can teach us. Okay, gotta run. See you at my house for dinner tonight?"

"Yes."

"Okay. Bye." Wolfe watched as she rushed to her car and then drove out of sight, giving him a quick wave as she left the parking lot. He didn't have much time to think about it, though, because he glanced over to find Oliver tapping his watch and beckoning him back with a fatherly wink.

It was not even noon yet.

—◯—

Dr. Hass was pleased he'd at least gotten part of his office assembled. A few books and knickknacks lined the shelves. He'd even lined his desk with office supplies. He had yet to hang his many awards of excellence. Apparently, this woman who'd run into him didn't need any credentials. She already thought he could solve all her problems.

Stuffing the wad of money in his pocket, able to smell it even from within the dark fabric of his pants, he invited her in and offered her the chair that had come with the house. He was a pretty good judge of char-

acter, but this woman, "Melb" she called herself, wasn't so easily sized up. She had a jovial smile and a gentle demeanor, yet her eyes sparkled with passion and determination.

"Don't you have a couch?" she asked, settling herself into the plush leather chair.

"Um…that's on its way."

She chuckled. "I guess I shouldn't be hard on you. You haven't even opened up for business! Besides, I'd probably fall right into a deep sleep if I stretched out on a nice couch. Hey, that's an idea! Do you hypnotize?"

"No."

"Okay, just asking. I thought that might be a good solution to my problem."

"What problem is that?"

"Oh yeah, right. The problem. You work by the hour, not the word count, eh? Anyway, I've got to lose weight. Four dress sizes. By Valentine's Day."

Dr. Hass remembered the new person he'd decided to become. In the old days, he would've laughed and made a wisecrack about the middle of the earth freezing over. But that was not who he was now. And surprisingly, without making that kind of wisecrack, he was really having a hard time coming up with anything else to say.

"Doctor?"

"Yes, um, sorry. Well…how much weight have you lost so far?"

"I've gained five pounds."

"I see." He decided he'd better get out a pad and take some notes. "Well, what kind of diet have you tried?"

"Um, I'm not sure what it's called, but it's where you try not to eat as much as you did before. I think it's low carb, medium protein, a little fat. Or is it low protein, high carb, and medium fat? I'm sure it's got some fancy name, but I can't think of it."

"Okay. Let me ask you this. Why do you want to lose the weight? Are you unhappy about how you look?"

"Heavens no! I'm a big-boned woman, and I always have been. Melb

Cornforth wouldn't look right in a size two pair of jeans. I'm voluptuous, and that's how God created me to be. Nobody is more secure about who they are than Melb Cornforth!"

"Then why do you want to lose weight?"

"Well, I found this fancy little wedding dress on sale, and in my haste to buy it, I didn't—what's the word?—acknowledge it was four sizes too small."

"Can't you return it?"

"It was on clearance. I got a good deal on it though." She smiled at that thought. "So anyway, what I'm realizing is that this is all in the head." She tapped her cheekbone. "And that's why I believe you're the perfect man for the job. Dieting isn't about eating right! It's about thinking right!"

Dr. Hass nodded, fairly impressed with her catchy phrases and smooth clichés. But concern grew inside him as he realized that he might not be able to help this woman. Yet he also knew there wasn't too much he couldn't sell, especially to a woman willing to listen.

"What's your favorite food, Melb?"

"Oh, that's easy. Pimentos."

"Pimentos?"

"Yes, I'll eat them on anything, which is my second-favorite food."

"What is that?"

"Anything."

"Okay…well, Melb, it seems to me that you are a very driven woman. What do you do for fun? What's your hobby?"

Melb shrugged. "I guess reading."

"Reading. Okay, Melb, it's time for you to find yourself a new hobby!"

"A new hobby?" The woman's eyes grew wide as if he'd announced she should try out for the swim team.

"Certainly. Right now your fixation is on food. Or rather, food you can't or shouldn't have. You need a new fixation." In the short time he had known Melb Cornforth, he had assessed that she was a woman easily fixated.

"A hobby..." He could tell by the way her eyes warmed that this idea was growing on her. "Why didn't I think of that? A hobby! Of course!" She looked at Dr. Hass. "What should I do?"

"Anything that you've never done before. Painting. Knitting. Writing. Jogging. Bird watching."

"Bird watching!" she shouted. Dr. Hass grabbed his heart, which had frozen in time momentarily but luckily started beating again. "That's perfect! I love birds! I have two of them. And there's been this old owl outside the house the past few nights. I've never seen an owl around these parts, to tell you the truth. And this bird just sits up there and says 'whoo whoo' over and over and over again. Why not pull out some binoculars and watch him?"

"Yeah...um...that sounds good."

"Thank you, Dr. Hass! You've been so helpful! Definitely worth the money."

"Oh, well..."

"No, really. It's great to finally find someone who knows what he's talking about." She stood and shook his hand heartily. "You're a godsend."

Dr. Hass smiled meekly as he escorted Melb out the front door of his home. She waved as she walked off, a cheerful grin easy to spot even at a distance. He just hoped he'd helped the poor woman. And that he never had to see her again. He had a lot of work to do, but it did not include helping the pimento-ly challenged.

## CHAPTER 12

THOUGH THE LONGTIME MAYOR of Skary, Indiana, sat at his desk in Bermuda shorts and a Hawaiian shirt in the middle of January, Martin Blarty tried not to let that distract him from the task at hand, which was figuring out, one, the history of Skary, Indiana. And two, where that history could be. Why would anybody steal Skary's history? Certainly he could talk to residents, see what they knew of their family history. But how accurate that would be, he didn't know. And he had to admit, his drive to uncover the town's origin was only intensified by his suspicion that someone was trying to hide Skary's history.

Admittedly, his first suspect was Mayor Wullisworth. If that man was capable of shorts in January, he was capable of anything.

"Martin!" the mayor called. Martin removed himself from the storage room where he'd been rummaging around for clues and went to the mayor's office.

"Yes sir?"

"Listen, I was thinking," the mayor said authoritatively, "we need some pep around this town. It's looking very bleak. Don't you think we need to start a city beautification program? Get some wildflowers growing. Have a nice landscape design somewhere in the town, maybe the city hall. Perhaps a fountain. You know, perk things up a little. My stars, by the looks of things around here, you'd think it was the dead of winter."

Martin didn't know what to say, so he stood there.

The mayor glanced up at him after several seconds of silence. "Don't we have a budget for that sort of thing?"

"Um…" Martin's words failed him. Not only did they not have a budget for that sort of thing, but they didn't have a budget, period. The town was going broke, and by the numbers he'd crunched last night, it looked as though salaries would have to be the next thing to go.

"For crying out loud, Martin, it doesn't have to look like the Rose Bowl parade. Just a few flowers for some color. How expensive can flowers be? See to it, will you?"

"Sure. Of course." He backed out of the mayor's office, his stomach in knots. Besides the budget crisis, there was also that tiny problem of the mayor going insane. Martin Blarty had to find this little town's purpose and find it quick.

He decided he needed to get some air, but just as he opened the front door to the building, he heard a bloodcurdling scream coming from outside. He ran out, his limbs trembling with fear. He'd never heard a scream like that. He scanned the area but saw nothing. The town was quiet now. Small flurries of snowflakes fell softly to the ground. He stood there for several more minutes, but there was only silence.

"Did you hear that?" Ainsley said, excusing herself from the makeup chair.

"What?" Alfred asked, checking his watch. Maude the Makeup Queen worked by the hour, and he was paying her a bunch of money to come make Ainsley Parker look delicate, winsome, strong, and smart. It amazed him what the right color blush could do.

Ainsley was at the front door. "That scream. Someone screamed."

Alfred shrugged. After living in New York for so many years, he guessed he had tuned out screaming a long time ago. "Ainsley, dear, let's get back to the task at hand."

Ainsley shut the front door, her brow furrowed. "I hope everyone's okay."

"Darling, you've only got one eye done, and I don't think you want to look like Boy George," Maude snapped.

"Who is Boy George?" Ainsley asked Alfred as she climbed back into the chair.

"Nobody you need to know about. Now listen, as soon as Maude is done here, we're just going to take a few pictures of you in your kitchen, doing various things. Just sort of your natural everyday life."

"For the portfolio, right?"

"Right. We want to put together a portfolio that will show your talent, your look, your 'brand.'"

"Brand of what? It depends on what I'm cooking."

"No, sweetheart. *Your* brand. It's how we're going to define you. You see, Martha already has a brand. We've got to make your brand similar enough that you appeal to Martha's followers, yet different enough so that you become your own product. Do you see?"

"I think so."

"I'm done," Maude announced, snapping her makeup case closed. She eyed Ainsley for a little bit. "So you're Wolfe Boone's lady, huh?"

Ainsley nodded. "Fiancée."

"I did Wolfe's makeup for a photo shoot for *Vanity Fair* years ago. Nice guy. You're lucky."

"Thanks."

Maude turned to Alfred. "You want me to stick around for touch-ups, or am I outta here?"

"Darling, at your rates, I'm going to have to send you packing. But good job with the makeup. She'll glow in the camera."

Maude winked. "But not shine. See ya."

Ainsley looked at Alfred. "We could've asked my friend Marlee to come over, you know. She does Mary Kay. It's not the way I'd wear makeup, but everyone else seems to like it."

Alfred drew her hands into his. "My sweet Ainsley. This is the big time now. You have to start thinking like that. Sure, we're just starting out. But if you don't think you're worthy of having your makeup done for a photo shoot, then the world may not think you're worthy of showing them how to bake manicotti."

"I have the best recipe this side of Lake Michigan."

He grinned. "Good girl. Now let's get in the kitchen and see what we've got. Philippe? Philippe?"

The photographer, a wisp of a guy in a black turtleneck and tortoise-shell eyeglasses, capered around the corner. "Are we ready?" he said in a French accent with a touch of Mississippi. Without the accent and trendy glasses, Philippe could have just as easily been Phil from down south.

"Ainsley, meet Philippe. He is one of the best photographers in New York."

"Did you ever take Wolfe's picture?" she asked, shaking his hand.

"I never had the pleasure. But my friend, Eric Boneham, have you heard of him?" She shook her head. "He is the one who took the portrait of Wolfe that's now on all the back covers of his books."

"Oh. Well, pleasure to meet you."

"All right, Ainsley, let's step around here, into your kitchen. Philippe, do you have all the lights set?"

"Heavenly," Philippe said, kissing his fingers and throwing them into the air.

"Okay, now, Ainsley, what I want you to do is take that pie on the counter, put it over here, so the camera can see you, and then we're going to get a shot of you cutting the pie."

"Okay." She took the pie, put it on the counter facing the camera, and cut the crust.

"*No!*"

Ainsley gasped, looking up at Alfred.

"I'm sorry, dear. I didn't mean to shout. Don't really cut the pie. Just *pretend* to cut the pie. I need you to look up at the camera, give that world-famous smile of yours, and pretend to cut."

"One should never cut something while looking elsewhere," she said.

"Martha can."

Determination sparked in her bright eyes. "Well, I guess since I'm not really cutting." She looked into the camera, smiled, and pointed the large knife to the center of the pie.

"Perfect!" Alfred clapped.

But Philippe said, "I'm not sure about the hair. Tied back like that?"

"Maude spent twenty minutes putting it in a sophisticated bun," Alfred said.

"I know, but it makes her look rigid. Don't we want more of an enchanting allure? The sprite of the kitchen, no?"

Alfred thought about this and then agreed. "Ainsley, let's take your hair down." They loosened a few pins, and her hair fell around her shoulders.

"Very nice," Philippe said with a smile.

Alfred sighed. "But the apron. It's hideous!"

"It was my Aunt Gert's," she said, looking down at it. "What's wrong with it?"

"Besides the fact it leapt out of 1965? Do you have anything else?"

She frowned. "A plain white one I got a few Christmases ago."

"Let's try it."

She removed the first apron and put on the second one. But it was much too big, hanging off her like a bed sheet. "No. Won't work. Too big. It doesn't show off your figure."

"What does my figure have to do with anything?"

"We like to give the image that you eat all day but still look like a model," Alfred grinned.

"Why would we want to give off that image?" she scowled.

"Because, Ainsley, we're creating an illusion. Just like Martha. I mean, we'd all like to live in Martha's world, but the truth of the matter is that it's impossible to create."

She crossed her arms. "I did it."

Alfred smiled. "And that, my dear, is why you will be the next person to encourage the world to tie up their linens with satin bows."

"What is going on here?"

Ainsley and Alfred turned around to find the sheriff standing there with his hands on his hips.

"Daddy! Hi! You're up from your nap."

"What's all this?" he said, gesturing toward the kitchen and eying Philippe.

"It's a photo shoot, Daddy. Isn't it wonderful? Alfred is putting together a portfolio for me. He thinks I can make it big."

The sheriff looked at his daughter, a small, sweet smile peeking from beneath his bushy moustache. "I know you can make it big too. You're the best cook I know."

"Thank you, Daddy."

"But sweetheart, we're going to have to be sensitive here."

"Sensitive?"

"All these flashing bulbs. This racket. It's not going to encourage Thief to come down and eat. And you know, he hardly eats anymore." The sheriff's sad tone quieted the room.

Philippe leaned to Alfred. "Thief?"

"The cat that practically used to run this town. Snippety-snip, though, and life's over for the poor guy," Alfred whispered.

"Daddy, give him time. He'll be okay. We'll be finished up here shortly, okay?"

"Okay," the sheriff sighed. "I gotta go in to work."

"Daddy, that reminds me. I heard someone scream earlier."

"Hmm. I'll check into it. Keep an eye on Thief, will you?"

"Sure, Dad."

The sheriff left, and Alfred pulled her back into the kitchen. "Now, let's get a shot of you whisking."

"It's called the Road to the Sale," Oliver said proudly, as his long metal pointer hit the poster standing on the easel. They were in the small conference room, Wolfe sitting in a chair in front of the presentation, while Oliver looked like he was ready to lecture a crowd of five hundred. "There are ten steps, and I've outlined them all for you. Let's get started, because I want to leave time for questions. Step One is called Meet 'n' Greet. And it's no joke, my friend, a car is sold in the first twenty seconds. It's at this point you have to analyze everything about the customer. What are their push buttons? Are they here for a family car, a

sports car, a utility vehicle? Once you figure out what they want, that's the last time they tell you what they want. From then on, you tell them what they want." Oliver gave a quick, definitive nod.

"Okay."

"Now, Step Two is The Walk-Around. This is where you walk the customer around the car and explain all the features. If it's a family, point out safety features. If it's a young guy concerned about his image, point out the sports features. Explain the feature. Illustrate the feature. Sell the feature." Oliver repeated this four more times until Wolfe finally nodded.

"Got it."

"Step Three is the Test Drive. Never ask if they want to go for a drive. You say, 'I'm going to go get the keys, and we're going to take this baby for a spin.' Or if it's a family, something like, 'We're going to take this car for nice, quiet drive.' And *here,* my friend, *here* is one of the most important tips: Once they're in the car, shut up."

"Shut up?"

"Don't speak until spoken to."

"Why?"

"Because *here* is where the customer becomes *emotionally attached* to the car. They feel it. They see it in their driveway. They can hear their kids talking in the back. Understand? Don't ruin the moment for them."

As Oliver was explaining Steps Four, Five, and Six, Wolfe realized there was quite an art to selling cars. Earlier, Oliver had told him that if you are going to come out and play it cool, and try not to act like a car salesman, you'll never sell a car. People want the show. They want the whole package. It's a love-hate relationship, but in the end, the salesman shtick works. "Trust me," he'd said. "I've tried the other way. I didn't sell a car for a month."

Now Oliver was rattling off facts. "There are 966 different makes and models of cars out there. Seventy-five percent of customers who say they will return after thinking about it, don't. You take up four hours of

their time, and at the end they think, *I don't ever want to do this again. I'll just take this car.*"

Oliver was continuing to give tips as Wolfe shook off his distracting thoughts and tuned back in to him. "When you're filling out the work sheet, always ask 'Whose name are we going to put this car under?' Why?"

Wolfe shrugged.

"Gives them ownership. Makes them feel like it's theirs already. You haven't even begun to close the deal yet. In fact, you haven't even talked price. You haven't even run a credit check! But already they're seeing their name on the papers."

"Interesting."

"Now, here's another important point. As you're filling out all the paperwork in order to start negotiating price, start naming off, out loud, all the features of the car. Why? Because right now they're thinking price. They're starting to get worried. You've got to get them emotional again. Remind them of the DVD player. The second-generation air bags that will save their lives if, God forbid, they were in an accident. The leather seats. The seat warmers."

Wolfe realized this was much more complex than he had anticipated. He was under the impression you went out there, greeted the customer, figured out what they wanted in a car, and helped them pick it out. This was practically an art form. Maybe he should be taking notes. He looked around for a pen and paper, but there was nothing.

"Now," Oliver continued, "when it's time to start the negotiations, never ever say the price of the car in hundreds or thousands. That completely freaks people out. Instead of saying, 'twenty-two thousand, five hundred,' say, 'twenty-two five.' You don't want people to realize they're getting ready to go into major debt."

"I see."

"And now, my friend, I am going to give you the most important piece of information yet on selling a car. It is something that is tried and true and can make or break any deal you are attempting to close. It is

the number one rule in the car-selling industry, and if you don't know this, you will never, ever be a success."

Wolfe moved to the edge of his seat.

Oliver glanced at his watch. "Oh my goodness! It's lunchtime! C'mon, let's go eat, and we'll finish up later."

## CHAPTER 13

WOLFE AND AINSLEY had bundled themselves up to take the dogs for a walk. Goose and Bunny frolicked ahead of them where a few patches of snow remained. They'd been theorizing over who might have taken the Wise Men, and why they hadn't brought them back. Ainsley sighed. "I hate this time of year, when all the Christmas lights come down and it's just plain cold."

Wolfe squeezed her hand as they walked. "Yes, but that just means February is around the corner."

"I know!" she squealed. "That's going to be the best day of my whole life."

"Me too. Hey, how'd the wedding shopping go today? Weren't you going to go pick out your bridesmaids' dresses?"

"Yeah. I didn't get to go, though."

"Why?"

"Well, the photo shoot took a lot longer than expected. The makeup lady put my hair back in a bun, then the photographer thought it looked better down, and so we did all these pictures until my hair fell into the soup I was stirring, so then they decided I'd better wear my hair back. That took fifteen more minutes, and then we had to reshoot everything. I'll go tomorrow, though. How was your day? Did you get to talk to any customers?"

"No, but Oliver walked me through the Road to the Sale. Pretty intense stuff. I didn't realize there was so much to know just to sell a car. I'm not sure I can do it."

"Sure you can! You're a smart guy. You'll figure it out."

"Well, thank you. I do know the secret to closing all sales now." He grinned.

"Really, what is it?"

"I could tell you, but then I'd have to kill you."

Ainsley laughed. "C'mon. Tell me!"

"It's actually pretty interesting. Once you have the customer in the office, and the customer tells you what they're willing to spend, and then you write down the figure that you're willing to sell the car for, which of course is always higher, you slide that piece of paper across the desk, and then you don't say a word. Oliver said the first person who speaks loses."

"Really?"

"He's says it's about ninety percent effective. He said one time he sat there for fifteen minutes while the man looked at the paper. Finally the man spoke. And he left driving a brand-new Cadillac."

"Wow."

"I just don't know if I'm going to be able to do the whole salesman persona. That's not really me."

"You'll do fine, honey."

"Maybe. I just hope a Folder doesn't come in."

"What's a Folder?"

"It's a customer who has done his or her research. They walk onto the lot, carrying a folder full of information on invoice price, features, and so on. Basically, they know what they want, everything they want in it, and how much we bought the car for. Oliver says they are the absolute worst customers because you never make any money off them."

"Huh. What kinds of customers does he like?"

"The couple who's driving around on a Saturday afternoon and decides to go look at cars, just for fun. He says seventy-five percent of the time he can get them to take a car home."

"Wow. Dad gave me my car ten years ago when I turned twenty. I don't guess I've ever had to buy a car."

"Mine was a gift from the publishing house."

Ainsley looked up at him. "Are you okay...not writing?"

He shrugged. "I guess I am right now. I miss it, though. Not the fame, and not the stories I wrote. But the process. That was the most fun for me."

"Trust God," she said, hugging him around the waist. "He will lead you in the right direction."

He squeezed her shoulders. "He's got a pretty good helper. You're doing a great job of taking care of me. I wish I'd met you ten years ago."

"Me too," she sighed. "But God's timing is perfect."

"Speaking of God, have you heard from the reverend lately? Seems like since Christmas he's been really busy or something. And for the past two Sundays, he hasn't stayed around to greet."

"I noticed that too. Maybe we should go by and see him later."

"Let's think about doing that," he said. "But right now I want you all to myself."

She giggled as he tickled her ribs.

"Ainsley! Hey! Wolfe! Ainsley!"

They turned around to find Alfred running toward them from across the street, his breath clouding in front of him.

"Alfred! What are you doing out here?" Wolfe asked as Alfred finally panted his way onto the sidewalk.

"Looking for Ainsley."

"What's wrong? Didn't the photo shoot go okay?"

Alfred smiled and handed her a set of pictures. Wolfe and Ainsley looked through them together. She laughed out loud. "My goodness! Look at me!"

"You look absolutely stunning," Wolfe said.

"I've never looked this good in my life."

"There's a lot to be said for lighting and a makeup artist," Alfred said.

"But honey, you're gorgeous without all this too, you know," Wolfe added.

"But look at me!" she exclaimed. "I mean, I look… I look…"

"Like you need to be in everyone's living room every weekday morning."

"Excuse me?" she asked Alfred.

"Ainsley, I've got a good feeling about this. I showed these proofs to a guy I know in television. He said you had the right look."

She was still staring at the pictures. "I look like I'm straight out of a home magazine, Alfred. I'm stunned."

"You shouldn't be. You're everything that this country needs, Ainsley. You're bright, funny, beautiful—"

"Yes, that's what this world needs, Al," Wolfe quipped. "We don't have any bright, funny, beautiful people anywhere in America."

Alfred and Ainsley shot him a look, and he found himself kicking snow chunks off the grass.

"Ainsley has that 'it' quality, Wolfe, and you know it," Alfred said.

"What's an 'it' quality?" she asked.

"It means, my dear, that you have what it takes to shoot straight to the top. And that's why I'm here tonight. I need you to pack your bags. Tomorrow morning we're going to Indianapolis."

"What?" Wolfe asked.

"There's a craft and bake trade show there, and God forbid, but Mary-Katherine Covington-Smith has the flu."

"Who?"

"Mary-Katherine is the premiere cookie baker in the Midwest. Every year she wins Best in Show at this thing. She won't be there this year, but you will be." Alfred was grinning from ear to ear.

"Alfred, how in the world do you know about a lady with too many names who bakes cookies at an Indianapolis bake sale?" Wolfe asked.

"It's a trade show, and to answer your question, I've been doing my homework. I had to understand the competition. And come up with a strategy." He looked at Ainsley and handed her a folder. "Here are the rules for the baking contest. Get your recipes together. Have three different kinds of cookies baked by 6:00 a.m. tomorrow. I'll see you at six sharp."

They watched as Alfred walked back across the street to his car. And Wolfe suddenly realized that Alfred Tennison knew more about selling cars than he did. He was particularly impressed with Alfred's keen deliv-

ery of 'telling, not asking' and his ability to conjure up the emotional side of this whole deal. And he also realized once Alfred put his 'offer' on the table, Wolfe had been the first one to speak.

Sighing, he watched as Ainsley headed back toward the house, skipping along and surely thinking about what kinds of cookies she'd be baking late into the night.

Melb Cornforth sat in a corner booth, away from the distractions of the crowded Mansion restaurant, with a book she'd picked up at the local library. It was on bird-watching. The more she read, the more she realized she wasn't really interested in watching any birds, but that silly old owl that hung around fascinated her. He almost seemed to taunt her with his questions. Well, go on and question. Who? Part of her just wanted to climb the tree and strangle it. But the other half of her, the nature lover she was sure dwelt inside her, sensed that there was something she could learn from this bird.

"Hi sweetie."

She looked up to find Oliver sliding in across from her, unwrapping the scarf from his neck and pulling off his gloves. She loved his hands. They were at once plump and strong. It was like putting her hand in a bed of marshmallows. Marshmallows on steroids.

"Sorry I'm late," he said, "but I stopped by the bookstore for a moment—wanted to pick up that new *Chicken Soup for the Salesman's Soul*—and got hung up with Dustin."

"Dustin?"

"The kid that works there, you know? He was telling me about some horror novel he's reading. Says it's terrific."

"Oh?"

"Yeah, some book about ghosts in a forest. Sounded kind of corny to me. But the way this kid talks, it's like he believes in that stuff. My goodness, the things that can get planted in one's head! I think Wolfe's books are responsible for a lot of it."

"So how was your day? Did Wolfe seem to catch on any quicker?"

"I think so." Oliver sighed. "I gave him a lot of information, and at the end he did look a little dumbfounded. I didn't even get a chance to tell him about After Market Presentations."

"What's that?"

"You know, where you sell them the rustproofing, the ten year warranty, and so on."

"Oh."

"And you know how I have that song about 'Buyers Are Liars.'"

She shook her head.

"Oh, you know, I've sung it for you before. It's to the tune of 'Get Down Tonight.' It goes like—"

"That's okay, honey." she held up her hands, looking around the restaurant.

"You know, KC and The Sunshine Band—"

"I know, I know." She smiled. "Yes, I remember." How could she forget? He had this insatiable appetite for disco. When talking about the wedding, she'd suggested songs by Whitney Houston or Celine Dion. Oliver had his mind set on the Bee Gees and Earth, Wind & Fire. He thought it would be great to play "I'm Your Boogie Man" while he walked down the aisle. They still hadn't come to an agreement on music yet.

And though she loved Oliver (a man for the most part very reserved), whenever any sort of disco tune came on, something happened to him. His body would start gyrating, his eyebrows would pop up and down on his forehead in what he thought was a seductive manner, and the next thing she knew, he was dancing. And it was the day he'd made up this jingle about "Buyers Are Liars" to some boogie song, that Oliver thought he might have a chance in the music industry. Fortunately, that was ten years before they met. And since then, he had found out that he didn't have much talent beyond catchy car jingles.

"Anyway," he said, "poor Wolfe has this very naive view of things. Black or white. Cold or hot. Evil or good. I mean, when I tell him that all buyers are liars, it might offend him."

"Are all buyers liars?"

"Of course they are! They either come in saying they're not willing to buy, and they do, or they say they won't pay more than *X*, and they do, or they tell me they want to get something conservative, and they drive off in a Corvette. People don't know what they want. Someone has got to tell them. That's me." Oliver grinned. She loved that grin. "And enough about me. How was your day? Did you put the money down for the caterer?"

"Umm…the what?"

"Hello? The caterer?"

"Yes…yes, of course." She scanned the menu. She was going to need a double cheeseburger. Maybe double onion rings.

"Good! Melb, this is so exciting. I can't wait until the day I call you my wife."

"I'm going to start owling."

"Excuse me?" Oliver asked.

"Owling."

"Howling?"

*"Owling."* Melb held up the bird-watching book. "I need a hobby."

"Why?"

Okay, this was going to be tricky. Oliver did not know that she'd bought a dress four sizes too small for $550 over budget. Or that she'd blown the caterer money on therapy. She would fix all this. She knew she could. That's why she was taking up owling. The therapist had told her to get a hobby. And that owl… It beckoned her.

"It's complicated, but trust me. It's the best thing."

"What's owling?"

"It's where you call to an owl and they call back."

"Why would you want to do that?"

"I don't know. It's a challenge. I need a challenge in my life." She tried to smile and ignore the confused look on Oliver's face.

"Isn't planning a wedding in this amount of time enough of a challenge?"

She laughed. "I'm sorry. Did I say challenge? I meant stress reliever."

Concern melted away from the turmoil in his eyes. "You're stressed? Why didn't you say something?"

"I'm fine. I really am. I just need a bit of a distraction. You know how wedding planning can be. You get so focused."

He took her hands. "Sweetheart, whatever you need. But tell me what's going on with you, okay? Don't hold it inside. We need to be honest with each other."

She smiled. "I agree."

"And encourage each other. That's what marriage is about, right?"

"Yes."

"And I want to encourage you and tell you how proud I am of you. You're doing a fantastic job planning this wedding."

"Really? Thank you!"

"I think if I had married any other woman, I'd probably have gone insane by now. But you realize things about me."

"Like what?"

"Like how important budgets are, for example. I mean, I can turn into a lunatic at the dealership when we go over budget. I mean, a real freak of a monster." He offered a smile. "But you sense these things, and that means the world to me."

"W-what, um, what kind of monster?"

"Sweetheart, I don't literally turn into a monster. You've read too many of Wolfe's books. What I mean is that I can get totally irrational and out of my mind, that's all."

"Oh." A weak laugh was all she could manage.

"What do you say we eat? What sounds good to you?"

"A double cheeseburger with a side of meatloaf."

Reverend Peck stood in the parking lot of his church with fifty orange cones in the freezing cold. It was Friday, and this was the last of his tasks. He was way ahead of schedule. It meant he could take tomorrow and

write his sermon, which he wasn't sure he was going to get to this week. But it didn't matter. According to his plan, he wasn't even sure he was going to need a sermon. Sunday was going to be a test run. He knew one thing for certain: The pews would be packed; there would be standing room only.

He finished up with the cones and traversed the small pathway that led from the church over to his parsonage. Inside, he fixed himself a bowl of stew and relaxed for a while on his sofa, trying to come up with a sermon topic.

After some thought, he realized exactly what he was going to preach on. It was brilliant.

Sex.

## CHAPTER 14

WOLFE GRUNTED OUT A SIGH as he rolled over, trying to peer at the clock on his night table. It was just past five. He'd gone to bed at midnight and had tossed and turned, tangled his emotions around the twisted covers.

It was their first fight. They would get over it. But it was also a good dose of reality. They were just like any other couple.

It had started that evening at his house, when they began discussing Ainsley's trip to Indianapolis. Wolfe had protested, questioning whether she knew what she was getting into with Alfred. He learned quickly that was not the best approach. The 'tell, don't ask' method might work with Oliver and Alfred, but Wolfe didn't have any luck. Telling her she was not going to Indianapolis did not go over well.

Soon the evening ended with Ainsley stomping out of his house, yelling something about cookies and dignity.

As he'd sat quietly in his empty house, Wolfe had to at least ponder the idea that his resistance to Ainsley's new journey might be due more to the fact that his own journey had seemed to end so abruptly. Spiritually, he was the best he'd ever been in his life. It did something to a person to know how much God loved him, how hard He'd worked to show that to him. But emotionally, Wolfe knew he was struggling. It was one thing to believe that an ordinary life was going to be his destiny. It was another thing to now be identified as Oliver's associate who still had not even talked to a customer.

Humbling. And he was sure that was where God needed him to be. Humble. He'd lived a life of glory. Now that was over.

But deep inside himself, he had to admit there was much of that life he loved. He even missed the nickname the town had given him. Boo. Who was Boo now? A salesman? A once-famous writer? Ainsley's fiancé? The reason the town suffered?

None of these identities told him who he was. He never thought at his age he would have to search for himself. But in reality he had no idea who he was or who he was supposed to become.

He rolled out of bed. Goose and Bunny's wet noses gave him an extra lift. He trotted downstairs and let them out into the cold. In two hours he was supposed to be at the car lot. He wanted to call Ainsley before she left for Indianapolis, but he had no idea what time she would be waking up.

So instead he put on some longjohns—on the off chance he might actually leave the building and be allowed to step onto the sacred grounds of the car lot—and decided to read his Bible. He knew one thing for sure: He was looking forward to church on Sunday. Maybe the reverend's sermon would really speak to him.

Ainsley shoveled one cookie after another with the spatula, sliding them into a beautifully decorated country-style basket. It was a little past five in the morning, and so far she'd baked one hundred and thirty cookies, seventy of those last night, mostly out of pure indignation. How could Wolfe not support her in this? What made him the authority of her life? This was her whole life's dream, wrapped up in a nice bow and about to be handed to her. How could he deny her that? Was he just jealous? Her thoughts had distracted her so much she'd put three teaspoons of vanilla in one batch of cookies, and then mixed the pecans into the wrong batter.

She had tried so many times to understand what in the world he was thinking, but rational thoughts were replaced by incensed emotions, which translated into another batch of cookies. Alfred had asked for three kinds. So far she had nine.

But it hurt her heart to know they were angry at each other. She shouldn't have stomped out of his house last night. Yet what more was there to say? She was going to Indianapolis, and he wasn't going to stop her with his petty worries of how Alfred Tennison was going to corrupt her. He'd done a lot for Wolfe. Why couldn't his talents be used for her dreams now?

Ainsley decided she'd better stop with the cookies. She turned off the oven and stood by the phone, thumbing absent-mindedly through the folder Alfred had given her last night. It was early, but she would be leaving soon. How could they go the whole day angry at each other?

She was just about to pick up the phone when she heard a scream. Gasping, she turned around, and then heard another horrifying scream. It was the worst sound she'd ever heard in her life.

"Daddy!" Ainsley ran upstairs. "Dad! Dad!" Opening his bedroom door, she found that he was just coming to. "Dad! Wake up!"

"What?" He jumped out of his bed, fully clad in his pawprint pajamas.

"Did you hear that?"

"What?"

"That screaming?"

The sheriff rubbed his eyes. "Screaming?"

"I heard a woman scream, Dad. I'm not imagining it. I wasn't even asleep. I was downstairs baking. I heard her scream twice. It was simply terrifying!"

The sheriff sighed, robed himself, and followed Ainsley downstairs, all the while beckoning Thief to come with him. The cat never left the bedroom. "What is it going to take with this cat?" her father complained. "He's like a zombie."

"Dad, focus. The woman. Screaming." Ainsley opened the front door and followed him outside, both with their house slippers on. Standing on the front porch, the sheriff looked around.

"I don't see or hear anything."

"This isn't the first time I've heard a scream."

"Sweetheart, I don't know what I can do until someone calls the police or we hear something else. Now come on back inside. It's freezing."

Ainsley followed her father inside, but not without one more look. She knew she'd heard someone scream.

*"Whoo. Whoo."*

Ainsley looked up. It wasn't yet 5:30 a.m. There, high in the trees, she heard an owl. She couldn't see it.

*"Whoo. Whoo. Whoo."*

"Who screamed?" she said flippantly, then went inside. Her father sat at the breakfast table, staring at the mound of cookies on the counter.

"You okay?" he asked.

"Yeah. I'm entering a baking contest in Indianapolis today."

The sheriff tried to look interested, but his eyes were puffy, and he was now staring at the kitchen clock. Ainsley quickly poured him a cup of coffee.

"I haven't been sleeping well," he admitted. "I'm worried about Thief. He's not the same cat. Half the time he doesn't want to come out on patrols with me. But when he does, he just sits in the car."

"Well, that's probably the best place for him, Dad. That way he won't get into trouble."

"I think he's depressed."

Ainsley joined her father at the table. "Thief will learn there is more to life than chasing lady cats."

Her father shrugged and sipped his coffee.

"Daddy?"

"Yes?"

"I got in a fight with Wolfe yesterday."

The sheriff looked up. "Thank goodness."

"What?"

"I was beginning to worry about you two, viewing everything through rose-colored glasses all the time."

"I feel horrible. I don't know what to do. What did you and Mom used to do when you got into a fight?"

"We'd take some time to ourselves, just to cool off. Then your

mom, she was always really good about bringing us back together to talk about it. Of course, I never wanted to. But once we started, we both realized why the fight started in the first place, and by the end of it, we were usually laughing about the whole thing."

"I've been reading Mom's diary about the wedding. I wish you two would've taken more pictures. It sounds so wonderful. Mom was so excited."

"It was the best day of my life. And it'll be that way for you too. Wolfe's a good man, Ainsley. I'm glad you're marrying him."

"Me too," she smiled. "I'll call him when I get back from Indianapolis. I'm sure everything will be fine. By the way, don't forget to go get fitted for your tuxedo, okay?"

"I already did. Yesterday."

"Really? Thanks!"

Outside, a horn tooted. "Who is that?"

"Alfred. He's taking me to Indianapolis."

"Well, be careful," he said, kissing her on the cheek. "I'll see you when you get back. Good luck!"

Ainsley looked at the baskets of cookies on the counter. "Um, Dad? I think I might need some help out with these."

~○~

Martin Blarty sat in the middle of the floor of the town's small library. Scratching his head, he rubbed his eyes and decided there was nothing more to find. This library contained everything except information about the town. The sun was now high in the morning sky. He walked down the street to the deli, once called Deli on the Dark Side, now renamed Deli on the Side, which actually fit since it was on the corner and there was always something "on the side," like a pickle or potato chips. After ordering a large coffee, he decided to pay the sheriff a visit. He knew the sheriff usually tried to be at the station on Saturdays. But when he got there, the dispatcher said he hadn't been in, so Martin decided to visit him at home.

On his way there, he noticed something very peculiar. There was a strange man walking through a grouping of trees. And as he drove by, he saw this man's expression, and it nearly scared the daylights out of him. This man looked like a ghost! His face was pale, his eyes gaping, his mouth hanging open like it'd been that way for a decade. And he walked swiftly. Back when Skary was the horror capital of the world, Martin wouldn't even have thought about seeing such a sight. But now—how creepy.

He quickly pulled his car over to the side of the road, locked his doors, and backed up a few yards. But when he got to the spot where he'd seen the man, there was nothing but trees. He could hardly catch his breath with his heart beating so erratically.

Should he get out of the car? Panting out his fear, he decided he might be able to see better if he stood closer to the trees. With trembling hands, he unlocked his door. But first he thought he should get a weapon. He looked around, but all he had in his car was a Kleenex box. He'd heard once that a man died in a car accident after being hit in the head by a flying Kleenex box. With enough fearful adrenaline pumping up his muscles, he had no doubt he could fling the thing hard enough to at least knock someone out.

Unless it was a ghost. Then he would need garlic. No, wait. That was for vampires. Maybe it was a vampire. He hadn't seen any fangs, and granted, the apparition wasn't wearing a black cape, but a blue flannel shirt. Still…

Grabbing the Kleenex box, he slowly got out of the car. He tiptoed along the side of the road and slowly made his way closer to the trees. Something moved behind some leaves. He gasped. Then he saw it. Just a cat. "Shoooo!" he hissed, and the cat bounded away.

He was beginning to get a grip. There was nothing to be seen out here. Maybe he'd imagined it. After all, he'd spent the last two weeks trying to find documents detailing the history of this town, but everything seemed to have vanished. Or maybe it had never existed. Whatever the case, he was a bit weary. He had lost a lot of sleep from the many concerns of his life: a town whose history had vanished, a mayor whose

mind had gone mad, and residents who didn't know what dire straights Skary, Indiana, was really in.

He pulled a tissue from the box and wiped his dripping nose. Maybe the mayor's hallucinations were now his own. Scanning the trees one more time, he decided there was nothing more to see. He walked to his car.

And then a heart-stopping scream made him drop his box of Kleenex.

Melb's double-decker sandwich was a work of art that defied gravity. Three kinds of meat, two kinds of cheese, plus lettuce, tomato, pimentos, and mayo, between two soft slices of French bread. Sure, probably a bowl of whole wheat flakes was a better choice for breakfast, but she'd decided that if she ate a lot in the morning, she wouldn't be hungry the rest of the day. Plus, she needed a lot of energy. This was going to be the first day of her hobby. She hoped it would distract her from her diet, which so far had added seven pounds to her weight.

Just as she was about to take her first bite, someone pounded at the door frantically. Melb hopped up and answered it, only to find Martin Blarty standing there, his eyes wide and startled. "A ghost! Dead people! Screaming!" he was saying.

"Martin, goodness, come on in. I was just…um…fixing myself some rice cakes." She opened the door, and Martin rushed by her.

"Is Oliver here?" he asked. She could see him shaking.

"No, he's at the car lot. Martin, whatever is the matter?" Since he didn't seem to be able to speak, she continued guessing. "Is it the mayor? He's claiming to see ghosts? Dead people? My goodness, the poor fellow is just off his rocker, isn't he?"

Martin was blinking and nodding and shaking his head all at once, and now eying the sandwich on the counter. "That's for Oliver," Melb said. "He likes me to bring him up a sack lunch sometimes." She smiled, but Martin still looked terrified. Melb leaned forward on the counter,

and in a hushed voice said, "Martin…whatever the mayor thinks he saw, it's nonsense. Is he saying he's seeing dead people? Because that was a very good movie, but dead people don't really walk around, you know? People who are losing their minds often think they see things that they don't. It's craziness, Martin. Don't be afraid, okay?"

"Craziness…," he mumbled.

She didn't seem to be helping. She knew it must be hard to see a friend fall off the deep end. Should she tell him about Dr. Hass? Should she admit she'd been to see a shrink? What would people think of her? Still…if she could help Martin and the mayor, she should. She knew that for sure. Telling herself to swallow her pride, she said, "Martin, I think I know how to help the mayor."

Martin looked up at her from his own distant thoughts. "You do?"

"But you must promise not to tell anyone who told you this."

Martin seemed to focus. "Okay."

"There's a new therapist in town. He just moved here. I went to see him because I'm having some…some…nightmares. Anyway, he's really good, and maybe Mayor Wullisworth could use that kind of help. I would imagine one's claim to have seen dead people would pretty much be reason to go see a shrink."

"Yeah…right."

She wrote down Dr. Hass's address and gave it to Martin. "Listen, Martin. This is just between you and me, okay?"

Martin nodded, thanked her, and left. Melb, however, still had the task of deciding whether or not to eat her sandwich.

## CHAPTER 15

WOLFE WAS JUST ABOUT to go to the bathroom to take off his thermal underwear that was doing nothing more than making him sweat in his cozy and warm office, when Oliver appeared with an enormous grin. "Well, today's your big day."

"Big day?"

"Just saw a car pull up. A woman is getting out. Think you're up to the task?"

Wolfe looked out and saw the top of her head bobbing through the lot. "Sure."

"Remember, the first twenty seconds are critical. That's when you sell the car. Got it?"

"Yeah."

"Remember the Road to the Sale. Remember the points?"

"I think so."

"Good. Now grin real big, offer the correct handshake, and go sell me a car!"

Wolfe stood. His heart was actually pumping dramatically considering he was just going out to speak to this woman. Taking a deep breath, he tried to muster up some confidence as he walked to where she was looking at a four-door sedan. "Hello!"

She looked up at him, gave him a smile indicative of annoyance, and looked back down at the car. "Hi."

"Looking for a car today?"

"No, I'm here because I'm shopping for shoes."

He swallowed. Ten seconds down the drain. He was just about to ask his next question when the woman suddenly started sneezing. Ten times. When she finally got ahold of herself, twenty seconds had already passed, and all he knew was that she was annoyed and apparently contagious.

"Sorry," she sighed. "I've had this for weeks."

"That's okay," Wolfe smiled, and then realized he needed to shake her hand, which had just managed to catch a million germs. He feebly stuck out his arm. "I'm Wolfe."

"Barbara."

"What can I help you with today?" No, that wasn't right. He should have said, "I can help you today." Good grief, this was falling apart by the second.

"My car broke down. It's going to cost a ton to fix. So I decided I should probably buy a new one."

"What did you have in mind?"

"Something reasonable, but I don't want compact."

He tried to size the woman up. She didn't seem to be the type concerned with image, and since she didn't want compact, perhaps safety was on her mind. "Well, I've got a nice Mercury Sable over here—"

"Don't bother," the woman said curtly. And then she pulled out a folder from the large handbag hanging off her shoulder.

He tried not to gasp. A folder. *A Folder!* On his first try!

She handed him a sheet of paper. "Here is a list of features I want, the color I want, and the make I want. Do you have this car on your lot?"

He looked at the sheet. "Well, we've got this car with all these features, but we only have it in maroon."

The woman scowled. "Maroon."

He was getting cold, and this woman's personality wasn't warming things up. He handed her back the sheet of paper. "I'm willing to bet you already know the price we bought this car for."

A smug smile was the only bright feature on this woman's face.

"Tell you what," Wolfe said. "It's cold out here. Let's save us both a

lot of time. Why don't you come inside, tell me what you're willing to pay for this car, and we'll go from there."

The woman moved past him. "I like your style."

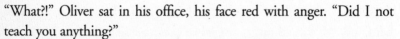

"What?!" Oliver sat in his office, his face red with anger. "Did I not teach you anything?"

Wolfe rocked on his heels. "But she's a Folder."

"So what? You've still got to go through all the steps. Now we don't have a snowball's chance of making a dime off this lady!" Oliver glanced through the glass window in his office to the lady sitting in the "negotiation" room. "Look at her! Her shoulders are back. Her head is high. She's got all the confidence in the world."

"But you said Folders are impossible. And she had already done her research. What was I supposed to do?"

"Steps *One through Ten!*" Oliver stood, pacing behind his desk. "Now she's got the edge. She knows we're desperate. I guarantee she's going to offer to pay a hundred bucks over invoice. A hundred bucks…" Oliver lamented.

Wolfe's gut swelled with desperation. "Let me work on her," he said, hoping Oliver would settle down a bit. The last time he remembered anyone being so mad at him was six years ago when he'd missed a deadline three times. Alfred finally called and yelled at him. Rushing back into the office, he closed the door and tried to offer a professional demeanor.

"What took you so long?" the woman snapped. "I don't have all day."

"Sorry. Just going over some paperwork." Wolfe sat down on the other side of the desk. "Now, whose name is the car going to be under?"

"Mine."

"Okay." He managed to find hope in that simple statement. "Well, let me do some figuring here."

She slid another piece of paper over to him. "I've already done that for you. Just to save you the time and effort. I broke everything down

by feature, and at the bottom you'll see exactly what I am going to pay for this car."

He took the paper. "Fifty-four dollars over invoice?" Dread washed over Wolfe for many reasons, not the least of which was the realization he'd spoken first.

~C}

Ainsley followed Alfred closely through the large Indiana Convention Center. Her nostrils began to fill with every delicious aroma she could think of as soon as they entered what was called the Sagamore Ballroom. In one corner of the building was the Casserole Bake-Off. In another was a contest for fried chicken. On the west end of the room was the cookie contest. With glee on their drive up, he had realized that she was going to be able to enter five different contests: chocolate chip, cookie with a nut, five-ingredient cookie, fifteen-ingredient cookie, and most original cookie, which was something she'd created years ago: Raspberry Orange White Chocolate with a Sprinkle of Ginger.

Alfred was also high on sugar, as he'd managed to eat the equivalent of an entire batch of cookies while driving. He was practically skipping along the convention floor as Ainsley briskly walked to keep up with him.

"I've never seen anything like this before!" she mused.

He slowed his pace and walked beside her. "Look at these women, Ainsley. Study them…their demeanor."

"What for?"

"This is your competition. Don't you think all these women want their own television show? Isn't that the dream of every woman in this building?"

A tall and thin woman caught her eye as they walked past her booth. She wore a thinly striped blue apron, her hair in a perfect bob. She looked up at Ainsley as they passed. A kind smile warmed her eyes. Ainsley grinned. But then the woman's eyes looked at the identification card around Ainsley's neck, the one that read COOKIE BAKE-OFF #101. The smile faded, and her eyes flashed an equal measure of elite

showmanship and severe competitiveness. A disapproving eyebrow rose while her eyes quickly scanned Ainsley's outfit. Then she smirked and went on about her business.

"Alfred!" she said. "Did you see that? That woman gave me a dirty look!"

His attention was on finding where they were supposed to be, but he glanced down at her. "Get used to it. When you win this thing, you will be the most hated woman in Indiana."

"Why?"

"Don't all women want to be the object of envy for other women?"

She was just about to retort when he pointed. "There! It's our booth! Come on." They toted the cookies over to the booth. She looked around. All the other booths were elaborately decorated. One woman's actually looked like a real kitchen! Another woman had music playing.

Alfred seemed to read her mind. "We're going simplistic," he announced. "Everyone has a theme. Your theme will be you. It will catch everyone's attention. Believe me." He lowered his voice. "Trust me."

"Okay." She smiled weakly at the woman next to her, who had a carousel of cookies spinning around on the counter. The woman didn't bother to smile back, glancing at her as though she were as important as a fleeting bug. "Alfred, this place...it's not me."

"I know. This is the big time. You're not used to the big time. But honey, you're going to have to get used to it. And I didn't tell you this before, because I didn't want to scare you, but we'll have company soon."

"Company?"

"Remember that TV exec I was telling you about? Harper Jones is his name. And he's due to arrive in about thirty minutes."

Wolfe stared at the woman. Never had he seen such cold eyes. The lady wasn't going to pay a dime above fifty-four dollars over invoice. Breaking the news to Oliver hadn't been pleasant. After five minutes of ranting, Oliver said he had to go back in there and get more money out of her.

Now Wolfe sat behind the desk, shaking hands folded together, stomach sour with stress. The woman looked quite relaxed, her purse sitting delicately in her lap, her eyelids slightly lowered. She looked like a lioness deciding whether the rabbit in the bush was worth the effort to get up and go mangle.

"Ma'am," Wolfe began, "I understand your thriftiness. It's natural to want a good deal. I can truly appreciate that."

"I'm sure you can."

"But what you're offering to pay here would barely cover processing the paperwork."

"Since when did filling out forms cost money?"

Was that a growl he'd just heard from her throat? "Ma'am, the people working here need money. They need to make a living. Oliver works very hard at running a reputable car dealership."

"Are you saying I'm taking advantage of that?" she purred.

"I'm saying that there's a difference between being thrifty and being cheap. You pay what this car is worth, and we'll take good care of you."

"I'm paying that number," she said, pointing to her handwritten figure on the piece of paper, "and not a dime more. Now, let's fill out the paperwork and get me the keys."

"No."

"No?"

"No. I'm not selling you this car."

"You can't do that."

"Sure I can."

"You're still making money off me! You're saying you're willing to throw away fifty-four dollars? I can leave here and you haven't made a dime!"

"I understand that. But it's the principle, ma'am. And the fact of the matter is that people have to eat. They have to make a living. I'm glad you've done your research. It's respectable for you to come in here well prepared. But it's ludicrous to think you're going to drive a car off the lot so the dealer can lose money."

The woman slammed her purse on the desk, causing him to jump.

"You can't do this to me! I've spent an hour and a half here, and now you're not going to sell me the car?"

"I will sell you the car, for this price." Wolfe wrote a new figure down, five hundred dollars over invoice, and slid it across to her with a smile. "And ma'am, that adds two dollars a month to your monthly payment. But it adds food to the table for the people working here."

The woman blinked and then took a deep breath, her hardened features melting by the second. "I never thought of it that way."

"So let me just fill out the rest of the paperwork for you, ma'am, and we'll have you on your way in a brand-new car that you're going to thoroughly enjoy."

Wolfe held out his hand to shake, and the woman took it, smiled, and then yelled, "*Ollie!* We're done in here!"

"Excuse me?"

The woman looked at him. "I just want to tell you, I am a big fan of yours. I've read all your books, have all of them neatly lined up on my bookshelf. I don't know what you're doing selling cars, but I sure wish you'd get back to writing."

Oliver walked in. "Well, did you sell the car?"

"He did. Talked me up to five hundred dollars over invoice."

"Really? Pretty smooth, considering you botched the entire Road to the Sale."

Wolfe stood up. "What's going on here?"

Oliver smiled. "Wolfe, meet my second cousin Lois Stepaphanolopolis, a.k.a. Barbara."

"What?"

"Listen, you don't think I'd send you out to the wolves without a test run first, do you? Lois took drama lessons in high school, so I thought she'd be great at pretending to be a Folder."

Wolfe sat back down in his chair, stunned. "This was just a setup?"

"Just a test run, my friend, just a test run. Now, I have to say, the first half was very shaky on your part. But boy, how in the world did you get her to up her price?"

"Emotions," Lois grinned. "He basically gave me this song and

dance about principle and food on your table." She shrugged. "If I were a real customer, I would've bought it."

Oliver eyed Wolfe. "So you were listening. Tapped into her emotions. Very good."

Wolfe wasn't sure if he was angry or relieved. "Why'd you start me off with a Folder?"

"Why not? From now on, every other customer is going to seem easy."

"Can I get your autograph?" Lois asked, an eager grin replacing the stout expression he had stared into for more than an hour.

He swallowed. "I don't know. Maybe I should be getting yours. That was quite an Oscar-worthy performance you gave."

Giggling, she waved a hand. "Oh, it was nothing. You should've seen me playing Sandra Dee in *Grease* in high school. You've never seen a death scene like that!"

He glanced at Oliver. "Um…Sandra Dee doesn't die in *Grease*."

"I know. But she did when I played her. I thought that would be a much more authentic and dramatic ending. Believe me, nobody ever forgot that performance, including my drama teacher, who I didn't tell before I did it. Let me tell you, there wasn't a person in that auditorium, including the cast, who wasn't shocked out of their socks. Not one of them forgot my name again."

"The meaning of Drama Queen isn't lost on you, is it?" Wolfe managed a smile.

"Well, Ollie, if we're done here, I've got to go grocery shopping."

Oliver gave her a hug. "See you soon, cousin."

When Sandra Demon left, Wolfe stepped in front of Oliver as he was about to leave the office. "Oliver, I can't say that I respect what you did back there. I was about to have a heart attack thinking how upset you were!"

Oliver shrugged. "I'm sorry, Wolfe. But I had to find out how you were going to do. At first, you had me worried. But you showed some ingenuity there at the end, and that has built my confidence in you. In fact, I feel so good about it that I'm leaving you here by yourself today."

Oliver walked past him, and Wolfe followed him to his office. "You're leaving me here?"

"Virginia will be here in about thirty minutes." Oliver was packing up his briefcase.

"Where are you going?"

Oliver glanced up at him. "You'll laugh at me if I tell you."

"I will?"

"You'll say I've been reading too many of your books."

"Oh."

"Well, aren't you curious about where I'm going?"

"Uh…sure."

Oliver lowered his voice. "Have you noticed a couple of strange people wandering around town lately?"

"No, not really."

"Well, I have. They look real weird too. Wide eyes. Pale skin. Screams from the bushes."

"No kidding."

"I'm just going to take some time off, go investigate what's going on."

"Shouldn't you just talk to Sheriff Parker about it?"

"The sheriff is about as useful these days as that cat of his. All he thinks about is Thief. His deputies are starting to get worried. Besides, I figured if I had more evidence, then I'd have a reason to go to the sheriff. So off I go. Hold down the fort for me. I'd say close up shop around five."

"Sure."

"And Wolfe, don't be mad at me. I do what I have to do to make sure my employees are thoroughly trained. Just ask Virginia what happened to her on her third day of work." Oliver winked, grabbed his briefcase, and went out the door, leaving Wolfe by himself to ponder whether he really wanted to know Virginia's story.

## CHAPTER 16

ALFRED WAS TALKING a mile a minute, and driving nearly two miles a minute. As they zipped along the Interstate out of Indianapolis, Alfred's ecstatic energy was hard to miss.

"You won four out of the five, Ainsley! That's never been done before! Ever! Did you know that? Harper was out of his mind. And he kept saying, 'She has the right look!' Over and over. I just can't believe it. I knew this was the right move. I knew it!"

She smiled at Alfred, who she wished would keep his eyes on the road. In her hand she clutched four blue ribbons, her fingers stroking the silky fabric. It had been quite a thrill, and the moment certainly wasn't lost on her, but it was dampened by the fact that she'd left Wolfe's house angry last night. And she wasn't sure if she was ever going to get used to all the nasty looks from all the other women in the cookie bake-off. Only one woman came up and offered her congratulations. It was her first year too. They spoke for about five minutes until Alfred ushered her off to meet reporters.

She tuned back in to Alfred, who was saying, "Harper and I talked at length, and we agreed that we're going to need to do a taping of some sort. Ainsley, I won't lie to you. There's a lot of competition out there. But if we do our best, and we make the right move at just the right time, we'll be in."

"If it's God's will," she said softly.

"Yeah, that too. So anyway, I'm going to have to take a few days and try to come up with a strategy. It's all about strategy." Alfred

reached to the back seat and snagged a leftover cookie. "My goodness, I'd weigh a ton if I lived with you!"

They drove awhile in silence. Thankfully, he had started to come down off his sugar high. When they came into Skary as dusk approached, she said, "Alfred, why don't you drop me off at Wolfe's house?"

"Sure."

The lights were on, and Ainsley felt relieved. She needed to say she was sorry, and soon. What good were four blue ribbons when things were left in turmoil with the person she loved most in this world?

"Thanks, Alfred. I could've never done this without you."

Alfred smiled, as if he'd longed to hear that statement his whole life. "Tell Wolfe hello."

As she walked up the front porch steps of his home, her heart beat in a way that reminded her of the very first time she'd climbed these stairs. She was so nervous, not knowing what to expect. She felt exactly the same this time. Would he forgive her? They'd never fought since getting engaged. Not even a little squabble. Her heart ached at the thought of how angry they'd been at each other. But maybe her father was right. Maybe it was good to know how they would react to such a thing.

She stood on his porch, swallowing back fear and pride and remembering the instructions of Jesus. She still wondered why Wolfe was so adamant about not wanting her to go to Indianapolis. But maybe if they sat down and talked about it… What if he was still mad, though? What if he refused to see her? What if—

The front door opened, and Wolfe was grinning. He spread his arms, and she ran into them. "I'm so sorry!" she cried. "I can't believe I left while we were fighting. That was horrible of me!"

He held her shoulders. "I'm sorry, Ainsley. I don't know what got into me." He stepped back from her and looked at the ribbons in her hand. "You won?" he asked excitedly.

She nodded and laughed. "Four out of five. It's a new record. And apparently a very good reason for a lot of women to hate me. How was your day?"

Wolfe shook his head and ushered her in. "Well, I almost killed Sandra Dee, but that's a whole other story."

Oliver had bundled himself up as if he were preparing for a blizzard. In actuality, he figured if he had enough layers on and someone tried to stab him, the knife might not even reach his skin.

His mind had been sifting dreadful thoughts of who these strange people might be ever since he'd left work. He'd seen three of them, and each time it had scared him out of his mind. He'd even been afraid to mention this to anyone until he overheard Martin Blarty talking to the mayor about a sighting of his own. They weren't doing anything particularly scary. But something about them was very frightful. Maybe it was the way they walked…slowly, methodically, as if waiting for something to happen. Maybe it was their expression, nearly frozen with alarm. Whatever it was, he knew something strange was going on. The thought had even crossed his mind that they could be spies from area car dealers, trying to learn his trade secrets. Whatever the case, he was going to find out the truth.

For twenty-five minutes he drove around and didn't see a single thing out of place. Skary, Indiana, as it always did in the early evening, purred like a contented cat. The streets grew quiet. Homes warmed from the inside out. And nothing exciting happened once dinnertime came.

Oliver decided he might have more luck if he got out of his car and walked around. But just as he was driving back into town, he thought he saw something, in a grouping of trees that led to the foothills.

His car screeched to a halt, and he got out. It was just a flash, a shadow that moved in already dark surroundings. Gulping so loud that he made a calico scurry away, Oliver clutched his fists together and walked straight into the trees. He could see nothing, so he stopped to listen.

*"Whoo. Whoo."*

*"Whoo. Whoo. Whoo."*

Over and over this went, and it sounded to Oliver like a male owl was calling to a female owl. If he didn't know better, there seemed to be some chemistry. But he didn't know better. He had no idea what the hooting of an owl meant.

He focused his attention back on finding the mysterious figure in the trees. Slinking forward as quietly as he could, he scanned the shadows for any movement. He was not going to be able to hear anything due to the racket these owls were making, but he always did have keen eyesight. And his father had always said the only weapon he needed was a sharp tongue. Although he seriously doubted a couple of quick one-liners was going to have any effect on these ghouls.

Oliver stopped and sighed. With all the whoo-whooing going on, he wasn't going to find a thing out here. "Get a room," he mumbled.

But then, out of the corner of his eye, a few yards away, Oliver saw something move. Gasping, he covered his mouth, trying not to scream.

~~~~~~

Dr. Hass couldn't believe how much cash was used in this town. Hadn't anyone heard of a credit card? Or billing? Not that he was complaining. How could he turn down cold, hard cash?

"You're terrific for seeing us at this hour," said the man who had introduced himself as Town Treasurer Martin (not Marty) Blarty, offering his hand for the third nervous time. It was seven in the evening, and Dr. Hass was beginning to realize why setting up shop at his own home might not be the best idea in the world.

"No problem." He reminded himself to smile. Perhaps his cheese might not be cheddar. Maybe it was Swiss, and he didn't know it. Or maybe he'd always known it and hadn't acknowledged it. Perhaps his was more like pimento cheese. At any rate, when he focused back on the two men in his office, he noticed Martin was staring at the large framed poster of Napoleon on the east wall.

Martin glanced at him. "Interesting…" He smiled uncomfortably.

"Some unique personality traits by which I've always been fascinated."

"Ah."

"So…what brings you two in this evening?"

Martin's eyes shifted nonchalantly to the mayor, whom Martin had introduced as The Mayor. "Well, as you can see, he's got some issues."

Dr. Hass wasn't sure what issues Martin was referring to. The mayor was wearing a Hawaiian-looking shirt, sunglasses, and Bermuda shorts. But Dr. Hass had come from L.A., so not many wardrobes shocked him.

"He thinks it's summertime," Martin said in a hushed voice, though the mayor hardly seemed to know where he was. "He's in complete denial."

"Denial about winter?"

"Denial about Skary."

"What about it?"

Martin's eyes averted to the ground. "You're new here, and I hate to put Skary in a bad light, but we're not doing well. And the mayor blames himself."

"Is it his fault?"

"No. It's nobody's fault. We used to be known for being Wolfe Boone's town, but he fell in love and became a Christian, so he's not writing horror anymore. But nobody blames him. Well, most people don't. But anyway, the town is not doing well."

"You mean financially?"

"Yes, among other things. We sort of lost our identity along the way too."

"But what about the national ad campaign? It said you were a thriving town perfect for cat lovers."

"An old woman's last-ditch effort to give the town an identity. Hardly anyone took that nonsense seriously."

Dr. Hass cleared his throat. Well, he was always one for nonsense. "I might be mistaken, but isn't this town full of cats?"

Martin nodded. "Oh yes. It used to be this crazy mystery too. Everyone had a theory about where all the cats came from. Last year, though,

we found out there was really no mystery to it. Apparently the sheriff's cat was responsible."

"No kidding."

"Yep. But that's been taken care of. Anyway, just before Christmas, the mayor began acting very strangely, and now, well…he's on the tropical isle of denial."

Dr. Hass nodded solemnly, wishing he had a couch or something. But it didn't seem that lying down was going to help this fellow.

"So basically what you are saying is that the mayor feels guilty about relying on one person to support this town rather than building up resources in other areas to see that the town was secure."

"Okay. Sure. But the fact of the matter is," Martin said tersely, "that he's the way he is now, and we've got to help him."

Dr. Hass swallowed. He'd tried to remind himself to turn up his sensitivity monitor, but he didn't always do a good job. His ex-wives would attest to that. "I'm sorry, I just wanted to make sure I understood." He offered a placating smile that seemed to be received.

"So what do you suggest we do, Dr. Hass? I have no idea how to get him back to reality."

"Sometimes when people experience high levels of stress or fear, they completely shut themselves off from their former identity, allowing their minds to heal."

"So we should just let him think it's summertime in Skary and there are no worries in the world?"

"Not necessarily. Sometimes, if the brain gets too comfortable in the imaginary world, the person won't come back. Why should he? There are no worries in the world there."

Martin's eyes widened as he stared at the mayor. "My lands!"

"Don't panic. We can get him back." Dr. Hass ran a hand through his hair…but stopped at the thought that this wasn't quite the best body language to show confidence in his statement. Luckily, Martin was still staring at the mayor, who simply sat there with a near-giddy expression on his face. But Dr. Hass had always had a motto which he'd applied often to his own life: *Face your fears.* It was this very idea that had caused

him to move from sunny California to a place that seemed perfect to test his theory. In a moment of truth, he did have to admit he was running himself, but running from something that could inflict horrible, bodily harm, so that was a different matter altogether.

"How?"

"We must get the mayor to face his fears. What's the worst-case scenario?

Martin thought for a moment. "Well, the town could financially collapse, leaving hundreds of people homeless and destitute, without running water or a school system."

Dr. Hass pondered. "Okay, well, we might not want to hit him with this all at once, but let's just offer him bits and pieces of the truth."

"What first? The fact that both of us are about six months away from not having a paycheck?"

"How about something like the fact that without some sort of intervention, Skary is in trouble."

"Well, those are the last words I spoke to him before he went haywire."

"I see." Dr. Hass sighed. "Listen, let's just keep working that angle. What the mayor is dealing with are huge feelings of inadequacy. The realization that he has failed. When he realizes that failing is a part of being human, he may forgive himself, which is what needs to happen."

"Ah." A light of acceptance popped on in Martin's eyes. "Forgiveness. Accept that he failed, and then forgive himself."

"Exactly. But first he has to accept it. For some people, failure is just a step above death."

And then the mayor stood up, surprising Dr. Hass enough that he rolled his chair back three feet. Martin gasped.

"If you're going to talk about somebody, you should do it when they're not in the room," he scowled.

Martin popped up. "Mayor! You're talking!"

"What's this about me being a step above death?" he growled, looking at Dr. Hass. "And what am I doing here?"

"Mayor, this is Dr. Hass. He's a therapist."

"The word *therapist* is so—"

"*A shrink!*" the mayor yapped. "What in the world am I doing here?"

Martin pointed to the mayor's shorts. "You've been acting a little strange lately."

The mayor looked down at his shorts, then at his Hawaiian shirt. "What's all this about?"

"It's what you got up and put on today, Mayor," Martin said.

Like slow-rolling tumbleweeds, five different emotions blew across the mayor's face. His eyes darted between Martin and Dr. Hass. After several moments, Dr. Hass stood up, gave Martin a knowing nod, then looked directly at the mayor and said, "Sir, the whole town of Skary, Indiana, could cease to exist, and it could all be your fault."

Silence tore through the room like a windstorm, erasing even the faintest sound. The mayor's mouth hung open. His eyes blinked very fast for five seconds, then stopped. Dr. Hass wasn't sure if he should try to say something profound, or call an ambulance. Was he even breathing?

And then the mayor spoke. "Who wants to go for a swim? It's topping a hundred today!"

Oliver screamed. A scream answered back. He screamed again. Then another scream came. This went back and forth until Oliver finally stopped screaming. The other screams went on and on, though. It sounded like a woman. And in fact, it sounded like...

Oliver pulled aside the brush and rounded a tree.

"*Melb!*"

"Oliver?" Melb was panting and about to cry.

Oliver rushed over to her and took her trembling hands. "Are you okay?"

"I-I-I'm fine. I heard screaming and then I started screaming. Was that you?"

Oliver nodded. "I thought I saw someone in the bushes."

"That's me!"

"What are you doing out here?"

Melb stood up, pointing to a book lying next to her. "I'm owling. Remember? I told you I was going to start a hobby."

Oliver shook his head. "I didn't realize what you meant, I guess."

"What are you doing out here?"

Oliver laughed a little. "Well, you're going to think I'm crazy. But I've been seeing some strange people around town. I took off work early to investigate, see if I could find one."

"What do you mean by strange people?"

"They're hard to describe. But there's something really off about them. They look like at any moment they're going to jump out from behind a bush and strangle you."

"They're hiding behind bushes?"

"Not really. They mostly just walk around aimlessly."

"Okay. Well, I'll keep an eye out for them. In the meantime, I'm not giving up on this owl."

"Melb, I don't think it's safe for you to be out in the wilderness by yourself at night."

"First of all, it's not a wilderness. And second of all, I am going to bond with this owl if it's the last thing I do."

"Why would you want to bond with an owl?"

"That's the whole point of owling. You hoot to them and they hoot back. It's this really nifty thing. But I can't seem to get the owl to show himself to me. He'll hoot, but he's being coy."

Oliver stood there in the middle of the brush, trying to understand Melb's sudden fascination with owls.

*"Whoo, whoo."*

Melb hunkered down, pulling Oliver to the ground. His face crashed into the leaves. "Shhh! That's the owl," Melb whispered. "We can't let him see us or he'll fly away."

*"Whoo, whoo, whoo,"* the owl said again, somewhere a few trees away, high on its top.

Melb smiled at Oliver. "He's looking for a mate."

"Oh."

*"Whoo, whoo, whoo,"* the owl said again.

"Whoo! Whoo! Whoo whoo whooooo-eeee-whoooo!" Melb replied, cupping her hands around her mouth. And then there was silence. Melb sighed. "See? Now he's not even responding!"

Oliver patted her on the back. "May I make a suggestion?"

Melb shrugged. "Sure."

"I'm no expert here, but it seems you might be coming on a little strong."

"How do you mean?"

"Well, you're wanting to come across as the loving lifemate and domestic set of feathers this owl can't live without, right?"

"Uh huh."

"I think you're making a slightly different impression. Maybe the party-all-night Britney Spears of all owl impressions."

"Really? The hooting's too aggressive?"

"I think so. I haven't read the book, but I imagine the male owl is looking for an owl that's, well, that's hard to catch but naive and innocent too."

"Really?"

"Sure. I fell so in love with you partly because I never thought I was good enough for you. When we got together, it made me love you even more, because I felt I'd really conquered something, which I did." Oliver smiled. Melb was grinning from ear to ear.

"Maybe we can practice owling tonight. You can help me be more subtle." She winked at him.

Oliver took her hand. "You are so cute when you hoot."

## CHAPTER 17

WOLFE PICKED UP AINSLEY from her house on Sunday morning. She was wearing a beautiful blue sweater and a matching blue skirt. "Wow!" he said as she climbed into his truck.

"What?"

"You look terrific."

"Thank you."

As they drove to church together, Ainsley told him some of what her mother's wedding diary said. "It was such a different time. Things seemed so much simpler then."

"How so?"

"Mom's diary is filled with dreams, just like mine. But it seemed like some of them were just dreams. She wanted a four-tier cake. I know she didn't have that. She wanted a silk dress. But hers was taffeta. Yet she wasn't upset. She was focused on what the wedding was about."

"Sounds like she was really in love with your dad."

"She was. I just wish she could've had the wedding she dreamed of. Dad said they'd planned on doing something really special at their twenty-year wedding anniversary. They were going to have all the things that they couldn't afford at their first wedding." Ainsley squeezed Wolfe's hands, indicating she couldn't say the rest of what she wanted.

"Sweetheart, your mother was very happy when she was alive, right?"

Ainsley nodded.

"She had you and your dad and your brother. So she never got a big wedding cake. I bet she wouldn't have traded anything in her life."

Ainsley smiled. "No regrets."

"No regrets."

"I guess I want to have a dream wedding partly because there's always the possibility that there isn't going to be a second chance."

"Our wedding is going to be perfect."

"What's that?" Ainsley said, looking out the front window of the car. She was pointing to a line of orange cones in the middle of the small church parking lot.

"Looks like they're blocking part of the spaces," Wolfe said, pulling in. There were only a few cars in the lot, but the orange cones were causing quite a bit of confusion. Cars were backing up and trying to pull around to the few empty spaces left.

"I wonder if Reverend Peck is going to have the parking lot paved?" It was currently gravel.

Wolfe found a parking spot and went around to the other side to help Ainsley out. Holding hands, they walked to the church. But when they got to the door, there was a teenage boy standing there, one they didn't recognize.

"Hi," he said, his hands full of bulletins. Wolfe smiled and held out his hand. But the kid said, "Sorry. If you want a bulletin, it'll be a dollar."

"What?" Ainsley laughed.

"A dollar. Cash only."

"For the bulletin?" Wolfe asked. "Does Reverend Peck know you're out here? What kind of scam do you think you're pulling?"

"The guy hired me. I get twenty percent commission." He smiled broadly.

"Forget it," Wolfe said. "Come on," he told Ainsley. "Let's go inside."

"But what if there's something important we need to know in there?" Ainsley asked. "Maybe there's a reason the reverend is charging for it."

Wolfe sighed and handed the kid a buck.

"Thanks!" the kid said.

Inside, they silently surveyed the once-familiar sanctuary that now contained only half the number of pews it used to.

"What's going on?" Ainsley whispered.

"I have no idea. This is weird." Wolfe took her hand and led her to one of the pews. "But we'd better sit down, or we might be standing for the whole service!"

They sat down, and Ainsley opened the bulletin. "Well, let's find out what's so interesting in this bulletin that would make it worth a dollar—*Oh!*"

"What?" Wolfe asked. Ainsley handed him the bulletin. Wolfe read the sermon title: *What the Bible Says About Sex.* He glanced at Ainsley. Her face was bright red.

Miss Missy Peeple, in her purple polyester suit complete with a green and purple scarf tied precisely around her neck, walked to church as she had every Sunday since she was able to walk. Nothing had ever kept her from church. She'd once trekked through a snowstorm. One time she even walked with a broken leg. She'd been born in this church, and she intended to die there too. Nobody would ever be able to accuse her of not supporting her local church.

As she made her way up Scarlet Hill, shooing cats that had the gall to get in her way, she could not help thinking of Marty Blarty and his quest to find the truth about Skary, Indiana. She'd seen him day after day at the library, at the courthouse, and at the town hall. The poor lad. He tried hard. And he sure was ambitious. Part of her felt sorry for him, for no matter how hard Marty Blarty looked, he would never be able to find the truth. She'd made sure of that nearly fifty years ago. Surely he would give up soon! Everyone who knew anything of the truth had died off years ago, except her. Besides, what this town needed was a good dose of inspiration. It could be famous again if given the chance. It was time to move forward, not get mired in a lot of ancient history.

She'd spent her life savings to promote to the world that Skary, Indiana, was the place for cat lovers. She'd expected people to come in droves. But instead, all she had noticed were some strange and unlikable

people wandering the streets. They'd come and gone for a couple of weeks now. She'd even spotted one in her backyard for heaven's sake! She'd called the police, but once they got there, the person had vanished. Of course, the police never believe little old ladies, and her complaint was met with skepticism. She knew what she saw, though, and from then on she kept a close watch out for them. And every once in a while, in the middle of the night, she would hear a scream that froze her to her bedposts.

Apparently, from what she'd heard, the sheriff hadn't noticed the strangers yet, nor heard a scream. Of course, he was too busy worrying about that furry fuzzball of a friend of his to notice anything about the town except that cats weren't multiplying by the dozens anymore.

An irritated grunt left Miss Peeple's lips as she climbed the final few feet of the hill that led to the church.

The first thing she noticed were the cars, parked every which way and on the sides of a nearby street. What in the world was wrong with people? Too much holiday cheer? Yeah, it's lots of fun putting up hundreds of dollars worth of lights. But then comes the time when you have to take them all down in the middle of the coldest month of the year. Nobody ever thinks of the takedown. Nobody but Missy Peeple.

The next surprise came when she shoved her way through a crowd of people near the front door. A pipsqueak sort of kid, with his hair gelled like his life depended on it, held up his hand. "Stop. Nobody else goes in. Sorry. We're full."

Miss Peeple was not accustomed to having people tell her no, nor hold up any sort of extremity in her face. "Step aside," she ordered the boy, waving her cane at him.

"Sorry. Can't. Maximum capacity is already in there. It's standing room only, from what I can tell. You'll just have to get here earlier next week. But," he said with a smile, "you're still welcome to a bulletin for a dollar."

"A dollar?" Missy hissed. "What nonsense is this?" She turned to those standing nearby. "What is going on here? Since when has anybody ever been turned away from church?"

She knew how to get a crowd going, and soon, after a few more derogatory remarks, heads were bobbing up and down. She could've said aliens were attacking, and there they'd be, agreeing with every word she said. She was just angry enough about this situation, though, not to be able to appreciate her sudden authority. "We will protest! That will show them! None of us will go to church! We'll start our own church!"

Suddenly the boy with the bulletins stepped forward. "A lady had to leave because her baby was crying, so whoever has ticket number seven can go on in!"

A man in the back yelped and then moved through the crowd, quickly hopping up the steps. The crowd began murmuring that perhaps their number would be called next, and soon nobody cared who Miss Peeple was or why she was there. All they wanted was their number called.

Missy turned and scowled at the church building. She knew one thing for sure. She had Reverend Peck's number. This was no accident. Miss Missy Peeple could smell a plot a mile away.

Reverend Peck hadn't actually read his sermon out loud, so when it came time to say the word he was preaching on, it got stuck on his tongue. The whole point of his sermon was that God created sex to be good, and that He had a plan for it, and that the Bible outlined exactly what that plan should be.

And in the monthly pastor's newsletter he received, called "Growing Your Mini into a Mega," it had told of a pastor who'd decided one day to preach on sex, and the next thing he knew he had five hundred people in the pews.

The Song of Solomon was certainly nothing new to him. It was a beautiful book of the Bible. When his wife was alive, he would often-times cite passages from this book and send it to her in a card.

Yet now, as he stood in front of a congregation half sitting and half standing, all of whom were looking at him as if he'd grown an extra head, Reverend Peck felt self-conscious. And perhaps it was because

deep down in his heart, he knew he was not preaching this sermon because he felt a passion for, well, passion. No, he'd come up with this topic for its pure shock value.

Well, it worked. He was completely shocked. And so was the congregation, that so far in the five minutes he'd been behind the pulpit, all he'd managed to convey was something about the *s* word, that it rhymed with a letter in the back of the alphabet, and that it was supposed to be within marriage. Looking down at his notes, he had three pages full of things to share! Why was he fumbling around here like an idiot?

Gulping down his newly formed stage fright, Reverend Peck realized he was going to have to do something, and do it quick. Murmuring had begun. He'd been around long enough to know nothing good ever came from murmuring. His whole plan was about to fall apart! He'd spent weeks on this…now for it all to crumble because he was embarrassed by his own sermon topic? He knew things were working so far. A crowd remained outside, anxious to get into the church. Everyone had a bulletin in hand, so he'd guessed correctly on that, too.

So with every ounce of boldness he could find in himself, he began reciting his notes. And not just in a conversational way, as he'd been accustomed to doing for decades now, but in a flamboyant, charismatic way. He used hand motions. He told jokes. He even walked the newly created center aisle where some pews used to sit.

Twenty minutes later, he'd covered everything anybody ever needed to know about sex. The basics were: God created it. It was good. Supposed to be for husband and wife only. Side benefit of reproduction.

When Reverend Peck came to the last sentence of his notes, he was relieved as never before. By the dismayed expressions staring back at him, he also realized perhaps that was a bit much for a small-town church to handle in one sitting. But he'd gotten their attention! Not once had he seen anyone yawn. And taking out the extra pews in the sanctuary made the place look packed. The people standing in the back didn't seem to mind. In fact, they looked simply happy to be here. When had anyone looked happy to be here?

So with a confident nod indicating he was indeed finished with the

*s* word, he then announced coffee would be served in the foyer for three dollars a cup. Cream and sugar were fifty cents more. And then he left the pulpit and quickly slipped out the back door of the church.

Sure, he used to greet everyone. But wasn't there more mystery to a person you never actually got to meet? People would wonder, *What's he like? Why doesn't he want to talk to us? He must be awfully important and busy.*

As he walked home to the parsonage, Reverend Peck knew he was making a gigantic gamble. In all of his years of ministry, never had he done a thing like this. The closest he'd come was deciding one day not to wear his robe. That had caused quite a stir among the community, which he thought was interesting since most of the community didn't attend. There was even an entire newspaper article about it, debating what kind of theology was behind the decision. Turned out it was simply because he'd gained some weight and couldn't zip it. But it took a lot of convincing on his part to settle everyone down. He did recall a slight surge in attendance, at least for a couple of weeks.

Opening the door to his home, he went inside, feeling emotionally fatigued. Desperation, he knew, made people do crazy things. He wondered how many people were rushing to get coffee right now.

Ainsley smiled as she peeked around the corner to see her father and Wolfe sitting in the living room watching the football play-offs together. How could she have ever imagined this day? And to think he would soon be her husband. A chill of joy tickled her.

Back in the kitchen, though, her thoughts turned once again to the missing Wise Men. In just a few days, she would have to put the Nativity set away. She still could not imagine who would've done such a thing! While her brother was here for the holidays, he'd done some minor investigating and hadn't turned up a thing. She thought swiping someone's Wise Men was pretty low, and if she ever found out who did it, they'd be hearing a word or two from her.

After putting the finishing garnishes on the meatloaf, and attending to the decor on the table, she finally announced that dinner was ready. Wolfe and her father joined her in the dining room.

When the sheriff finished saying grace, she said, "Dad, I'm worried about Reverend Peck."

"Oh?"

"Church was crazy today. Weren't you there?"

The sheriff had stuffed his mouth, so he shook his head. After swallowing he said, "No. Thief wasn't doing well this morning. I had to bring his food bowl to him and his water. After I scratched his tummy for over an hour, he finally decided he might want to go outside. But ten minutes later he wanted to come inside."

"Yes, well, back to Reverend Peck. He'd taken out half the pews, marked off only a handful of parking spaces, and made everyone pay a dollar for a bulletin."

"Really? Sounds like we have a newly converted entrepreneur on our hands." The sheriff snorted out a laugh.

"Dad, this isn't a joke. Something's wrong."

The sheriff sighed. "Something's wrong with this whole town, Ainsley. Can't you feel it? Can't you *see* it? Mayor Wullisworth is just one example. Thief is another."

Ainsley stared at her food. "What are we going to do?"

"Thief's going to see a shrink."

Her mouth fell open. "Excuse me?"

"Apparently he takes mammals as well as humans."

"Who? What are you talking about?"

"He just moved to Skary. Dr. Hass." The sheriff lowered his voice. "I only heard about him because Melb told Martin to take the mayor there. I don't know how Melb knows about him, one can only guess. But he comes highly recommended."

"You're taking your cat to a therapist."

"Look at him, Ainsley. He hardly moves. Remember how vibrant and alive he used to be? He's near dead now. What would you propose that I do?" The defensiveness in her father's tone made her try her best

to be supportive. She glanced at Wolfe, whose expression could not hide the shock in his eyes.

"Whatever you think will help, Daddy."

"I'm only telling you this, because maybe that's what Reverend Peck needs. Maybe his head needs a doctor."

She sighed. "All I know is that in all my years of knowing Reverend Peck, he has never preached on the *s* word before."

"Shame?"

"No. It rhymes with *x*."

"Extra shame?"

"Sex, Dad."

With wide eyes, the sheriff diverted his attention to his potato salad and then matter-of-factly said the therapist's phone number was on the refrigerator if she wanted to hand it along to the reverend. Then he took his meatloaf and went to the living room to finish watching the ball game.

Ainsley looked at Wolfe, who was staring down at the table, deep in thought. "You okay, Wolfe?"

"I can't help but think this is all my fault," he said, not looking at her.

"What's your fault?"

"This town depended on me. I've let them down."

She grabbed his hand. "Wolfe! Don't talk like that. None of this is your fault. This town has always struggled. For a few years you brought us prosperity, but it's not your job to do that. And God has a plan for you away from your old life. You must know that, right?"

Wolfe nodded. "But Ainsley, I'll be honest. I'm miserable selling cars."

"You haven't sold a car yet, have you?"

Wolfe shook his head. "Not a real one, anyway. Maybe if I do I'll understand that high Oliver keeps talking about. But right now, it's all I can do to roll out of bed and get dressed." He shrugged. "Maybe I should be grateful. Maybe that's what's wrong. I'm not being grateful for what I have. Instead I want something different. I thought I wanted an ordinary life. Now I'm not so sure."

"I'm sorry. I don't know what to say. I don't know how to make this better."

He smiled as he looked in her eyes. "You make it better just by being by my side. I can't wait for you to be my wife. I can't wait to see you in your dress on our wed—"

"*Dress! Oh no!*"

"What?"

"I forgot! I was supposed to go to the tailor yesterday! I made the dress an inch too long." She hopped up from the table. "I'm going to have to reschedule. But when? I'm supposed to go pick out invitations and design the cake—oh and get bridesmaids' gifts. Have you booked the rehearsal dinner yet?"

"Already done."

Relief settled her panicked heart. "Okay, good. At least that's done." She went to the kitchen and got her folder. "I have to keep up with this list. I've got to pay attention, or I'm going to forget something important. Sweetheart, will you excuse me? I've got to go write out exactly how we want our invitations worded, okay?"

Wolfe nodded, and she bounded upstairs, her mind stretching itself in ten different directions. She was usually so organized. Why did things seem so discombobulated?

She went to her desk drawer to get the invitation catalog. But after five minutes of searching, she couldn't find it. A familiar tightening of the throat made her sit on the bed and try to hold back the tears.

She didn't remember reading anything about a meltdown in her mother's diary.

## CHAPTER 18

MELB DABBED THE TISSUE to the corner of her eye, the way she knew a proper woman should. If she could say anything for those romance novels she used to read, they'd taught her some manners. Because what she really wanted to do right now was wail and carry on and blow all of her problems into a Kleenex.

She looked at Dr. Hass, who seemed somewhat dismayed that she was even shedding tears. What kind of therapist hadn't seen a person cry before? Maybe it was that she got splotchy. Since she was a kid, she'd been plagued by splotchy crying. Her friends would cry and look adorable. She would cry and look as if she'd rolled in poison ivy.

"I'm just desperate," Melb continued. "I have less than a month to my wedding day, Dr. Hass. And I keep eating and eating."

"Did you start a hobby?"

"Oh yes. And I've been faithful to it. It's actually fun. I've been owling."

"Howling?"

"Owling. It's this thing you do with owls. Anyway, it has relieved a lot of stress. But I'm still tempted to eat what I shouldn't, and when I shouldn't. I think, *Don't eat that cookie.* And my body hears, *Eat three cookies.*"

"You say you're stressed. About the wedding?"

"Well, not just about the wedding. That's part of it. Certainly trying to drop this much weight to fit into my wedding dress has been stressful. But I'm also feeling guilty."

"About?"

Melb tore up her tissue, then looked at Dr. Hass, her bottom lip quivering. "The wedding budget. Oliver and I sat down and agreed on a budget, and I've completely blown it."

"He'll understand."

"Oh, I don't know. He runs a very tight ship at his car business, and if there's one thing I know about Oliver, he doesn't fool around about money."

"But if you two are to be wed, don't you think honesty is the best way to start out the marriage?"

Tears streaked Melb's cheeks as she nodded. "That would be nice, Dr. Hass. But obviously you've been reading too many self-help books. Sometimes in real life, the truth is better left buried until one can fix it so that the other one never knows what happened."

"What's your plan to fix it?"

Melb rubbed the bits of Kleenex up and down her cheeks. "That's why I'm here."

"Melb," Dr. Hass said, "I can't fix your problems by lying for you, or coming up with a scheme. But I can tell you how to find peace in your heart about this situation, and possibly lose weight too. You say that you've been getting stressed. A lot of people eat when they are stressed. You say you are under stress because you are hiding this secret about overspending on your wedding budget."

"That sounds right," Melb admitted.

"So it seems to me, the solution lies in confession."

"Confession?" Melb choked on the word.

"You must confess to Oliver what you have done."

Melb shook her head. "*No!* I can't do that!"

"Melb, do you believe you will find peace in your heart if you don't?"

"I may not find peace in my heart," Melb retorted, standing up, "but I will find a piece of pie!"

"Excuse me?" Dr. Hass asked.

"I'm hungry. And our time's up anyway. Don't you watch the clock?

For crying out loud, we're fifteen minutes over, and I'm not paying another dime!"

"Melb, please, wait."

"Dr. Hass," Melb said, "if I wanted to hear the word *confession,* I'd go see the reverend!" She slammed the door behind her.

Martin Blarty was feeling slightly self-conscious as he sat on the back porch of the mayor's house in a pair of shorts that hadn't seen the light of day in three decades, along with his legs. Pasty didn't really begin to describe his skin, and though it was just he and the mayor, it was still mortifying nevertheless. Not to mention the fact that the scene was complete with beach towels, Hawaiian breezes (a concoction of red punch, pineapple juice, and rum, but since the mayor had forgotten two out of the three ingredients, it was really just punch), sunglasses, and a Beach Boys tape playing in the background.

The mayor had insisted Martin join him, and Martin, trying to remember Dr. Hass's advice, decided to let him continue his fantasy, while at the same time dropping subtle hints about reality.

A little hard to do in this bizarre setting.

The mayor was chitchatting about this and that, and Martin decided this might be the time to drop some sort of remark about how broke the town was. But suddenly the mayor blurted out, "Maybe I need to find a wife."

Martin's mouth was wide open because his words had been stopped in their tracks. But it remained wide open as he tried to process the mayor's words.

"It's time. I've been a bachelor for far too long, Martin. And what good are the sunny days without someone to share them with?"

Martin thought he was doing awfully well sharing the sunny days with his friend. Who else would wear shorts in forty degree weather?

Martin was glad when the mayor got up to go fill their glasses with

punch. His emotions ran the gamut, from being utterly angry and despising the mayor for being completely incapable of handling Skary's dire situation, to feeling sad that the man he thought was so strong had turned out to be so weak.

When the mayor returned to the porch, with a fresh layer of sunscreen on his nose and two glasses of punch, Martin decided to try again at bringing up the strange new visitors he'd spotted.

"Probably tourists," the mayor quipped. "You know they all look the same. Wide-eyed, cameras ready to take a picture of anything deemed interesting, fanny packs wrapped around their bulging waists."

Martin wanted to retort, but it was useless. The mayor was only an echo of who he used to be, and though he didn't want to ignore Dr. Hass's advice, he also felt that the only way to truly get the mayor back on his feet was to figure out how to save this town. And figuring that out, he believed, meant getting back to the basics of what this town was originally about. He felt sure the town's history was the answer to its future. In the back of his mind, he outlined a plan to call a town meeting in hopes of gaining more information.

But finding Skary's history was going to be the trick.

There was one person in this town old enough to know and keen enough to remember. But a visit to her house was like walking under a ladder. Bad things were going to follow. First he was going to have to get some pants on.

"Come in, Marty," Missy Peeple said, surprised by the visitor but nonetheless cordial.

"Martin," he said. "Please, not Marty."

"Why can't I remember that?" she chuckled. "I guess I've always been a sucker for rhyme, Mr. Blarty."

"I'm sorry for stopping by unannounced." He entered, taking off his coat.

"You smell like sunscreen," Missy said, raising a suspicious eyebrow. Marty always was a strange one.

His eyes darted away. He shrugged and took a seat on the couch. Only her curiosity about his visit made her decide to drop the sunscreen inquisition. "Coffee?"

"No, thank you. I'd like to get to the point of why I'm here."

"All right." Missy managed to make it to her chair without her cane. She covered her legs with her quilt and then put her attention on Marty, who looked anxious. "What is it?"

"As far as I know, you are the oldest resident of Skary."

"It is true."

"Well, as you know, the town is in trouble."

Missy Peeple could not help the expression she knew tightened her skin and narrowed her eyes, drawing her mouth into a straight line. Of course she knew! It was because of this town's sudden interest in conscience that she was not able to save it in the first place. Now, of course, he needed her help.

As far as she was concerned, she'd done all she could. Her life savings was gone, and she was still eagerly awaiting Skary's transformation into a haven for cat lovers. Yet this town was all too willing to accept another fate. Why should she risk anything more to help save it?

"What about it? Shouldn't you be talking with the one man who is responsible? Boo could've stopped all of this from happening if he'd had the sense not to fall in love. Have you heard the man is selling cars? What is wrong with him?"

Marty cleared his throat. "I don't blame Boo. A lot of things have happened over the years to make Skary what it is and isn't today. But I still think there is hope to save our town."

An eternal optimist always prompted a lengthy sigh. "So why are you here?"

"I believe in the deepest part of my heart, Miss Peeple, that the key to our future lies within our past."

"Is that so?"

"If we understood our roots, maybe we could find an identity again. Maybe we could understand why we were born, so to speak."

Missy threw off the quilt and rose, gesturing for Martin to get her cane. After he did, she walked over to the table where she always kept a pitcher of water. Pouring herself a drink, she cleared her mind of anxieties, trying to convince herself she held the power in this situation. But that wasn't exactly true anymore. In a desperate, perhaps noble, attempt to save Skary, Indiana, she may have made one fatal mistake.

She turned back to Marty, forcing calm into her voice. "Martin, do you really believe anybody cares why this town was born? People go about their day-to-day business, forgetting who is responsible for their well-being, mindless of who might help them in their future. All they know is how to get through the day."

"I agree. But maybe knowing about this town could spark something, you know? Maybe it will cause a resurgence."

"Every day more and more people leave. I noticed just yesterday that the fish and tackle shop is closing."

"I know," Marty sighed. "That's why I'm desperately seeking the truth. The trouble is, the truth does not seem to want to be found."

"Oh?"

"Records, documents, everything related to Skary's history seems to have vanished. Rather, it has been taken. I don't know why, but I intend to find out. Right now, I was hoping you would know about this town, Miss Peeple. I was hoping you'd heard stories your forefathers had told, that perhaps you'd written something down, or maybe had a journal passed down through the generations. I know the basic history of Skary, like when it was founded and what was built where. But I need to know the heart, do you understand? I want to understand *why* it came into being."

Missy shuffled over to a nearby window, staring out at her limited view of the town. People and cats scurried here and there. Marty wanted the truth. But the truth would mean everything she had worked a lifetime to achieve would suddenly be ripped from her. It meant a sacrifice she was not willing to make.

Besides, she reminded herself, she no longer held the keys to the truth. She'd entrusted those to Wolfe Boone. She wasn't sure why. She only knew that perhaps the man who had wrecked their town should hold a new burden on his shoulders. Maybe that burden would be to find out the truth and then to decide what to do with it. Or maybe the burden would come in finding out the truth too late, and knowing he could've done something about it.

At any rate, she'd wiped her hands clean of it. She had told him that the key to the town was inside the pages of his book. Whether he wanted to find the truth or not was up to him.

Missy turned to Marty. "I'm sorry, dear. I don't know anything. My family did not share any secrets, if that's what you are after."

"Not secrets. Just truth."

Missy shook her head. Her body told her to sit back down. "I have no stories to tell. Only the story of my own life, which may come to an end very soon."

Marty's perpetually dull eyes lit with interest. "Why would you say that?"

Missy dismissed the thought of drawing sympathy…more like pity…from Marty. "I am old, after all. That is why you're here, isn't it?" She smiled.

Martin rose and went to the front door. "Thank you for your time." Heavy disappointment rang in his tone.

"I'm sorry I couldn't help more."

Her visitor nodded and then left quietly. Missy could not identify the emotion that strained her throat. Remorse? Relief? Whatever the case, it was nothing a good hard peppermint couldn't cure.

## CHAPTER 19

WOLFE HAD TO WORK LATE, and Ainsley's father had decided to take Thief to a therapist, so she found herself alone in the house. Which was probably a good thing. She'd spent the day running around the town trying to play catch-up on all the wedding plans she'd failed to make in the earlier weeks. She'd accomplished only half of what she needed to do.

By the afternoon, she found herself trembling from anxiety, and exhausted. She took an hour nap before getting up and realizing she hadn't even planned dinner yet. She threw together a simple casserole and then sat in the living room, sketching out her ideas for flower arrangements.

The Nativity set caught her eye. She observed it, trying to find a way to reconcile herself to the fact of the missing Wise Men. After all, the most important figure of the entire set was there: Baby Jesus. Mary and Joseph didn't seem bothered by it. The shepherds were probably happy about it, no rivaling porcelain figures on the other side of the mantel.

As she stared at the scene, she found herself observing the fact that everybody up on that mantel knew all they should about themselves. The shepherds had their role. The angels had theirs. The animals knew where to stand. Mary and Joseph's whole life had been defined for them. And Baby Jesus…his whole life's work was to help others define themselves as children loved by God.

And Ainsley Parker knew what hers was too. It certainly wasn't as noble as being the mother of the Savior of the world, but nevertheless, it gave her an identity all her own. And according to Alfred, she would be doing it on a much larger scale very soon. It was nice to have some-

one believe in everything you'd suspected about yourself for years but
didn't have the courage to articulate. Nobody would've believed in her
talents. Not even herself! She just knew what she was good at, and she'd
tried really hard to be even better. Now it was paying off.

She walked over to the mantel and gently picked up Jesus. The mystery of how a little Baby Boy could hold her in His hands was tucked
deep into her heart.

A knock came at her door, and she gently set the figure back where
it belonged. At the door, she was surprised to see Alfred.

"Hi." She smiled.

"May I come in?"

"Of course."

Alfred led the way into the living room. "I have good news," he said.

"What?"

"Harper Jones is very interested in seeing more of you."

"Really!" She reminded herself that jumping up and down like a
schoolgirl was not going to portray the right image. She clasped her
hands and smiled graciously.

"It's true. But he needs to see you in action."

"What does that mean? Should I have him over for dinner?"

"No. More like we need to find that big event you can be in charge
of. We'll bring a TV crew out to tape it. We'll edit it up and format it
like we would a TV show. It would be a sort of pilot. If they like what
they see, Ainsley, you could be on your way to stardom."

Ainsley shook her head. She could hardly believe it. Looking at
Alfred she said, "But what kind of event?"

"I don't know," Alfred admitted. "We're going to have to find something. I'll be thinking about it." Alfred took her hands and smiled
warmly. "This is it, kiddo. This is your moment. Time for you to shine.
All these years you've been in that kitchen working your tail off, probably
for the most part underappreciated. But it has all paid off now. Thanks to
Martha's little downfall, my friend, you may be rising faster than a loaf of
basil-tomato bread."

Ainsley nodded, but she couldn't help but feel a little grief. It was

hard to take the place of someone so great. Alfred squeezed her hands. "Don't fret, Ainsley. This is what you were born to do."

Thoughts of big kitchens, fancy serving dishes, and gourmet foods were interrupted by Alfred looking up at the mantel and saying, "Hey. Where are the Wise Men?"

Wolfe was trying his hardest to control his emotions. But right now all he wanted to do was berate this impossibly indecisive customer. For five hours now this man, Mr. Hyatt, had been on the car lot. The Road to the Sale had taken an hour. Since then, they'd been haggling over pennies. And it wasn't just Mr. Hyatt, though he was a penny pincher if there ever was one. But it was also Oliver, who refused to consent or even meet halfway. Sure, they weren't going to make a ton of money off the deal, but wasn't a little money better than nothing? Looked as if they could bring in about four hundred dollars.

And so Wolfe was the go-between, which was completely exhausting. The charismatic smile Oliver insisted he wear in front of all customers could not reflect less what he was feeling on the inside.

Wolfe plodded back to the office where Mr. Hyatt sat, his face pinched as tightly as the twisted folds of a belly button.

"Well," Wolfe said heartily, inserting happiness into his tone. "Looks like we may have finally come to a deal."

Mr. Hyatt nodded, though his eyes dulled with skepticism. "I would hope so."

"Looks like Mr. Stepaphanolopolis will come down that extra five hundred dollars. But only if you'll agree to purchase the All-Weather package, which will provide a rustproof sealant on the bottom of your car in case of—"

"What?" Mr. Hyatt fumed. "I've been sitting in this office for *five hours* while you bat this deal back and forth like a Ping-Pong ball. Mister, I have given you my final offer. Take it or leave it!"

At this point, Wolfe knew exactly what he was supposed to do. A friendly smile. An understanding nod. A polite response about how he would have to go back to the finance manager and "see if the numbers would fly."

But Wolfe was supposed to be off two hours ago. He should be at home finalizing honeymoon plans. Instead, he was, in Mr. Hyatt's words, the Ping-Pong ball being batted.

"Tell you what," Wolfe said, leaning across the desk like he might just whisper a secret. Mr. Hyatt leaned forward in anticipation. "Rock, paper, scissors."

"Excuse me?"

"Three times. Whoever loses consents to the other's deal."

"What in the blue moon are you talking about?" Mr. Hyatt asked.

"Well, I'm a little tired, frankly, of going back and forth to the Great Wizard. And actually, he's just an ordinary guy trying to make a living. I'm sure you're fed up with the process. Rustproofing your car is hardly what you had in mind, is it? So let's just settle it here and now. Do I need to remind you how to play?"

"What is going on here?" Oliver was standing in the doorway, his arms crossed.

"This man is nuts!" Mr. Hyatt said, standing and gathering his coat and hat. "He wants to play kid games with me."

Oliver's eyes cut to Wolfe, and Wolfe realized that because he'd gotten fed up, he was getting ready to lose a deal for Oliver.

"Wait, please, Mr. Hyatt," Oliver was saying, following the man out the door. Wolfe watched through the window as Oliver scurried after him and out of sight.

Sighing, he fell into his chair. He'd made a grave mistake out of frustration with an industry he had little tolerance for. Oliver had instructed him on what to do, and he had failed. He wasn't cut out for this, and he knew it. Whatever his new destiny would be, it wouldn't be in the car business.

He looked up to find Oliver stomping toward the office, the skin on

his face slowly turning a purple-red. Pointing his pudgy finger at him, Oliver yelled, *"You're fired!"*

Dr. Hass had been in Skary, Indiana, for a month, and every day seemed more bizarre than the one before. He was making a nice living so far, but had barely started his business. Plans were taking shape, and he thought his experiment was going quite nicely, but other than that, all he did was listen to people's problems, which turned out to pay pretty well. But goodness, this town was a mess! You would think with all the cats running around, people would understand their soothing nature and adopt one or two as their own. It was well documented that a pet, especially a cat, was able to lift a person's spirits. So why was everyone so upset over all these petty problems? Next week alone he already had five appointments set up, not including Melb Cornforth, who insisted on being seen twice a week until her wedding. That, of course, was before she'd stormed out of his office in pursuit of pie.

His newest patient was going to prove to be quite a challenge. He sat in the chair across from Dr. Hass, eyes narrow and uninviting, hanging over the arm like he owned the place. But it was this patient Dr. Hass had the most hope for. And, indeed, the most passion for.

"You say he's like this all the time?" Dr. Hass asked Sheriff Parker. The sheriff, a burly guy with a thick mustache to counter his smiling eyes and easygoing demeanor, nodded solemnly.

"Ever since he had that surgery, all he does is lie around. He has no spunk to him. You should've seen him before. He'd bound out the door every day, a smile on his face, bounce to his step. Now look at him."

Dr. Hass studied the cat. There was not too much he could conclude by looking at him. He'd curled himself up in the chair, haughty like most cats, which is why Dr. Hass loved them so much. He could relate to the feline race's thoughts of superiority. Though he was work-

ing on trying to combat egotistical feelings, there was always comfort knowing the cat was out there not trying to combat his in the least.

Sheriff Parker was staring at the poster of Napoleon, but didn't say anything.

"So did this begin right after the operation?"

"Yes. At first I thought it was just due to the physical soreness of the operation. But then, as the wound healed, I realized he wasn't getting any better. I don't even think Thief would eat if I didn't spoon-feed him," the sheriff said, a slight tremble in his voice.

"You're, um, spoon-feeding your cat?"

The sheriff nodded solemnly. "He used to eat the dry cat food, but that's hard to fit on a spoon, so I bought the moist stuff. I have to take it up to him, along with his water, every morning and every night. I've been doing some massage techniques on him, trying to relax him so he'll feel better, but that doesn't seem to work either. Doctor, I believe he is depressed."

"Depressed."

"His—well, his recreation has been taken from him. Now he's lost his meaning in life, do you know what I mean?"

"I think so," Dr. Hass said carefully. "Can you give me any more details?"

Sheriff Parker shrugged. "Well, I've tried catnip. I've groomed him endlessly, hoping he'll still feel like he has cat appeal, you know? That's important for a cat like Thief. I bought this CD of soothing cat noises that I play all the time. Still, nothing." The sheriff leaned forward. "Dr. Hass, I'm desperate. I want my cat back. Can you help him?"

Dr. Hass tried to smile reassuringly. Yes, he could help. But the problem wasn't with the cat. And breaking the news to this kind of fellow was going to take some finesse. "Sheriff Parker, I can help your cat. But you're going to have to follow my instructions without fault."

The sheriff's eyes grew round. Thief was unimpressed and had fallen asleep in the chair.

"I am going to write down five things you must do, and if you do these things, you will see Thief return to his old self."

The sheriff grinned, thanking him profusely as Dr. Hass wrote down these things on a piece of paper. He folded it and handed it to the sheriff. "Now, don't share this plan with the cat. Simply do what is on this list, and you will find Thief back to his normal self."

The sheriff nodded eagerly, scooped the cat up, and pumped Dr. Hass's hand as if he were a well of endless knowledge. "Thank you! Thank you, Dr. Hass!"

"You're very welcome," Dr. Hass said, escorting them to the door. Watching them leave, he could only shake his head.

The cat wasn't depressed. He was spoiled.

## CHAPTER 20

"WAIT!"

"Ainsley!" her friend Marlee complained. "Do you want to do this or not?"

Ainsley twisted her long locks around her fingers. "I don't know."

Marlee set down the scissors and came around to sit in front of Ainsley. "Honey, you're white as a ghost. I think you'd better think about this."

Ainsley shook her head. "If I think about it, I won't do it." Ainsley held up the mirror and gazed at her reflection. She'd had long hair her whole life. She couldn't even imagine what she would look like otherwise.

"Alfred said it would make me look a little older, a little more sophisticated."

"Why do you trust this Alfred guy?" Marlee asked.

Ainsley set the mirror down. "He's going to make big things happen for me."

Marlee smiled at her friend. "Honey, big things already are happening for you. You're marrying a handsome millionaire that thinks you hung the stars. Isn't that everything you ever wanted?"

"Yeah, but I never dreamed I could have this, Marlee. This is going to change my life. I'm going to be somebody. Not just Sheriff Parker's daughter. Or my mom's spitting image. I'm going to be recognized for being my own person."

Marlee stood and grabbed her scissors. "I always knew you'd be bigger than this town," she said. "So what are you thinking? Short bob? Layered?"

Ainsley's skin went clammy. Marlee had been to beauty school a while back but was fired from a local salon when she burned a lady's hair off while attempting to give her what she'd deemed the Perm for Life. Apparently, Marlee found out, you can't double the solution in order to get a firmer curl.

But she'd let Marlee trim her hair here and there, and others still had her cut their hair. Marlee had always had a sense of style.

"I don't know," Ainsley admitted with a long sigh. "I don't even know what look is up-to-date."

Marlee's fingers were tangling through her hair. "Do you trust me then?"

Ainsley closed her eyes. Open heart surgery might be less nerve-racking. "Okay…cut it."

After a brief assessment of her facial shape, her forehead, and her ears, Marlee made the first cut. Then gasped. "Oh…no…"

"Marlee! What!"

A chuckle was followed by, "Just kidding. I thought we'd get that out of the way."

Ainsley groaned. "Very funny."

But with each snip of the scissors, Ainsley couldn't decide whether the anxious feeling inside her was excitement or dread. Reinventing oneself was certainly exhilarating. But she'd stared into the same face with the same hair for years. Who would she be staring at now? "Not too short," she said.

"Trust me," Marlee said authoritatively, sounding like a sculptor attending to her clay.

After what seemed like hours, but was only thirty minutes, Marlee announced she was done. Pumping the hairspray bottle overhead, she then held up the mirror for Ainsley to see.

"Ah!"

"Do you like it?" Marlee smoothed her own hair repetitively.

Ainsley's eyes could not grow any bigger. She threw the mirror down and ran into Marlee's bathroom. Marlee ran after her.

"You hate it!" Marlee's eyes filled with tears.

So did Ainsley's. But she didn't hate it. She loved it. Marlee had cut it two inches above the shoulders, layered it a little so it flipped up slightly on the ends, and then cut a few wispy bangs. Ainsley had come looking like a girl ready for womanhood. Now, for the first time in her life, she looked like a woman. A real woman. A beautiful woman. She turned and hugged Marlee. "It's perfect!"

"Really? You really like it? You're not just saying that?"

"Marlee, it's stunning. I look like a model!"

Marlee jumped to her side and turned her back toward the mirror. "You can still play around with it and wear it in different styles. You can tuck it behind your ears, wear it in an updo, pull it into a low ponytail. There are tons of options."

"Thank you," Ainsley said, squeezing her friend's hand, unable to take her eyes off the image in front of her.

"Wolfe is going to love it," Marlee beamed.

"Wolfe!" Ainsley gasped, slapping her hand over her mouth.

"What's wrong?"

Ainsley's mouth fell open. "I didn't even think about Wolfe!"

"What about him?"

"He loves my hair long."

"Ainsley, it's your hair. You can do with it what you want. Besides, it's not his head that has to carry around an extra pound of hair, which is surely what I cut off today!"

Ainsley swallowed and turned back to the mirror. She prayed Wolfe's day had been good.

A pounding headache had led Wolfe to grab some coffee on his way home. He'd never been fired from a job in his entire life. Admittedly, the feeling was somewhere between relief and remorse. He hated how angry Oliver was at him, but he was probably only a few days away from quitting anyway. Now he didn't feel like diving into his honeymoon project either. All he wanted to do was find some quiet.

As he left the deli with his coffee, he noticed a horde of people walking to the community center. Curiosity brought him in stride with them. Walking in, he asked the lady next to him what was going on.

"Some town meeting," she said. "Probably about feeding the cats. But I swear if you don't feed 'em, they sit outside your house and meow until the cows come home." She lowered her voice. "Rumor has it that the owl was brought in to get rid of the cat problem, if you know what I mean." She didn't wait for Wolfe to nod. "Owls eat cats. On the food chain, I mean. Some owls do. The big ones anyway." A hunkering smile revealed this woman might just like to see that happen. "You seen the owl?"

Wolfe nodded.

"Yeah. Kind of weird. Lotsa weird things been happening around here. You seen the people?"

"People?"

"You haven't noticed them? My lands! They walk around here, real scared looking, kind of like ghosts. And sometimes you'll hear this scream—it'll freeze your blood." She smiled mildly at him. "'Course, I suppose you're used to that sort of thing."

"Pardon me?"

"Ghosts and screaming and such." She paused. "Because of your books."

"Oh." Luckily for Wolfe, the crowd making their way into the community center had now dispersed into the meeting hall, so the woman walked through a different doorway and disappeared.

Wolfe stood in the back, his height making it easy to see all that was going on, which presently was nothing but a group of people chattering away. But soon, Martin Blarty was moving toward the front microphone.

"Folks, thanks for coming on such short notice. That's the great thing about a small town—news spreads quickly." He smiled, but it wasn't without uneasiness. Was he going to tell the town about the mayor?

On the other side of the room, Wolfe noticed Missy Peeple. For

such a small woman, she'd always had a big presence. But observing her now, he thought she looked so frail, the way a woman her age should look. She leaned on her cane, her full attention on Martin. If Missy Peeple were a character in one of his novels, he couldn't imagine what motivation he would create behind such a perplexing personality.

"Okay. We just need to get some urgent information out, and town meetings seem to be a good place to do this. So please tell friends and neighbors who aren't here today. Also, the mayor sends his apologies for not being here himself... He's on vacation in a...tropical locale. He hopes everyone had a terrific Christmas, and as always, he looks forward to a fantastic new year. Speaking of new year, has anyone noticed the strange people who've been seen here and there?"

Heads bobbed while Wolfe tried to figure out Martin's transition, or lack thereof.

"Well, folks, nobody seems to be able to make any sense out of this. They don't seem to be doing anything wrong, so we can't make arrests, but let's just keep an eye out for them, and report anything strange...um, beyond their appearance and the bloodcurdling screams...to the authorities. The second reason this meeting has been called is to see if anyone has any information regarding Skary's history..."

As Martin continued, Wolfe noticed a man near one of the side doors, observing silently, standing with the crowd but not really part of it. He was wearing a bright blue silk shirt, a matching tie, and dress slacks. He certainly did not fit the profile of a Skary resident. He nervously scratched at his neck and pulled at his collar.

"...so if anybody here would like to give me any information you have on Skary, it would be greatly appreciated. Like I said, I think all of us would love to know the history behind the history, so to speak. Wouldn't you say?" Martin's enthusiasm was greeted by a few claps.

"Well," Martin concluded, as Wolfe watched the man he'd been observing slip out the side door, "thank you for coming. It's always nice to see such support from our residents. I hope you have a terrific day!" Martin walked into the crowd and out of sight.

Wolfe finished off his coffee, tossed his cup on the way out of the

community center, and found his car. He just hoped nothing else surprising happened today.

For a reason Melb Cornforth could not identify, her deepest emotions seemed to emerge over food. Today, the chicken-fried steak was no exception, providing a nice pad for the tears that fell from her face. The more she blotted, the more emotional she became. Sitting in the middle of The Mansion, she tried to hold it together but could not.

She was probably reading into things. Oliver had called earlier, telling her he had to work late and would not be joining her for their usual Saturday evening dinner at The Mansion. His tone was cold; he said he would explain later.

Had he found out? Had he discovered what she'd paid for a wedding dress she could not wear? Had he discovered she'd blown the money for the caterer and the wedding day beautician on therapy? Each day Melb tried to make things better, they just got worse. What was she to do? How could she tell Oliver the truth? And if he had found out the truth, would he still want to marry her? Would he still love her?

Her sobs had moistened what was admittedly a fairly dry piece of meat, so Melb took a bite. It had needed some salt, too. Did she eat when she was stressed? Was it true, what Dr. Hass said? He was a therapist, after all. Weren't they paid to see in people what people couldn't see in themselves?

The hobby, though not diminishing her appetite, was a nice break. She could've never guessed how much she would like owling. But it was quite a challenge. It was as if she bonded with the owl, and every night wanted to get closer and closer to it. A mysteriously deep satisfaction came from hearing that owl hoot back. In her life, Melb had never seemed to be really good at anything. She couldn't cook that well. She'd never been pretty, though Oliver seemed to think she was the next Miss America. She'd never enjoyed sports, watching or playing. And it was becoming clear that she couldn't manage money very well.

But who would've guessed she could hoot! According to the book she had on owling, not everyone in the world could get an owl to hoot back. And each night, she seemed to refine the skill even more. She would climb higher and higher into the hills, more dedicated with each step.

All the hooting in the world, though, was not going to get her into a dress or make money fall from the sky. What was she going to do? Desperation caused tears to spill again, and this time into already moist peas.

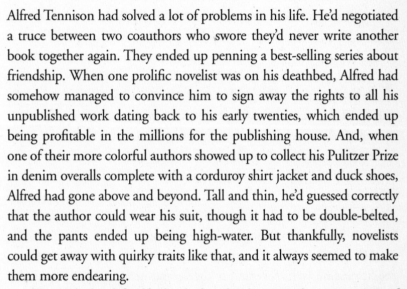

Alfred Tennison had solved a lot of problems in his life. He'd negotiated a truce between two coauthors who swore they'd never write another book together again. They ended up penning a best-selling series about friendship. When one prolific novelist was on his deathbed, Alfred had somehow managed to convince him to sign away the rights to all his unpublished work dating back to his early twenties, which ended up being profitable in the millions for the publishing house. And, when one of their more colorful authors showed up to collect his Pulitzer Prize in denim overalls complete with a corduroy shirt jacket and duck shoes, Alfred had gone above and beyond. Tall and thin, he'd guessed correctly that the author could wear his suit, though it had to be double-belted, and the pants ended up being high-water. But thankfully, novelists could get away with quirky traits like that, and it always seemed to make them more endearing.

However, that left Alfred naked, unless he wanted to wear a pair of farmer overalls, which was awkwardly the better solution. So Alfred sat out in the limo in overalls and ate a Big Mac. It wasn't that bad. These ceremonies were endlessly boring. And it proved Alfred Tennison would do just about anything to be successful.

So he was finding it quite annoying that he was unable to come up with a good solution to put Ainsley in the spotlight. The producer he'd talked with wanted her to pilot a show, something that would "show her stuff." Alfred knew instantly it would need to be a gigantic catering gig, but what that was, he didn't know. Creating an event just to showcase

Ainsley would look too staged. He needed to plant her smack dab into the middle of a planned event.

He'd created a skeleton budget and secured financing. He knew how much it would cost to hire a film crew. There were some non-essentials he'd like to have but could live without. Now he just needed that event. And until he found it, he couldn't begin to estimate a total cost.

Complicating his thought process was the woman in the booth next to him. He recognized her, but couldn't recall her name, though he'd spent Thanksgiving and Christmas with her. Back in his city, the name (he was bad with names anyway) wasn't as important as the position. Here in Skary, Indiana, there weren't really any important positions that he could see. He did recall it seemed to be an incomplete name, like Kather or Lind or Elizab. Something strange like that.

Anyway, between bites of her meal, she was crying, at times actually wailing. The waitress would come over every once in a while, but instead of asking her to calm herself down, she'd refill her tea and, therefore, her seemingly endless supply of tears.

Alfred tried for several more minutes to concentrate on the task at hand. But it was useless. All he wanted to do was go tell this woman to shut up and eat! Finally, exhausted with both the battle of failure and frenzy, Alfred stood and approached her booth.

She glanced up at him, tears oozing from her eyes like tree sap. Bright random welts covered her cheeks and neck, and he wondered if it was contagious.

"Yes?" she asked, blowing her nose into a napkin. Alfred took a step back. Surely skin disease wasn't airborne.

"Well, um…"

"You're Alfred," she said suddenly. "Wolfe's editor, right? Alfred Tennison, from New York City!" Her damp face brightened as she offered a cheerful smile and enthusiastic hand to shake.

Alfred swallowed, taking it limply and wondering if he had his antibacterial lotion in the car.

She said, "Boy, somebody's going to have to show you how to shake hands in this part of the country. My Oliver, now that man can crush your knuckles if you're not careful."

"How do you do?" Alfred said as politely as he could. "Good to see you." Lie, lie, lie. *Nice to see you with duct tape over your mouth.*

"Look at me. I'm a mess. Excuse the fluster," she said, waving her hands across her face.

It occurred to Alfred that maybe she was crying because she was dying of some horrible skin disease, and then of course it would be heartless to say something like, "Can the sniveling, lady."

"Was there something you wanted?" she asked.

"Um…are you okay?" Alfred's fingers climbed over the skin on his own face as he tried to articulate exactly what he was seeing on hers.

She looked confused for a moment, then said, "Oh. The splotching! My face, right? Looks like I got stung by bees?"

*Bees. Or the plague.*

"I must look like a real mess. I'm a splotcher."

"Excuse me?"

"A splotcher. I splotch when I cry. Always have, even when I was a baby. For the longest time my mama thought I had the mumps. Anyway, it's a Melb Cornforth trademark," she said with a trying smile.

Melb! Right. Thank goodness for that, and the fact she wasn't dying of a contagious skin disease.

"Well, um… Listen, I'll just leave you to be. I just wanted to…to, um, make sure you're okay."

Melb's watery eyes dried instantly. "You did? You came over to see if I was okay? That is so kind of you!"

"Oh. Well, glad you're okay."

"Okay?" she chuckled. "Hardly." Melb shook her head, and the waterworks started again. Alfred's newly grown conscience told him an eye roll would be inappropriate at this moment. She looked up at him. "But the last thing you want to do is listen to my problems."

That was a trick question. He knew it.

"I probably wouldn't be able to help you anyway," Alfred shrugged. "Not unless you can pull a caterer out of your hat."

Wolfe was barely over the shock that his beloved fiancée had cut eight inches off her hair when he was struck with the news that they were going to therapy. It had all happened so fast.

After an intensely long day, he'd arrived at her house before she got home, so he spent an hour listening to his future father-in-law explain how Thief was making progress.

"By moving his food and water bowl from his usual spot in the kitchen to a different location, like the laundry room, I've found him starting to improve."

"No kidding."

"But the doctor was very precise... He said the food and water must be kept in that same location for three days without being moved an inch." The sheriff's eyes were as wide as Butch's when he told those covert operation stories.

"Fascinating."

"There are four other things," the sheriff whispered, twisting his head to see if Thief was anywhere in sight. "But I tell you, Wolfe, I'm encouraged. This is the first sign of hope I've had. I swear, this doc knows what he's talking about."

"What's his name again?"

"Hass."

"Does he dress kind of flashy?"

"Yeah, I think so. Brightly colored shirts."

"So what's the next step?" Wolfe said, nodding toward the paper in the sheriff's hand.

"This one," the sheriff admitted, "is a little strange. It says here that under no circumstances shall I stroke his fur."

"Really?"

"Very strange, but I guess it has to do with something concerning nerve endings. You know, this new-age sort of touchy-feely medicine."

Wolfe nodded, trying to be agreeable, but in the back of his mind, he had to admit this was one of the weirdest things he'd ever heard.

And that was exactly what he was thinking when Ainsley walked through the door. Between his jumbled thoughts on Thief's strange medical regimen to his first glimpse of what Ainsley had decided to do to her hair, he knew a somewhat questionable expression likely flickered across his face.

But whatever his expression, he thought her reaction—hysterical tears—was a bit extreme. Then she yelled at him, something about finally being a woman, and marched upstairs. He was just unwinding from that whole scenario when she proceeded back down the stairs.

"You don't understand!" she wailed.

That was an understatement.

"I've had long hair my whole life. My *whole life.*"

He was nodding. "Ainsley, it's just that—"

"You hate it! I can see it in your eyes!"

"No…no… It's just a surprise."

"Please," she nearly sneered, "I know disappointment when I see it."

"You have to admit, you would be shocked."

Her eyes narrowed. "If what, you cut your hair above your ears?"

"Why are you so mad at me?" Wolfe asked, which was when the sheriff decided it was time to go upstairs and not stroke his cat. "I'm sorry I had a shocked look on my face! It's shocking! You've cut your beautiful long hair. Your new haircut is fine, but your hair has been your pride and joy forever."

Ainsley sniffled and turned away from him, shaking her head. "I love it. I think it makes me look sophisticated."

Wolfe took her shoulders and gently turned her around. "Ainsley, you will always be beautiful to me. It has nothing to do with that. It was just shocking, okay? Just surprising."

Teary eyes stared into his. "I should've told you."

"It's your hair," he smiled. "You don't have to ask or tell me anything. And besides, you're right…you do look sophisticated." Then, without thinking first, he continued, "Wait a minute. You said sophisticated."

She nodded.

"Wait just a minute. Did…Alfred put you up to this?"

She didn't agree, but she didn't deny it either. By the way her eyes grew wide with hesitation, he didn't need her to say it. He let go of her shoulders. "He did! Alfred told you to cut your hair, didn't he?"

"He may have."

"Alfred Tennison!" he fumed.

"It was just a suggestion, Wolfe! He didn't handcuff me and take me to cut my hair, if that's what you're suggesting."

His face flushed with anger. "Not with literal handcuffs anyway."

"What's that supposed to mean?"

"It means that ever since Alfred began whispering his little plan to you about making you the world's next great homemaker, all you can see is the stars in your own eyes."

"I knew it! You are jealous!"

"I'm worried, Ainsley. You are supposed to be planning our wedding, yet everything is getting shoved aside for Alfred and his big dreams."

She teared up. "They're my dreams too."

"You are my dream, Ainsley. And I won't throw away my dream."

And with that, they were now on their way to therapy. Ainsley had recalled her father's mention of Dr. Hass and the wonders he'd performed for Thief. So she declared them in crisis and struck out for Dr. Hass's home. But to Wolfe's everlasting thankfulness, the good doctor was apparently not in his office on this Saturday evening. Relief didn't begin to describe his emotions, though. Not only did he not want to see a therapist, but he also did not want to see *this* therapist. Any therapist who practiced on cats couldn't possibly have a talent for counseling couples.

They stood on the sidewalk in front of the doctor's home, trying to avoid each other's eyes while clearly each wanted desperately for the

other one to signal all was well. But instead, Ainsley offered folded arms, and all Wolfe could do was sigh.

"Well, he's not here," she said. "But I still think we should get counseling."

He tried to steady his expression, which apparently could set off fireworks this night. "Why not see the reverend? We don't know anything about this Dr. Hass."

"He's helped everyone who has come to him! Thief. The mayor is slowly coming around. And...and...Melb!"

Wolfe rolled his eyes. "Is this why you want to come? Because all your friends are in therapy?"

"Look, I think there are going to be issues about being married to a celebrity that we're going to have to address."

"I'm not a celebrity anymore, Ainsley."

She scowled. "Not *you*. Me."

Wolfe realized he had not yet told her he'd been fired by Oliver. He looked up at her to say something, but she was stomping back to the car, her shoes nearly striking sparks against the concrete.

## CHAPTER 21

REVEREND PECK HAD never in his career dreaded a Sunday. While there had been disappointments and such, every week always brought new hope that maybe this time a life would be changed.

But this Sunday morning, as he ironed his shirt and picked out a tie, dismay was his breakfast companion instead of his usual bowl of Cream of Wheat. He couldn't describe last week as either disastrous or successful.

And he'd had enough preaching on the kind of topic he'd preached last week. For crying out loud, God had created it from the beginning of time, and nobody needed a preacher to tell them what it meant or how to do it right.

Yet all week he'd been having trouble coming up with something to rival last week's shock factor. So he'd prepared three sermons and was trying to decipher his mood about them when a knock came at his front door. It surprised him enough that at first he thought he was hearing things. In all his days at this church, he couldn't recall ever having a visitor *before* church. But when the knock came again, he went to answer it.

Standing in his doorway, dressed snazzier than a Pete's Steakhouse sirloin topped with grilled onions and peppers, was a man trying to smile and swallow and blink all at once. "May I help you?"

"You're the reverend of this town?"

"Yes, Reverend Peck."

The man looked distraught and couldn't seem to find the words he was looking for. So the reverend invited him in. It was cold as the North Pole outside anyway.

"Tell me your name."

"Dr. Hass," he said softly. "I'm new in town."

They sat at the breakfast table. Dr. Hass declined coffee. "Thinking of coming to church this morning?"

"Not really," he sighed. "I should, don't get me wrong. But I'm not the kind of person who belongs in church. I just needed someone to talk to this morning."

"Everyone is welcome in our church, Doctor. Incidentally, what kind of doctor are you?"

Dr. Hass smiled a little. "The successful kind."

"I see. Well, then, what can I help you with?"

"I had this grand life out west. I was rich, respected. I lost it all. And I thought I could use a change of pace. So I moved here. You know, everyone assumes life in a small town is better, simpler. But I have to say, from what I can see, you all are as messed up as any of the rest of us."

The reverend laughed. "Oh yes. You could certainly say that."

Dr. Hass leaned forward on the table. "There are things I fear, and it's those things that I suppose corrupt my heart."

Fear! He could preach on fear! He'd never preached on fear before because he was afraid it was too heavy of a topic for a congregation that thought "Jingle Bells" had a lot of spiritual significance and should be added to the Christmas hymnal. But he suspected, in fact he knew that many people struggled with fear and that fear drove numerous actions that caused trouble in their life.

But one thing Reverend Peck knew about himself: He had to be prepared. He'd always known that he was not one for speaking on the fly. Many years ago, he had a friend who would not select a topic until the morning he was to preach. And without a single note, he could get up there and talk until he was blue in the face. Reverend Peck had always envied him and his church a little bit. There were only twenty members, but they were always very excited come Sunday morning. They'd dance in the aisle to the organ, shout out amens, and wave white hankies. Nobody had ever shouted amen in his church, and almost everyone here thought dancing was wrong, though these same people

could be found in the county dance hall from time to time. And hankies were for blowing noses.

"I know what fear can do to a person," Dr. Hass said. "And it's not pretty."

"You seem like a guy who enjoys helping people," the reverend observed.

Dr. Hass nodded humbly. "I suppose I do, though maybe I didn't know that about myself all along. But I happen to think if you face your fears, you can conquer them."

"Is that so?"

"Oh yes. I've actually tested this theory scientifically."

Reverend Peck engaged his guest's eyes. "I want you to be at my church this morning. God loves you. And He has a purpose for you."

Dr. Hass smiled. "My grandmother used to tell me that."

"No, I mean, He has a purpose for you this morning."

"Excuse me?"

"How would you like to be a guest speaker?"

Melb marveled at how quickly some problems could be solved. Of course, sometimes solving one problem created another problem, which was the case this morning. But she was trying not to think about that as she sat next to Oliver, waiting for Sunday morning's service to begin.

They'd had to arrive forty minutes early. Last week, due to odd construction in the parking lot and the fact that half the pews were missing inside the church, Oliver and Melb had had to stand near the back. They'd nearly been turned away.

This morning, everyone else seemed to have the same idea, arriving early. The house was packed, and there was already a line outside.

From across the aisle, she observed Ainsley, who sat with her father. Had she cut her hair? *Yes, she did! Goodness, nearly to the scalp! Well,* Melb thought, *I hope she donated the rest of it to the place that makes wigs for cancer patients. No need to waste beautiful hair like that.*

She wondered why Wolfe wasn't with Ainsley. Late last night, squelching the fears she had about Oliver knowing her budget fiascos, he'd shared with her that he'd fired Wolfe that day. Though still upset by the firing, by the time he'd gotten home, Oliver had cooled off a bit.

By then, Melb had found a solution to her budget problems. The kind and thoughtful Alfred Tennison, who had come over to ask if she was okay, had been looking for a big event to film, complete with a "celebrity" chef and caterer, he'd said. When Melb told him she couldn't afford anything like that, Alfred explained he would pay for it all.

"What's the catch?" she'd asked.

"No catch, except you have to be willing to have a lot of cameras and extra people around. And there may be times parts of the reception will need to be rearranged slightly for continuity control. Just things like that."

She had hesitated, but Alfred said, "You will have the most gorgeous wedding cake you could dream of. Flower arrangements you see out of magazines. Enough food to feed the whole town if they show up."

"Yes! Yes! I'll do it!" she exclaimed. How could she turn it down? It was now her only hope of having her dream wedding to match her dream dress.

There was the slight problem of explaining to Oliver why all the cameras and extra people were there, but maybe he wouldn't notice, or perhaps he would be so bedazzled he wouldn't care. She'd spent the early evening owling while going over her options in her head. She hadn't quite come up with a good idea about sharing this with Oliver, but there was still time. She was just relieved there was going to be food at the wedding!

Dr. Hass had struggled his whole life with looking down on people. His mother told him that even as a child, he would rather play by himself than have to tolerate the behavior of other children. It was this kind of attitude, he supposed, that had brought him success in life. But perhaps

it was also this attitude that had brought such bad luck onto his personal life and led to his escape from people seeking to "do him in," as they liked to say.

So the irony of all this was not lost on him as he stood behind a church pulpit to preach a sermon to a group of people who looked as though they'd just seen someone raised from the dead.

Dr. Hass had declined the reverend's first offer. After all, he was wearing far too many hats in this town as it was. But then Reverend Peck sweetened the deal. Offered an honorarium. And that's when Dr. Hass realized that inside him was a speaker just dying to come out. And after all, he was passionate about the topic he would be speaking on, though, again, the irony wasn't lost on him that he was running from things, or people, he feared.

So at fifteen after seven, arriving at the reverend's doorstep hoping for—what, he wasn't sure; perhaps spiritual grace?—he'd left with spiritual responsibility.

The crowd, even standing at the back wall because there weren't any pews left, was understandably shocked when Dr. Hass announced he would be the special guest speaker for the morning. But it didn't take him long to get warmed up. It amazed him how energizing it felt to stand in the presence of people whose ears were locked onto his every word. He stumbled through his first thoughts, trying to remember to pay equal amounts of attention to all corners of the room. But before long he was on a roll, gesturing, speaking loudly enough that his voice reverberated off the walls. He overplayed his expressions, but it seemed to add just enough emphasis to regain the lost attention of some of the church members.

He'd forgotten most of the scriptures Reverend Peck had suggested he should use, but he did find certain phrases like *antiquated nebulous truisms* and *irrelevant platitudes of sanity* helped him seem qualified, as well as sharpening the dull minds before him. And by the end of the twenty minutes, he felt as if he'd made a difference. Of course, he wasn't exactly facing his own fears and, in fact, had seemed to forget all the

resolutions he'd first made after leaving the West Coast to come to small-town America. But that was neither here nor there.

It felt good to stand in people's awe again. He'd forgotten the feeling.

Afterward he greeted the parishioners, each of them offering a hand along with a skeptical smile. He'd given no explanation to where the reverend was; the reverend had asked him not to. That was sure to make people uneasy.

An attractive blonde with hair cut just above her shoulders shook his hand and said, "Is the reverend okay?"

Dr. Hass remembered to smile in an easy manner. "He is. I'm just filling in. He'll be back next week."

"I'm worried," she said, though not necessarily to him.

Sheriff Parker, who stood beside her, said, "Dr. Hass, you'll be glad to know that Thief is getting better! Your suggestions worked."

"Good." He smiled.

The blonde said, "My fiancé and I are going to come in next week. We've been having some…some problems."

Sheriff Parker grinned. "You know these young kids," he winked.

Dr. Hass said he would be glad to see them, and then he turned to acknowledge other people waiting to shake his hand.

He could get used to this kind of friendliness. He could only imagine how it felt to always be liked.

Like an overfilled pie crust, Ainsley's heart was bursting with the many troubles she faced. She had hoped church would lift her spirits; it usually did, but today it only added to her anxieties. Dr. Hass had focused on overcoming fears…

Was that her problem? She feared too much? She wasn't facing her fears, as Dr. Hass put it? Her insides trembled at the thought of what was happening to Reverend Peck. Was he abandoning the church, the ministry?

Then her mind would drift to Wolfe, who hadn't even bothered to show up for church today. Was it to spite her? They'd left each other's presence in a huff yesterday.

Then there was the matter of her transformation. Exhilaration didn't begin to describe her feelings. For the first time, she felt she had purpose. Everything she'd worked so hard at was now paying off. There had been people in her life who'd thought her attention to detail was absurd. But they loved to come to her house and enjoy those same special touches.

And that personality trait was now convincing her she needed to take down the Nativity set. She could hardly stand to look at it without the Wise Men. And admittedly, it was far past Christmas.

She was walking to the garage to get the box that held the figures when the doorbell rang. Her father was upstairs implementing the third step to Thief's therapy, which was not to acknowledge Thief's presence.

She went to the door, hoping it was Wolfe.

"It's you," she smiled.

He smiled back and took her hands. "I hate when we fight."

"Me too." She embraced him and said, "Where were you this morning?"

"Standing in line, trying to get in. There wasn't enough room, though. And it was freezing outside, so I came back home."

"Oh, that's so sad! What is the reverend thinking? It wasn't even the reverend speaking. It was Dr. Hass." She pulled him inside. "It's too cold to stand out there."

"I just wanted to come by and see if we're okay."

"We're fine. I thought about you all last night and this morning."

"And you know what I thought of? That I should be helping you."

"Helping me?"

"Plan the wedding. There are some things I could do, you know. I don't even have a job now, so I have plenty of time. I got fired yesterday."

"You did?" she gasped.

"Yeah. I wasn't cut out for that trade, I'm afraid. What can I do to help you with the wedding?"

She squeezed his hands. "Honey, you don't need to do anything. I know I've fallen a little behind, but I'll catch up. I spent a lot of this weekend mapping out what I need to be doing. If I have a list, there's no stopping me."

"You're amazing," he said. "You have this remarkable organizational ability. I've never known anyone who can multitask better than you."

"You know just how to make a girl blush," she giggled.

They kissed, and relief flooded her body. Everything was right with the world when she was inside this man's embrace.

"So what are you up to?" he asked.

"I was just about to go to the garage and get the Nativity box. I can't stand the vacant spot where those Wise Men should be any longer."

"I can't imagine why anybody would take them and then not bring them back." He followed her into the garage, where she retrieved the box.

On their way back to the living room, she said, "I tell you, Wolfe, it makes me lose faith in humanity. It really does."

"We'll pick out a new Nativity set for you."

She set the box down and went to the fireplace, caressing one of the shepherds with her finger. "This was my mother's."

He embraced her from behind. "I'm sorry."

She smiled up at him and patted his cheek. "You are my wise man."

He laughed and helped her gather a few of the figurines off the mantel. Setting them down on the coffee table, she opened the box up, pulling out the Styrofoam where every figure had its proper place.

And gasped so loudly it sounded like a tire losing air.

"What's wrong?" Wolfe rushed to her side, then looked down. "The Wise Men! You found them!"

Ainsley had slapped her hand over her mouth. It fell to her chin as she said, "They've been in the box the whole time. I…I…I forgot to put them out."

"Well, that's okay. At least you know they're safe and sound." His face beamed with relief.

She nearly dropped Joseph and the angel. His hand slipped below hers and took them away. "Are you all right? Why aren't you happy?"

"I just…just can't believe I forgot to put them out. I never forget to do things like that."

He laughed. "Well, you've had a lot on your mind, like our wedding. Don't be hard on yourself. The main thing is that we found them."

She grinned to defuse his worry and said, "Will you grab the donkey? And the manger?"

Apparently satisfied that he'd comforted her, he returned the grin and went to the mantel. She didn't expect him to understand. He couldn't possibly know why she was upset.

But inside, her spirit was agitated with uncertainty. For as long as she could do it, she'd been in charge of putting the Nativity set out. And not one time had she forgotten any of the figurines. To Wolfe, it represented simple forgetfulness. But to her, it represented much more.

The stress of everything was taking more of a toll on her than she'd thought. What would she forget next? The room swirled around her as her mind tried to adjust itself into the multitasking machine she thought it was. Her whole talent depended on the fact that she could do more than one thing at a time. How could she forget something like putting the Wise Men out?

"You okay?" Wolfe had returned with figurines in his grasp.

She smiled. "Just going over a menu in my head for tonight."

"That's my girl."

The phone rang, a perfect excuse for her to drop her facade and turn the other way. She answered it in the kitchen.

"Hello, Ainsley, it's Alfred."

She glanced behind her. Wolfe was busy finishing the Nativity set. "Oh, hi."

"I have terrific news."

"What is it?"

"I've found a major event for you to cater. I've already hired the film crew and one of the best directors around."

Her knees grew weak. "I…I can't believe it."

"Believe it."

"What's the event?"

"Melb Cornforth's wedding."

"What?"

"Yeah, she agreed to have the film crew there and everything. It will kind of have a reality TV flavor to it, but I think it will work."

"That's only a few weeks away. Valentine's Day."

"I know! It's perfect! We can have this in the can by the first of March. Timing is everything, Ainsley. This is the perfect solution. By the way, I didn't tell Miss Cornforth it was you. I thought that would be a great surprise."

"Um…yeah…"

"So here's what I need from you. You've got to plan the entire menu for the wedding, plus design the cake, flower arrangements, and reception decorations…" Alfred kept talking, but her mind blocked out all he was saying. She squeezed her eyes shut and nearly felt dizzy. Something inside her was screaming no, but even louder than that was determination, and she knew its origin.

Memories of her mother had slowly faded over the years, but one remained, and it hovered in her mind like a beautiful butterfly in front of an orchid. With complete clarity, she could see her mother pulling out freshly baked cookies from the oven as Ainsley arrived home from a hard day at school, turning with a smile on her face, that same perfectly pleasant smile she always wore without fail. And without effort. She wondered what sacrifices her mother made in her own heart to be able to offer that kind of smile on every occasion.

"Ainsley?"

"Yes, I'm sorry. Yes. That's um…that's fine. It's the week before my own wedding, though."

Alfred paused. "Ainsley, to make it big, there are a lot of sacrifices to be made. You can ask your fiancé about that. He knows what it means to sacrifice. Now I have to know right now if you're willing to make those sacrifices. If you're not, there are plenty of other women ready to step into Martha's shoes."

A single tear rolled down her cheek, and she wiped it away. "I'm ready, Alfred. You know that."

"Okay. Good. I like your attitude. Now listen, you will have two chefs helping you, plus a cake designer, ready to do your will."

Ainsley could hardly believe it. "That's amazing."

"You'll receive a shipment of designer catalogs, probably tomorrow. Look through them. Create a budget. I have a lot of resources, but we're still going to have to watch what we spend."

"Okay."

"Ainsley, I'll be in touch. Call me if you need anything."

She hung up the phone, nearly paralyzed by the dozens of thoughts clamoring for her attention.

"Okay, I put the box in the garage," Wolfe said, clapping the dust from his hands. "What do you want me to do now?"

She opened her mouth to speak, but too many words wanted out at once.

## CHAPTER 22

MARTIN WATCHED THE MAYOR, in his fancy sunglasses and tropical shirt, walk past his office. To Martin's extreme relief, he didn't stop in. Earlier, he'd spent an hour listening to the mayor's thoughts about starting to jog every day, just to get in shape. Martin thought he was subconsciously aware how much his legs were showing.

Martin held his breath until the mayor went into his own office and shut the door. Last night, he'd found a fascinating clue to the town's history. And maybe clues to some other mysteries as well.

He'd found an old map of the town dating back to the late 1800s, buried underneath a loose board in the library. An *X* seemed to show the location of something in the foothills. Late in the night when he'd hiked up to investigate, he'd found five shacks, nearly dilapidated. He'd been aware of two of them, but according to the map, there seemed to be a precise reason for their location.

They were all laid out exactly the same, with an area for bunks, a small wood-burning stove, and heavy wooden bars to lock them from within. As Martin had stood inside one, the walls seemed alive with whispers. These shacks meant something, but he didn't know what.

Beyond their location, there were few clues left. He'd found an old and torn blanket, an empty milk jug, and a letter that was now only inky smudges. All he could make out from it was, *I have found a place…* Whatever it said, the letter did not seem to have been sent. He'd found it tucked in an unmarked envelope that had slid between two floor planks.

In the still night, cold beyond measure, Martin had stepped out of

one of the shacks, intending to go home. But he heard someone in the woods, causing a frightful stabbing in his heart. He rushed back into the dirty shack and closed the door, opening the peephole slightly to try to catch a glimpse. He'd been so excited by his discovery on the map that he'd forgotten about the ghost people wandering around.

At first there was nothing, though his pounding heart told him to stay put. And then, in the shadows, a figure moved. Martin covered his mouth, trying not to scream. As his eyes focused in the dark, he realized he was about to encounter one of these strange people who'd now invaded their town.

He started hyperventilating and stepped away from the peephole. But curiosity drove his eye back to it, and what he saw through it nearly made him faint.

Melb Cornforth, of all people! Her long shadow trailed behind her as she slowly walked through the woods, head tilted high as if she might just start howling. What in the world was she doing in the woods at this hour? When she'd finally passed out of his line of sight, Martin fell backward into a nearby post and let out a yelp. He felt as though he'd traipsed smack-dab into one of Wolfe Boone's novels.

Was Melb one of those people? Had she been captured by them and now turned to the dark side? How was he going to tell Oliver? Should he even tell Oliver? Maybe Oliver was one of them too!

Martin gasped. Maybe the mayor had succumbed to them as well. Maybe he hadn't lost his mind… Maybe he'd lost his…his…soul!

Opening the door slowly and praying he wouldn't be captured, Martin ran down the wooded hill as fast as his white legs would carry him and slept only minutes the rest of the night.

*No wonder I'm so tired,* he thought. At the front office door, just a few feet from their desks, there was a knock. The mayor, carried away with thoughts of island women, hardly noticed. Martin sighed and wondered who would knock at the front door of the mayor's office. He opened the swinging glass door, but there was nobody there. A crawling feeling of fear, reminiscent of last night, made him shiver. Looking down, he noticed a small envelope at his feet, tied up with brown string.

He looked around once more, then picked up the envelope and opened it carefully.

His hands were shaking so badly he could hardly read the small words: *Your answer lies in the pages of* Black Cats.

"What are you doing?"

Martin gasped, stumbling forward while trying to turn around. The mayor stood behind him, trying to see what he was up to.

"N-nothing." Martin stuffed the note in his pocket. "Nothing."

"Well, listen, I'm going to take an early lunch, maybe take a jog in the park. It's a beautiful day; why not soak up some sun, eh?"

Martin couldn't even begin to nod.

"You want to join me?"

Martin shook his head. "No. Um, I've got to go to the bookstore."

Wolfe stood on the sidewalk outside what used to be Sbooky's bookstore. When Wolfe announced his retirement, the *S* had been taken down, and it now just read Booky's, which had conjured up a lot of rumors in the gambling community.

In the afternoon chill, Wolfe debated his next move. He didn't need the money, but he needed a sense of self-respect and, on a practical note, something to do in the middle of the day. Oliver's job offer, at the time, had seemed reasonable. Now he understood why the job market was so tight. There were jobs out there, but some were more desirable than others. And the fact of the matter was that Oliver was very good at what he did, had a gift for it. Wolfe, on the other hand, was gifted in other areas.

As he stared through the shop window, he felt a certain exhilaration. He loved books, always had. Why not be surrounded by them every day? And he could certainly sell a book!

Without any more thought, he entered the store. A simple jingle alerted the manager, who was busy with a box of books. When he looked up, his eyes grew wide. "My golly, it's you!"

Wolfe extended his hand. "Wolfe Boone."

"Of course I know you! Your picture is all over the place here." He smiled and pointed to the various posters. "When you retired, we thought we were going to have to change focus, and we did. We're opening up a new romance section. But to tell the truth, your books still sell very well."

"Thank you."

"I'm Hardy Bishop, the manager."

*"Dude!"*

Wolfe glanced up to find Dustin, the usual "dude behind the desk." He remembered he had quite a fondness for vampire novels.

"It's *him!*" Dustin jabbed his finger toward Wolfe, gawking shamelessly. Mr. Bishop tried to maintain his pleasant candor.

"And this is Dustin," he said without enthusiasm.

"Actually, Dustin and I have met."

"Sure have," Dustin said. "Took that Polaroid of him." Dustin pointed to the taped picture hanging from the counter.

"So Mr. Boone, what can we do for you?" Mr. Bishop asked.

"Well," Wolfe said with a chuckle, "I'm looking for a job."

"No way...," Dustin said, and was curtly hushed by Mr. Bishop.

"You're looking for a real job?" Mr. Bishop asked.

"Writing is actually a real job, believe it or not, but since I'm not writing anymore, I thought I might be good at selling books other people have written."

"You'd be a dream," Mr. Bishop said, cutting his eyes to Dustin, who was using two bookmarks for drumsticks.

"I'd love to work here," Wolfe added, after Mr. Bishop was silent for a moment.

Mr. Bishop's eagerness turned solemn. "Mr. Boone, I'll be honest with you. I simply do not sell enough books to justify having two employees."

Wolfe's heart sank. "Oh. Sure. I understand."

Mr. Bishop paused at a private thought, glanced up at Wolfe, turned to Dustin and said, "Hey, Dustin, can you go clean the toilets?"

"Ah, man...," Dustin moaned.

*"That's it! You're fired!"*

Dustin's mouth fell open. "I'm fired?"

"I've had all the backtalk I can stand from you, Son. 'Dude' this. 'Man' that. You're lazy and unreliable, and I keep thinking one of these days you might get a clue and step it up a notch, but you never have."

"But...but...," Dustin's cool evaporated like his sense of vocabulary.

"Wait a minute," Wolfe said. "Mr. Bishop, you don't need to fire Dustin."

"But you'd be a much better employee."

"True," Wolfe smiled, "but you can hire us both. Tell you what. I'll work for free. You don't have to pay me until I increase your business enough that you can afford me."

Mr. Bishop slapped the counter with a stout laugh.

"Is it a deal? Can Dustin keep his job?"

Mr. Bishop looked Dustin up and down and sighed. "I guess."

"Thank you!" Dustin hollered. "I won't let you down!"

"You're welcome," Mr. Bishop said. "Now go clean some toilets, will you?"

"Ah man...," Dustin sighed and shuffled to the back room.

"When can I start?" Wolfe asked.

Mr. Bishop stared into the air. "Hmm. You can start tomorrow if you're willing to tackle my newest problem."

"I'm willing to do whatever you need, Mr. Bishop."

"Terrific," he sighed. "Because to tell you the truth, I was not looking forward to it."

"Well, anything has got to beat selling used cars," Wolfe said.

"Okay. I need you to read all the new romance novels coming in and pick out the top twenty."

Martin was so deep in thought that he nearly passed the bookstore. Backtracking a couple of steps, he turned and walked in. To his right, an entire shelf lined with Wolfe Boone books immediately caught his

attention. He stood in front of a selection of what looked to be hundreds of books, *Black Cats* dominating most of the space. The store carried hardcover, softcover, and audiobooks, just for starters. Martin was scratching his head trying to decide what he should do when the manager approached.

"Hi there. Looking for a new Wolfe Boone book, I presume?"

"I know I want *Black Cats,*" Martin said. He studied the bookshelf. "Looks like a mighty thick book."

"Four hundred and ninety pages," the manager replied. "Each page more tantalizing than the last."

Martin sighed. If he'd been talking about an appetizer, he might've sold him. "You don't know if there happens to be CliffsNotes to this book, do you?"

The manager chuckled a bit and said, "Not that I know of. But I know how you can get a quick summary."

"Really?"

"Hey Wolfe, over here."

Martin looked over the shelf to see Wolfe's head moving toward him. A warm blush began at his neck.

"Martin," Wolfe said, shaking his hand. "How are you?"

"Um…fine. I didn't know you were in here."

"Starts work tomorrow," the manager said.

"Oliver fired me," Wolfe said sheepishly.

"Oh. Sorry to hear that."

"He asked me if there were CliffsNotes to *Black Cats,* and I told him I thought you could give him a pretty good summary."

Martin was horrified, and he knew his coloring showed it. "Listen, it's not how it sounds. I'm a big fan, Wolfe. Really. I just, well, it's just that…"

"No need to explain," Wolfe smiled. "It's okay."

Martin glanced at the manager and said, "Can I have a second with Wolfe?"

When they were alone, he leaned in toward Wolfe. "This is quite embarrassing. It's just that I need information, and quickly."

"Information about what?"

"Black cats," he said, then wished he'd had a better answer. Should he tell Wolfe? Could he trust him? These days, everything—everyone—seemed so bizarre.

"You know my book is fiction," Wolfe said.

Martin nodded. Now he looked like a fool. What was he going to do? "Listen," Martin finally said, "let me buy you lunch. I'd just like a summary of your book, a little more detailed than what's on the back cover."

Wolfe hesitated, and Martin could see perplexity strain his warm smile. But then he agreed.

After they'd ordered their food at The Mansion, Martin said, "I know this sounds strange."

Wolfe nodded. He couldn't imagine what Martin was up to. The man seemed to be reading his mind.

"There are just some strange things happening in this town," Martin said. "I know I'm not the only one noticing the weird people walking around, coming in and out of the woods like ghosts."

"I've seen a couple," Wolfe said. And indeed they were strange. Enough to spark a book idea, if he wrote such books anymore.

Martin nodded. "I've seen more than a couple, and"—Martin said, lowering his voice, his eyes shining with mystery—"some of ours..."

"Really."

"I don't want to talk about too much of what I know," Martin added as Wolfe started to ask a question, "but something is going on with this town, and I'm going to get to the bottom of it."

"So what does my book have to do with it?"

"I'm not sure, except you wrote this book about black cats, and we have a lot of black cats, and maybe you answered some questions about our town without knowing it."

Wolfe had to laugh. "You're suggesting a prophecy of some sort?"

"Well, nothing that dramatic, but I'm just curious about the story. Maybe it holds the key."

*The key.* Missy Peeple's strange allusion whispered in his ear. "I'll help you in whatever way I can."

"Tell me what it's about."

"Basically, people in a town full of black cats begin experiencing bad luck. The residents decide they need to get rid of the cats, thinking them responsible for the curse. But it seems the harder they try to rid the town of the cats, the more bad things start to happen."

"That hit the bestseller list, did it?" Martin said with amusement.

Wolfe laughed. "Somehow, yes."

"Okay, well, what types of things started happening to the town?"

"Different things, in and of themselves not strange. But when they all started happening at once, people believed something was going on. For instance, the well went dry. And there were grass fires. The church burned down. People from other towns heard rumors about the corn they sold and stopped buying it. Different things like that."

"How did they figure out it was the cats?"

"They didn't. But out of desperation they decided the cats were cursed and they needed to leave."

"Were the cats cursed?"

Wolfe grinned. "Maybe they were, maybe they weren't, but the people's paranoia caused even greater things to happen. The very thing they feared came upon them."

"Well that sounds creepy," Martin grimaced.

"You should read the book," Wolfe winked.

Martin's eyes widened. "The black cats don't start possessing the spirits of the townspeople, do they?"

"No—that'd be silly."

"Right."

"Martin, does this have anything to do with your search for the town's history?"

Martin leaned forward. "I can't say much. But yes. I believe there

are many things missing about this town, and I want to know why they're missing and what they are."

"The makings of a good mystery."

"It's more than that," Martin said. "It could even be scandalous."

Wolfe laughed. "Even better."

Martin smiled, but then it faded into shadows of thought. His blank stare was replaced by a gaze directed at Wolfe. "Unexplainable things are happening around here. But I happen to believe all things have an explanation, if you dig deep enough."

Wolfe said, "Then let's find this town a happy ending."

Martin's tired features revived. "What do you mean?"

"I mean that I think you're onto something. The problem is, there is a lot of mystery surrounding so much of this town…and many of its people."

Martin nodded. "But something about what you wrote will give us the answers."

"Why do you believe that?"

He paused. "I got a note. Don't spread this around, okay? But this morning a note was left at the office telling me that my answer lies in the pages of *Black Cats*."

Wolfe leaned back in his chair and rubbed the back of his neck. Deciphering an encrypted message in his own book was going to be somewhat daunting. He sighed, and his gaze found its way toward the front windows of the restaurant.

There, standing in one of the windows, was Missy Peeple, her beady eyes staring back at him. Martin seemed oblivious to everything but his hamburger. An eerie chill raced down Wolfe's back, and with one blink, she was gone.

Martin looked up and stopped chewing. "Are you okay?"

Wolfe nodded and picked up his tea. If he didn't know better, he would think Missy Peeple was a character that might have leapt straight out of the dark corners of his imagination.

## CHAPTER 23

"Dr. Hass!"

The shrill sound of his name being screamed nearly caused him to fall out of his chair. All morning he'd been working on a plan to open the practice he'd meant to start in Skary. And his next appointment wasn't scheduled for another fifteen minutes. The only noise he'd heard was that cat trying to convince him to let her in.

*"Dr. Hass!"* The scream came again, this time closer. He jumped up from his chair, running outside of his office. The next thing he knew, his head was pounding and now somebody was screaming, *"What are you trying to do, kill me?!"*

When he regained his focus, shaking off the pain and rubbing his forehead, Dr. Hass saw Melb Cornforth standing there, one hand rubbing her own forehead, the other on her hip.

"I…I thought you were… I…"

"Thought I was what?" Melb asked.

Dr. Hass sighed. "Another patient. What in the world are you doing screaming like that?"

Melb's face clouded with huffiness. "Well, I did have good news until you almost killed me."

Dr. Hass walked back into his office, plopping into his chair. "Isn't it still good news, since you're not dead?" That was the best he could offer, because what he really wanted to do was tell this crazy woman to keep her money and find sanity somewhere else.

Melb thought about that for a second. "I suppose so." Her jovial grin returned. "Guess what?"

Dr. Hass could only throw his hands in the air and shake his head. He couldn't imagine what would justify running down the sidewalk screaming like that.

"I lost twelve pounds!" She emphasized this point by hooking her thumb under her waistband and pulling it out an inch.

"Really?" Dr. Hass could not conceal his surprise. "So the diet has been working!"

"Well, not really. That's the weird thing. I've been eating everything in sight." Melb placed her hands on Dr. Hass's desk and leaned toward him, then used a finger to tap her cheekbone. "It's psychological, I think."

"Psychological?"

"You said it yourself. It's in my head. So," Melb said, "maybe I don't have to eat less, I just have to see myself skinnier. The brain has a lot of power we don't recognize, you know." Melb stood upright and noticed her figure in the reflection of the nearby window.

"How's the hobby?"

"Fun, though I'm not sure it's really helping me with the weight loss. But I tell you, I'm going to bond with this owl if it's the last thing I do."

Scratching his head, Dr. Hass wondered how in the world Melb could be losing weight while eating more. Was it possible to psych yourself into losing weight? He scribbled notes on the pad in front of him.

"Melb, that is good news indeed."

"So I'll see you on Thursday?"

"You're losing weight. What do you need me for?"

"It's got to be the combination of talking about my feelings while imagining myself losing weight. Don't you think?"

"Um…sure…"

"So see you on Thursday."

"Melb?" he asked, as she started to leave his office, "did you ever tell Oliver about your budget problems?"

"No," she smiled, "but it all worked out." Winking, she added, "It always works out in the end, Dr. Hass. Oh! I probably just lost two more pounds with that positive thought!"

And out the door she went. Dr Hass watched her confidence build with each bounding step.

He had barely processed Melb's magical transformation when his next clients arrived. Admittedly, he was intrigued. The sheriff's daughter, Ainsley, and world-famous novelist Wolfe Boone, who was called Boo around these parts, walked in, tentatively peeking around the door.

He beckoned them in with a wave. Standing, he greeted each of them with a handshake, trying to assess the situation.

As far as he could tell, this was Ainsley's idea. Her expectant manner showed enthusiastic hope for something troublesome in her life. Wolfe, on the other hand, displayed no enthusiasm in his handshake, his facial expression, or his words. "Nice to meet you, Dr. Hass."

Offering them the two chairs in front of his desk, he said, "Mr. Boone, it's a pleasure to meet you in person. I'm a big fan."

"Wolfe, please. And thank you."

"I've read a couple of your books. Delightful." It was a standard line. He'd used it in many social circles. *I've seen a couple of your movies. Delightful. I've been to two of your homes. Delightful. I've dated both your daughters. Delightful.*

But in this instance, in a small town where small talk was a way of life, he instantly realized this was a huge mistake.

"Oh? Which two?" Wolfe asked.

Surely his large gulp gave him away, but he tried, nevertheless, to recover. "Oh, you know, let's see here... I'm terrible with titles...but it's the one where the guy's in the house, and there's that scary ghosty-thing, and everyone is scared to death but nobody knows what it is."

"Sounds like the plot to all his novels," Ainsley said, laughing. Wolfe, however, shot her a look that indicated he didn't find the humor in it. Her laughter faded, and luckily for Dr. Hass, so did the present conversation.

"So," he said quickly, "what brings you two by?"

Ainsley cleared her throat and said, "Well, we're supposed to be married in less than a month, and there are some issues we're trying to work through. Maybe that's putting it lightly."

Dr. Hass noticed Wolfe was giving his attention to the wall where Napoleon hung. "Napoleon," he mumbled, glancing at Dr. Hass. "Interesting choice of art."

The doctor smiled up at his inspiration. "Well, sometimes there's more to a person than meets the eye."

"True," Wolfe said. "Did you know that Napoleon was ailurophobic?"

"What's that mean?" Ainsley asked.

"He feared cats," Dr. Hass answered. "But let's get to the fears you two are obviously facing in light of your upcoming wedding."

Wolfe sighed, finally turning his attention from the framed poster. He looked at Ainsley, suggesting that he'd rather she explain it all.

"All right," she sighed. "It's like this. We are happily in love, can't wait to get married, but things have dramatically changed in our lives, and we're both having trouble dealing with that."

"What has changed?"

"Well, Wolfe has decided to stop writing, so he's trying to find a new niche in life. It's not going so well. He got fired from selling cars."

"I see. Suppressed homogeneity neurosis."

"And I'm trying to pursue a new career in the entertainment-home-making business, and it's taking up a lot of my time. Wolfe's having a hard time with this."

Wolfe shook his head. "Let's be clear. I completely support Ainsley in whatever she does. However, we're supposed to be planning our wedding, and she's been so busy with all this other stuff that it's been pushed aside."

"It hasn't been pushed aside! He's afraid we're not going to have a wedding! I'm capable...*perfectly capable*...of juggling more than one thing, Wolfe."

"Then why hasn't anything been done that is supposed to be?"

"It's just been shifted around, that's all."

Dr. Hass held up his hands. "Okay, listen, let's start over here. I think the best thing both of you can do is simply be honest with each other about how you are feeling. I hear that's what makes a marriage strong. Wolfe, why don't you begin? Be honest with Ainsley."

He felt for the guy. The last thing under the sun any man wants to do is attend therapy with a woman. The way Wolfe's fingers scratched over the skin of his neck, Dr. Hass felt his own skin crawl with an itch. But he had to give it to the guy…it was more than he would've done to save a marriage.

Then again, Dr. Hass had reinvented himself. After all, he'd just preached at a church service!

He tuned back in to Wolfe, who was in the middle of describing his fears that Ainsley's whole focus had shifted from him to success.

Dr. Hass nodded, smiled assuredly at Wolfe and said, "Good job, Wolfe. I know sometimes it's difficult to be that honest." Wolfe looked like he wanted to beat something up. A rose-colored flush of anger tinted his tan complexion.

"Ainsley, it's your turn."

Wolfe and Dr. Hass both watched her trying desperately to release a hangnail from her finger. With no luck, she smiled sadly and glanced up at them both.

"Go ahead," Dr. Hass encouraged, after she still had not spoken.

"Well," she began, but couldn't seem to go on.

"It's all right. Just be honest."

Through teary eyes she looked at him, then at Wolfe. Then she said, "Okay. Here it goes. I've taken on the job of planning Melb's entire wedding reception for a video that Alfred wants me to make to show to several TV executives who think I might be good enough to be Martha's replacement."

"What?" Wolfe's brows furrowed.

"Who's Martha?" Dr. Hass asked.

"Stewart," she answered, though her eyes remained on Wolfe, who had now risen from his chair and walked to the other side of the room.

"I'm sorry, I'm not following," Dr. Hass said.

"It's a big opportunity for me," she said. "Wolfe's former editor thinks that I could be the next Martha Stewart, so he's been putting together a plan to put me in front of some television executives who

might be interested in giving me my own show." She stared at Wolfe's back, then looked at Dr. Hass. "It's a really big deal for me. A lot is at stake. But Wolfe doesn't support it."

Wolfe turned. "How could you not tell me this?"

"Because I knew you'd be mad! And here you are, mad!"

"How can you handle somebody else's wedding when you can't even manage to handle ours!"

Ainsley stood with a gasp. "How dare you! This is all because of the Wise Men!"

Dr. Hass was thoroughly confused as these two ranted back and forth at each other. For starters, what wise men was she talking about? And why would anybody want to be the next Martha Stewart? Many questions swelled to the surface of Dr. Hass's mind, but he knew there was definitely one thing he was going to have to clear up.

He stood, waving his arms to get their attention. Finally, their words dropped off one by one until they stopped talking and looked at him.

"I'm sorry. I need to know, are you talking about Melb Cornforth?"

Wolfe stomped out of the office. Ainsley nodded tearfully at Dr. Hass, then grabbed her coat and purse and followed him, calling his name.

Thankfully all the tension had just marched out the door and Dr. Hass could think clearly. One thing he immediately realized—a lot more counted on Melb fitting into her dress than he'd realized.

"Wolfe! Wolfe! Wait!" Ainsley stumbled down the porch stairs of Dr. Hass's office, calling after the one man she'd ever loved. Tears nearly froze to her cheeks as she ran after him. He walked swiftly, several yards ahead of her, and looked like he did not intend to stop. Her breath crystallized, and she ran as fast as she could. She finally reached him, circling in front of him to stop his stride. "Please," she begged.

On the brims of his eyes, tears threatened to escape. He couldn't even look at her. His hands were deep inside his trench coat, and his scarf clung to the front of his chest like a wall in front of his heart.

Finally, he looked at her as she grasped his arm with both hands. He said, "It's not what you think it is. Fame is nothing you want, Ainsley, I assure you."

Sniffling back threatening emotions, she replied, "It's not the fame I'm after, Wolfe. Surely you know me well enough to know how little I care about that sort of thing."

"I thought I did."

"Then believe me. It's not fame I'm after. And I realize it's hard for you to understand what it feels like to grow up in a small town with hardly any hope of ever following your dreams. I've watched Martha Stewart do everything I've always wanted to do. And I became really good at what I do too. Why is it so bad to want success in that?"

Wolfe stared into the winter sky. "It's not bad. But at what cost do you want this success?"

"Why does it have to cost anything? I've already sacrificed for years. People never understood me, never understood why I cared so much what length the flower stems were in a vase. Why I cared so much about using real butter. Why I cared so much about growing my own herbs. Maybe people thought I was trying to be like my mom. Maybe I was. But for me, I thought, maybe, just maybe, someday I might go beyond this small town."

Wolfe finally took her hands in his, warming them between his gloves. "I don't want to lose you. I fought too hard to get you." His determined, quiet smile carried her anxieties away like a strong wind.

"You won't lose me," she said. "I promise that."

"I hope you know I want the very best for you. I want you to be successful. But I also want you to understand what this kind of success would mean. Your life will never be the same."

"If you're in my life, my life will be just fine." The tears that came blurred Wolfe as if he stood in a misty rain. She wiped them away.

"Ainsley, I just hope…"

"Hope what?"

He fingered the ends of his scarf. "I'm just an ordinary guy. You know that, right?"

"Wolfe…you're perfect."

But this didn't seem to bring any comfort to the deep concern that swallowed the light in his eyes.

## CHAPTER 24

AINSLEY HAD TRIED to spend the morning picking out flowers for her wedding, but the florist was on vacation, and her granddaughter, who didn't seem to know a rose from a tulip, was filling in.

Even though their fight had been a couple of days ago, Wolfe's angry words rang in her ears. Was she taking on too much? Was this the life for her? It was hard to imagine turning it down. After all, how many times had she found herself in her own kitchen, imagining she was baking a pie in front of millions? Yet how could that compare to being loved by the man of her dreams? Her emotions swayed like the top of a wind-whipped tree. Couldn't both be her destiny? Why did she have to choose?

The granddaughter, aptly named Daisy, was trying to suggest pairing purple carnations with orange lilies. Ainsley was quite sure she didn't want her bouquet to look like a football jersey. She walked around the florist shop for a while, trying to imagine what she might carry down the aisle on her wedding day. But in the back of her mind, she knew she also was going to need a beautiful centerpiece arrangement for Melb's reception table, plus smaller arrangements for each of the dinner tables.

"Anything you like?" Daisy asked from the counter.

Ainsley shook her head and said she'd be back later. Besides, what she really needed to do was start planning the menu. Thankfully, hers was going to be catered, so she didn't have to worry about that. She drove home and noticed Alfred's car outside.

"Hello?" she said, entering the house.

"In here, honey," her father said.

The two were sitting in front of the TV. Alfred hopped up from the couch like he'd just been rescued from watching home movies. "Hi there," he said, taking her hand into a gentle handshake.

"Hi Alfred. What's going on?"

"Oh, I just dropped by to see if you were home. Your dad thought you might be home soon. We were watching…um…sports." Alfred's candid smile made Ainsley laugh.

"What's going on?" she asked again.

"Well, I thought if you weren't doing anything, we could work on speaking to the camera. I know you don't have any experience doing this, and it does take some practice."

Ainsley's eyelids fell closed at the thought of doing one more thing today.

"Alfred," she began. The words she knew she should speak became tangled with the words she knew she wanted to speak, and what fell out of her mouth was a mess of mumbling.

Alfred leaned toward her, trying to understand. "I'm sorry, Ainsley. I didn't catch that."

She sighed. "Nothing. Sure, we can do that. How's an hour sound?"

A grin stretched across his face. "Plenty of time to teach you to engage the world through one small lens."

She hoped it was easier than picking out the perfect flower arrangement.

Reverend Peck felt like he had made a terrible mistake. The peace he held in his heart dripped away with every thought he had concerning Sunday. How could he have turned over his entire church service to a total stranger? He'd lost his mind! Regret seeped through the wall of ambition he'd built so high, and now he realized what a grave mistake he'd made. Sure, his numbers had increased. But when were people going to grow bored with expensive coffee, scarce parking, and missing

pews? Every week he would have to reinvent himself and that was no easy task.

Finally a break in the weather had brought in mild temperatures, so the reverend left the house with only a light jacket and a scarf his wife had knitted for him years ago. The chill of the day returned when the wind picked up. The reverend's eyes teared up a bit, whether from cold or concern he didn't know.

The dust of the sidewalks seemed to part as he walked, the breeze gently blowing it from side to side. His hands burrowed deep into his jacket pockets. In his heart, despair dug itself equally deep. Perhaps it was time to stop ministering to this town. There seemed to be nothing he could offer, no way of helping them out of mediocre spirituality. Of the few who even came, most wanted to come on Sundays and then be done with it for the rest of the week. There were exceptions to that rule, but exceptions certainly weren't enough to build a church on.

Reverend Peck looked up just in time to see a familiar face. It was Dr. Hass, heading up the porch steps of a large house.

"Dr. Hass!" he called.

The man turned, saw the reverend, and waved his greeting. "Hello!"

The reverend approached and looked at the house. "This is where you live?"

"And work. My office is in here." Dr. Hass shook the hand the reverend offered. "Sir, you look troubled."

"Do I?" The reverend sighed and nodded. "I suppose I am."

"Sit here with me on the porch," the doctor said. "It's a nice enough day to enjoy outside, don't you think? Especially with some hot tea and good company." Dr. Hass smiled warmly at the reverend, offered him a seat in one of the two rockers on the porch, then went inside for the tea.

Reverend Peck gazed out at the town. From the porch view, he could see the tops of the buildings on Main Street, the steeple on his church, the top of Wolfe's house, and the trees at the park. Not a bad view. Nobody had ever thought too much of prime real estate in this town. If you weren't four blocks from the store, you were eight. Of course, he'd

lived in the old parsonage since his ministry began, though he'd always imagined a horse ranch with twenty acres might fit him nicely.

"Here you are." Dr. Hass offered him cream and sugar for his tea, then fixed himself a cup. He sat down.

"Thank you." A single sip warmed his chilled body.

"I wanted to tell you," Dr. Hass said, "that I really enjoyed preaching for you Sunday. I don't often get a chance to stand up in front of people and speak. It was quite exhilarating, if I do say so myself! I suppose you're used to it."

"Well, thank you for filling in on such short notice. I don't suppose that's what you had in mind when you came to my house that morning."

Dr. Hass chuckled. "Well, it did revive me."

The reverend sipped his tea and said, "The truth of the matter is that I don't have any business counseling anybody's spirit. I'm a dried-up old has-been."

"What?"

"It's true. I seem to have nothing more to say. Or maybe nobody wants to listen anymore." A heavy sigh filled the pause. "My whole life I thought I was supposed to be a pastor. It never occurred to me to be something else. But I have to admit that either I've lost the anointing or there's no hope for this town."

"An identity crisis."

The reverend glanced at Dr. Hass. "I guess so. Who's having the identity crisis might be up for debate."

"It might be time to reexamine your cheese."

"Excuse me?"

"I read this book called *Who Moved My Cheese?* It's all about dealing with change in our lives. There are some who work their whole lives resisting it. There are others who take unexpected change and use it for their advantage."

The reverend held the teacup close to his face, allowing the steam to warm his skin. "Whatever could I do except preach about God's love? I don't have any other skill."

"That's what everyone says...in the beginning. But in the end, we're

all able to find things we're good at. Adapt. Become chameleons to our environment. I, in fact, have had my cheese moved all the way from California to a small town called Skary, Indiana."

"What in the world brought you to Skary if it wasn't our famous resident, Wolfe Boone, who is becoming less and less famous now that he has retired?"

Dr. Hass refilled his teacup. "I like cats."

"Hmmm. Well, we've got plenty."

"Cats are great companions, and they have actually been proven to release stress in humans who take care of them."

"Maybe I should get a cat," the reverend said. "But then I'd end up having to adopt its eight hundred siblings." The reverend chuckled. "Used to be legendary, a real mystery that added to the allure of a town called Skary. But ended up being the sheriff's promiscuous cat, Thief. The problem is fixed now."

For a moment, they were silent. The reverend studied his transparent face in the puddle of tea at the bottom of his cup.

"I've heard we can change who we are," the doctor said. "For the better, I mean." He patted the reverend's shoulder. "And you, sir, seem to bring out that side of me. You're a good man. I can see that. I want to be a good man too." He shook his head. "It's hard to be a good man after years of being, well, not-so-good."

The reverend set his cup down and looked at Dr. Hass. "You need a clean slate."

"Skary, Indiana." Dr. Hass smiled.

"Yes, but you've followed yourself here. I'm talking about a clean spiritual slate. You came to my house the other day. What for?"

Staring at the wood beneath his feet, he said, "I suppose I have noticed the old me is hard to shake. He's like a shadow. And the brighter the light gets, the bigger he seems to grow."

The reverend nodded. "The light does seem to expose things the darkness likes to hide. Eventually, though, he won't be able to hide anymore."

Dr. Hass's fingers began fidgeting with every part of his teacup. The

reverend patted him on the arm. The man looked like he was not used to being touched, but he accepted the gesture with a small smile. "There is one who can walk inside of you, who can fill you with good that you cannot find within yourself. A Houseguest, I suppose you could call Him, who can put things in order."

Dr. Hass bit his lip. "My house is old, Reverend. Full of dust. And rotting wood is stealing its sturdiness."

The reverend said, "I'm not talking about this house."

"Neither am I." Dr. Hass stood. "The house that cages me is not fit for a King."

The reverend squeezed the man's arm. "But He became a lowly servant."

The reverend continued, "Doctor, come Sunday. Come to church." He grinned. "And you won't even have to preach the sermon!"

Dr. Hass's eyes lingered on the reverend's. Then he went inside.

Missy Peeple imagined it was sometime in the afternoon. She'd never kept a clock in her bedroom, as she always woke up at precisely the same time every morning. But now it was late afternoon. Soft light shone across the room, and she watched the hazy, dusty air swim through the beams of light, weightless and carefree.

Her long gray hair lay across her shoulder, exactly the way it had all night. She slept on her back, always had, right in the center of her bed. There were times at night, as she drifted off to sleep, when she imagined the mayor as her bed companion, though she wondered how he would fit on the slice of bed to her left. Or how he would take to the rock-hard mattress she insisted upon.

Lazily, her eyes opened and closed, and she wondered how she would eat today. Her strength these days seemed to flee like the night moon as the sun tipped itself over the horizon. And all day today, she'd floated between sleep and wakefulness, with hardly even the energy to stare at the ceiling.

Her mind was alive, as it always had been. And though her body would not obey a single command, her thoughts ordered themselves to come to attention. Yet what good were they, captive inside her head?

She could call out, but nobody would hear her. Scarcely a soul ever came to her home. Was this her moment to die? Alone? Starving to death over several days?

She gasped at the thought, her eyes popping open as if shaking off death's impending approach. She had hardly thought of dying all her life. And even old age had not hinted at taking her life.

The gasp she had taken in flowed out in the form of tears, trickling down her temples and dropping onto her pillow. "Not like this," she mumbled. "I can't die like this."

Clutching the edge of her sheet and blanket, she pulled them toward her chest with all the effort she had in her. The soft cotton tickled her chin, and it reminded her of what she might've felt like wrapped up in the soft blankets her mother had held her in.

She hadn't thought of her mother in years. Closing her eyes, she imagined herself a swaddled baby, tight in her mother's arm. Yes, she was close to completing the circle of life. Death had cracked the door open, wondering if she would come quickly or kick and scream on the way out.

Miss Missy Peeple whispered to the silent walls, "I don't want to die like this. Give me a chance, and I will make things right."

The rest of her words garbled themselves into dreams only a deep sleep can spawn.

Wolfe sat in the back room of the bookstore, a box of books next to his chair. Thumbing through the pages of *Petals of Destiny*, he was not sure his life could sink any further. He'd been fired from selling cars, which was fine with him, but now found himself in charge of reading and selecting romance novels for the bookstore. He'd moved a notch lower on the totem pole of dream job descriptions.

Yet he saw how passionate Oliver was about selling cars. He wondered if the passion came out of desperation to love an unlovable job, or if Oliver truly *loved* selling cars. He certainly was good at it. He'd stayed in business for years.

Should he try to find a passion for whatever he was doing and love it? Or find what he loved and the passion would follow? Glancing at the top of the page, his heart sank. He was only on page thirty-four and had been reading for two hours! Reading his own thoughts...

Trying to refocus, he began reading *Petals of Destiny* again:

Stella watched him walk along the edge of the water, his thin white shirt ruffling against his hard body. His golden hair, swept side-ways by the cool breeze, glimmered as brightly as his tanned and sweaty skin.

When he saw her, he smiled, the one that spoke a thousand different words to her heart. She wanted to run to him, throw her arms around his neck, kiss him until waves washed away the sorrow she felt in her heart.

Yet, how could she love a man such as this? And with Christoff's voice still beckoning her home?

Several times he found himself laughing out loud. Did women really read this stuff? But it wasn't long before the laughter faded, and Wolfe found himself staring at his own reflection in the small window across the room. His fingers thumbed the one-pack that was supposedly called his abs. He flipped the book over and looked at the stunning machine of a man on the front cover, tanned, sculpted, with perfectly aligned ears. Wolfe touched his left ear, sharply aware of the half-inch lower it was than his right. He stared at his face, fingering the pages of the book, wondering if he should start working out.

"Wolfe?"

Wolfe turned in his chair. Mr. Bishop stood at the doorway. "Can you come out and help on the floor? We've got a few customers, and I need to send Dustin on an errand."

Wolfe hopped up and walked swiftly to the door, happy to be able to close the book. He laughed. With a few slight changes, these books could easily become horror novels. They were plenty scary as it was. Surely women didn't really buy in to that junk?

Out on the floor, Wolfe was happy to help a few customers while Mr. Bishop handled the register. Maybe if he stuck with it long enough, he'd be relieved of his romance novel duties.

"Wolfe?"

Wolfe turned at the voice. "Hi Martin."

"Listen," Martin said, his tone quietly serious, "I have to know how your novel ends. I didn't ask before. But I need to know. I know it sounds crazy, but maybe there's something in there that could save the town."

Wolfe led Martin to a vacant aisle. "Martin, I know my book. I know everything I wrote in there. I made up a story. It couldn't possibly be relevant to what this town is going through."

Martin nodded. "I know, I know. But I'm desperate, Wolfe. I won't lie to you. Mayor Wullisworth loses touch with reality more and more every day. And I'm losing this town. In the not-so-distant future, we might be a ghost town." Martin's eyes shone with urgency.

Wolfe sighed, looking around to make sure there were no customers in need of help. "Okay, fine. But I'm telling you, there's no secret mystery locked in the pages of my book. I know what I wrote, and it's just a story. That's all. Nothing more, nothing less."

"So how's it end?"

"As I told you before, the town realized how strangely the cats were acting and believed them to be cursed. Finally, after a lot of effort, the cats vanish, nearly overnight. And the town seems to be heading toward recovery. But then, tragedy strikes."

"What happens? Do the cats come back in bigger forces to kill the humans?" Martin's eyes widened with each word.

Wolfe smiled. "No. In fact, most everyone in the town dies in an earthquake."

Martin's hands found his hips. "What? What kind of ending is that?"

"The cats weren't acting strangely because they were cursed. It was

because they were trying to warn the people an earthquake was coming. It is documented that many animals, including cats, have the ability to sense weather changes and impending seismic catastrophes. The town lay on a fault line, and it was well known throughout the town that it had a chance of succumbing to that sort of disaster. In fact, that is why the forefathers of the town kept a lot of cats around. They knew the cats would forewarn them of disaster by their behavior. But through the years, the people had forgotten this. They'd focused primarily on their future and forgotten their roots. If they'd remembered what their forefathers had done for the town, they might have known why the cats were acting in such a strange way and then escaped in time."

Martin rubbed his chin. "So…the cats were trying to warn them. That's why they were acting strange." Martin's eyes darted to the window.

"Martin," Wolfe said calmly, "our cats aren't acting strangely. They're just being cats. Remember, this is just a story."

"But the note said the answer to this town's problems is in your book." Martin's fingers fidgeted with the buttons on his shirt. "Maybe the black cats will start acting strangely."

"Martin, Indiana isn't exactly known for its earthquakes."

"You know as well as I do that an earthquake can strike anywhere."

Wolfe scratched his forehead, trying to figure out how to convince Martin his book did not hold the secret to this town's future. "Martin, look, the only thing my *fictitious* town and Skary, Indiana, have in common is their search, or lack thereof, for their history. My town didn't care about its roots. Skary is searching for hers. That is the only correlation between the two books I can see."

"Other than the plethora of black cats."

"Yeah, but I got my idea for the book from our problem. Don't you see? It's just a story. That's all. A horror novel. Nothing more, nothing less."

Martin did not seem convinced. He was staring at a large poster of the book hanging from the ceiling.

Wolfe decided to tell Martin something he'd convinced himself was not necessary before. "I know who sent you the note."

Martin's head snapped around toward Wolfe. "You do?"

"Yes. I wasn't going to tell you before, because mingling with this person can only cause one trouble. I learned the hard way."

"Who sent it?"

"Miss Peeple."

"How do you know?"

"Because she visited me on Christmas, handed me a copy of *Black Cats,* and told me the key to the town's future was in my book."

"Why didn't you tell me this before?" Martin demanded.

"Because it's absurd. I know my book, and I know it has no such mystical solutions to a town's problems. It's just a story!"

Martin scowled, but upon further thought, his expression softened and he looked at Wolfe. "Maybe I should go see Miss Peeple anyway. Find out what her agenda is."

"I'm sure she has one. It's usually to cause trouble."

Martin buttoned up his coat and shook Wolfe's hand. "Thanks for the information."

"Be careful," Wolfe said, escorting Martin to the front door of the store.

"Of the cats?"

"No, Martin. Of Miss Peeple."

"Oh."

"And Martin?"

"Yes?"

"The townspeople caused their own troubles through paranoia. Their fears drove them to be blinded to reality and to create things that did not exist. In the story, I mean."

Martin pulled his gloves on, swept his scarf around his neck and continued out the door. Headed in the direction of Miss Peeple's house.

## CHAPTER 25

MARTIN KNOCKED several times, each time more furiously than the last. Eventually, he was pounding, which caused a neighbor to step outside and take a peek. Martin offered a friendly wave, and the neighbor smiled and pretended to need something on the porch.

"Miss Peeple?" Martin called. He peered through the window and didn't see any movement. Maybe he should break in, see what he could find before she returned. Of course, that would be illegal…if he was caught.

Martin squeezed his eyes shut to the tempting thought. *It's illegal even if you don't get caught,* he reminded himself. Still, something urged him and his heart raced at the thought. He'd never done anything illegal in his whole life!

He looked around. The inactive street behind him seemed to nod in approval. "What am I doing?" he breathed, but went ahead and rattled the doorknob. To his surprise, it twisted, popping the door open. "Oh!" he cried, then quickly shut it. Sweat trickled down his temples.

He turned his back against the door, his fingertips nearly clawing its wood. His head whipped back and forth as he scanned the streets for any sign of a potential witness. Only a cat here and there.

Martin could hardly breathe. With one hand he clutched his chest. With the other he wiped his sweat. This was it! He could go in, find some clue about why Missy was sending him secret notes, and be out of there without a trace.

He checked his watch. He would give himself five minutes. If he found nothing, he would leave.

Reaching behind him, he opened the door and slid backward into the house, shutting the door quietly. He glanced out the window once before hurrying through the house. What he was looking for, he did not know. He decided there was really no need to tiptoe, though his paranoia nearly demanded it. Walking lightly across the room, he tried to take in everything at once. He wished the smoking gun would stand up and announce itself, but he knew he was probably going to have to sift through some drawers.

In the kitchen, he opened one drawer, looked in it, decided there was nothing there, and closed it. He did this several more times before realizing a minute had passed because he was being so careful about everything.

As he walked into the living room, a pungent mixture of stale mothballs and dust caused him to sneeze. Luckily, he had quite a petite sneeze, which had embarrassed him in high school but was now coming in pretty handy. Nobody was going to hear him.

He'd never been any further than the living room in Miss Peeple's house. Walking down the hallway nearly seemed like a crime by itself. He peeked into the bathroom, but the sight of a pair of stockings hanging from the tub was all he needed to quickly shut the door again.

Then he decided to venture into the bedroom. The thought caused him a seismic tremble from head to toe. But it was the only room he hadn't been in. And he had two minutes left.

The door was halfway closed. With a single finger, he pushed it open, and it creaked to a standstill a few inches from the wall. He could see a vanity table, a dresser, and a small window from where he stood, plus the end of the bed, where a quilt was neatly folded.

"What am I doing, what am I doing?" He pushed the palm of his hand into his forehead, as if this might shift his brain enough to make him think clearly. What kind of person breaks into people's homes? Of course, what kind of person sends eerie, anonymous messages? Miss Peeple knew something, and he was determined to find it out.

He stepped into the room and looked around. Taking one more step in, he decided he would look in the—

*"Ahh!"* He stumbled backward, knocking himself into the vanity. *"Ahhh! Ahhh!"* His high-pitched squeal scared him as much as the sight before him. But when he finally got ahold of himself, he realized something even more horrifying.

Before him, tucked quietly into her bed, was Missy Peeple. Her eyes were closed, and she wasn't moving. Like a hungry seagull, his mind dove into dark waters, fishing for reason. Was she dead? And he had broken into her house... This wasn't going to look good! His fingerprints were everywhere! He gasped for air. He was going to be a murder suspect! Maybe he should just sneak out of the house. But...but he didn't murder her. And if someone saw him sneaking out of her house, then he'd look even more guilty.

"Oh dear, oh dear." His fingers came to life and crawled up his chest and over his chin to his mouth, where he nibbled at a fingernail that had already been tattered earlier when he received the note.

Then. A moan. He resisted the urge to squeal again. She was alive! Alive! Alive? Now what? Obviously something was wrong. Miss Peeple was always quite ashen, but her skin tone was completely devoid of color. She moaned again, as if in pain.

His hand clapped over his mouth to keep the shriek down in his throat. He ran out of the room and back to the living room, panting in fear. He couldn't just leave her here, could he? He must call for help.

He walked over to the phone and closed his eyes. *This* was why he never did anything wrong in high school. He knew he'd get caught.

He dialed the police.

Oliver ran out of the shed as fast as he could, slamming the door and fumbling with the lock until it closed. He stood in his backyard, wondering what he should do, so frightened he thought his knees might collapse. He backed up until his hands found the brick of his home, keeping an eye on the shed.

What *should* he do? He'd caught one, but now what?

He ran into his house, locking the back door. He didn't know why. He'd tied it up with rope and gagged its mouth.

He leaned on the kitchen table, trying to catch his breath. He could feel his heart straining under the intense adrenaline that pumped it. Blowing like a woman in labor, he managed to at least stop shaking and sweating.

"Oliver?"

With a yelp he turned around, his face contorted in a paralyzed expression of fright. Luckily he didn't scream, "Don't kill me!" because it was only Melb.

"Melb," he breathed.

"Are you okay?" she asked. "You look like you've seen a ghost! Are you feeling all right?"

He nodded, managing a weak smile. "W-when did you get here?"

"Just a few minutes ago. Went to the bathroom. I saw your car was here, so I figured you were out puttering around in the shed."

He nodded and gulped. "Yes. Just, you know, messing around."

"Why are you breathing so hard?"

"Went for a jog."

"In the shed?"

"No. No." He tried to laugh, but his lungs didn't hold enough air yet, so it sounded more like a wheeze. "Just, you know, back and forth in the yard."

"Why are you jogging?" Her hands were now on her hips, and he knew that was the last place you wanted any woman's hands.

"Um…you know…to get in shape. For the…for the…wedding!"

Melb's expression turned furious. He was shocked. Did she know about the thing in the shed?

"Are you saying I'm *fat?*"

His jaw fell. He shook his head. Had he just said that? Wait a minute. Didn't he just say *he* was fat? He looked at her. "I was doing the jogging."

"I know!" she said, startling him with her sharp tone. "But are you trying to insinuate that I should be out jogging?!"

"No, no, Melb, please. Why are you getting so upset?"

Her hands dropped off her hips, and she shook her head. "I'm sorry." Tears welled up in her eyes. "I didn't mean to accuse you."

Though Oliver was trembling from head to toe with stress, he managed to walk over to Melb and take her cheeks into his hands. "Sweetheart, I love everything about you. Why would you say something like that?" He sort of impressed himself with how caring he could be while knowing he'd locked a monster in the shed.

She wiped away a tear. "It's not you. I guess I'm just feeling a little stressed." But she grinned at him. "No concern, though, okay? It's not prewedding jitters or anything like that."

He stroked her curly hair. "I know planning a wedding is stressful."

"It's going to be beautiful," she said, her eyes dreamy with thought. "There'll be a few surprises."

"I like surprises. Sometimes. Just don't surprise me by not showing up," he chuckled. Speaking of surprises, he couldn't help but glance out the back window to make sure the shed was still shut.

"So what are you doing home so early?"

"Oh, slow day. Plus I had some honeymoon things to take care of." He said all this while praying God would forgive him for lying.

She grinned. "Well, don't let me keep you."

"Are you, um, going somewhere?"

"I'm going to go owling. I've been having some luck at dusk."

He stretched his lips into a fanciful grin. "Well, don't be too long."

"Okay," she laughed.

"Exactly how long will you be?"

She pinched his cheek. "Listen to you, all worried about me."

He shrugged. "So, um, how long?"

"Oh, I'd say about an hour. I'll be home in plenty of time to cook dinner. We'll have it here tonight, right?"

She pecked him on the cheek and grabbed her purse, then walked out the door. As soon as he heard her car pull out of the driveway, he nearly collapsed. "An hour. An hour. Okay, what do I do?"

He paced the length of the living room, and then came up with an

idea. He'd call Martin. Martin always did have a good, solid head on his shoulders.

From the time he'd called the police until the time he'd watched Missy Peeple rolled away on a stretcher with an oxygen mask nearly covering her whole face, Martin had envisioned himself in jail, in the electric chair, and in hell. He was sure he had the face of a criminal, the way the deputies kept looking at him on their way in and out. And Sheriff Parker stopped once and observed him from across the room.

But to his surprise, nobody asked him what he was doing there. Sheriff Parker asked if he was feeling okay. Martin could only nod. He was afraid if he opened his mouth, a confession might drop out.

So there he was, twenty minutes after he'd made the phone call, standing alone in Missy Peeple's home. Nobody asked what he was doing there. And nobody asked when he was leaving. They'd simply asked about Miss Peeple and her condition, to which he could only answer with shrugs and nods.

The house creaked with the wind outside, and he felt so jumpy he decided to leave the house and go back to work. Missy Peeple might not be there, but even without her presence, the house still seemed cold.

At his office, he dropped his coat into his chair and tried to calm himself down with an extra large cup of coffee. His hands were shaking so much, though, that he spilled some of it down the front of his shirt.

A curse word jumped to the tip of his tongue, wanting to be released. But instead, he held his tongue, bit his lip, and flared his nostrils to try to hold in his frustration. A curse word was not going to help the moment settle.

He collapsed into his chair, wishing his mind would stop revisiting various scenarios of what would happen to him if he were accused of murder. He tried to think rationally. One, Missy Peeple wasn't dead. She just looked that way. Two, nobody seemed at all concerned that he was there. In fact, one deputy shook his hand and thanked him for finding

her! So what in the world was he worried about? His conscience. He'd always had that dratted conscience.

The phone rang at his desk. He smiled. Thankfully, something else to put his mind to.

"Martin Blarty."

"Martin! Thank heavens!"

"Oliver? Are you okay?"

"Martin, get over to my house. Now! Hurry! Hurry!"

And the phone went dead.

Martin's ears were burning like he'd lit them on fire, so he knew his blood pressure had spiked to levels he hadn't seen since he thought he'd witnessed a cat raised from the dead.

Oliver's eyes were bulging out of their sockets, slicing back and forth between Martin and the shed, where supposedly he'd tied up a "ghosty-thing."

"What'd he look like?" Martin asked.

"Well, I don't know, average build. Real creepy looking."

"Creepy how?"

"Pale. And shaking like he was possessed."

"Really?"

"And wearing a coat."

"A coat? Ghosts don't need coats, do they?"

Oliver shrugged. "I guess it depends on how long they've been dead."

Martin folded his arms in front of his chest. "Why would that matter?"

"Maybe you get cold right after you're dead because you're used to your blood keeping you warm."

"Oliver, I'm afraid I don't completely agree with your theory. Ghosts are invisible, apparitions, phantomlike."

"Well, how do you know? Have you ever seen one?"

Martin shook his head. "But sometimes things happen to people that we don't understand. Maybe it is dead. Or maybe it's…possessed."

They stared at the shed, then Martin whispered. "Unlock it."

Oliver's hands were shaking so badly it took him over a minute to finally get the key in the hole. A click indicated the lock was undone.

"You're sure he's securely tied up?" Martin asked.

"I'm sure."

They took simultaneous deep breaths, and then Oliver opened the shed door.

At first, in the darkness, Martin could only see two knees and the front legs of a chair. But as his eyes adjusted, there it was, sitting, tied up and gagged, its eyes wide with…with…fear, was it? It looked the same as when he'd seen the others in the forest. Wide eyes. Pale skin. And that strange facial expression.

It appeared to be male.

As Martin approached, the creature started whimpering, shaking his head at some horrible thought of what he might do to him. He glanced at Oliver, who stood a few feet behind him.

"You're sure it's one of them?" he asked.

"Positive. Just like the others, he was sneaking through the forest, then screaming bloody murder."

The man tried to wriggle loose, but to no avail. His wide eyes stared at Martin, who suddenly felt a surge of confidence and approached him.

"I don't know what you think you're doing in this town, but I can tell you, we won't die without a fight."

The wriggling stopped, and the man's eyes went wide with bewilderment. Martin felt a sense of superiority.

"You heard me right. Now I don't know what you think you're doing in this town. Probably trying to bring some kind of crazy curse. Is that what you're trying to do? Curse this town?"

The ghost shook his head vigorously.

"We've heard your screaming. We've seen you sneaking around here at all hours of the day and night. But let me tell you something. This

town does not welcome ghouls, goblins, witches, ghosts, mummies, vampires, or anything else that requires a stake or garlic."

Oliver leaned over and whispered, "Martin, ghosts don't eat steaks because they don't have digestive tracts."

Now the It simply stared at Martin. Maybe this thing was getting the point.

"Oliver, what do you think we should do to it?"

"We can't kill it. It's already dead."

Color drained from the ghost's already pale face. His eyes darted back and forth between Oliver and Martin. And then it suddenly panicked, thrashing about, trying to kick its legs. Its head whipped back and forth so ferociously that the chair fell over, and to their horror, the rope Oliver had used to bind his hands to the chair came loose. The ghost stood up, screaming as he ungagged himself.

Oliver screamed. Martin opened his mouth, but nothing came out.

"You're crazy!" the It screamed. "I'm from Kentucky! You all are a bunch of loons around here, I tell you!"

And then it fled, knocking Martin to the ground. Oliver stepped aside as it raced past them and started to hop over the fence. They watched as a cat jumped up on top of the fence. The It knocked it off without hesitation, leapt over the fence, and was gone.

Martin and Oliver tried to catch their breath for a few moments. Oliver dabbed his forehead with a hanky. Martin could only lean against the shed and repeatedly touch his body to make sure he hadn't been killed. Finally Oliver said, "We're a bunch of loons? That guy's dead and he thinks he's from Kentucky! In Indiana, everybody that's dead knows it!"

Martin closed his eyes. His body slumped in fatigue. Something crazy was happening to this town, something out of a horror novel. Who would believe such craziness? He glanced at Oliver. And how could Martin explain his suspicions that Melb had succumbed to the same fate?

His ears were hot again.

## CHAPTER 26

ON MAIN STREET at dusk in Skary, Indiana, there was the most marvelous view. If you stood right in the middle of the street, usually the last two weeks of January, it looked as though the road continued right into the setting sun. Even on a cold day, the sun's rays warmed the street, sending an amber, hazy glow along the pavement.

There wasn't much traffic in Skary, so Wolfe was able to stand there, observing the splendor of the sunset. While he'd always had a remarkable view from his home, he'd discovered this particular view by accident a few years ago when he'd decided to take a walk to battle writer's block. He'd stood there for forty minutes, taking in every little detail until the sun finally buried itself on the other side of the earth.

Today it wasn't writer's block that had caused him to walk. It was Ainsley. They had planned to meet after Wolfe got off work, to discuss some wedding plans, in particular the groom's cake. But she'd called right before he left, explaining she was supposed to meet the two New York City chefs, who were flying in on a different schedule than originally planned. Alfred was whisking her off to meet at a restaurant near the Indianapolis airport, and she had an hour to come up with at least some sort of menu for Melb's reception, and on and on. He had tuned her out, his thoughts clouded by envy, anger, and disappointment.

He felt as if he was losing her, and as rationally as he tried to think about it, the fear still stood firm in his mind. And in a moment of honesty, he wasn't sure he was marrying the girl he thought he was. To him, Ainsley had always been a picture of stability, of simplicity and purity and family. Now she was off chasing dreams of stardom. Though he

thought her shorter haircut was fine, it was the principle of why she'd cut it that disturbed him. It was like she was trying to become somebody new, but it was the person all those years before that he'd fallen in love with.

Of course, these days he seemed to be a shadow of who he used to be. At the point he'd decided that his life had become completely empty, he'd found hope. He'd found purpose. But he couldn't dismiss how odd it was to find purpose for your life while losing the very purpose you thought you were born for. Never in his life had he doubted he was supposed to be a writer. Now, there was a strange fulfillment in his life, coupled by a rare feeling of dismay. How could he feel purposeful and lost all at the same time?

He'd wanted to visit with the reverend about this, but these days, the reverend seemed as lost as anyone. But Wolfe knew from experience what a quiet moment of meditation could do for one's soul. And there was nothing like staring into the fiery blaze of the earth's light to scorch away misguided fears.

Ainsley had reassured him that she could do both: plan their wedding while following Alfred's twelve steps to becoming Martha Stewart. But Wolfe could see the stress in her eyes, the way she strained to hold that charming smile he so loved to see.

He stepped out of the street and onto the sidewalk as a slow-moving car passed by. The sun wasn't quite tucked into bed, but its warmth had left and the chill of the streets had returned. He turned and walked back toward his house.

And he found himself praying.

He found it remarkable how prayer worked. Before, he'd thought it included a heavy amount of time on the knees, bowing and mumbling words one imagined the Lord wanted to hear. But he understood it now to be more conversational, not in an irreverent way, but in a comfortable way. He found it easy to praise, sometimes harder to ask for help.

Now, though, his life's wishes seemed to be falling apart. His wedding day was looking shaky. And indeed, the woman of his dreams seemed to have other dreams she wanted to pursue. Not to mention that

his own passion for writing had not diminished, although he now had no idea what to write. He'd also discovered, sadly, that he really didn't have any other talents that would be useful in the work environment. He knew for sure he was not cut out to sell cars, and he was beginning to suspect after his third romance novel that he was also not going to enjoy reading that genre for any reason.

He liked working at the bookstore, though the pace was horribly slow. At times he prayed for at least one customer to come in needing help, even if just looking for a romance novel.

Instead, most of his time was spent chatting with Dustin, who loved detailing the habits of his two pet snakes.

Oh Lord, how he wanted to marry Ainsley. He couldn't imagine his life without her. His body ached at the thought of losing her. Then he almost laughed aloud, recalling those horrid romance novels he'd been reading. Maybe they weren't so far from the truth after all.

As the midnight blue color of the night sky sketched itself over Skary, Wolfe felt very lonely.

The restaurant's electric atmosphere seemed to feed the crowd around Ainsley. She was trying to pay attention to the conversation while taking it all in.

On her left was Chef Danté Elouise, well-known New York restaurant owner, who had not quite achieved the status of fame. Alfred had explained to her that many chefs were looking for opportunities to become the next Rocco or Emeril. On her right sat Marc Yeager, a Boston chef who had some short-lived success on the Home Shopping Network before one of the products he was touting ended up having a short in it that burned up seven kitchens across America.

Ainsley was enjoying some of the most exquisite food she'd ever tasted. The restaurant specialized in Hawaiian food, and she tried what they called butter fish. It melted in her mouth. But her appetite waned out of nervousness, especially as Alfred was going on and on about what

a superstar she would become. The two chefs seemed to buy it. They talked to her with a respect she'd never known from the professional world.

When it came time for her to share her desired menu for Melb's reception, the two chefs praised her selection of recipes and the way she chose all the foods to complement one another. They gave subtle suggestions, which she approved of, and at the end, she thought this was going to be the best reception she'd ever attended.

They began discussing some of the particulars of shooting the pilot, and Alfred said, "You know, Ainsley, we are going to have to separate ourselves a bit from Martha Stewart. It will be considered old school after we're finished with it. There's a new show in town, and it's going to outshine the rest. What I'm saying is that we have to be a little different. I think one way we do it is to have more of the reality aspect. Reality is hot right now. Seems like the trend will continue for a while. On our show, we'll be set apart because we'll actually have people eating the food. It's not just for show, you know? It's for enjoyment. You'll really be cooking, not just pulling something out of the oven that's been sitting there for an hour. Part of the show will be the real, live interaction of people. What do you think?"

Chef Danté spoke up. "Sounds like a lot of pressure." Then he looked at Ainsley. "Pressure I am sure you can handle."

Chef Marc said, "A lot can go wrong, but sometimes that's what makes it interesting."

Alfred nodded. "Exactly. And we don't always have to have the high-paced atmosphere of a wedding reception. Sometimes it will be a dinner for friends. Or a picnic with children."

Ainsley laughed. Already she could see how much fun this was going to be. Alfred squeezed her hand. "This is your moment, lady. Everything you've been working for."

Chef Marc said, "It will be a pleasure working for you."

"Indeed," added Chef Danté.

"I know Melb is going to be so excited about all this. It will truly bless her."

"Who is Melb?" Chef Marc asked.

"It's her wedding we're doing," she said, a tinge of sadness clinging to her heart as she realized these men didn't even have a clue how special this day would be for Melb. She cheered up by reminding herself that *she* knew, and that was all that mattered.

Alfred said, "I'll call Melb tomorrow and tell her the menu. She'll be ecstatic. I'm also going to have to tell her she'll need to extend her guest list. We're going to need a lot of people there."

Chef Marc wiped his mouth with his napkin. "All right. We'll get to work. There will be a lot of planning on this. I'll be making the ingredients list. Danté will put together the timetable."

"I can't believe this. It's almost like a dream!"

Alfred laughed. "It's going to be a lot of hard work. Are you up for it?"

She nodded. "I wouldn't have it any other way."

Alfred checked his watch. "We better get you two to the airport. Wish we could meet longer, but I know you're busy, and I appreciate your time here." All four stood and shook hands. Then Alfred said, "Ainsley, I'm going to go hail them a cab."

"Okay. May I use your cell phone?"

"Sure." He smiled and handed it to her. After the gentlemen left, she dialed Wolfe's number, excitement building with every ring. But his answering machine picked up. "Wolfe? Wolfe? Are you there? It's me... Hello?"

Only silence answered back.

"Okay, um, I just wanted to tell you about my evening. It was incredible. I was afraid I'd be home too late to call you tonight, so I'm using Alfred's cell phone. I miss you. I'll call you tomorrow. You're not going to believe some of the stuff that's going on! It's so exciting. I love you. Bye."

Wolfe sat in his living room, listening to her voice over the recorder. The cell phone static emphasized his feelings of disconnection. He didn't

want to talk with her. He didn't want to hear her exciting news. He just wanted her back in Skary, planning their wedding, loving him.

He closed his eyes as she hung up the phone. Part of him wanted to jump up, grab the receiver, and talk with her. But mostly he was disgruntled and angry. Admittedly, he was still feeling betrayed that she'd agreed to plan Melb's entire reception without telling him. As far as he could tell, she didn't have a thing planned for theirs.

Goose and Bunny whimpered their request to go outside. He sighed, wishing for an ounce of their eagerness. Instead his body felt heavy, burdened. He got up and let them outside, and decided to make some hot tea. While his tea steeped, he glanced over to his bookshelf and saw the copy of *Black Cats* that Missy Peeple had brought by at Christmas. He shook his head, holding the little tea string and bobbing the bag up and down in the cup. It was an odd thing to say there was a secret message in something you wrote and you didn't even know about it. Common sense told him this was a bunch of nonsense. But the imaginative side of him wondered if it could be true.

He added cream and sugar and took his tea to the bookshelf, thinking of the story of *Black Cats* and wondering if there was any kind of significance to it. Sure, he'd gotten the idea by living in a town filled with cats. But that's where he'd thought the similarities ended. Everything else had come straight from his imagination, or so he thought. Could he have been influenced by some unseen circumstance that had caused him to write a book about the mysteries behind a town?

The warm tea he sipped seemed to melt away these crazy theories. He smiled. It would make a great plot for a novel, though.

He took the book off the shelf, looking at the cover. It was the last book he'd written, one of his best. He'd enjoyed the process of it so much. As he sat back down, the blinking red light of his answering machine caught his attention, pulling his thoughts back to Ainsley. He flipped the pages of the book with his thumb. He didn't want to feel this way about Ainsley, but these days it seemed the only way out of it was to not think of her at all.

Staring down at the book, he decided to flip it open. It was rare that

he even looked through a book of his once it was published. It was satisfying to see it in print. But he knew the book so well, there was never a need to look through it once it arrived between hard covers.

When he opened it, though, shock electrified his body. His jaw dropped and he let out a surprised laugh. There, in the middle pages of the book, was a small space cut out, just large enough for a...key. A key! It was taped to the inside of the hole.

Wolfe jumped up from his chair and hurried to the kitchen. He set the book down and carefully untaped the key. It was no bigger than his thumb. He checked the time. It was just after nine. He looked up Martin's phone number and dialed it.

"Hello?"

"Martin, it's Wolfe."

"Hi Wolfe. What's the matter? You sound—"

"Can you come over right now?"

"Sounds urgent."

"It is."

"I'll be right there."

## CHAPTER 27

"I CAN'T BELIEVE IT," Martin said. He stood in Wolfe Boone's kitchen staring at the tiny key.

"So let's go confront Miss Peeple about this. She's given us some key, now let's find out what it means."

Martin grimaced. "One problem. She's, well, sort of…possibly dead."

"What do you mean?"

"She had to be rushed to the hospital this afternoon."

"What?"

"I was breaking into her house at the time," Martin said quietly. "Don't tell anyone. But I had to know why she sent the note. I was try-ing to find clues."

"You *broke* into her house?"

"I didn't think she was home," Martin emphasized. "I had knocked several times, and nobody answered. The front door was open, so I went in." He threw up his hands and shrugged. "How was I to know she was actually lying incapacitated in her bed? I probably saved her life," he said, trying to convince himself. "She was alive when they were wheeling her out."

"Well, let's go. Let's go to the hospital," Wolfe said, grabbing his coat off the back of his chair. "That woman has been at death's door before and come back."

"It's a forty-minute drive to the county hospital."

Wolfe turned to him. "Martin, aren't you the least bit curious about

why she went to all this trouble to hide a key in a book and give it to me? And then when I didn't find it, drop a hint to you?"

"Of course I'm curious," Martin replied. His fingers tore through his hair, and he closed his eyes. "It's just been a hard day. I'm not sure I can stand any more surprises."

"Surprises?"

Martin opened his eyes and rolled them, exhausted at the thought of even trying to explain what else had happened. "Can I trust you not to spread what I say around?"

"Sure," Wolfe said. "What is it?"

"Oliver caught one today."

"Caught what?"

"I don't really know what to call it. Ghost doesn't seem right. Goblin, well, I don't even know what a goblin is, really. Heck, you're the expert on these things."

"What are you talking about?"

"Oliver caught one of those people that are wandering around the outskirts of town. You know? Screaming every now and then? Looking like the walking dead. Technically, is there a difference between the walking dead and ghosts?"

"Martin, I make ghost stories up. They're not real. And what do you mean Oliver caught one?"

"Had him tied up in the shed when I got there. I interrogated him—"

"You interrogated him?"

"Yes. Real weird. Eyes wide," Martin said, his fingers and thumbs circling his eyes in an O shape. "Shaking. Sweating. Claims he's from Kentucky. How bizarre is that?"

Wolfe had covered his mouth with his hand, as if holding in a thousand questions that wanted to escape. His hand slid down to his chin, where he scratched it in thought. Then he said, "Where is he now?"

"Oliver?"

"No…the…the…"

"Oh. Escaped. Chair fell over. Rope slid off. Up he jumped, and out he went."

Wolfe zipped up his jacket. "Come on. We're going to see Missy Peeple."

It was a little hard to decide, there were so many to choose from, but Dr. Hass decided on a black cat with white paws that he named Blot. Blot had been hanging around his porch for several days now, since the first day he'd arrived, in fact, and they'd seemed to have a certain connection. For some odd reason, the cat really wanted in his house.

Thrilled to finally be invited inside, Blot had hardly left his side. She'd tangle her tail between his legs, circling each ankle with a soft meow. Only once did she leave the room he was in to go investigate an owl hooting nearby. She returned only minutes later, though, and was now curled up on the corner of his desk, where he busied himself with back paperwork in the late evening. All this therapy was putting him behind! He'd spent an hour with Melb Cornforth and her weight-loss saga. To her astonishment, she'd been losing weight and believed it was because of their twice weekly sessions. He didn't dispute her, but instead pocketed the $150 and told her he'd see her the next week.

He was just closing a folder when he heard his front door crash open. Blot hopped to her feet, but Dr. Hass froze in his chair. He could hear footsteps stomping across the floor. He wished suddenly that Blot was not a cat but instead a pit bull.

Just as he was about to scream for help, a man came around the corner, bundled in his coat, emotions scrambled on his face. His eyes were pleading, his mouth in a tight, angry grimace. Overall, it was clear that he was not a very happy man.

"Dr. Hass!" his voice boomed through the office. Blot's tail sprang toward the ceiling, and she moved a few steps closer to Dr. Hass. It was Leroy Hurgison.

"Leroy. Hello. Good to see—"

"This town is crazy! You know what happened to me today?! I got tied up in a shed, and these people were claimin' I'm a ghost! I swear I thought they were going to kill me, except then they were discussin' how one might kill a ghost. I've never seen two crazier people in my life. They looked at me like I was some sort of vampire. I don't know what kind of crazy town this is, but I'm leaving! Do you hear me? There ain't nothin' here in this town that's worth my life, and the last thing I'm gonna allow to happen is gettin' myself murdered by a bunch of towns-folk who think their town's being haunted!"

Dr. Hass stood up, nervously stroking Blot. "Leroy, I certainly understand why you're upset. You have every reason to be. But—"

"Don't even try to convince me I need to stay. You should've seen the looks in their eyes. 'Oliver, what should we do, kill him?' 'Why, I don't know, Martin. Can you kill a ghost?' I can't believe I'm standing here alive to tell you about it. I can live with who I am and what I have wrong with me. What I can't live with is the fear of being hunted like a deer. I'm scared to death! Good-bye!"

Leroy marched out of the office and left without closing the front door. Dr. Hass fell into his chair as Blot leapt onto his lap. "Good grief," he mumbled. Coming from the city, he hadn't realized how much small-town folks paid attention to things. In the city, nobody even noticed when something was different. Everyone was into their own business and nothing more. But it was not the same out here. Business was fair game, no matter whose it was.

Blot nuzzled her face into his shoulder. "Wait!" he shouted. "Oh! *Oh!*" He carefully set Blot down and stood, clasping his hands over his head and laughing. He had just realized something, something astonishing! Leroy didn't even notice because he was so mad!

"Blot! This is amazing! Amazing!" Blot's slit eyes indicated she was far less impressed. But it didn't matter. Something huge had happened tonight, something unforeseen.

He scrambled back to his desk and flipped open his calendar. He

was still two weeks from Phase Two, but his gut told him it was time to proceed. Phase Two would begin the day after tomorrow—and include an added twist.

It was past ten when Ainsley unlocked the front door of her house. Alfred had dropped her off about ten minutes ago, but instead of going in, she'd decided to drive over to Wolfe's house to see if he was still awake. Not being able to speak with him while she was in Indianapolis had disappointed her. And his tone had been less than enthusiastic when she'd phoned him at work to tell him she'd have to cancel that evening.

She was hoping that with all the good news from the day, he'd be able to understand and join in her excitement. But to her astonishment, even this late at night, he was still out. So now thoughts of where he might be plagued her mind.

At home her father was awake, sitting in the kitchen with a ball of yarn.

"Ainsley! Watch this!" Her father rolled a yarn ball across the floor, and Thief tackled it with charisma. "Can you believe it? Thief's back! The therapy worked!"

Ainsley smiled, unloading her stuff on the couch and joining her father in the kitchen. "That's terrific, Dad."

"Amazing, if you ask me. I always thought shrinks were a crock of you-know-what."

"Aunt Gert's stew?" Ainsley smiled.

Her father laughed. "No, but close. Anyway, I just thought those guys didn't know what they were talking about, you know? I figured they were just there to rake in the money. But this shrink fixed my cat! I followed all the steps he told me, and it worked."

"I'm so glad. It's good to have Thief back on his feet."

"So how was Indianapolis?"

"Fine. A lot of fun. I'm a little in awe of all of this, to tell you the truth. Dad, did Wolfe call, by any chance?"

"Nope. Haven't heard from him today. But your cake lady called."

"Nita?"

"Can't remember, but the one who is doing your wedding cake."

"Yeah, that's Nita."

"Well, she said you waited too late to give her your cake choice, and that she's going to have to special order something-or-other, and it will take about a month to get in."

"That's too late."

"That's what she said. So she wondered if you had another idea for your cake."

Ainsley sighed. "Okay, I'll call her tomorrow."

"She said she'd definitely need to know something by the weekend. Her calendar is filling up."

Outside, a faint scream could be heard. Ainsley gasped and turned toward the door. Her father rolled the yarn across the floor.

"Dad? Did you hear that?"

"What?"

"That scream."

Her father shook his head.

"You seem to be the only one around here not to notice there have been some strange things happening, Dad."

Her father clapped his hands loudly while Thief retrieved the yarn. "Honey, people scream for all sorts of reasons. And so far, nobody is reporting any sort of crime, so I don't really see what I can do. Fetch, Thief!"

"All right then. If you're not concerned, then I guess I shouldn't be," she said. "I'm exhausted. I'll see you in the morning."

"Okay, sweetheart."

She made her way upstairs, changed into her pajamas, scrubbed the makeup from her face, and fell into bed. But she knew as tired as she was, sleep would not come easily, because all she could think about was where Wolfe might be this late at night.

"You're relatives?" the male nurse asked.

Wolfe glanced at Martin, then shook his head. "No, she has no living relatives."

"We can't let anyone see her but relatives."

"Sir," Martin said, "she is a lonely old lady. Her only chance at survival may be the comforting words of those who…um…"

"Care about her," Wolfe finished.

"Yes, that."

The nurse glanced toward the room where Miss Peeple was apparently 'resting comfortably,' as he'd put it earlier. "Well, I have to say I've been a little disappointed nobody has been up to see the poor lady. She seems so sweet and lovely."

Martin and Wolfe tried not to flinch.

"How is she?" Wolfe decided to ask. That would be an appropriate question if she were sweet and lovely.

"Honestly, it's not good."

"Is she sick?" Martin asked.

"Well, basically what I can say is that she's simply dying of old age."

Martin glanced at Wolfe. "People don't actually do that these days, do they? Die of old age?"

The male nurse smiled a little. "It is rare. You're welcome to go in and see her. But I must warn you, she hasn't woken up since she arrived."

Martin followed Wolfe into the room. She lay in the bed, so white she nearly blended into the sheets. Her breathing was shallow but steady. With those menacing eyes closed, she nearly looked peaceful. Wolfe kept his distance, though. Something told him she might just fly out of bed with a scream.

"This isn't good," Martin whispered.

Wolfe pulled the key out of his pocket. "Miss Peeple? We found your key. Now we want to know why we have it and what it belongs to."

The only reply was the constant beep of the heart monitor. Martin was all but huddled behind him.

He sighed and turned to face Martin. "Now what?"

"Maybe you can help me with something."

"What?"

"I found a hidden map. It shows five shacks up in the foothills. I've visited all the shacks, but there doesn't seem to be much up there. Maybe tomorrow we can go up there together and you can take a look around. See if you can find anything."

"Sure. After work."

The male nurse approached them as they left the room. Martin said, "If she wakes up, please call this number," and handed him a card.

## CHAPTER 28

OLIVER COULD HARDLY SLEEP that night.

He'd warmed some milk, sat up and read, even sipped some Nyquil, but to no avail. Rest would not come. All he could see was the Kentucky ghost's startled eyes staring back at him.

In the morning, he rose so early he decided to go eat a big breakfast at The Mansion. But the food tasted like cardboard. So he left most of it and went to work. He was sitting at his desk when he heard someone at his door. A knock came, and then another knock. Oliver swallowed and in a strained voice said, "Come in?"

The door opened, and a middle-aged, suave-looking guy peeked his head around. "Was that a question?"

"No, please, come in." Oliver fumbled the pen in his hand and tried to stand up, banging his knees on his desk. Wincing in pain, he did manage to shake the man's hand.

"Are you Oliver?"

"Yes. Oliver Stepaphanolopolis."

"Goodness. Going to need a flashcard for that one."

Oliver tried to politely smile. "Just call me Oliver."

"I'm Dr. Hass."

"Are you looking for a new or used car?"

"No. The reason I'm here, Oliver," he said, going over to the door and quietly shutting it, "is of a private nature."

"Oh?"

"Yes. First of all, I have to know, are you the kind of person who can keep a secret?"

"Well, I'm certainly the kind of person who is always willing to hear one." Oliver offered a bashful grin. The doctor smiled mildly. "Um, anyway, I guess so. But if you're going to tell me you murdered some-body, I'd have to turn you in to the police. So don't confess anything."

Dr. Hass sat down in a chair across from Oliver, who also sat down. "It's nothing of that sort. But I have to know if I can trust you."

"I'm not sure if you can. I don't know why you're here, and quite frankly, you're making me feel kind of eerie."

"Sorry, didn't mean to do that," the doctor said with a warm wink. "Okay, I'll tell you why I'm here. I'm sure you've noticed a group of people around town that don't belong."

Oliver jumped out of his chair with a yelp. "So it's true! I caught one! Those creepy little twits are wandering around our town, ready to take it over, or do whatever they're going to do! So I caught one! Scared it, too, if you want to know the truth. He screamed like a girl, and I don't think I'll ever see him around these parts again, whatever kind of 'him' he is." Oliver blinked away the frightful scene and looked at the doctor.

"Oliver, I know. That's why I'm here."

"It is?"

"I need somebody brave enough to catch them and bring them to me."

Oliver tore off one fingernail after another with his teeth, barely paus-ing to comment. "Brave enough. I wouldn't exactly call myself brave."

"Oh, I think what you did was incredibly brave, Oliver."

"How do you know about that?" Oliver felt his skin crawl.

"It's not important how, but just know, I have faith that you're the right man for the job."

"I'd like a little more information about what you plan to do with these…these…whatever they are."

"A little more information? How does a hundred and fifty dollars sound? For each one you bring in?"

Perspiration collected over his brow line. "Are you trying to buy my silence?"

"Just your trust."

"Well, I'll take one twenty-five if I can tell my friend Martin."

"Martin. Hmm. The only other person who knows about the 'shed.'"

Oliver gasped. "Are you psychic?"

"No, no. But I do know Martin. Have met him once. Seems to be an admirable fellow. Sure, why not. But only you two. And you must bring them to me discreetly. Without harming them." He handed Oliver a card. "That is my address. Martin knows the place."

"How do you know Martin?"

"Oliver, I'm a counselor of sorts."

"You are?"

"Yes. Martin is not a patient, but I have met him."

"So what does a psychologist want with a bunch of ghosts?"

"Are you certain they're ghosts?"

"I'm not sure what they are!" Oliver said, pounding his fist on his desk. "All I know is that I want them out of my town!" Oliver shook his head. "I'm sorry. I'm normally a pretty docile man. I've been surprising myself lately, though. Over the past few months I've done everything from scheming to keep two lovers apart to asking the woman of my dreams to marry me." He looked at Dr. Hass. "I could've probably used a shrink...I mean head doctor...a few months back."

Dr. Hass said, "You want these people out of your town?"

"Yes."

"I can guarantee that if you'll help me."

"You're not going to do anything...illegal, are you?"

"I'm going to help them."

"How do you help a ghost?"

"Oliver, do you want them gone or not?"

"I do," Oliver sighed.

"Are you going to help me?"

Oliver swallowed. "I will."

"Good. Then I can guarantee you'll be rid of them soon." Dr. Hass stood. "Oh, and Oliver. They'll be coming into town disguised as tourists."

Ainsley was not sure if she was hyperventilating. But she did know that she couldn't catch her breath, and she felt as if her heart was going to pound right through her chest wall.

"Hello? Ma'am?"

She nearly dropped the phone, but managed to put her mouth to the receiver. "Y-yes. I'm here. I'm…um…just…"

"I'm sorry, we just don't have the banquet hall available for that night. You really should've called sooner."

"Thank you…" Ainsley reached out and tried to hang the receiver up, missing twice before finally lifting it high enough for it to hook. "What am I going to do?" she cried to herself. This morning she'd worked on Melb's reception. But she knew that left her plenty of time this afternoon to work on her own wedding. Except everything she was doing kept leading to dead ends. Marlee had even called wondering when her bridesmaid's dress was going to be ready. Ainsley could hardly believe she'd forgotten to sew it! She'd picked out the pattern many weeks ago, and gotten Marlee's measurements, but that was it. The pattern lay in a corner, ready for material.

*Material. Go get material.*

She grabbed her purse off the table and went outside. As she drove to the fabric store, her mind swirled with everything that was going wrong. All she had right were her wedding dress and invitations. Besides that, she had yet to pick out flowers, had not planned the reception or found a caterer, hadn't found a new wedding cake or attended to all the minute details that came with planning a wedding in general. And she was flabbergasted to realize she might not be capable of it all. Never in her life had she not been capable of planning something. But now everything seemed to be crumbling before her.

"No," she said to herself. "I can do it. I've always been able to do it, and I still can." She wrapped her fingers around the steering wheel and leaned forward in steely determination.

Once at the fabric store, she told herself to get in and get out. There

was no time to waste. She had still not talked with Wolfe, and it picked at her. She'd decided not to call him. She'd left a message. She wasn't going to beg him to understand. If he didn't understand her passions and desires, maybe he didn't understand her at all.

"Hi Ainsley!" Alma Hayes, the store owner, said.

"Hi Alma." Ainsley smiled through her distressing thoughts.

"Let me guess! You're making some new aprons? We just got in this fabulous chili pepper pattern."

"No aprons."

"A table runner?"

"Actually, a bridesmaid's dress. For Marlee."

Alma frowned. "Really? This late?"

"I know, I'm running a little behind."

"Well, nobody I know can sew faster than you can."

"This shouldn't be hard. I already know what I want." A dreamy smile stole over her lips. "Powder blue silk."

Alma smiled and went behind the nearby counter. "Five yards?"

"Yes, that should be fine."

Alma was jotting all this down. "Powder blue silk. Okay, I'll put in an order for it."

"An order? You don't carry it in the store?"

"Not silk. We carry only white. Everything else has to be special ordered since it's so expensive."

The next question came out as barely a whisper. "About how long would it take to get it in?"

"About four weeks."

Her face warmed as she tried to hold back tears. "Four weeks."

Alma grinned. "But we have a lovely selection of blue taffeta."

Reverend Peck could hardly sleep, could hardly eat. He was exhausted, for one. He'd spent a week trying to put all the pews back in. The bolts that were so easy to take off didn't seem to want to go back on.

But he also knew he was losing hope. The passion that had for so many years put him behind the pulpit and provided him with a message few wanted to hear was dying. He could no longer look into indifferent faces. He could no longer pretend what he was doing was making the slightest difference.

But something deep inside told him he couldn't leave Skary. True, it was home to him. Yet there was something more about this town, something he couldn't quite put his finger on.

In all his years of ministry, he had kept every single sermon he'd preached. He simply filed them by date. He had nearly a thousand, stored neatly in his basement. Reverend Peck made his way down there, pulling the string that illuminated the single light bulb.

Without much trouble, he found the very first box from twenty years ago. Opening it, he thumbed through the folders and found it. Holding it up toward the light, he laughed. His very first sermon at this church! *Learning to Love Those Who Are Different.* He sighed. It was probably useless to preach. Everybody in this town was exactly the same!

Martin leaned back in his chair, folding his arms together, looking around the donut shop to see if anyone else was listening. Oliver was practically stretching all the way across the table, staring at him for any sign of reaction.

"Oliver, this is crazy!" he whispered.

"I know, I know," Oliver whispered back. "I'm scared out of my mind!"

Martin's eyes narrowed. "This Dr. Hass... There seems to be something off about him, doesn't there?"

Oliver shrugged.

"You didn't ask why he wanted us to catch these people?"

"He didn't seem to want to give the information. In fact, the money was incentive to trust him."

"Trust him."

"Yeah."

They sighed at the same time, then studied each other. Finally Martin said, "I have a theory."

"You do?"

"Yes, about all these people. I don't think they're ghosts or goblins or even possessed."

"That's what he said!" Oliver exclaimed.

"There's only one thing that makes sense to me."

"What is it?"

Martin shoved his half-eaten donut out of the way. "They're clones."

"Clones?!"

"Shush!" Martin said.

Oliver whispered, "Clones?"

"Yes, clones. Don't you remember what Missy Peeple has always said about Garth?"

"Garth Twyne the vet?"

"She's always maintained that he cloned pigs. Some even thought cats, until that little mystery was solved."

"It was just a crazy rumor!"

"Maybe, but maybe not. From all I can tell, Missy Peeple holds a lot of secrets about this town. You've said it yourself: These people don't look normal. Perhaps they're clones, throwaways, experiments that went awry."

Oliver's eyes bulged. "Dr. Hass might be involved with this cloning experiment?"

"It would make sense as to why he was so secretive about it. And why he has suddenly shown up in town."

Blinking rapidly, Oliver covered his mouth in a frightful, private thought. Then he looked at Martin. "Could be why that guy thought he was from Kentucky. He was cloned from somebody in Kentucky!" Oliver gasped at his own words.

Martin stared at the table. "I don't know if I can believe it myself, Oliver. But I intend to find out the truth. As soon as Missy Peeple wakes up."

Oliver swallowed. "And I intend to catch myself a clone. And then use it for ransom to find out what Dr. Hass and Dr. Twyne are up to." Oliver gobbled up his donut, chewing through one thought after another. He then said, "It is a little odd to think of Dr. Twyne cloning, though. I mean, from what I understand, he has trouble performing basic neutering operations."

"True," Martin said. "But it could just be a disguise. And now he's cloning people. Except the experiment isn't going well. He's got to figure out what to do with all the duds."

Oliver shook his head in disgust.

"One thing I know, Oliver. I will find out what's going on with this town, and what happened to it long ago, if it's the last thing I do. It's the only way to save Skary and Mayor Wullisworth."

"How is he, by the way?"

Martin shook his head. "Well, last time I saw him he was sitting in his bathtub on the 'beaches of Bermuda.'"

"Goodness," Oliver said. "It's sad to see someone lose his mind."

Martin nodded and smiled. "At least *somebody* around here is thinking clearly."

They reached across the table and shook hands.

Ainsley could not stop sobbing. For at least thirty minutes now, all she was able to do was sit on her bed, look through her wedding planner, and cry. Her dream wedding was falling apart piece by little petit four. Whenever she finally got herself together, she would turn the page in her wedding planner and start to cry all over again.

Marlee was going to be wearing blue taffeta.

The wedding cake was going to be coconut something-or-other. The cake lady assured her it would be terrific. Terrific for a luau.

She still hadn't found a suitable place for the reception. The only spot in town she liked was mysteriously booked. The woman wouldn't

say who'd booked it, only that it was firmly in the schedule. Ainsley thought it was a tall tale if she'd ever heard one.

She still had hopes for a caterer. She'd called one about thirty miles away; they thought they could do it and said they'd get back with her.

Her groom-to-be wouldn't call her back.

Uncontrollable sobs filled the bedroom again. She lay back on her bed and turned on her side. When the tears cleared enough for her to see her bedside table, she noticed her mother's wedding diary. Picking it up, she dried her tears and flipped open the diary to May 9, which would've been about three weeks before her parents' wedding.

If it were possible to have a wedding without relatives, it should be done!

She laughed, sitting up on her bed.

The only person who seems not to have lost her mind is Gert, who is simply being a wonderful and supportive sister. She's fallen in love too. A man named Wilbur. I've begged her to elope. It's truly the only good way.

Oh, I'm being harsh. I love it all, truthfully. My wedding dress is so beautiful, it's nearly indescribable. I've never seen anything like it. It took me four months to make it, but it was worth it.

There hardly seems to be an adequate way of celebrating what will be a lifetime of love.

Tears rolled down Ainsley's cheeks. How could her mother have known how very short her lifetime of love was going to be? And Aunt Gert, too. Wilbur was lost just as tragically, before they even had children.

She whispered to her mother, pouring out her grievances and fears. *"I love him,"* she cried. She did, more than she could say. But did he love her anymore? Could he accept who she'd become? Could he accept who *he* had become?

Grabbing at a tissue, she wiped her tears and blotted her cheeks, gasping for fresh air that was not polluted by her self-pity. How she was going to pull off this wedding, she didn't know. But she would do it. She *had* to do it. She'd dreamed of this day her whole life.

She just hoped the groom would show up.

The phone rang, and she eagerly grabbed it.

"Hello? Wolfe?"

"Ainsley, hi. It's Alfred."

"Oh. Hi."

"Well, what did you think of Indianapolis? Did you ever dream you'd have two elite chefs at your beck and call?"

She shook her head. "It was quite an experience." She didn't know what else to say. They'd already talked all the way back that night.

"Ainsley, there is a lot of buzz about this. People are talking, and in this business, talk is good. Everyone is waiting to see what you're like, who you are, what you're up to. And I think I've come up with a tag line for the show: 'Ainsley Parker: This Isn't Your Mother's Kitchen.' What do you think?"

She closed her eyes. She didn't know what to think. "You're the expert, Alfred."

"I think it delivers the message that this show is new and fresh, that you're new and fresh."

"Like a ripe tomato plucked off the vine," she sighed.

"Anyway, I may be out of touch for a few days. I have to fly to New York to tie up some financial backing. Ten days, my friend, and you're on your way to the top."

"Alfred, um…I need to talk to you about something."

"Yes?" Urgency made the word almost a hiss.

"It's just that…well…" Her fingers tore through her hair. She wanted to quit all this! All of it! What did all this matter in the light of her love for Wolfe?

"I've waited my whole life for a talent like you, Ainsley. I was born to make stars out of fire. And you've got the fire, the passion, that is needed to make it big. And now, behind you, is the person who can put

all the pieces into place. Of course, I don't have to remind you how much of my own money I've invested into this."

She couldn't say a word.

"My darling," Alfred said, "you are the next domestic diva. I'll talk to you soon."

She hung up the phone, rolling her eyes and throwing herself backward into her pillows. She plopped her mother's diary onto the bedside table. A flurry of papers swooshed to the ground. Retrieving them, she flipped through a handful of articles that Alfred had clipped for her to use as inspiration. In between articles on "Feng Shui for Your Backyard Barbeque" and "I ♥ Vintage T-Shirts," she noticed the cookie bake-off rules from the competition in Indianapolis. She couldn't remember reading them the night before the event when she was mad at Wolfe and baking nine different kinds of cookies. That seemed like such a long time ago. In an effort to distract herself, she tracked her weary eyes over the fine print.

But her mind reeled with anger toward Alfred, who certainly didn't care about her feelings or concerns. All of his friendliness, had it been a setup to woo her? to trap her? Her fists clutched the papers.

He wanted a domestic diva? Then he was going to get one.

Wolfe sighed, hanging up the phone in the back room of the bookstore. It was busy. He'd been thinking of Ainsley all day, but he had been in charge of distributing stock onto the shelves and had not had an opportunity to call her. Now Martin was waiting at the front of the store for him, eager to go explore the secret map.

Wolfe shook his head and decided he couldn't delay Martin any longer. He'd have to call her again later tonight.

"Have a good evening, Wolfe," Mr. Bishop said with a wave as Wolfe left the store. He waved back and joined Martin on the sidewalk.

"Let's eat an early dinner, and I'll show you the map," Martin said.

After they'd ordered at The Mansion, Martin took the map out of his briefcase and laid it on the table. He turned it to face Wolfe.

"These are the five shacks I found," Martin said, pointing to their location on the map, indicated by a box.

"How far apart are they?"

"I'd say about a half-mile from each other."

"It's odd, they look like they're in a circle."

"I noticed that too," Martin said. "Probably coincidence."

"I don't know," Wolfe said. "It could mean something. What about this *X* here in the center? What was this?"

"Nothing from what I could tell. There was not a shack there."

"What is there?"

"I think just trees and brush."

"What have you ever heard about these shacks?"

Martin shook his head. "Nothing, really. We've talked about tearing them down, we don't want kids getting hurt. But for the most part, nobody seems to bother them."

The waitress brought their meals and Wolfe folded up the map. "As soon as we can, let's get up there. It's going to be hard to see in the dark."

"I brought flashlights."

Huffing and puffing her way up the small hill, Melb murmured her discontent with the owl. She'd tried everything. She'd read books at the library, hoping she was simply using the wrong dialect of owl. She'd spent hours owling softly, in order not to intimidate Mr. Sensitive. But nothing worked. The owl would not have her. And it was ticking her off.

Every book she'd read said that a little patience and a whole lot of hooting would get an owl to connect. But this owl was stubborn beyond belief. Well, he hadn't met stubborn.

She stomped up the last part of the hill and stood there, catching her breath. After a few moments, she listened.

*"Whoo. Whoo."*

Her brow furrowed. "Right back at ya, pal." She knew the owl was too far, so she kept walking, listening every so often to make sure she

was tracking in the right direction. "Mister owl, playing hard to get," she mumbled. "I hardly think I'm being aggressive enough for you to run like I'm dragging you to the altar."

She stopped once more and listened. She could hear the hooting and knew she was getting closer. Something told her tonight was going to be the night she heard that continuous hoot back…that connecting hoot.

"Come to mama." She smiled. Then she took one step forward, but the ground vanished, hurling her into nothingness.

## CHAPTER 29

THEY'D VISITED THE FIFTH SHACK, which was nearly identical to the first four. Wolfe looked around it as best he could, then joined Martin outside, who was on the lookout for anything strange.

"I didn't find anything," Wolfe sighed. "Do you have any idea how long the shacks have been around?"

"I'd say since the town was founded, which was 1870."

"They look about that old. You feel if you breathe hard they might collapse."

"Must've been built pretty sturdily to survive for this long."

"I'll say," Wolfe said. "Well, now what? Should we go explore what this *X* means?"

Martin looked south. "I know for sure there is nothing out there but trees. No buildings anyway. But I guess it's worth a try."

"If this map is accurate, I'd estimate we're looking at a half-mile walk due south."

"I'd agree."

"Let's go."

They turned on their flashlights and started walking.

Melb massaged her flesh for several seconds, assuming she was dead. But it sure hurt when she pinched herself. Debris and limbs and twigs covered her hair and face, and she coughed as she tried to loosen herself from the mess on top of her head. Looking up, she could see the night

sky and realized she was in a hole, about three feet wide and six feet deep.

"My heavens!" she exclaimed, trying to catch her breath. "How am I going to get out of this?"

She slowly stood up and to her relief realized the hole was not six feet deep, but only about four feet. Her shoulders were just above the edge of the hole. "What kind of beast would dig this kind of hole?" The word *grave* blew through her mind. Suddenly feeling very claustrophobic, she realized she was going to have to get out of this hole before she started hyperventilating. She braced one foot against the wall of the hole, but it slid down, the mud too slick to get a good foothold. Then her leg bumped up against something. She screamed, but then realized it didn't feel furry or slimy, so she was probably okay. Was it a log? She bent down, trying to feel it with her fingers. When she finally did reach it, to her surprise, it was metal. With more investigation by her hands, she realized it was a metal box. After three attempts, she managed to lift it up to about her chest, where it nearly knocked a new dimension into the side of the mud wall. It was very heavy but not too big, and straining like a weightlifter, she managed to lift it up out of the hole and set it on the ground. There, the moonlight illuminated it. A safe! With a lock!

She squealed in excitement. She didn't know why. But she did. Then, with dread, she realized she might have just taken out the only thing she could've stood on to lift herself out. But after several attempts, she managed to get a foothold into some tangled tree roots and lift herself out of the "grave." She knelt next to the silver safe, which glimmered in the moon's white beam. "A treasure," she whispered. "A buried treasure." She'd found a buried treasure! "Oh heavens!"

*"Whoo. Whoo."*

"Shoo, bird," she said and then tried to figure out a way to get the treasure chest down the hill.

Martin's legs were aching as he followed Wolfe, whose stride was twice as long as his. It seemed they'd been all over the hillside, and he felt only

disappointment they'd been unable to find anything of significance. He didn't really want to go find the invisible *X*. But Wolfe had been kind enough to come out here with him, so he didn't want to shoot down any ideas.

"Key still around your neck?" Martin asked.

Wolfe tapped his chest. "Got it right here, safe and sound. Hopefully we will find something that needs a key!"

"How much longer, you think?" Martin asked between bated breaths.

"I'd say not long now. Be on the lookout for anything strange. We could be near it and not know."

"Near what?"

"Whatever the *X* marks."

"Maybe it's just the center of the map."

"Maybe."

They continued walking, both men looking around them for anything significant. Then Wolfe stopped. "Wait." He held up a hand. "Did you hear that?"

"What?" Martin asked. All he could hear was an owl.

"Over there." Wolfe pointed to their left. "I think I heard something."

"Probably an animal," Martin said.

Wolfe shook his head. "It sounded more like…"

"Like?" Martin's skin shivered.

"C'mon," Wolfe said, walking in the direction he'd just pointed. Martin followed closely behind.

After they'd walked about thirty yards, Wolfe stopped and looked around. The trees hovered over the low fog, illuminated by the moon's light. Wolfe stood there with his hands on his hips, his face as serious and still as a bird dog's. Then his eyes focused on something. He squinted through the dark, took a couple of steps, and held up a finger indicating Martin should be silent.

"What?" Martin asked, ignoring the finger.

Wolfe pointed to something on the ground. Through the fog, all

Martin could see was brush, but of course he was half hiding behind Wolfe.

"What?" Martin asked again.

"That hole!" Wolfe whispered back. "See it?"

Martin peeked around Wolfe and saw it. It looked like a pretty large hole. "A grave?" Martin asked, his voice high like a little girl's.

Wolfe slowly walked forward, Martin hunkering behind him. When they came to it, Wolfe looked around carefully, then bent down. "It's huge," he observed.

Martin stepped aside so he could see it. "Not long enough to be a grave."

"Too deep. Look at all these broken limbs around here, and on the inside. Looks like it was covered at one time."

"What would a covered hole be doing all the way out here?"

"This is the $X$," Wolfe said. "Exactly where the $X$ is on the map." He pointed his flashlight down into the hole again. "Look!"

Martin flinched. "Shhh! What?"

"Down there," Wolfe whispered. "Footprints! Fresh footprints!"

Martin got on his knees and peered down into the hole. Sure enough, footprints. Large enough to be a man's, pressed a half inch into the muddy bottom.

"And look!" Wolfe aimed his flashlight at the sides of the hole. "How odd."

Two deep lines cut into the mud, going from the bottom all the way to the top, plus a handprint here and there.

"What do you suppose those lines are?" Martin asked.

"Looks like something was taken out of here by somebody," Wolfe said, standing and pointing his flashlight in every direction into the woods.

Martin could not calm his beating heart. Never in his life had he been on this kind of adventure.

Wolfe looked at him. "We've got to find out who's been out here and what they took."

Melb was pretty sure she didn't have asthma, but the way her lungs refused to squeeze adequate air in and out, she felt like it. Wheezing all the way into the house, she nearly dropped the safe on her toe twice before it came to rest in the middle of her living room. The house was dark. Oliver wouldn't be at her home until later. He'd called earlier to inform her he had something to do after work.

She switched on a single light, causing her parakeets to chirp a greeting, and stared at the safe. Heavy as it was, it was small, luckily, or she wouldn't have been able to move it. She figured it was about two feet on each side. From the sound of things inside, she had deduced that a pile of money was waiting for her.

She almost wept at the idea. Just days ago she had no idea how she would pay for her wedding. Now, not only was her entire wedding paid for, but she might've just found enough wealth for them to retire! She laughed out loud.

Then stared at the padlock.

The only thing standing in the way of all her dreams coming true was a heavy-duty padlock. Calling a locksmith was not an option. There was only one in Skary, and he was her half-cousin. Jimbo would ask too many questions and want a reward.

Any other locksmith would need proof, she assumed, that the safe was hers.

A small keyhole on the bottom looked as dark as the hole into which she'd fallen. She let go of the lock and sat on the couch, trying to get herself together. Excitement tingled every inch of her, but fear followed with the numbing realization that she had a big secret, and she didn't know exactly what to do with it. Her birds chirped, wondering why she hadn't greeted them.

She justified all this in two ways. First, the person who had this money probably was long dead and gone. And second, if not, he shouldn't have been stupid enough to bury his money in the woods.

There. Now that her conscience was clear, she could focus on how

she was going to get that padlock off. She went and grabbed a hammer. She drew back and with a steady hand, let the hammer fall on top of the lock.

It hardly budged. She tried this three more times, but the lock was too sturdy.

Then she heard Oliver's car pull up outside. Scrambling to her feet, she put the hammer up and ran back to the safe. Bending at her knees, not her waist, she lifted the safe with all her might and as fast as she could heaved it to the pantry, where she piled a bunch of stuff on top of it. She knew it was fairly secure there, for now. Oliver hardly ever went in the pantry because he couldn't stand the smell of garlic. In fact, at his own house, he didn't even own a spice other than salt or pepper. Covering it up as best as she could, she was just coming out of the pantry when she heard him opening the front door.

Oliver hated lying to his soon-to-be wife, but it was a little hard to explain that he was out scouting the suspected clones. Besides, this was dangerous work, and he didn't want her involved. He fumbled with the doorknob from lack of attention.

As he was doing this, he noticed muddy tracks leading all down the sidewalk and to the front door. He smiled. Melb's large feet, for sure. After several attempts, he got the door unlocked. Melb was in the kitchen, leaning on the counter in a very relaxed fashion.

"Hi there, good-looking," she smiled, but sounded out of breath.

"Hi. You okay?"

"Why?"

"You sound out of breath." He looked down, and mud was tracked all over the floor. "Melb, look at this muddy mess!"

Her eyes darted to the floor, and her excited expression turned grim. She opened her mouth to say something, but he cut her off. "I support your owling efforts, honey. I really do. But maybe you should take your shoes off before you come in."

She nodded and smiled. "Of course. Yes. Owling."

"How's that going, by the way?"

"I'm getting closer."

"Good." He grinned.

"How about something to eat? A sandwich?"

"That'd be terrific!" he said. As she got all the ingredients out of the fridge, he could not help but let his mind wander to what he'd seen today. Three times he'd witnessed the "clones" wandering around town, trying to infiltrate themselves as regular Skary citizens. One was shopping, though her behavior was anything but normal. She kept looking over her shoulder every few seconds. Another one sat drinking coffee, but in the darkest corner booth he could find, and from what Oliver could see, he wasn't there for the coffee. The whole time he kept looking around, out the window, as if he was expecting something to happen. And a third one, another male, was walking along the street when suddenly he screamed and ran down an alley. Oliver tried to chase him, but he was gone.

Melb handed him his sandwich. "So, anything exciting happen to you today?" She smiled.

He smiled back. "Nah."

"Me either."

## CHAPTER 30

AINSLEY HAD SPENT the evening busying herself, going back and forth between tasks for Melb's wedding and for hers. And crying. Wolfe still had not called. And she refused to call him. So she found herself alone.

Well, nearly alone. Her father poked his head in once to see what was for dinner.

"Pete's Steakhouse," she replied with a small smile.

"Gotcha. You okay?" He opened the door wider. Thief came bounding in and joined her on her bed.

"Yeah. Just stressed. I'm fine, though."

"Okay."

"Dad?"

"Yeah?"

"Was mom stressed before your wedding?"

He grinned. "Well, your mother was never one to show any signs of stress. That was the way back then, you know. You kept your emotions to yourself. These days everyone encourages emoting and going on and on about how you feel as if that's going to solve every problem in your life. So I don't really know. She seemed poised to me." He paused. "You want to talk about it?"

"Uh, no. Thanks. Have a good dinner."

She found herself staring at the phone more than once, hoping it would ring. She checked it twice, just to make sure there was a dial tone. Anger always did make her more productive, and by the end of the evening, she'd completed the food arrangement for Melb's wedding, and...well, nothing for hers. She hated to admit that her energy for

planning her own wedding was slowly deflating. She wondered if he still wanted to marry her. She wondered if Wolfe would ever be able to see her true heart again.

Wolfe couldn't believe how sore he was when he rolled out of bed. Goose and Bunny, eager to greet the morning air, nudged him down the stairs, where he opened the back door and let them out. He stretched his arms up with his usual morning yawn, but yelped instead. "Ah!" He was going to need a long, hot shower to knead the soreness out of these muscles. He poured himself a cup of coffee and went to the front window of his home. The morning sun, low against the horizon, had not yet covered up the night sky. A few stars, like pinpricks through dark fabric, glimmered to the west.

Even with all the excitement last night, his mind was on Ainsley. He desperately wanted to talk to her, but wasn't sure who he would be talking with. He longed for the Ainsley who wanted nothing more in life than to be his wife. But the new Ainsley did want more in life. Was that so bad? He sighed and stared into the beauty of the morning. He spent most Saturdays with Ainsley. He wondered about today. Would she have time for him?

Turning to his bookshelf, he studied the top, where all his books were lined up. Walking closer, he looked at each spine. He could remember holding each one in his hand for the first time. It never got old. He loved getting that first book. They always told him it was the first one off the press. He didn't know if that was true, but he believed it anyway.

He was realizing something dreadful, though. His mind was growing stagnant. For years it had been a playful child, eager to get up in the morning, eager to tackle the world. Had it grown out of that stage? Was it time to move on, mature? He shook his head at his heavy thoughts.

Life was so perplexing. A door closed. A window opened. All throughout life, closing doors, opening windows.

Deep inside his spirit, like a tiny fish engulfed between the mighty waters of the sea, he heard a voice whisper *patience.* He laughed. He thought his whole life he'd been a patient man. Now was he being tested?

"You mean, God," he said aloud, "that you're not going to deliver my answer to the front door?"

Just as he finished that sentence, to his surprise, someone knocked. Rushing over to the door, he hoped it was Ainsley. However, he found the reverend standing there, looking small and meek, hunched over with his coat buttoned up, trying to stay warm.

"Mind inviting a crazy man into your house?" he said with a smile.

"Reverend, come in! I've been thinking about you."

He took his coat and offered him coffee, but the reverend declined. Wolfe said, "You look thinner. Are you eating?"

"Enough to get me by," the reverend sighed. "I haven't had much of an appetite lately."

Wolfe joined the reverend in the living room. Through an appealing smile, Wolfe noticed his begging eyes. "I never questioned it, Wolfe. My whole life I thought I should be a pastor."

"You should be," Wolfe said emphatically. "What would I have done without you in my life?"

His eyes were glassy with tears. "I just don't know anymore."

"Know what?"

"I think it's over."

"You're thinking about quitting?"

He laughed a little. "I'm cleverly calling it retirement, so I don't feel quite as bad."

Wolfe stood. "Reverend, no! You can't!"

The reverend leaned back into the couch, looking Wolfe in the eyes. "All our lives we are molded, you know? By what our parents tell us about ourselves, what our classmates tell us, what everyone we come in contact with tells us. You'd think by my age I would understand who I am, but I'm not sure I do. I thought I was put on this earth to help

people, but I'm not helping anybody, Wolfe. All I'm doing is providing a place for people to go one morning of the week."

"But Reverend, you helped me. Isn't it all worth it if you've just helped one person?"

"Would one book have been enough?"

Wolfe sighed, then quietly said, "No."

The reverend smiled at him. "You're a good man. You weren't hard to change. You just needed a little direction. God did all the work anyway."

Wolfe joined him on the couch. "You know, perception is a funny thing. I always thought how lucky you were to know your calling."

"Don't you know yours?"

"I thought it was to be a writer. But now I don't know."

"Don't you still love to write?"

"I'm not sure. I thought it would never leave me, but I sit down to do it, and the passion is gone."

"Be patient, my friend," he said. A tingle slid down Wolfe's back.

"Patient."

"God will show you in due time."

"Who am I supposed to be until then?"

An amused expression lifted Reverend Peck's eyes. "Who are any of us without God? Lost souls."

"And with God?"

The reverend thought for a moment. "Souls with purpose, but sometimes without plans."

Wolfe smiled. "I hope I get my orders soon. Right now I'm reading romance novels at Booky's."

The reverend laughed. "Well, I guess you can see where I've landed." He shrugged. "I put all the pews back this week. And decided to stop the nonsense I created. But I don't have a thing to say anymore, Wolfe. So I'm starting with the first sermon I ever preached. Used sermons." He shook his head. "I've never preached a sermon twice in all my life."

Wolfe knew he couldn't say anything to help the reverend, but he

placed a hand on his shoulder. The reverend smiled in appreciation and said, "Well, at least I am looking forward to one thing."

"What's that?"

"Your wedding!"

Wolfe looked away.

## CHAPTER 31

"COME! ON! YOU! STUPID! PIECE! OF! SHINY! METAL!" As hard as she pried, though, the lock would not come loose.

Melb wanted to scream. For days she'd tried to open the safe, and without success. And as time passed, she was becoming more and more paranoid. She thought her life might even be in danger, if the owner of this money found out it was missing.

Plus, the way Oliver was acting these days, she wasn't sure if he knew she was hiding something or not. When he was around, his mind seemed occupied with everything but her. He'd start a sentence and then not even finish it, deciding instead to just stare into space.

She tried to convince herself that he just had a lot of wedding stuff on his mind. Four days until their wedding! She threw the pliers down and rested, smiling at the thought. She wasn't sure how much weight she'd lost, but she knew it was significant. She had one more appointment with Dr. Hass before the big day.

And she'd decided not to try the dress on until the day of the wedding. She knew she would become obsessed with trying it on to see if it would fit, and she thought this would be the perfect time to implement that faith thing Reverend Peck was always talking about. Walk by faith, not by sight. Her waistline said the dress wasn't going to fit. Her faith told her it would. And from that moment on, she began thinking of herself as a size 10/12 and not an inch bigger.

She was getting a lot of comments from people about the weight

she was losing, and each week she had to notch her belt one tighter to keep her pants up.

She also realized she had only four more days to bond with that owl. After the wedding, she'd have no need for a hobby anymore.

Shoving the safe to the back of her closet, she glanced at her watch. It was almost time to meet Oliver for church. As she dressed, she thought of how lovely it was going to be to tell him they were rich. She imagined the look on his face when she surprised him on their wedding day. Those eyes would twinkle. That little mouth would drop wide open. He would squeeze her tight and jump for joy!

She zipped up her dress, pulled on a pair of pantyhose that hadn't fit in four years, and whisked herself off to church where she hoped the sermon wasn't going to be about lying.

Wolfe saw Ainsley as he walked in, sitting in her favorite pew, looking through the bulletin. His heart skipped a beat, for several reasons. Her beauty always did something to him. He never grew tired of it. But also, the conflict that had arisen between them. They hadn't talked since Indianapolis.

"Throw down your pride, you mutt," he growled to himself. She was truly the woman of his dreams. Was he really ready to throw all that away? But she seemed so different these days.

"Hi," he said, approaching her.

She looked up at him. Her eyes cast a defensive look. She scooted over in the pew and let him sit.

Wolfe was just about to try to explain how he was feeling when a finger tapping on the back of his shoulder interrupted his thoughts.

They both turned to find Melb sitting behind them.

"Have you seen Oliver?"

"No, sorry," he said. Ainsley shook her head.

"Well, it's just that usually he's here very early. He likes to get his

favorite seat, you know, and it's almost time to start, and well, as you can see, I'm here alone."

"Don't worry, Melb," Ainsley said, "I'm sure he's just running late. Maybe making some last-minute wedding plans or something."

"No, he wouldn't be doing that. He was in charge of the honeymoon, and as you know from experience in working for him, Wolfe, he had that done weeks ago and under budget."

Wolfe nodded, detecting a tinge of bitterness. "Could he have overslept?" he asked.

"Ha!" Melb blurted. "Oliver? Oversleep? The last time that man overslept was at four months old."

Ainsley and Wolfe looked at each other, trying to decide how to make Melb feel better. But before they could say much more, Reverend Peck took the pulpit.

Bespeckled Douglas Brewer, at five foot seven, barely had enough meat on him to hold a T-shirt on. He'd gotten his thin frame from his mother, Agnes, and his poor eyesight from his father, Truman. What nobody ever could figure out, though, is from where Douglas Brewer got his temper. The shock that would come when it was even casually displayed was priceless, and over the years, Douglas had grown somewhat amused by this.

He didn't like it about himself, and could truly identify with the Hulk. A bad temper was nothing to brag about. But occasionally, it did come in handy. He'd not yet had a chance to save the world, but apparently he'd just saved his own life.

The balding man who called himself Oliver looked remarkably like a fish out of water, wide eyes, gasping for breath. Douglas knew the man was shocked. Douglas supposed he'd been picked because of his appearance and size. He'd noticed this man a few times over the past couple of days. And of course, everybody had now heard the rumors about Leroy.

"Don't have a heart attack. Sheesh." Douglas pushed his glasses up

his nose and shook his head. The rope Oliver had brought to tie him up now tied Oliver to an old water pump that stuck out of the ground. Without much trouble, Douglas had managed to pull the guy behind the local dump (though he was sure Oliver weighed twice as much as he did), careful not to drag him through the poison ivy he'd encountered a week ago. The misery of fighting fear *and* flesh was nearly indescribable.

Oliver, shiny from sweat, shaking like a hairless Chihuahua in winter, could do nothing but suck tiny drafts of air in rapid succession.

"What did you plan on doing here, mister?" Douglas said. He was normally not this bold. He had a conscience, after all. And really preferred computers over people. "What'd you bring that rope for?"

"A-a-are you from Kentucky?" was all Oliver said.

He was actually from Arkansas but had moved around so much that it was too complicated a question to get into right now.

"I've seen you following me," Douglas said. "And you come after me with this rope. I can't imagine what you'd planned to do with it."

Oliver's skin tone faded to putty. "D-don't kill me."

Douglas crossed his arms. Don't kill him? What kind of freak was this man? Had he planned on killing Douglas?

Douglas sighed, stepping back a few paces to think. Was it all worth it? Really? Couldn't he just live with his problems and deal with them? His mother had convinced him it was time to address the situation, especially with what happened several months ago at the zoo, which managed to embarrass his entire family, but in the end, did it really have to be this difficult? He glanced at Oliver, wondering what in the world this man was thinking.

He'd been told by Dr. Hass to integrate himself into this town's society and try to live normally among the things he feared, but the things he feared, which he could scarcely mention, didn't hold a candle to its citizens. Leroy knew that firsthand.

Douglas looked at his watch. He was late. Since getting the instructions to enter into society, Douglas decided why not try church? A few others had mentioned it too. There didn't seem to be too much else to do around here. He glanced at Oliver, who seemed to be holding his breath.

"I'll deal with you later," Douglas said. Thankfully, the man was wearing a wool coat and a stocking cap. He'd be okay for a little while. Maybe it would be good for him to sit here and think about what he'd done...or had attempted, anyway. Douglas tied a bandanna he had in his car around Oliver's mouth.

He started to walk off, but then turned and looked at Oliver. "I'm sorry I yelled at you," he said. "I shouldn't have done that, even though you were apparently trying to kidnap me. It's just that I have a temper, and sometimes things trigger it that just make me fly off the handle like a trapeze artist." Douglas shrugged. "The fact of the matter is that I have a lot of things wrong with me, and I suppose I should crawl off and die somewhere, but there's just that certain human instinct that makes you say to yourself, *I'm okay.*" Oliver's expression did nothing to make Douglas think he was tracking with him, so he turned, happy to have confessed his anger before going to church, and started walking away.

And for a few moments, he'd forgotten all about why he was in this town, altering his entire life to try to make it whole. Unfortunately, it didn't last. Walking to church, he found himself holding his breath and praying he wouldn't scream like a banshee.

At least he was praying.

Reverend Peck had dreaded this morning right up to the time he approached the pulpit. The idea of recycling his sermons was just so preposterous that he nearly felt ill. And of course the first sermon he ever preached was so bad that he could hardly preach it without some revisions, which did help him feel a little more useful.

It did bring back good memories, days filled with hope and faith. He had been young, feeling as though God would use him to conquer the world. It didn't occur to him until just a few years ago that not only had he not conquered the world, but he'd barely conquered a hillside. And from that point on, he likened his hope to a shriveled raisin. Once a beautiful, plump grape, food of kings. Now a fruit old people eat to

keep their bowels moving. It didn't have that Camelot-like notion he'd dreamed of years before.

He began his sermon as dryly as possible, with hardly an acknowledgment of a congregation seated out there. He read from his notes without much excitement. He really just wanted to be done with it.

But then he noticed something, as he'd glanced up at the congregation by pure accident and habit. New people. *New people.* Usually new people came only when there was a birth. Once he'd been lucky enough to have a member give birth to triplets. Then, of course, there was Thanksgiving, when the town looked as if it'd had a spark of renewal. But it faded as quickly as the smell of turkey the next day.

He picked out four, sitting there quite attentively. And then, to his surprise, another one walked in, a skinny guy who sat in the back. An unexpected fervor made him stand a little taller. And suddenly the lifeless words on the pages before him became something more than words. They translated themselves into a *message.*

Perhaps it was a corny idea for a sermon: loving people different from you. But back in his twenties, when so much hate transcended America because of differences, it made perfect sense. He remembered he'd preached to only a half-dozen people that day, but he thought if he reached them, maybe they'd reach a half a dozen more, and so on. Oh, those were the days, when nothing seemed impossible for God.

That same kind of restless hope now filled his words, and he realized that the congregation had begun to sit a little straighter, pay a little more attention, widen their eyes enough to take in the entire scene before them.

Pretty soon, charisma rang in his voice, and his eyes filled with the light of a dreamer. He looked at each individual, sure his words were meant just for them. He was on quite a roll, making his third point about nothing God created being an accident, when something very unexpected happened.

A woman he did not recognize on the fourth row raised her hand.

At first, Reverend Peck kept going. For not in all of his many years of preaching had anybody raised a hand. And he did not know what to do.

But she kept it high, flickering her fingers as if he had not seen her the first time. She was a mousy woman, with big glasses, stringy, oily hair, and a dress out of the seventies. And though he tried to continue, the distraction was more than his exuberance could ignore. His words trailed off as he stared at her.

Finally, clearing his throat of the rest of the words that were soon to follow, he said, "Um…yes?"

She stood up, an expectant, wide-eyed expression behind the glasses that nearly covered her whole face.

"Does that include cats?"

"What?" the reverend asked, amidst the many whispers that were now circulating the small sanctuary.

"Cats? Did God create cats, or did the devil?"

He could hardly believe his ears. For a moment he tried to concentrate, thinking maybe he was in a nursing home and having senile delusions. Is that what was happening? Was he really in a wheelchair, murmuring incoherently?

"I-I'm sorry. I didn't quite…"

"Cats. Did God make them, or did the devil?"

He focused his attention on this woman, and interestingly, the whole congregation seemed to be waiting on his answer. "Well, ma'am, God did."

"Huh." She folded her arms in front of her chest, deep in thought. But she was still standing, and he wondered if he should continue. But before he had any more of a chance to think, she said, "So does that mean we should accept the little critters, even though they're wicked rodents who deserve to be burned at the stake?"

The reverend made eye contact with Wolfe, trying to send him a signal that if anything bizarre happened—anything more bizarre than what was currently happening—Wolfe should stand up and help him out. Wolfe's eyes told him he was watching carefully. The reverend looked back at the woman.

"I know, I know," she said, holding up her hands to ward off the mumbling, "some people don't share my view. And I guess that's what

I'm getting here from your speech, is that I should like people who like cats, and I should try to like cats, the disgusting, pitchforked beasts that they are."

At this point, Reverend Peck, more than he had his entire life, wished God would just take him to heaven. A heart attack would be fine. A slight discomfort, but soon over. Here he was, trying to change the world, or at the very least forty people, and this woman wants to talk about cats? What on God's good green earth was he doing here? Wasting oxygen!

But then the woman said, "It's just that I've never heard anything like this before, and I've heard a lot of people talk and say a lot of things, sir. But your words…they're touching me right here." She pounded her fist against her chest so hard that he thought she might knock herself over. "Maybe that's been my whole problem all my life. Maybe I just didn't love them enough."

*Them* was not clearly identified, but nevertheless, Reverend Peck couldn't help but smile. And as he glanced across the congregation, he noticed they were smiling too. Whoever this woman was, whatever it was she didn't love but now thought she could love, she was transformed. Maybe it was a small transformation, but it was there. He looked at the woman, as directly as he could through the magnification her glasses provided, and said, "Ma'am, what is your name?"

She smiled. "Elsie Czychzyl."

Though he didn't understand the last name, and was pretty certain she'd not used a vowel when she'd said it (in fact, it sounded remarkably like a slot machine handle being pulled), he nodded and said, "Well, Elsie, I've got the rest of my sermon. How about I finish up here, and then you and I will visit afterward?"

Elsie's face shone like her hair, and she nodded, grinned, and then promptly sat down. Elsie What's-Her-Name had renewed his identity.

Dr. Hass sat in his living room, dusty from weeks of neglect, staring at his cat, Blot. Though he did love cats, he'd never owned one before,

mostly because of how often he moved. So he was slightly concerned at how quickly Blot seemed to be gaining weight. He'd been feeding her fancy cat food. After all, he could afford it at the rate he was making money these days. Perhaps the food was too rich? Whatever the case, her belly was ballooning like his bank account in the '80s, and he was pretty sure she was getting lazy. All she wanted to do was sit around and nap or meow. *Oh!* The meowing had become incessant.

He had not gone to church this morning. Too much on his mind. A little guilt, yes. But his thoughts were consumed with his new strategy, which was bold but perhaps not wise. Especially with the group of people he was dealing with.

So far, Oliver had not brought him a "catch," and he was beginning to worry he'd put too much strain on his subjects. Whatever the case, he was going to have to monitor very carefully. He was certainly taking a risk, one that he'd never expected. But he also believed he'd found the key.

So as patiently as he could, he sat and waited, watching his cat gain weight by the minute.

Though the church service was as bizarre as they came, not even that could distract Wolfe from the disappointment he felt in his relationship with Ainsley. Things were tense, and they were just getting worse.

Afterward, they walked together, but in silence. Ainsley seemed as though she wanted to talk, but her mouth was closed tightly in a straight line across her face. Wolfe didn't want to be the first one to speak.

Suddenly Martin rushed up next to them. "Wolfe!"

"Hi Martin," Wolfe said, then frowned. "What's wrong?"

"She woke up." Martin caught his breath. "Missy Peeple woke up."

## CHAPTER 32

DOUGLAS BREWER HAD decided he'd left this Oliver fellow out in the cold long enough, so with intimidation (he had to fake it since his temper had now faded), he'd moved him to his car and driven him twelve miles to the small hotel at which he was staying.

Once inside, he left his hands and ankles tied, but sat him on the comfy chair in the corner of the room. Undoing the bandanna, he watched as Oliver gasped for breath, staring up at him angrily.

"I have allergies!" the man shouted. "I could hardly breathe because my nose is stopped up, and you have that stupid thing tied around my mouth!"

Douglas observed him from a distance, folding the bandanna neatly in the palm of his hand. "Sorry."

Sniffling, Oliver looked away, noticing for a moment his surroundings before giving his attention back to Douglas. "You let me go, and you let me go now."

Douglas said, "Why would I let you go? You tried to kidnap me."

"I was taking you back to your owner, you idiot!" Oliver spat.

"My owner?"

"Yes! Whether you know it or not." Oliver said this with hesitancy in his eyes, unsure, Douglas assumed, of how he might react to that statement. Douglas didn't even know what it meant. "You need help," Oliver said softly.

"I need help?" Douglas laughed. "For what?"

"You may not even know it. That's the sad part. But I was simply

trying to help you. And, I'll admit, it was for selfish reasons. I wanted you folks out of town."

Douglas crossed his arms. "That's how small towns are. Never wanting to include people."

"Hey, that's a stereotype! We include all sorts of people. Just…just not people like you."

He could hardly believe his ears! People like him? Computer geeks? Is that what he was implying? Pushing his glasses up his nose, he managed to get his glare across. Oliver looked away.

"You know," Douglas said, "one day you'll be sorry. Because one day we're going to take over the world." It was a mantra he and his computer buddies always said for fun, but apparently Oliver didn't think it was funny, because he turned a shade whiter. "Settle down, dude," Douglas said. "First we have to get a date." Again, he laughed. He and his buddies could hack into the national defense system but couldn't get dates. They always thought that was funny. But Oliver flinched, blinking rapidly.

Douglas shook his head and sighed. He sat down on the edge of the bed. "What am I going to do with you?" he asked.

"Let me go?" Oliver offered meekly.

"With no consequence for your actions?" Douglas stated. "I don't think so."

"I'm going to call the police!" Oliver said.

Douglas thought this was strange for two reasons. One, Oliver was tied up. Two, that was exactly what Douglas was thinking about doing. But Dr. Hass had told him to keep a low profile, to stay out of trouble. He'd said he didn't want any "extra factors" involved. So maybe calling the police was a bad idea. And why would Oliver want to call the police? He'd just tried to kidnap somebody. How was he going to explain that?

The two men stared at each other, processing their own thoughts. Then Douglas said, "Well, I'm hungry. I'm ordering a pizza."

Wolfe had told Ainsley he would explain everything when he got back, then rushed to Martin's car. Driving eighty miles an hour, they got there in about thirty minutes. At her room, the same male nurse that had been there before noticed them walking down the hall and stopped.

"You two got here fast."

"Is she still awake?" Wolfe asked.

"Sort of. She's basically mumbling incoherently, though once she asked what day it was. I told her Sunday, and she cried."

"She cried?" Martin asked.

"Said she'd never missed a day of church."

Martin cocked an eyebrow. "You wouldn't know it from some of the things this lady has done."

The nurse looked as if he would love the juicy details behind that remark, but Wolfe said, "Come on. Let's get in there."

The men entered her room, and Missy Peeple didn't even acknowledge someone had opened the door. Her head was laid to the side, and she was staring out a small, lightless window. Martin glanced at Wolfe for reassurance, then went to her bedside. "Miss Peeple, it's Martin. Marty...Blarty."

She whispered something without turning her head. Martin looked at Wolfe as if to ask, *Did you catch that?* Wolfe shrugged.

"I'm sorry, Miss Peeple. Did you say something?"

Another whisper. Martin sighed and shook his head. He walked to the other side of the bed, but she seemed to stare right through him. She whispered again, and again Martin couldn't understand her.

"Lean closer," Wolfe urged, but he wasn't sure he would be able to muster up the courage to get that close to the woman. Martin's expression reflected the same sentiments, but after a few moments, he leaned in, putting his ear up to her lips. He stayed like that for several seconds, his brow lowering with each word she muttered. Finally, he raised up and looked at Wolfe.

"Well? What'd she say?"

Martin moved alongside the bed and joined Wolfe by the door. "I'm...I'm not sure."

"You're not sure? You didn't hear her?"

"No. I heard her. I just don't understand it. She said, 'May the Lord safely keep and restore you.'"

Wolfe frowned. "May the Lord safely keep and restore you?"

"That's what she said. Twice. The second time she said, 'Safely keep and restore you.'"

"What's that supposed to mean?"

"I don't know," Martin sighed. "It's a nice thing to say, but it doesn't make any sense. And as you and I both know, rarely does Miss Peeple say anything without some sort of agenda behind it."

Wolfe shivered at that thought, then looked at the old woman, tiny against the bed. What a different look she had without her hair slicked tight against her head. The deep line of age on her face had softened, and her hard eyes twinkled with sadness.

"Safely keep and restore you," Wolfe said aloud, trying to under-stand what that meant. Then, to his surprise, the old woman turned her head and, with a shaky arm, beckoned him over to her bed.

"Go ahead," Martin said, shoving him forward a little when Wolfe didn't budge. Swallowing deeply, one heavy foot after another, he made his way over. She stared right through him. "Um, yes?" he managed.

Then suddenly her eyes moved, startling Wolfe. She looked at him, then down at the middle of his chest. He wasn't sure what she was star-ing at until he looked down himself. The key! He'd put it around a chain to keep it safe. His buttoned up shirt revealed a tiny part of it before it disappeared behind the fabric.

"The key?" Wolfe asked, taking the chain out and holding it up for her to see.

She looked at it, then at him. "The key…," she whispered.

"I found it. In the book you gave me."

Her eyes grew wide. With labored breath, she said, "Then…then… you found the…" A hefty cough delayed her next words.

"The *X*? Yes, we found it." He cleared his throat. "How did you know to put it in a book?"

She spoke with great effort. "I knew a writer could never throw away his own book."

He looked at Martin, who'd casually moved up beside him. But Missy's sole focus was on Wolfe. Something passed through her eyes, a mysterious acknowledgment of some sort. Then she closed her eyes and seemed to fall asleep.

Wolfe rubbed his forehead furiously and turned to Martin, guiding him away from the bed. "That was bizarre," Wolfe said. "But now we know. This key goes to whatever was in that hole. I wish I'd had the chance to ask what was in that hole, though."

Martin shook his head. "Who else would know something is there? And why would they take it?"

"Whatever is in there is important," Wolfe said. He looked over at her, now in a restful slumber. "And she wanted me to find it."

"Then she had to have known you'd seen the map," Martin said.

"I don't know how. But she also wanted you to know about the map. You found it."

"That woman knows a lot of things. She always has. And nobody ever asked why. I guess everyone assumed it was her business to know."

Wolfe fingered the key. "Maybe it is."

Then Martin said, "I've got an idea."

The woman could wail. And she did. Ainsley tried her best to comfort Melb, but to no avail. The deputies that had accompanied her father to Oliver's house were getting a little irritated by this, and had finally thrown up their hands and told Sheriff Parker all they'd gotten out of her is that Oliver was missing.

Sheriff Parker walked across the room and addressed Melb. "Ms. Cornforth." She looked up at his voice, blotting her tears. "You're going to have to get yourself together, ma'am, if you want to help Oliver."

She nodded, an emotional gurgle causing her to choke. The sheriff

glanced at Ainsley. "I knew something was wrong," Melb said, drying her cheeks with a tissue. "When he didn't come to church. I knew it. I should've gone to check on him earlier."

"Let's focus on where he might be," the sheriff said. "Did he make any unusual comments, or tell you he was going somewhere? Maybe you've forgotten?"

"No. I saw him last night. He said he'd see me at church."

He jotted down notes. Deputy Kinard came over and said, "Sheriff, we've located his car on Main Street near the road to the junkyard. Nothing unusual about it. Locked up. Doesn't look like any foul play."

"Okay," the sheriff said. He then looked at Melb. "He probably got distracted somewhere. The fact that his car is still in town is a good sign. I'll have a couple of my guys roam around, see if we can't locate him, okay? I'm sure he's fine."

This brought a small smile to Melb's worn features.

"By the way, do you know of anyone who would want to hurt Oliver?"

The smile dropped into a line of dread across her face. "Hurt him?

"For any reason?"

She burst into tears and Ainsley rubbed her back, looking at her dad and shooing him away with her hand. He sighed and left the house.

"There, there," Ainsley said, and prayed her father would find Oliver soon.

Dr. Hass found himself whisked out of his house and down the front steps by these two rambling men: Martin Blarty, the town treasurer who'd brought the mayor in for a psychological examination, and Wolfe Boone, famous novelist who couldn't accept his fiancée's new plans. Both were babbling on about an old woman in a hospital who held the key to the town's crisis.

On the way there, at a West Coast pace of eighty miles an hour, the two were explaining that Missy Peeple, a Skary resident, seemed to

know more about this town than she had previously said. But now she was in this mildly demented state and not making much sense.

"At one point she said, 'May the Lord safely keep and restore you,'" Martin said, glancing in his rearview mirror at Dr. Hass, waiting for a reaction, so Dr. Hass stuck out his bottom lip as if examining the statement carefully. How was he supposed to know what an old woman's chattering was about? Maybe she was just trying to be nice on her deathbed.

"Do you think you'll be able to tell whether she's coherent or not?" Wolfe asked.

Dr. Hass rubbed his chin in a delicate manner. "Hard to say." Wolfe glanced back at him. "But I'll give it my best shot." Dr. Hass looked at the two men in the front seat, half contemplating whether he should jump from the car and make a run for it. Then he said, "What does this woman know?"

"That's what we're trying to find out," Martin said.

"The town depends on it?" he asked.

They exchanged glances before looking at him. "You're on a need-to-know basis," Martin finally said.

Oliver did not have an appetite for the pizza this man had offered him and was now gobbling down. He'd never seen a man so skinny consume a large pizza that fast. His mind raced with possible escape scenarios, but at the end of all that thinking, he really didn't have a plan, except to hope that Martin would find out he was missing and put two and two together. He was, after all, the only person who knew of Oliver's plan to nab one of the clones.

Oliver raised his eyes, ever so carefully, to study Douglas, as he called himself. So much of it made sense. Of course he was a clone. Skinny, probably had digestive problems due to the cloning. Strength that was really inhuman. How Oliver had ended up tied to a water pump he was not sure. All he knew was that this Douglas's face turned bright

red and the next thing he knew, the rope that had been *in* his hands was now *around* his hands.

Maybe the poor guy had no clue he was a clone. How would he know if no one told him? Oliver tried to think back on all the signs that Garth Twyne was involved in this. Really, there weren't any, except Miss Peeple's years of insistence that he'd cloned pigs. Why didn't anybody listen? Now here he was, staring at a clone in the flesh and blood.

Still, it was so hard to believe Garth Twyne the vet was smart enough for all this. The dumb lad had spent most of his time courting a woman he would never have, and then scheming to try to get her anyway. So, Oliver concluded, this Dr. Hass must be involved somehow. Oliver admitted that he did have a strange feeling around the man, as though there was something not quite right.

But enough of that. Oliver's immediate problem was how to get out of this predicament. And as he thought of this, an even more sickening thought overwhelmed him. Maybe Douglas was not planning on killing him. Maybe he was planning on *cloning* him!

"Ah!" Oliver shouted.

Douglas looked up, in the middle of licking all his fingers. "You okay?"

"I'm...uh... Can you please tell me what you're planning on doing with me?"

Douglas stood, throwing the napkin he hadn't bothered using into the pizza box that sat on the bed. "Well, why don't you tell me what you were planning on doing with me?"

Oliver bit his lip. How much should he say? Would it cause him to be in more danger?

"Earlier," Douglas said, "you mentioned my 'owner.' What in the world did you mean by that?"

Oliver swallowed. "Nothing."

Douglas took a step closer to him, his small eyes narrow with determination. "Oh yeah? You want to reconsider that answer?"

"Okay, okay," Oliver blurted. "It's exactly what I said. Your owner told me he'd pay me a hundred and fifty dollars to bring you to him."

"What owner?! You're acting like I'm a dog!"

Oliver formed his words carefully. "What exactly are you?"

Douglas put his hands on his hips. "What exactly do I look like?"

Oliver said, "Out of curiosity, do you look exactly like the one you came from?"

Douglas shook his head. "What in the Hellmann's Mayonnaise are you talking about?"

"You don't know, do you?" Oliver said sadly.

"Know what?"

Oliver sighed and realized the only way of potentially getting out of this was to tell the guy the truth. He gathered his thoughts before speaking. "There is one before you."

"One before me?"

"Maybe more. But I suspect one."

"One what?"

"Man. The man you came from."

"My father?"

"Oh, is that what they call it? Is that what they told you? He's your father? You poor fool," Oliver sighed.

Douglas laughed, shaking his head and staring at the ceiling. "You know, I have to say, this is the most wacked-out, dripping-with-crazy town I have ever seen in my whole life. I mean, you travel cross-country, you go through these small towns, and you think, What kind of people could live in such a small town? And now I know. Crazies! Crazy lunatics!"

"I'm sure they brainwashed you," Oliver said calmly. He didn't want to upset the guy any more. "But take a look at yourself. I mean, ask some hard questions, sir."

"Hard questions?" Douglas asked, amusement lighting up his features. "Like what hard questions?"

"Well, I mean, have you noticed that the other people in this town don't suddenly scream for no reason? Just out of the blue. Look, I don't hold that against you. It's probably just a glitch from the cloning process—"

"Cloning process?!" Douglas laughed, yet his eyes registered nothing but bewilderment.

"And why do you wander around the woods at night? Looking like the walking dead? You see, it's not your fault, I'm not blaming you, but these are simply not normal, everyday behaviors of a human being."

Douglas stared at Oliver, laughed, stared some more, and then his laugh faded. "What exactly are you saying here?"

Oliver lifted his head with courage. "Douglas, I don't know how else to tell you this, but you're a clone."

"I'm a clone."

"Yes. And we're not a prejudiced town, you should know that, but I just don't think we're a good fit for you. You and your buddies might try someplace like New Orleans. You'd fit right in."

Douglas was laughing hard. "You think I'm a clone?"

"It's okay, I know this is going to take a while to sink in. I should've known Dr. Hass didn't tell you."

Douglas stopped laughing. "Dr. Hass?"

"Yes, your owner. Dr. Hass."

"My owner?" Douglas shook his head. "Wait a minute, wait a minute. I think there's been a big, big, big misunderstanding here."

Oliver tried not to look disappointed. He supposed if he were a clone, it would be hard to accept. Douglas had a very serious look on his face.

"You okay?" Oliver asked, trying to be sensitive.

"You said that Dr. Hass paid you to kidnap me?"

Oliver nodded. "We sort of had a deal. If I kidnapped you, he'd make sure you wouldn't return to this town."

And then Oliver's heart stopped. Because Douglas's face was turning bright red.

"Hmmm. Huh. Mmmmm." Dr. Hass leaned over the old woman, holding his breath as he did so. But the mothball smell still penetrated his nostrils, so he tried not to make ugly gagging noises.

"Safely keep and restore you," she mumbled. By the expression on Wolfe's face, this was supposed to mean something. What in the world was he supposed to say?

"She's crazy," he finally announced. "Certifiable. *Loco y loco.* Howard Hughes's sister." The two men stared at him. He tried to act casual. "It happens with old age, you know. What is this lady? About a hundred?"

Wolfe stepped forward, crossing his arms. "How can you tell she's crazy just by looking at her?"

"Well, do you know what 'safely keep and restore you' means?"

Wolfe shook his head.

"Well, then, I would conclude she's senile."

Martin said, "Don't you need to do some more tests? And isn't there anything we can do to bring her out of it?"

Dr. Hass said, "Well, you can always try a mixture of lemonade and vodka."

"Excuse me?" Wolfe said, his face stern.

"Look," Dr. Hass said when nobody laughed at his joke, "the mind is a delicate thing. What did you expect? I was going to come in here and wave a magic wand, making it all better?"

Martin sighed. "I'm sorry, Doctor. We're putting too much pressure on you."

"Psychology is as much common sense as it is medicine. I've proved that over and over again."

"Where did you say your degree is from again?" Wolfe asked.

Dr. Hass stared into Wolfe's engaging eyes and said with a confident smile, "Life, Wolfe. The same place you got yours."

## CHAPTER 33

THEY DROPPED DR. HASS back at his home office and headed toward Wolfe's house. "Don't you think there is just something off about that guy?"

Martin shrugged. "I guess."

"I didn't see any diplomas in his office. Strike you as odd?"

"Well, he did just get to town. Maybe he hasn't put them up yet." Martin glanced at Wolfe. "Maybe we were expecting too much out of him at the hospital, like I said."

"It's not what he didn't say, but what he did say," Wolfe began but then noticed something peculiar. "Martin, look at that!"

Three police cars were parked in front of Melb Cornforth's house. "Pull over!" Martin said and hastily exited the car. Wolfe followed.

When they got inside, Melb was sitting on her couch, crying, Ainsley's arms draped around her. "Wolfe!" Ainsley said, jumping up and rushing to him. "I'm so glad you're here."

"What's going on?"

"Oliver's missing," Melb said between sobs.

"Missing?"

Ainsley nodded. "He didn't show up for church. They found his car near Main Street but haven't found Oliver yet." She looked at Melb. "They'll find him, Melb."

Suddenly Deputy Bledsoe rushed in, looking for the sheriff, who was just stepping out of the bathroom. "Sir, we found Oliver's stocking cap."

The sheriff's eyes lit up with annoyance as he glanced around the room, realizing everyone had just heard that, including Melb, who was

whimpering with the visible effort to control herself. Deputy Bledsoe didn't seem to notice.

"Behind the junkyard, near a water pump."

The room grew silent as the sheriff rubbed his brow. "I don't understand this. We've never had a kidnapping in this town," he muttered.

Suddenly Martin was pulling Wolfe alongside him, up to the sheriff. "Sir, we need to talk. Outside."

Dr. Hass was not one for taking long walks, but since he didn't have a car this was his only option. He'd probably walked a mile, careful to track where he was going so he wouldn't be lost in the backwoods of Indiana forever, when he finally decided to give some thought to his life. Truthfully, it wasn't something he did much. But being around crazy people tended to make one reflect. He wasn't sure why. Maybe it was fear of turning out like them.

He was certainly shocked by what he'd found in small-town America. There was a sense of community, albeit an unhealthy one, from what he could see. Back home, people didn't care about anybody else's business unless it would somehow help theirs. Here, everybody cared about everyone else's business, even if it hurt theirs. Strange.

Yet with all the unexpected dysfunction, he couldn't help notice the tremendous loyalty—the care—that everyone displayed. In the circles he ran with, everyone was too busy searching for themselves to notice anybody else existed. Here, sure, there seemed to be a real lack of self-awareness, but that was nearly transcended by the thoughtfulness. Who in the world cared if the mayor of your town went nuts? In his old life, that would be considered scandal worthy of the front page. Here, he was a protected citizen.

Dr. Hass continued to walk.

It was true that though he'd moved halfway across the United States to explore new cheese, he had been experiencing the strange realization that the part of him he'd wanted to leave behind had indeed followed

him. He'd no sooner driven into the town limits when his other half had joined him.

Sighing, he looked at the beautiful pines. The woods that surrounded this tiny town nearly seemed to envelop it with their beauty. He walked the trail in the woods, bundled in his coat, scarf double-wrapped around his neck, listening to the most enjoyable silence.

But he knew with silence would come thoughts prompted by conscience. For so long he'd surrounded himself with the noisy chaos of big cities—that way he would never have to listen to himself, at least with his heart engaged.

Now, though, it whispered to him, as softly as the sound of snow being blown across the hillside. He closed his eyes and stood still, trying to understand what it was about himself that he never liked. He was always trying to be somebody else, never confident enough to own up to who he'd been born as.

He'd had a loving mother, though she'd had poor judgment on many things, like naming him after his father, who he'd turned out to be exactly like. He'd been a creative child, innovative in such a way that his teachers always liked him. So how did he end up like this?

*"Whoo."*

Dr. Hass looked up into the sky. The clouds moved so fast it made him dizzy.

*"Whoo. Whoo."*

He smiled a little.

"I have no idea."

Sheriff Parker's foot tapped furiously against the cement sidewalk they all stood on. Martin kept glancing at Wolfe, as if to ask him for some help, but Wolfe could do nothing but stare in disbelief.

*"Cloning?"* the sheriff whispered harshly, though all the others were still inside.

"I know it sounds crazy," Martin said. "But I'm telling you, I believe it."

"Martin," Wolfe said. "That's crazy!"

"I know it is," Martin said. "But you didn't see the guy Oliver got. He really was something else to look at." Martin stared hard at the sheriff. "And you know the rumors that have run around this town for years now."

"They're rumors, Martin," the sheriff said.

"Then how do you explain all the crazy people walking around this town? Huh? Screaming at all hours of the night? Suddenly coming into our town, trying to fit in?"

The sheriff stared at his feet. "I'll admit, I haven't been too engaged because of Thief's ordeal and all. I figured if they weren't breaking the law, they weren't my concern."

"Four of them were at church this morning," Wolfe offered, though he didn't really know what that meant or how it might help the situation.

"So you're saying Oliver kidnapped one of these people, he got away, and this Dr. Hass offered Oliver money to kidnap the rest of them."

"And he assured Oliver he'd 'take care of them,' which Oliver understood to mean keep them out of our town…by whatever means possible." Martin's eyes shifted back and forth between the sheriff and Wolfe.

"What would a psychologist want with a bunch of clones?"

Wolfe laughed out loud. "Folks, they're not clones!"

Neither of the men acknowledged him.

"I have a theory that Dr. Hass might be involved in this…with Garth."

Wolfe laughed…again unnoticed by the two other men.

Martin continued, first glancing back at Melb's house. "And I'll tell you something else. I think Melb's been cloned."

Wolfe threw up his hands, though he really couldn't wait for this bizarre explanation.

"Melb?" the sheriff asked.

"I haven't had the heart to tell Oliver, but I've seen her, Sheriff. Out in the woods in the middle of the night!"

The sheriff's eyes were widening.

"And has anyone but me noticed how much thinner this 'new' Melb is? Doesn't that make sense? If you're cloned, you'd be thinner?"

Wolfe narrowed his eyes, looking hard at Martin. "And how exactly does that make sense, Martin?"

But Martin didn't have a chance to answer, because the sheriff said, "Let's go find us a Dr. Hass."

With the house surrounded, and guns pulled in a showdown-like setting worthy of Clint Eastwood, everyone was quite disappointed when Dr. Hass was not home.

"Now what?" Kinard sighed, placing his unloaded pistol back in its holster.

Sheriff Parker thought for a moment. "Kinard, you stay here, wait for the doctor. Everyone else, over to Garth's place."

Wolfe stood there and watched Martin follow the rest of the deputies. He slapped his hands over his face and shook his head. Surely they didn't believe this nonsense!

Just as in his book, in the end, everything had an explanation. Wolfe sighed. Well, while the rest of the town chased phantom clones, Wolfe was going to find out what the key around his neck belonged to.

Martin couldn't quite decipher what was going through Garth Twyne's little head. Garth stood in a small operating room, surrounded by the cohorts, white as a ghost. And there was an unconscious cat on the table everybody kept eying.

Martin thought the sheriff might repeat his demand, since Garth wasn't inclined to say anything.

And he did. "Well?" the sheriff said. "Are you involved in this or not?"

Garth's skinny frame trembled as he shook his head.

"So you're trying to tell me you have no idea what this cloning business is about?" the sheriff said, his arms folded authoritatively. Martin decided to fold his own arms.

Garth frowned. "Did Missy Peeple put you up to this?" he asked. "First it was pigs, now people?"

"Oliver Stepaphanolopolis is missing, Garth, and if you know something about it, you'd better speak up."

"You actually think I'm cloning people?" Garth asked, trying to show a confident smile but looking more like he was about to be sick.

"I don't know what to think," Sheriff Parker said. "All I know is that I have a citizen missing, a bunch of weird people walking around, and the doctor I think is mostly responsible for this is now AWOL. Give him up, and your punishment could be less severe."

"Who up?"

"Don't pretend you don't know Dr. Hass."

"I don't know Dr. Hass."

Martin thought he was doing a pretty good job of pretending.

"See? That's just the sort of thing I'm talking about," the sheriff sighed.

"You know me!" Garth protested. "Since I was a little kid!"

"True."

"Then don't you think I would be the kind of person who would brag about this sort of thing?"

The crowd in the room sort of agreed on that point.

"Unless the money was right," the sheriff said suddenly, and then everyone was back to agreeing with the sheriff.

"Do I look like I have a lot of money?" Garth said, and the room quickly scanned his tattered khakis, flannel shirt, and stained doctor's robe. He looked the sheriff in the eyes. "If I had a lot of money, I'd have bought Ainsley the kind of ring she deserved."

The sheriff sighed and said, "Enough about your dating woes, Garth. I'm going to get to the bottom of this, and if you're not going to

help me, that's your choice. But if in the end you are involved with this in any way, I suggest you get your business in order, because you're going to be spending a lot of time in a cellblock the size of a cat carrier."

Garth licked his lips but didn't seem to have too much more to say.

The sheriff leaned in, and so did everybody else, just to hear what he was going to say. "Garth, you had better remember one important thing: I'm a tough cookie."

And then the cat on the table meowed, and everyone screamed like sissies, including the sheriff who had nearly hopped into Deputy Kinard's arms. A small, satisfied smirk quickly appeared on Garth's lips. "Amnesia must've worn off," Garth said casually.

The sheriff adjusted his shirt and plopped his hat back on his head. "I'll be back," he said, pointing a shaky finger at Garth. "I'll be back."

Oliver had never been one for electronics, but sitting in the middle of the seedy motel room, he sort of wished he had one of those fancy phones that takes video, because never in a million years would anybody believe what he was hearing.

All around him were clones.

"So can you believe this?" the one that called himself Douglas said, after explaining the whole kidnapping plot.

The other seven shook their heads. One said, "I wondered what happened to Leroy!"

"That Dr. Hass, he's sick! Crazy!" Douglas's finger traced circles in the air beside his ear, and someone let out a long whistle for emphasis. "None of us knew what we were getting ourselves into, but now's the time to get ourselves out."

"Wait a minute," one lady said, standing up. "I spent a lot of money with this guy. And my problem ain't solved. I ain't leaving town until I get my money back!"

And the room erupted in rowdiness. Oliver held his breath. He hoped their aggression wasn't about to turn on him. After all, he'd deliv-

ered the truth. He sat there wondering what kind of problem they were talking about. That they didn't have souls?

Douglas hushed the crowd. "I don't know about the rest of you, but these past few weeks have been the worst of my life." Emphatic nods indicated it was true for everyone. "I swear I don't even know who I am anymore!"

Tears sprang to Oliver's eyes. What a sad life to find you aren't who you think you are, and that you're just a cheap copy of someone else. Oliver had been through hard times in his life but had always known who he was. He guessed it was partly because he had two doting parents who always took him to church. These people, if you could call them that, had nothing of the sort. Probably raised on a cloning farm somewhere in east Indiana, now thrown into the world to try to make a living. But can one really live without an identity? Oliver knew from experience it wasn't making a living that caused one to have an identity. It was a deep reassurance that came from the inside…a reassurance that there are no accidents and…he sighed…that you are one of a kind.

He glanced up and noticed everyone staring at him. He also noticed that he'd been crying a little louder than he'd thought.

"Oliver, we're not going to kill you," Douglas said with exasperation.

"I know," he said. "I'm not scared."

"Then why you sheddin' tears like a rain forest?" one woman said. She had a heavy accent and big glasses. *And bad metaphors,* thought Oliver.

He looked at all of them. "I just feel for you, that's all."

The lady said, "Well, you should. It's an awful thing that happened to us."

Oliver nodded. "I'll say." He sniffled. "I'd say I'd be praying for your souls, but…" He couldn't finish his sentence. The poor people didn't have souls to pray for.

Douglas shrugged when everyone looked at him. "See what I've been dealing with all day?"

Oliver said, "You just seem like such kind people, and I know it's hard having this problem. It's as big of a problem as anything I've ever

seen, frankly. But I want you to know, if I weren't so freaked out by all of this, I'd try to lend a helping hand."

Douglas, somewhat moved by Oliver's strange compassion, glanced around the room and then said, "Well, thank you, Oliver. But I don't think you can help. Many of us have been trying to get help for years, and this was sort of a last resort. Now we've been double-crossed, and that has just made things worse."

"But we'll get ours!" someone shouted, and the room was rowdy again. Oliver sighed. Well, at least he wasn't going to die. Now his best hope was to not get cloned.

## CHAPTER 34

DR. HASS HAD once seen a movie called *Breakdown* where a wife was kidnapped by a group of truckers who held her for ransom. The idea behind the movie was to cast suspicion on what kind of odd people might populate rural towns. He'd thought the idea was somewhat corny.

Until now.

As he sat in a small jail cell in the middle of Skary, Indiana, Dr. Hass had thought he'd seen it all. But he hadn't.

The sheriff, who had once heartily thanked him for curing his depressed cat, now was interrogating him.

It had been odd. The sheriff had asked him if he wanted to confess. And Dr. Hass thought about that. He knew confession was good for the soul. And after all, he'd spent a lifetime going from place to place, living really no kind of life at all, though at times he'd had everything a man needed to make him happy. But he never really was happy. And he learned, in the end, he always lost it all. Despite how much sense that whole cheese analogy made.

So in the middle of a place called Skary, Dr. Hass thought it might just be very appropriate to confess. For years he'd been able to avoid the law. By one fluke or another, he'd worked it out.

But now, things did seem rather dire. He'd been just about ready to confess, nearly opening his mouth to do so, when the sheriff said, "You been cloning people, mister?"

And that was when the movie *Breakdown* had flashed through his mind, and when he got really worried. He didn't have an opportunity

to say much more, because the sheriff then spouted off a whole bunch of evidence about why they thought he'd been cloning people, and that he was in with some vet named Garth. This amused Dr. Hass, since he'd been a vet for three months.

Anyway, he didn't really know what to say, especially since they all seemed to have their minds made up. In a town like this, he decided it wasn't going to do much good to ask for a lawyer, since he was probably part of the whole weird mix. Besides, he'd been a lawyer once, and he knew what to ask and what not to ask. So instead, he asked to see Reverend Peck. This brought an amused reaction from everyone standing outside his jail cell. And off they went to get Reverend Peck.

So now a lone deputy watched his cell, slumped over in the chair, half asleep. The sheriff's cat had taken a strange interest in him, soliciting looks and rubbing up against the bars of the cell as if he would like an invitation in. Dr. Hass wasn't sure why the cat liked him, but he was glad somebody in this town did.

Melb had excused herself from the crowd in her living room, going to the bedroom and shutting the door. Inside her closet, she moved the clothes that covered the metal safe.

"Ohhhh, Oliver," she moaned. "Is this the reason something has happened to you?"

Through her tears, she stared at the lock she had not succeeded in breaking. Her mind bounced from telling the authorities of the treasure she'd found to the hopes it would help bring Oliver home to making the mistake of confessing about it only to find it was not connected to Oliver's disappearance. She bawled like a baby at having to make the decision.

Something else muttered at her heart. That Oliver had gotten cold feet. That Oliver had decided not to marry her. That Oliver had run for the hills.

And if that was true, she was going to need every cent that was inside this box.

Melb steeled herself, gathered up all the clothes she now couldn't wear due to her tremendous weight loss, and plopped them on top of the safe. Then she stood and wiped her tears.

If Oliver wouldn't have her, she thought with her nose high in the air, perhaps the delightful but annoying Dr. Hass would. After all, something about his magical words had made the impossible possible.

She stared down at her waistline. Oliver or no Oliver, she was going to fit into that wedding dress!

Reverend Peck, escorted by a deputy and Sheriff Parker, arrived at the jail. Reverend Peck did not know what to expect. It seemed to him it was Sheriff Parker and the gang that had lost their minds. But according to them, Dr. Hass was the mad scientist, a "cloning doctor" who was using their town as bait. As they were walking up to the jail, after the deputy was out of earshot, the sheriff added, "And we believe they may have taken Melb."

"Melb Cornforth?"

"Yes. The person we've been calling Melb might be her clone," the sheriff whispered.

And Reverend Peck thought *he* was having a midlife crisis.

Once inside, the sheriff instructed Reverend Peck to be at the very least coy. "I'm not expecting you to be a professional interrogator," he said, "but try to get a confession out of him. You're a pastor. People like to confess to pastors."

The reverend glanced at the sheriff. "So you're expecting something like, 'I've been cloning people for years. You finally caught me'?"

The sheriff smiled. "Something like that."

A deputy led the reverend back to the holding area. In the fourth cell down, he could see Dr. Hass sitting on his cot with nothing to do but stare at the sheriff's cat that was pacing outside the bars.

Dr. Hass's face lit up when he saw him and he stood. The deputy unlocked the door and the reverend entered. So did Thief.

"Thief, not so fast," the deputy said, swooping the cat up and carrying him outside. "Ten minutes, gentlemen."

Dr. Hass sat back down on the cot. "Thank you for coming."

Reverend Peck stood by the door. "This is pretty odd. What are you in for again?"

"Cloning."

"Cloning." The reverend shook his head. "So...that's kind of different."

"Yeah," Dr. Hass said with a smile. "Never been accused of that before." He laughed, but his face was tinged with sadness.

The reverend leaned forward, placing his elbows on his knees and clasping his hands together, giving his full attention to Dr. Hass. "Well, I suppose there is a reason you wanted me to come today, isn't there?"

Dr. Hass nodded somberly.

"Is there something you want to tell me?"

Dr. Hass nodded again.

"Something hard?"

"Yes."

Reverend Peck swallowed. He'd seen a lot of things in his years in the pastorate, but if this man confessed to cloning, that might be enough to do him in. "Go ahead," he said, his heart thumping against his chest.

Dr. Hass looked up at him, looked down at the floor, glanced up at him again, sighed, bit his fingernail, ran his fingers through his hair, winced, chewed his lip, and then looked very distant.

"Take your time," the reverend said, morbid anticipation about to eat him alive.

After a few more minutes of silence, the reverend couldn't imagine what this man was about to tell him. So he said, "Dr. Hass, let's start with something simple."

"Okay."

"You know, I must confess something myself."

"Oh?"

The reverend smiled warmly. "I don't even know your first name."

"Oh." Dr. Hass sighed and stared at the cement again. "Well, that's not simple either."

"But it's a start, right?"

Dr. Hass sighed. "Yes, it's a start."

"Okay, well, go ahead. Tell me your first name."

"It's Jack."

"Jack. There you go. Jack!" The reverend said heartily. But then he frowned. "Your...your...um... Your name is...Jack..." The reverend cleared his throat. *"Jack Hass?"*

Dr. Hass shrugged. "Let's just say I've spent a lifetime living up to my name."

Ainsley had finally gotten Melb to lie down for a while. In the kitchen, she leaned against the counter, pinching her eyes closed to try to hold in the tears.

So much was happening, and never in her life had she felt more overwhelmed. She was trying to stay strong for Melb, trying not to think of the many implications attached to Oliver's disappearance. Yet there was nothing else on her mind. Melb was devastated, even hinting of her fears that he had left her.

Someone knocked at Melb's front door, so she went to answer it, hoping it was Wolfe. Instead, Alfred stood there grinning.

"Ainsley, my dear, you have been a hard woman to track down!"

"Alfred," she breathed, trying to muster up a smile. She couldn't. "What are you doing here?"

"We were supposed to meet this afternoon, remember? Talk about final design?"

Ainsley stared through Alfred. "Oh..."

"Hello? Anybody in there?"

She looked at him. "I'm sorry. Something came up."

"Hmm. Well, looks like you're free now, so why don't we—"

Ainsley lost it. Tears streamed down her cheeks. "I'm not free,

Alfred! Okay? Something terrible has happened, and I'm trying to help my friend!"

"Oh," he said. "I'm sorry. What's wrong?"

"Oliver is missing!" she cried.

"Missing? The Oliver of the Melb and Oliver wedding?"

"Yes," she said. "That Oliver."

Alfred practically shoved his way inside the house, closing the door behind him. "Ainsley, this is not good!"

She blinked through her tears.

"We have to have a groom! The whole show is centered around a wedding!"

"Alfred, that is the least of my concerns right now," she sniffled.

"Well, it's my first concern," he said gravely. "I have sunk a lot of money into this, Ainsley, and I am not going to let it just fall apart four days before it's supposed to take place."

She went to the kitchen, her trembling hands trying to grab a glass to get a drink of water. "I don't know what to tell you."

He sighed. "Keep me posted, please."

"Fine, I'll keep you posted." She felt so incredibly fatigued at that moment the room spun around her, and she quickly slid onto a barstool to steady herself.

He walked to the door, smoothing out his expensive coat and pulling on his leather gloves. "Ainsley, are you up for all of this?"

She managed to look at him. "Up for all of what, Alfred?"

"When you hit it this big, things get really difficult. You hit problems, and you deal with them. I know that sounds hard-core, but it's the way it works."

"We're talking about a human being missing here, Alfred. I'd say that's more than a problem." And add to that the fact that she and Wolfe were hardly speaking.

"It's a problem like any other problem."

"Does it take a cold heart to get to the top?" She could not help but glare at him.

"Of course not," he said, his charming smile returning. "Just a brave one."

And with that, he left. She put her head on the counter and shut her eyes.

Oliver was not privy to the plans the eight were making concerning Dr. Hass, which suited him fine, to tell the truth. The motel room door opened suddenly, and he gasped.

Douglas entered, looking around the room for something, barely acknowledging Oliver. "Okay," he finally said. "Come with us." He took Oliver's elbow, pulled him out of the chair, and guided him firmly out the door. The rest of the clones stood gawking at him.

Oliver was so terribly frightened he wanted to scream. But they screamed, and he thought maybe that was some odd sort of ritual or something, so he thought it better to keep his mouth shut.

"We're traveling in two cars," Douglas said, to nobody in particular, and then they split up in two groups. Douglas took Oliver.

In about fifteen minutes, they were in front of Dr. Hass's house. Oliver wanted to stay in the car, but instead he was pushed out the side and led up the sidewalk. Douglas knocked on the screen door, with everyone behind him. He glanced at Oliver. "You better fess up, Oliver," he said. "That's the only way we're going to get this guy, you understand me?"

Douglas knocked again, but again there was no answer.

"*Hey! Hass!* We know you're in there!" Douglas yelled, scaring Oliver half to death. He then yanked open the door and marched inside. After a few minutes, he returned. "Nobody's there, except a really fat cat."

Suddenly he frowned, a deep, anxious frown. And so did everyone around Oliver. They were looking at one another with complete astonishment, exchanging emotions that he could not understand.

Douglas shook off the moment and looked at an older woman who had approached. "You looking for the fella who lives here?" she said.

Douglas nodded.

"Took him to jail earlier." She pointed in the direction of Main Street.

"Thank you," Douglas said, then looked at the others. "Let's go."

Reverend Peck could hardly believe what he was hearing. Dr. Hass was talking a mile a minute, and though he had not confessed to cloning, he'd confessed to nearly everything else under the sun.

He'd been married a number of times, had been bankrupt twice, and was in the middle of telling Reverend Peck of the twenty-year drug habit he'd kicked a decade ago, when a bunch of people came into the jail. The two men could hear their voices echoing through the corridors.

"Stop!" That was Sheriff Parker's voice. "Oliver?"

"Stay back," came another voice, unfamiliar. "I said stay back!"

"Oliver, are you hurt?" asked the sheriff.

"I'm fine. Do what he says though, okay?" Oliver said.

Reverend Peck was very confused about what was going on as he and Dr. Hass stood at the cell bars.

"We're here to see Dr. Hass!" the voice said, and then a bunch of people agreed.

Reverend Peck looked at him. Dr. Hass was shaking his head. "Oh no," he said with evident dread.

The reverend didn't have time to ask questions, because before he knew it, a crowd of people was coming around the corner, headed straight for their cell. He recognized a few of them from church that morning, especially the lady who'd inquired about cats.

"*You!*" a skinny man said, pointing a stern finger toward Dr. Hass.

Dr. Hass held up his hands, gave a shifty smile, and backed away from the bars. Reverend Peck decided he'd better do the same thing.

"Douglas, hello," Dr. Hass said in a quavering voice.

"Don't you 'hello' me," Douglas said back at him, now fully in front of the bars. "What do you think you're up to? Huh?"

"Up to?" Dr. Hass grinned.

Suddenly Oliver was shoved to the front, and Dr. Hass's eyes shifted back and forth between the men. Douglas said, "He told us everything."

Oliver stared at Dr. Hass. "Unbelievable. I should've known what you were up to."

Dr. Hass sighed, sitting on his cot and slumping.

"You deceived us," Douglas said through gritted teeth.

Dr. Hass nodded, sadness plaguing his features.

"How could you do that to us?" Douglas said.

And suddenly Oliver spoke up. "Don't you understand what you've done to them?"

Dr. Hass looked at Oliver. "You were the one willing to take money to get them out of your town."

"True," Oliver said, "but that was before I knew what was going on! You said you could help them. I thought you could help them! Instead, you've created a nightmare!" Oliver looked as though he was about to cry. "They keep saying they want their money back, but I imagine what they really need back are their souls!"

Douglas sighed. "Look, Oliver, let me handle this. Since the start, you've been a little overly dramatic, haven't you?" Douglas looked at Dr. Hass. "We've spent weeks here under your little plan, believing you were our friend. Believing you were trying to help us. Instead, you were just sucking us dry."

Oliver gasped and shut his eyes.

Reverend Peck was very confused. "I'm sorry," he said, speaking up, "but I don't quite know what's going on here. You're saying...are you saying... What exactly are you saying?"

"They're clones!" Oliver cried. "And Dr. Hass let them loose in our town to try to see if they would adapt! But they didn't. They just went nuts. So Dr. Hass paid me to kidnap them and bring them back to him. Heaven knows what he was going to do with them then!"

Silently, everyone stared at Oliver. And then Douglas said, "What?"

Oliver looked at Reverend Peck and whispered, "They don't know they're clones."

Dr. Hass laughed. "Are you trying to tell me, Oliver, you think they're clones and I'm the one who did it?"

"Aren't you?" Oliver said with a huff.

Dr. Hass shook his head and stared at the ceiling for a moment in some private thought. "You people are something else, I'll tell you that."

"You're denying it?" Oliver asked with a skeptical expression.

Dr. Hass sighed. "They're not clones. They're ailurophobics."

Oliver looked around at all the people standing near him and seemed to get the heebie-jeebies. "Well that sounds contagious."

Dr. Hass grumbled, "They're people who have a horrible fear of cats."

"And this man," Douglas raged, "claimed to be able to help us! Claimed he had the solution to solving our phobia! Instead we paid him tons of money and found out he was going to try to have us kidnapped!"

Dr. Hass stood, causing everyone to take a step back. "Look, you all have got a lot wrong here." He looked at Douglas and everyone else. "I was trying to help you."

"By kidnapping us?"

Dr. Hass leaned against the far wall of his cell and said with great heaviness in his voice, "My mother was ailurophobic."

"So what does that have to do with the price of tea in Japan?" the woman with large glasses asked.

"It always hurt me to see her live with that. I helped her, and I thought I could help you."

"Dr. Hass," the reverend said, "I believe you."

"I am a doctor, but I don't have a PhD in anything concerning psychology. My doctorate's in organic agriculture bionics from the Beverly Hills Massage and Homeopathic University."

Stunned silence soaked the room.

And then the lady with large glasses said, "What in the world can you do with that kind of degree?"

"Run a spa."

Douglas stepped forward. "What exactly are you saying here?"

Jack Hass looked everyone in the eye before saying, "I couldn't even run a spa right, but I found I was really good at one thing. Being a con man."

"A con man!"

And then everyone started yelling hateful things at Jack. The reverend felt badly for him but didn't know how to stop it. Jack finally held up his hands angrily. "Wait just a minute!"

Douglas shushed the crowd and folded his arms, waiting for an explanation.

"I know you all think I'm some sort of crook, and maybe I am, but I came to this town with the best of intentions! I wanted to start over, wanted to be a good person. I truly believed I could help all of you. So I decided to start a business here to help people get rid of their cat phobias. But then all these people in Skary went crazy on me, thinking I was some sort of psychologist. The next thing I know, people are shoving cash in my hand and paying me to analyze them. To be honest with you, most of their problems could be solved with a little common sense! And I know it was wrong to take their money, but I thought I was helping them, and they thought I was helping them, so I decided why the heck not? So one little lie turned into one huge lie.

"I'll be honest here: I've spent a lifetime being deceptive. Ever since my dad ran out on my mom and we had money troubles, I learned I had a knack for becoming people I wasn't. When I became an adult, that never left. So I've just pretended all these years to be people I'm not, and I've made a pretty good living doing it. I even cheated to get my degree. Then even though I tried to leave that kind of life, turns out it has followed me anyway."

Everyone looked completely stunned, but Douglas broke the silence. "Good for you, Hass. But you know what, I don't really care about all that. What I care about is that I've spent weeks running around here, doing everything you said to find a cure for myself. Scared half out of my mind, to tell you the truth. And in the end, I'm out a thousand bucks!"

Dr. Hass smiled a little. "You can have your money back. All of you. It's underneath a loose board in my office at the house."

There was a collective, relieved sigh.

"You conned us, Hass," Douglas said, "and you're going to pay for it."

Dr. Hass nodded as if he expected the anger. Then he casually pointed to Douglas's feet. Douglas glanced down. There, at his feet, was Thief, Sheriff Parker's cat, gliding back and forth against the bars. "It's…it's a cat…," Douglas said softly.

The rest of the ailurophobes carefully looked down, and relishing the attention, Thief walked between their legs, hoping someone would bend down and pet him.

But nobody screamed. In fact, they looked hopelessly relaxed, although astonished.

"I'm not screaming," one woman said.

"I don't even feel my heart racing!" said another.

"Are we cured?" another asked.

Everyone looked at Jack, who only smiled humbly. "The reason I was going to have you kidnapped was to redirect your fears. I found this out with Leroy when Oliver kidnapped him, mistakenly thinking he was some kind of ghoul. Leroy was so shaken up over the incident, he totally forgot he was scared of cats. I thought I might try my theory on you all as well. But," he said, looking around the cell, "looks like things didn't end up quite as I expected. Except, of course, you all are cured."

"How?" Douglas asked.

"Your attention has been redirected, that's all. Cats are no longer your primary concern."

Everyone seemed truly astonished by this, and then Sheriff Parker, who'd been standing near the back, stepped forward. "What about Thief? You cured him. How did you know what to do?"

"That one was easy," Jack said. "Thief was simply spoiled. I just put him on a regimen to unspoil him."

Reverend Peck said, "Well, you have quite a speaking talent."

"Thank you," Jack said. "Probably from that lawyer stint I did a few years back. Anyway," he said, looking at everyone, "go get your money. It's all there. I haven't spent a dime. I haven't had time since listening to

this town boohooing itself to death! I'm truly sorry for deceiving you. Please accept my apology."

Nobody knew what to do. A few nodded. One woman cried. And then, slowly, one by one, they left. Sheriff Parker stood in front of the jail cell door.

"Dr. Hass… I mean, um…"

"Call me Jack."

"Okay…" There was a slight pause as the sheriff processed that. Then he said, "Sir, I'm not sure what to do with you. But right now, I just can't let you go. I'm going to need to consult a prosecutor."

Jack sighed. "I understand."

"You have the right to a lawyer."

"I won't need one. Studied the law, know what I need to know."

Sheriff Parker and Reverend Peck couldn't help but smile. The sheriff then looked around, presumably for Thief. "Okay, gotta go find my cat. I'll check on you later."

Jack turned to Reverend Peck. "Thank you for your kindness." He extended his hand, and Reverend Peck shook it warmly. "I wish I could be the kind of person you are. Maybe I could learn." He noticed Jack had tears in his eyes.

"None of us can ever be good enough, Jack," the reverend said. "For no matter how hard we try, in some way or the other, we are all really good at conning. Either ourselves or others."

Jack laughed a little, wiping at his tears. "Is there any hope for humanity? Any hope at all for those of us who are so flawed?"

The reverend sat there for a moment, nodding his head, but filled with sudden and severe emotion. Tears filled his own eyes, and as he looked up at Jack, he saw the very reason he'd been assigned the task he was about to abandon.

The reverend said, "Let me tell you about an apostle named Peter. And another one named Paul. And what happened when they encountered a man named Jesus."

## CHAPTER 35

WOLFE AND MARTIN sat in the early afternoon hour of Valentine's Day on a bench facing Main Street. For a while they watched in silence as the town's citizens scurried from flower shop to gift shop to the post office, preparing for the romantic holiday.

Wolfe hadn't seen Ainsley that morning. She had Melb's wedding reception to prepare. As they sat on the bench together, he knew there was not much he could do to cheer Martin up.

Martin was trying to make light chitchat. "I've always despised this holiday," he said, though his voice sounded cheery.

"Oh?"

"Sure. So commercial. If there's someone special in your life, you feel pressured to do amazing things. If there's no one special in your life, you feel like a loser." He glanced at Wolfe. "So what are you doing to celebrate?"

Wolfe shrugged. "Nothing, really. Going to Melb's wedding."

"Yeah. I hate weddings. If you're married, you're reminded of how all the romance has left your life. If you're not married, you feel like a loser."

Wolfe was beginning to get the picture that Martin was quite depressed. "You okay?" he asked, squeezing his shoulder.

Martin nodded solemnly. "Yeah, I guess." A large sigh escaped. "I really thought we had a chance at saving the town. I thought if we could just find that one thing, you know? That one thing that would make a person proud to be a Skary citizen."

"I wish Miss Peeple could've been more helpful," Wolfe said. "Things are looking pretty dire for her."

" 'May the Lord safely keep and restore you,'" Martin said with a chuckle. "Of all the things that have come out of the woman's mouth over the years, it's interesting that's the only thing she can seem to mumble."

"Yeah."

And there was silence again. Then Martin stood up. "Well, I guess I better go shower and change for the wedding. At least there's going to be free food there."

Wolfe laughed. "Really great food, actually. Ainsley's doing a surprise reception for Melb, and the food is going to be gourmet."

"Oh! Well, that brightened my day a little." He shook Wolfe's hand. "In about two weeks, I'm going to have to tell everyone that Skary is going to be bankrupt. Pray that God prepares their hearts."

He turned and walked slowly down the sidewalk toward his car. A heavy burden of sadness filled Wolfe, and he prayed instead that God would save Skary.

For a woman about to be married to the man of her dreams, Melb Cornforth's emotions were not holding up very well. She'd already dealt with the guilt of believing Oliver had left her. Though traumatic, when the dust had settled, Oliver was by her side, and all was well. She'd learned long ago you had to forgive yourself or you weren't going to get far in life.

But what had nearly shocked the mascara off her eyelashes was the news about Dr. Hass. Jack, as they were calling him now. Ever since she'd learned he was a con man and not an actual psychologist, she'd felt nothing but a hungry dread. And hungry she was. It was as if she'd gained a pound a day. Everything he'd taught her was a farce. And now she was completely psyched out.

She'd tried to get her mind off it by preparing for her wedding day. She'd decided to groom her eyebrows. But thanks to some overly

ambitious plucking, she was now nearly hairless above each eye. Of course, this brought her to tears also.

Finally, after much solitary discourse, she decided she had to see Dr. Hass. Bundling herself up, she made her way to the jail, which, thankfully, she'd only been in once, back a few years ago when she had intoxicated a cat by feeding it too many rum cookies and beer-battered fish all in one day. And they say the alcohol cooks off!

The deputy pointed her down the hallway and to the left, where she found Dr. Hass reading something. His eyes grew startled when he saw her.

"Melb," he said. "What are you doing here?"

Sniffling, she removed her coat and scarf and stood before his cell. "I came to confront you. You helped me. Truly helped me. When no one else could. And now I'm afraid everything's going to fall apart, Doctor. I'm really afraid. I'm afraid I'm not going to be able to fit into my wedding dress. And it's all your fault! Because you're a fraud!"

"Look," Dr. Hass said, "I don't mean to be rude, lady, okay? I'm really working on not being rude. You must know that. But ever since I met you, you're the one that has created the illusions here, not me. I mean, from the very beginning you just assumed I was a shrink, and empowered yourself by believing every word that came out of my mouth! I could've said go throw yourself off the cliff, and you would've smiled and told yourself that was certainly a way to lose some pounds."

She felt her face puff into a ball of rage. "How dare you! You are the one who deceived me! You're a con man, for crying out loud! How can you justify this?"

"I'm not justifying it, lady. But I'm telling you that you didn't need me to motivate you. You did the whole thing yourself."

She crossed her arms. "What are you talking about?"

"Melb, do you want to know how you lost all that weight?"

"I know!" she said. "Because of you! You helped my brain trigger something that made the pounds just fall off."

"No," he chuckled. "It was nothing I did. It was pure and simple. Exercise."

She laughed. "Exercise? You've lost your mind. I haven't exercised a day in my life!"

"Oh? What do you call owling?"

"Owling? That's the hobby you told me to get!"

"Yes, but don't you realize how much walking and climbing you do every day to follow that silly owl all over the place?"

She blinked three times.

"It's true, Melb. There are no secret solutions in life, no magic words. It's just practical stuff, like exercising, that shows results."

Her mouth fell open. But then her eyes blazed. "Are you telling me I've been paying you all that money, and the reason I lost weight was because I've been exercising?!"

Dr. Hass shrugged, an amused look accompanying a wry smile. "Con men aren't con men for no reason. People are gullible. I've made a career out of that human fault."

"Well. Well! Ah!" She found herself speechless. "I...I spent nearly all my wedding budget on you!"

He swallowed. "I promise to pay you back."

She shook her head, disbelief stopping anything else from coming out of her mouth.

He said, "And Melb, you look really good. Your wedding's tonight, right?"

She nodded.

"Then why are you here? Go get ready for the best day of your life. Only a few get to find the love of their life, you know."

Tears welled in her eyes, and she took his hand. "Thank you. I think."

"You're welcome." He smiled.

Ainsley found herself dizzy with stress. The reception hall was filled with lights and cameras and tons of people she'd never seen before in her life. She'd been disgusted by Alfred only four days ago, but now she longed to see his familiar face. Instead, she had a person every minute coming

to ask her questions. She felt as though she was directing traffic on the freeway.

The last thing she was concerned with was how she looked, but she was now being whisked away by her hair and makeup person, Maude, who insisted she was the most important part of the team. "What every woman wants," Maude explained, "is to see a woman do all this... this... this homemaking with perfect hair and makeup. They say they hate it. But then they try to do it themselves." Ainsley smiled mildly.

The woman dusted her face, ratted her hair, and made a fuss over her, rambling on about how she couldn't understand why, with all that help, Martha Stewart could never get her bangs out of her eyes. But there was only one thing on Ainsley's mind. One person. Wolfe.

Her heart longed for him. But right now, it was time to get into character. Alfred wanted a show. He was going to get a show.

Oliver was on the top floor of the community center, adjusting his tuxedo and staring out the window. He turned to find Martin standing in the doorway with a big grin on his face. "Martin!"

Martin enfolded him in a big hug. "What are you looking at?" he said, walking over to the window.

"All the news crews out there. I've been watching tons of people walking in and out with microphones and lights and cameras. Poor fools," Oliver said. "Probably heard about that cloning thing and rushed out here for the big story. Who has the heart to tell them it's not true?"

Martin turned back to him. "I'm happy for you. What a grand day."

He grinned. "I never thought I'd marry a woman as beautiful as Melb."

"You two will have a wonderful life together."

Oliver looked into the full-length mirror that stood before him. "You know, I can't imagine much can go wrong in a marriage when it's based on truth and honesty and love."

Martin smiled. "Yeah, I guess you're right."

"Don't worry, Martin. You'll find the right woman some day."

Martin gazed out the window. "That's the least of my worries right now."

Ainsley finally got to a breathing point. The chefs were in the kitchen, complaining about the double ovens but seemingly under control; the cameras and lights were set, the tables were decorated. She stood and took it all in. It was the most gorgeous thing she'd ever seen. Candles would soon be lit all over the place, creating a mystical and glowing palette for the room. The tables were decorated with delicate sophistication, each with a red rose, red votive candles, and greenery.

Staring at it all, she sensed the sad reminder that her wedding was going to be nothing of the sort. She was going to have to pull things together in a week, and that was going to produce nothing but the basics.

She comforted herself, though, that it was not about the fancy table linens or the gourmet food. It was about her love for Wolfe, and that had not diminished an iota.

Still, a sadness lingered at her failures. She'd indeed not been able to do both. Something had to be sacrificed, and in the end, it was her dream wedding.

"How's my superstar?" Alfred said, slipping up beside her. He threw his hand out dramatically and flung it around the room. "Perfection."

She smiled. "It is beautiful, isn't it? Are you sure Melb hasn't a clue?"

"Not a clue," he said. "I told her not to come in here until after her wedding."

"She's going to be delighted!"

He guided her away from the tables. "Now, there are a few more things we need to—"

She held up her hands. "Alfred, there's a time when nothing else can

be done. I'm going to go upstairs, visit with the bride-to-be, and wish her blessings. You *can* handle everything, can't you?"

He forced a smile. "Sure. You're the boss," he winked. "You'd better start thinking like that. From this day on, your life will never be the same."

Not even excitement stirred in her spirit. But she smiled at him, then headed upstairs. Carefully opening the door, she spotted Melb in a chair with Marlee in front of her.

"Ainsley!" Melb said. She was wearing a denim shirt and blue jeans.

"Hi there, soon-to-be bride!"

Melb gushed. "Marlee here offered to do my makeup for free."

Ainsley smiled. "Marlee will do a good job for you."

"Right now she's trying to pencil in the eyebrows I nearly yanked completely out this afternoon. I guess I'm a little nervous."

"That's normal," Ainsley said, sitting next to her. "Everyone gets nervous about the idea of spending the rest of their lives with someone."

"Oh, I'm not nervous about that. I know Oliver is the one for me. I'm concerned the dress won't fit." She looked at both of them. "I haven't actually ever tried it on."

Ainsley's eyes popped. "Melb! Never?"

"Never," Melb sighed. "I just decided to have faith that it would fit. I had to drop four dress sizes, and I think I've done that. Now it's a matter of getting it all zipped up, you know?"

The other two exchanged glances.

Melb said, "But girls, it's the most beautiful dress I've ever seen. Ever. And I got it for a heck of a deal."

Ainsley checked her watch. Forty-five minutes until the wedding. "Melb, um, what do you say we go ahead and get that dress on you. Just to make sure."

Melb nodded. "That's probably a good idea." She looked at Ainsley. "You're looking awfully sophisticated."

"Thanks," she said, managing a smile.

Melb went to the table and unzipped the garment bag. She pulled out the satin white dress, and Ainsley thought she'd never seen a more

frilly wedding dress. She thought it looked like a Cinderella dress! "Melb! Oh! That is beautiful!"

"Isn't it?" she said. "Well, let's see if I can get this thing on, shall we? If not, I guess I'm going to be marching down the aisle in denim!"

They helped Melb slip on the dress. With all the ruffles and such, it was not an easy dress to get into. But finally, with her arms through the armholes, it was time to zip it up.

"All right!" Melb breathed. "I'm sucking it in! Let's go for it!"

Ainsley carefully tugged at the zipper. At first, it wouldn't budge, and the room seemed void of all oxygen. But then, with a slightly greater tug, the zipper moved, and everyone's eyebrows shot up. "Keep sucking, Melb!"

She did, and before they knew it, the zipper had climbed all the way to the top! Ainsley and Marlee cheered and turned Melb to the long mirror in the corner of the room. She took a long look at herself. Ainsley could hardly contain her excitement.

"Well?" Marlee said. "What do you think?"

Melb looked at herself from the top of her head to the bottom of her feet and said, "It makes me look fat!"

Missy Peeple wished the nurse had pulled the covers a little more over her shoulders. Her whole body was cold, and now her shoulders felt like ice. But she was too weak to do anything about it. Her mind drifted and she hardly knew if it was day or night or if things were real or imaginary.

It was as if her soul had left the very center of her body and was now clinging to the outer edges, wanting to escape the prison that had kept it tied to this earth.

If ever there was a time to believe in heaven, this was it. And she did. She always had. She believed everything the Bible said. For heaven's sake, she could nearly quote every part of it.

But she also knew she'd fallen short of what it had asked of her.

All because of secrets. Lies. Pride. Yes, pride. The center of it all.

She'd done all she could now. She'd given the key away. They knew where to find the secrets. She prayed she'd be gone from this earth when they did.

"Safely keep and restore you," she mumbled. It came from the recesses of her mind, far away, like a distant country.

"Miss Peeple?"

She heard her name called, but she couldn't open her eyes. It echoed through her mind as if spoken through a tunnel.

"Miss Peeple?"

Again. *Lord? Is that you?*

"Miss Peeple? It's Reverend Peck."

She couldn't open her eyes. Her mind would not allow her to come out of her dizzy sleep. But she wished she could. She wanted to hold his hand, tell him she was sorry she'd missed church. But her lifeless body only sank further into the bed.

"Safely keep and restore you," she heard him say. "Yes, my dear. The Lord Jesus will safely keep and restore you. Do not be afraid. He stands waiting for you, my child."

But something kept her soul nailed to this earth, and what it was she did not know.

## CHAPTER 36

AINSLEY SAW ALFRED rushing down the stairs and into the reception area, heading straight toward her. She was standing behind the wedding cake where a director named Dolph was shining lights on her and setting up cameras. "Don't squint your eyes!" he'd instructed, but how could she not with all the lights?

"Okay, darling, the wedding upstairs is about to begin! We're going to do some of the first part of the script now, and then the real heavy stuff starts when everyone gets down here."

Her stomach flip-flopped, but she ignored the fear. "Darling, this is child's play." She deepened her voice too.

Alfred's face froze in a stunned expression, but then he smiled. "I like it. Good. That's good. My goodness, woman, you wrecked the whole career of the most famous novelist alive, simply with your charm."

She flashed a grin and winked at him.

"That's my girl! Hold your head high, have confidence that you are the perfect person for this, and make love to the cameras."

She frowned. "Excuse me?"

"It's just a term," he said sheepishly. "A bad one."

"I'll say." She eyed him. "I can't imagine Martha putting up with that sort of language."

"Sorry. Anyway, just do your best."

"I am the best, Alfred," she said, facing the camera directly in front of her. Dolph was standing next to it, giving her hand signals she didn't understand. But Alfred moved out of the way, and within a few seconds Dolph pointed at her, and a red light glowed on top of the camera.

She looked at Dolph and said, "Can you stop smacking your gum?" Dolph's eyes widened and he nodded a little, handing his gum to the man next to him. Alfred's mouth was wide with awe.

Smiling, she pushed her shoulders back, commanded her hands to stop shaking and said, "Good evening. And welcome to *The Ainsley Parker Show*. Tonight I will be demonstrating how to create the most divine wedding reception you will ever see. And with some easy tips and extra planning, you can have the reception of your dreams too. Just remember, this isn't your mother's kitchen."

"Cut!" the director yelled.

She stared at him.

He added, "Perfection."

～◯～

Alfred watched from behind the cameras as his protégée prepared to charm the world. It was just a matter of time. Arms folded in front of him, he laughed to himself. Once, just a few short weeks ago actually, he'd thought his life was over. He was to the point of questioning his very existence. The one man he'd relied on had failed. And in failing, had wrecked the career of a very successful editor. It did amaze him how quickly everything one builds up can come tumbling down. A lifetime of building. A second of destroying. But now, he was back on top, with the lady who was soon to be crowned Queen of Croissants, or something like that. He was going to have to come up with a more catchy title if he was going to base his whole life's happiness on her success.

He caught her eye and gave her a reassuring nod. It was like a new Ainsley had arrived. She barked orders. She stared down incompetent people. My goodness, she was fabulous! Dolph said, "Okay, we're going to do the wedding cake part now." And Dolph, a normally edgy person, seemed to be trying to be overly polite, apparently afraid of what might happen if he wasn't.

Ainsley smiled confidently and waited for Dolph's finger to point at her. As soon as it did, she said, "Welcome back. At any wedding recep-

tion, you'll always find the wedding cake, which is a true reflection of the bride and groom's personality. These days, you'll find all sorts of different cakes at weddings, some of them sophisticated, some charming, and some just downright crazy!"

Alfred smiled at her whimsy. That was going to win hearts.

With perfect timing, she used her hands to guide the camera lens to the tall cake standing beside her. "Now," she said, "as you can see, this cake is three-tiered, with white icing and delicate gold and silver flowers all around it, appearing to free-fall off the edge of the cake like a waterfall." She grinned at the camera as though it were a person. She was a natural! "What a fine job our caterers did, don't you think?"

*"Cut!"* Alfred hollered. Everyone turned to him, Dolph waving his hands and shooting him irritated glances.

"What's wrong?" Dolph asked.

Alfred stepped toward them both. "Ainsley, my dear," Alfred said with a chuckle, "you can't refer to caterers or chefs or anything like that. The illusion has to be that you're doing this all yourself."

Ainsley frowned. "Alfred, trust me. I am the best. The best. Do you hear me? Don't question me again." Her eyes flashed rare confidence. A tense smile was all he could muster.

"Okay, then. I guess you can say that." He nodded to Dolph and then stepped out of the way. Turning his back, he gathered himself.

What he hadn't counted on was the small-town values side of Ainsley that apparently he was going to have to wrestle to death. Looking up, he saw Wolfe standing in the doorway. Had he been watching the whole time? By the look on his face, he wasn't happy, and when he caught Alfred looking at him, his eyes blazed with anger and he turned and left.

Wolfe stood for a moment, taking in the scene before him. The front of the church was thoroughly decorated with beautifully colored flowers of all kinds, and there was also a unity candle to one side. An arch decorated

with white roses, centered on the stage, was where Oliver and Melb would soon stand to become one. He felt his entire body become rigid. What he'd seen downstairs was nothing short of grotesque. The beautiful woman he'd known and loved had become another product of Alfred Tennison. It made him sick. He didn't even recognize the woman down there, shouting commands, nose in the air.

He turned to find Reverend Peck looking very frazzled. "It hasn't started yet, has it?" he said, out of breath.

"I don't think it can start without you, my friend."

Reverend Peck nodded, zipping up his black robe and running his fingers through his windblown hair. "Right. How do I look?"

"Just fine, sir," Wolfe said, adjusting his robe slightly. "You've got three minutes to spare."

The reverend seemed to settle a bit. "Okay, good. I've been at the hospital with Miss Peeple."

"Oh? Did she say anything, um…meaningful?"

He shook his head. "Not really. She just kept mumbling, 'Safely keep and restore you.' Over and over. I think she's near death."

Wolfe sighed. "You better get up there."

"Right," he said, and rushed to the front. Wolfe spotted his future father-in-law and went to sit next to him.

"Hi Wolfe," the sheriff said, greeting him with a firm handshake.

"May I sit here?"

"Of course." The sheriff scooted over.

"How are you?"

"Well, I'm okay, except I can't find Thief."

"Really?"

The sheriff nodded somberly. "He used to leave for a day or so. But he's been gone for three days now, and I have no idea where he could be. I'm getting really worried."

"I'm sure he'll turn up. Now that he's feeling better, maybe he just needed to roam around."

The sheriff nodded, though not convincingly. Then he turned to

Wolfe. "I wanted to tell you something else. I'm not sure I should, because sometimes a father should just stay out of his daughter's business, but I think you need to know this."

Wolfe's heart skipped a beat. "Okay."

"Ainsley is a mess. She's been trying to do this secret reception, and I'm assuming she's pulled it off, but what she hasn't done is…"

"Is what?"

Regret flickered across his face. "She's hardly done a thing for your wedding, Wolfe."

Wolfe looked down at his feet. Emotions tickled at his throat.

"And I know Ainsley, and I know she's going to try to pull all this off next week. I just wanted to warn you, since she might seem a little crazy."

Wolfe tried to smile. *Crazy* was a bit of an understatement considering the way he'd seen her act down there. "Thanks. Good to know." He stared up at the reverend, who was getting ready to begin the ceremony. "But she still wants to marry me, right?"

He looked surprised by the question. "Wolfe, of course she does. You must believe that."

Wolfe nodded, but then had to decide exactly what he believed. Because inside his soul there were many theories vying for the top slot.

The wedding music began, and he settled into his chair. Oliver came out, proud as could be in his tuxedo. He gave quick smiles to those he managed to make eye contact with in the audience, and then he looked down the aisle, waiting for his beautiful bride-to-be.

With a small transition, the music changed to the wedding march, and the back doors opened. There Melb stood, in a beautiful, though very puffy, gown, smiling with the radiance of someone completely loved.

She walked down the aisle with that kind of confidence. And in fact, Wolfe had never seen her look so confident. Her curly hair was pinned up under her headband-veil, and she smiled at everyone she saw, then at Oliver, who had never stopped smiling.

Wolfe tried not to think about the other wedding that might not take place.

"My dear, you are sweating!" the makeup lady said, aghast.

Ainsley shot her a look. "People don't sweat in the big city?"

She smiled tolerantly. "It's just that we can't have shine. On camera, a little perspiration on your forehead can look like a frying pan waiting for an egg. Come, dear."

Ainsley sighed, flustered beyond belief. It was hard being this hateful and moody. It cut directly against the grain of who she was. And it seemed to be backfiring. She thought she'd be such a monster nobody would want to work with her. But instead, she seemed to become everyone's hero.

"Ainsley!" Alfred stood in front of her as she was being powdered.

"What?" she said, bringing herself back into reality.

"We've got about ten more minutes, and we've got to cover the main dishes."

"She's sweating like a pig," the makeup lady growled. "Give me a second."

A splintering pain shot through Ainsley's head and she rubbed her temples. Martha made this all look so easy.

Reverend Peck turned to the audience and said, "And now, my friends, these two will say their vows to each other. They wrote their own, which I always think is so precious. Oliver, we will begin with you."

With a shaking hand, Oliver smiled and pulled out a piece of paper from his pocket. He stared Melb in the eyes, as if there were nobody else in the room. Then he looked down at his paper. "My beautiful Melb, whom I had admired from a distance for so long, and who is now going

to be my extraordinary wife—I love you. I will always love you. Our love is based on truth and honesty, commitment, loyalty, friendship, and most of all, on Jesus Christ. My dear and lovely Melb, you are my most prized treasure, and I will never stop loving you."

Oliver folded up his paper as a collective "Awwww" came from the crowd. Melb was moved to tears.

Reverend Peck said, "Beautiful, Oliver. Melb, go ahead."

Melb was shaking worse than Oliver, and was wiping her tears and looking extremely nervous. Wolfe imagined Melb had not had much opportunity to speak in public. She opened up the piece of paper in her hand, looked at it for a long moment, making the crowd slightly uncomfortable.

"Melb, go right ahead," the reverend said again, giving her a re-assuring nod.

"O-okay. I'm sorry. I'm…I'm just a bit nervous."

"Understandable," the reverend said, glancing at Oliver, who had plastered his smile on by now.

"Okay. Here I go." Her voice was shaky. "Oliver, you are the light of my life. You have brought such joy and meaning to my life. I can't believe I'm lucky enough to be with you." Melb was reading her words like an eight-year-old doing a book report. Wolfe winced a little. He hoped Melb wasn't going to go on too long like this. "And I'm just so thankful that you love me and…and…and…"

The crowd moved to the edge of their seats. Melb seemed to be stuck like a broken record.

"Yes?" Oliver finally said.

A large sigh escaped from Melb and she threw down the piece of paper in her hand quite dramatically, causing a gasp from the audience.

"Oliver," she said, squeezing his hands, "I wrote down some words, and they are true, and I mean everything I was going to say. But…but…"

"But?" Oliver asked.

"Here's the thing. This wedding is the most exciting thing ever to happen to me in my whole life. When I found out you loved me, my

whole life changed. And it's good to know that you will never stop loving me, because I have to confess a few things."

Oliver's Adam's apple popped up his throat and slowly sank back down.

"Here's the deal. I spent way more money on this dress than I was supposed to. And then I lied to you about that, because I knew you were a stickler for budgets. But I wanted the dress, and so I bought it, without even trying it on. So that's when I decided to go into therapy to try to lose weight, which worked, because as you can see, I'm very skinny now."

Oliver's mouth was hanging open.

"And I wish I could say the deception ended there, but it didn't. Things just kept getting worse, because I was blowing the whole wedding budget on a shrink, who ended up not being a shrink at all. But then I didn't have enough money for a caterer or to get my hair and nails done, or pretty much anything you'd given me a budget for."

Oliver was still catching flies with his mouth.

"Oh, and then I accidentally spelled your name wrong on the invitations, so I had to reorder those. But don't worry, I've been practicing, so I've got that down now."

Oliver was speechless.

"So anyway, what I'm trying to say here is that I've been horrible. Just horrible. But then this amazing thing happened, and I was offered the chance to have my wedding reception done by a television show with some celebrity caterer, and so what I'm trying to tell you here is that everything worked out. Unbelievably, it worked out. Downstairs there is a glorious wedding reception waiting on us, and if you'll still have me as your wife, I want to go downstairs and celebrate our love together. There will be a few cameras and things, but we'll just ignore that, okay?"

Oliver glanced out at the audience, who was equally shocked. Wolfe was sure nobody in that room had ever heard vows like that before. Oliver managed to close his mouth and pull himself together. Taking a deep breath, he said, "Melb, I just have one question for you."

"Yes?"

"Do you love me?"

Melb smiled. "Yes, Oliver. I love you more than anyone else in the world."

Oliver nodded, and then took her hands. "Then yes, I'll still have you as my wife."

Melb grinned, and Reverend Peck looked more relieved than he had in his whole life.

Melb said, "Oh, thank goodness."

Reverend Peck said, "Yes. Thank goodness. Okay, shall we continue?"

"Not quite yet," Melb said, and the room was stunned into silence again.

Oliver cleared his throat. "Um, Melb…what…what are you doing?"

Melb lowered her voice as if no one else could overhear. "Speaking of the treasure you'd mentioned before, me being the treasure, I think is how you put it, I have a bit more news for you."

Oliver looked like he couldn't take a bit more news.

"You see, my love," Melb said with a dramatic flare, "I have found a treasure."

In nearly a whisper, Oliver said, "Me?"

"Well, yes, you too, of course, but I'm talking about a true-life, *Pirates of the Caribbean* treasure."

A mutter swept through the room, and the reverend held out his hands to hush everyone.

"What are you talking about?" Oliver asked.

"I was out owling one night and fell into a hole with a buried treasure. It's a safe with a whole bunch of money in it, though I haven't actually been able to get it open because there's this heavy-duty lock on it. But anyway, I kept it to myself for the longest time, because I was afraid it might belong to somebody, but nobody had mentioned losing a treasure, and you know how fast news travels around this town." Melb looked as though she was about to cry with joy. "Oliver, we're going to be rich! Can you believe it? Rich!"

Oliver's face contorted with multiple emotions. Though he was trying to smile, his eyebrows drew together with worry. He opened his mouth to say something, but nothing came out.

Then Reverend Peck said, "Well, let's get you two married before anything else jumps out and surprises us." He laughed nervously.

Wolfe's gaze found Martin across the room, who in turn was looking at him with intense eyes. Wolfe nodded, trying not to leap from his seat.

CHAPTER 37

MARTIN'S HAND SHOOK as he wiggled Melb's front doorknob. Wolfe was trying not to pressure him, just wondering why he wasn't using the key Melb had given Wolfe before the wedding, so he could feed her birds while she was gone on the honeymoon.

Martin glanced at him. "It's just that the last time I broke into somebody's house, the door was open, so I didn't technically break in. I guess I'm getting good at this sort of business." A nervous laugh followed.

"Is it technically breaking in when you've got the key?" Wolfe tucked his hands into his jacket, trying to keep warm while Martin wrestled with his conscience.

"I guess that's a good way to look at it," Martin said. He took the key from his own pocket and inserted it into the lock. After a gentle click, the door popped open. They glanced at each other.

"Now what?" Martin whispered.

"Nobody's home, so you don't have to whisper."

"Yeah, that's what I thought when I broke into Miss Peeple's home."

Wolfe urged him in and shut the door behind him. He turned on a single lamp in the living room. Melb's parakeets chattered in the corner of the room. Martin seemed frozen by the door.

"Well, let's start looking for it," Wolfe said.

But Martin didn't move.

"What's the matter?"

Martin paused, looking down. "What if we're disappointed?" He looked up at Wolfe. "What if it won't save the town?"

Wolfe walked over to Martin and put his hand on his shoulder. "We won't know until we open that box."

Martin nodded reluctantly. "What will be will be."

In the midst of a crowded room, with cameras in her face, people yelling directions at her, and friends mingling nearby, Ainsley Parker remained completely poised. Flawlessly, she'd done every take with energy, grace, and intelligence. Even Dolph, who'd seemed nearly unemotional, was now showering her with one compliment after another.

The highlight of the evening came when Alfred opened the doors and allowed Melb in. Ainsley watched as Melb screamed with excitement and Oliver grinned from ear to ear. She could see how pleased they both were. The cameras were equally pleased, eating up the perfect scene before them. Then Alfred introduced Ainsley as their "celebrity" caterer, and Melb just broke down, hugged her, cried, and hugged her some more. "Ainsley, this is the most beautiful, perfect thing I have ever seen. I feel like I've walked into a castle, and I'm a princess."

"You are a princess, and this is your evening. Enjoy everything about it."

And then it was back to work, explaining the salmon recipe as if she'd just made seventy plates herself.

*"Here!"* Wolfe heard Martin cry. *"In here!"*

He rushed through the house toward the hallway. He ran into Melb's bedroom and found Martin in the closet.

Martin turned to him. "I found it," he breathed.

Wolfe stepped forward, and there, underneath a pile of clothes, was a small silver safe with a padlock on it.

"It's not too heavy," Martin said, pulling it forward, out of the closet. The men knelt on either side of it.

Wolfe took the chain from around his neck and held the key in his hand, looking at Martin, who urged him with watchful eyes.

After two tries of getting the key into the hole, Wolfe finally did it and clicked the lock open easily. He pulled the lock off and took a deep breath. "Here we go."

Opening it up, both men peered in. Grabbing for the contents at the same time, their knuckles crashed into each other. They both yelped.

"I'm sorry," Wolfe said. "Go ahead."

Martin shook his head. "No, I want you to."

He carefully stuck his hand in and pulled out what looked like a diary. And then another diary. Four of them. The men looked at each other.

"Journals," Wolfe said, handing two to Martin.

"Whose?" Martin wondered. Then he said, "Look! On the front of each of them!"

In faded handwriting, on the front of each journal, were neatly printed, _Safely Keep And Restore You._

Wolfe could hardly believe it. "Safely Keep And Restore You! SKARY. It's an acronym!"

Both men flipped open the journals and began reading.

Ainsley's knees felt so weak she thought she was going to have to sit down. But she didn't ever have a chance, for she moved from one place to the next, the cameras always on her, the lights bright and stunning her senses.

But she felt weary.

And she couldn't help but notice Wolfe was nowhere to be seen. Had he left?

She told Alfred she needed a few minutes to recuperate, and though he obviously didn't like the idea, he managed to smile and step out of her way. She moved to a quiet corner and sipped a glass of water, while the cameraman and director were taking an interest in Mayor Wullisworth and his Bermuda shorts.

She shook her head, trying to make sense of Wolfe. On one hand, he professed his love for her and said he supported her. But why wasn't he here, at her big moment? She put a finger below her lashes to catch the tears, hoping she wouldn't smear the fancy makeup job.

"Wolfe, where are you?" she whispered. She felt he was so far away from her heart. His words rang in her ears, but she needed him by her side.

"Ainsley!" she heard Alfred shout over the crowd noise. "Let's go! We need your commentary on the table designs! And Melb and Oliver are getting ready to cut the cake!"

Ainsley closed her eyes and prayed to God for peace in her soul.

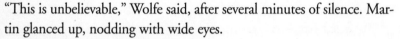

"This is unbelievable," Wolfe said, after several minutes of silence. Martin glanced up, nodding with wide eyes.

"What's in yours?" Martin asked.

"This looks like the entire story of how Skary came into existence."

"What does it say?"

"Apparently Skary was created as a safe haven for moral rejects of society. It was created by three pastors, who built those shacks up in the hills. They would take in prostitutes, bootleggers, those accused of being witches, and give them food and water and protect them from being executed. That's what I'm getting from all this, anyway. The handwriting is a little hard to read."

Martin said, "I know who wrote these."

"Says Clara here."

"Yes. Clara is Miss Peeple's grandmother. And according to this, a prostitute who was saved by these pastors. She had a daughter by one of the men who paid her for her services. That's when she was taken in by these pastors, because she wanted to save her child, and the authorities had found out she was a prostitute. She ran for the hills. Literally."

After a moment's thought, Wolfe said, "Which means Miss Peeple's mother was that child."

Martin nodded, gazing at the pages in front of him. "That's why she didn't want anybody to know the town's history. Because we would've found out her grandmother was a prostitute."

"But it also explains why she has fought so hard to keep this town alive, using any means possible. It is this very town that saved her mother's life."

Martin thumbed through the pages, awe in his eyes. "This is how our town came into being, Wolfe. By saving misfits and rejects."

Wolfe smiled. "And I guess it's still doing that today."

Garth Twyne stared through the community center basement windows, watching the festivities. He'd been invited, but he hadn't felt like going. It was just a reminder that Ainsley's wedding was soon to follow. He wasn't sure what all the hubbub was about, but there were lights and cameras everywhere. He found Ainsley and watched her, sadness in his heart. He had tried to fall in love with Ginger, but there just wasn't a spark there. He had always loved Ainsley's poise.

He did have things to be thankful for, he supposed. He was no longer accused of cloning people, so that was a plus.

He decided to go home and order a pizza. But behind him, he heard a noise in the brush. His first instinct was to run like crazy, but after a moment, he realized it sounded like an animal caught up in something.

He cleared the brush and, to his surprise, found the owl that had been hooting for the past few weeks around these parts.

"Hey," he said, gently pulling back the brush. "It's okay." He could tell that it had a broken wing. "Shsshhh. It'll be okay."

The poor owl was thrashing nervously. He ran to his truck and got out a pair of gloves and a blanket. When he returned, the owl seemed to have lost strength and stared up at him with helpless eyes.

"Don't worry," he said. "I'll take care of you."

Wolfe and Martin had been reading entries in the journals for an hour or so. Wolfe rubbed his eyes and laid down the journal in his hands. "This is a lot to take in," he said. Martin nodded, still into whatever he was reading. "The last thing I read explained how they would go out and help these people."

Martin looked up.

"They'd go into certain towns and find, say, a prostitute that was in trouble. And they would shake her hand and say, 'May the Lord safely keep and restore you.' And everyone knew that was the code word for being saved, though nobody knew where this place was. Apparently they'd pack up a small bag of things they owned, what they could carry on their backs, and then the pastors would sneak them out of town at night. Nobody knew where Skary was, because it was up in the hills, hidden away. But soon their numbers grew, and they made themselves a town. Became official in 1870."

Martin said, "In here, which looks to be the last journal, it says that after they'd been a town for about two years, they destroyed all the evidence linking them to their past and started anew. The only thing that remained was the name, Skary. They knew through the generations, the word-of-mouth history would be lost."

Wolfe shook his head. "But I guess in some way we're always linked to our past. It shapes us to be who we are today, right?"

Martin nodded. "And I guess perhaps that is why Skary struggles. We lost the purpose that we were created for in the first place." Martin's fingers traced the edges of the journal in his hand, and he looked up at Wolfe. "Do you think this is enough?"

"To save Skary?"

"Yes."

"I don't know," Wolfe said softly. "I hope so, Martin."

"Some may look at it as an ugly wart on our nose."

"Others may see it as noble and good."

Martin sighed and rubbed his eyes. "Whatever the case, it's our last chance. To save Skary. To save the mayor. This is what our town is about, and either we're going to embrace who we are, or we're going to run from it."

"What's going on here?"

Wolfe and Martin scrambled backward, and then looked up to find Melb and Oliver standing over them. Melb's face was twisted with anger. Oliver just looked shocked.

"Melb!" Martin jumped to his feet. "What are you doing home?"

She crossed her arms. "Well, what in the world do you think we're doing home?" Martin and Wolfe both noticed at the same time the champagne glasses and bottle in Oliver's hand. A bashful blush crossed Oliver's face.

"Oh," Martin said. "Um…this isn't what it looks like."

"Where's the money?" Melb's face was drawn in panic.

Wolfe said carefully, "Melb, there is no money. There never was."

"Oh yeah, right!" she screamed, even startling Oliver. "You stole it!"

"This is all that was in here," Wolfe said, holding up a journal.

Tears formed in her eyes. "I don't believe you," she said. "You stole it. You stole our money! You broke into our home and stole our money!"

Oliver's eyes were cutting from one face to the next.

She asked, "How'd you get that lock open, anyway?"

Wolfe held up a key. "This safe belongs to Missy Peeple. She gave the key to me. She wanted us to find what was in here, which is information on the town's history. Martin has been trying to find it to help the town out." It was the most he could explain while being stung by the fiery darts shooting from her eyes.

Suddenly she broke down and cried. "I thought I'd found… I thought we were going to be… I just thought…"

Oliver set down the champagne bottle and glasses and reached for Melb. "Honey, it's okay. Please don't cry."

"I know it's stupid," she said, staring at the open, empty safe. "I just thought something truly magical had happened."

"It has," Martin breathed, staring at the journals.

Oliver took his thumbs and wiped her tears. Then he said, "My dear Melb, you do not have to worry. I'm a millionaire."

It took her a second to register this. She stared at the floor, then looked at him. "What?"

"I'm a millionaire. I made a fortune back years ago when I sold my old car lot over in Gary. You don't really think I make a living selling a couple of cars every two weeks do you?"

She was not the only one in the room with her mouth wide open. Oliver glanced around sheepishly. "I just do it for the challenge. I make some money off it, but every year I think I can do better, and I do." He shrugged.

A relieved laugh burst from Melb. Oliver smiled and said, "I know you would've married me if we were the poorest fools around."

She nodded eagerly. "Of course I would've."

Oliver laughed too. "But according to your vows, sounds like I'm going to have to put you on a strict budget and teach you some money-managing skills."

Everyone in the room laughed.

Then Oliver picked up the champagne. "Well, if you don't mind, Melb and I would like to be alone, since we can be now that we're officially married. I've been waiting a long time for this."

Melb blushed. Wolfe did too. Martin grinned and gathered the journals. "Have fun on your honeymoon at the…Bass Pro Shop."

"We will!" they both said.

Wolfe was leaving the room, and Oliver said, "And Wolfe, we'll be back in plenty of time for your wedding." They smiled at each other, for the first time since Oliver had fired him. Wolfe nodded.

Outside the house, Wolfe and Martin stood there, trying to make sense of it all.

"What are you going to do?" Wolfe asked.

"The only thing I can do. Go share all this with the mayor, see if it will bring him back to reality. Give him a purpose again for being our mayor."

Wolfe checked his watch. "Kind of late, isn't it?"

"He's on Caribbean time."

"Oh."

"What about you?"

Wolfe thought for a minute. Something he'd not felt in a long time stirred inside of him. "I'm going home. I'm going to write."

The two shook hands. "Take these," Martin said, handing him the journals. "I see something in your eyes that tells me you're going to need them."

He watched Martin return to his car and back out of the driveway. His fingers twitched, eager to get home.

A few lingering guests mingled around the reception hall, but the event was winding down. The makeup lady was done powdering Ainsley's face, thank goodness. She was allowed to perspire out her nervousness at last. Leaning against a table, she drew in a deep breath and smiled.

"You're satisfied," Alfred said. She hadn't even noticed him walking up. "You should be. You were terrific. The best."

She laughed. "I can't believe I pulled it off." She was talking more about her candor than the reception. She'd said some pretty brutal things to Alfred through the evening. Yet here he was, still admiring her. It struck a sour note inside her.

"I've already sent the tapes off for editing. You know, Dolph, a man of few words, even said you were naturally talented, that you shone for the camera. I have a feeling about this, Ainsley. You're going to make us both very—"

Alfred stopped. Both of them saw a group of three executive types walking through the reception hall doorway, looking around for something or someone. The lady, a head taller than the two men with her, looked familiar to Ainsley, but she couldn't quite place her.

One of the men asked a guest something, and then the guest turned and pointed to the table where she stood with Alfred.

"Who is that?" Alfred asked.

"I have no idea," she replied.

The three made a beeline toward them. Alfred stepped in front of her in a protective manner, extending his hand toward the first man. "Hello, Alfred Tennison. I'm Ainsley's manager. We're not doing any interviews tonight, but you're welcome to call my office tomorrow and schedule an—"

"We're not media," the man said. He was looking at Ainsley when he spoke. All three of them were looking at her. The woman made eye contact, then looked around the room with a insidious smirk on her face.

"Who are you?" Alfred asked, and Ainsley noticed his voice cracked.

"I'm Robert Barry. This is my assistant, J. R. Stepford, and this is Elizabeth Carson-Cummings."

The woman's name hung in the air, and Ainsley swallowed. She knew her from the bake-off in Indianapolis. The man was explaining he was from some sort of committee that was in charge of rules and regulations. He made it sound very official. But all Ainsley could do was stare into the woman's cold eyes.

"And what is your business here?" Alfred said, mustering up professional confidence again.

"We're here to inform you that Miss Parker will be stripped of the four blue ribbons she was awarded in Indianapolis."

"Why?" Alfred asked.

The woman finally spoke, her voice low and guttural, her eyes narrowed like a Cheshire cat. "You cheated."

"Cheated?" Alfred gasped. "What in the world are you talking about? She did no such thing!"

"Oh, I beg to differ," the woman said. "We have laboratory tests that prove it."

"Prove what?" Ainsley managed.

"Prove that you used Brach's butterscotch candies in your Butterscotch and Chocolate Deluxe cookie."

Ainsley looked at Alfred, who was growing pale.

The woman continued, "The rules clearly state that every ingredient put into your cookie must be *homemade*. That includes candy."

"What?"

"Or didn't you read the rules that were sent to you before you entered the contest?"

Ainsley glanced at Alfred, whose stupefied face was paralyzed.

The woman said, "It's in paragraph two point seven, sub-section C."

Alfred looked at Ainsley. "You used Brach's candy?"

Ainsley nodded. "I did."

The man named Robert said, "Then I'm sorry, young lady, you've been disqualified, and the title will be given to the runner-up. We'll notify the press immediately."

Alfred said, "Is that necessary? Really? To run the story? To—"

"Expose her for the cheater she is?" the woman said, smiling. "Why yes, it is."

Ainsley said, "It was an honest mistake."

Robert said, "Whatever the case, you will be banned from the contest for life and will need to give back all your ribbons too."

Ainsley thought Alfred was going to weep.

"I guess the next Martha Stewart has chosen her same fate," the woman said.

Alfred managed in a quiet voice to ask, "H-how…how did you find this out?"

The woman said, "An anonymous tip." Then her heels clicked against the floor as she headed to the door.

The room quieted around them as they watched the woman walk away. Ainsley turned to find Alfred sitting alone at a nearby table, his face distraught. He glanced up at her. "It's over. The media exposure on this will be too detrimental, too controversial."

Her throat tightened. "I'm sorry, Alfred."

"I know," he said softly. She could see tears shimmering in his eyes. He sniffed back his emotions. "A dream died here tonight, though, you know? A dream for both of us."

"I'm so sorry," she said, her own tears dripping down her face. She took his hands. "But it was only a dream for you, Alfred. My dream is to be with Wolfe."

Alfred shook his head in disbelief. "I'll never understand it, I guess." He looked at her. "But I know I was right. You were going to be the It girl. You would've made it, Ainsley. I have no doubt about that."

She smiled through her tears. "Thanks for believing in me. It made me believe in myself."

"The only saving grace about all this is that hopefully you'll remain the innocent woman that you are. That world, Ainsley, it can corrupt people. Even the people with the best intentions. It makes them, well… just look at me." A sad smile crossed his lips.

"Alfred, you are not bad. Please don't believe that about yourself. And you know what? There is a real kind of saving grace that doesn't depend on the shortcomings of other people. Alfred, I made that anonymous call. I tried to tell you I didn't want all this, tried to back out, but I couldn't get myself to tell you the truth. I'm sorry. It was wrong of me not to be honest."

He sat stunned, his arms limp in his lap, his back hunched with defeat. Even the wrinkles in his face seemed to deepen with each passing second.

His eyes looked up with pleading sincerity. "You are so at peace with the world, Ainsley. I have always been at war with it. But it just keeps beating me down."

She squeezed his hands. "Alfred, the world has nothing to offer but disappointment. It will fail you until the day you die. God will never fail you, though. Never."

He patted her on the back and wiped a stray tear that strolled down his face. "Thank you, my dear. You are both lovely and wise." He stood, gathering his coat.

"Where are you going?"

"Well, I have some things I have to take care of, loose ends to tie up."

"Oh, Alfred, can't all that wait until the morning?"

"I meant with God." He shook her hand and said, "I will see you at your wedding." And then he walked out of the reception hall.

Ainsley sat for a moment, taking in all that was around her, which now was crumpled napkins, dirty floors, a half-eaten cake, and lipstick-stained coffee cups—a perfect picture of how she was feeling. Just two hours ago, life was a room full of gorgeous candlelight, cheery friends, plump roses, and toasts to success and love.

Yes, how quickly things could turn.

She gathered her coat and bag and left the community center, glad to be done with the charade that had backfired anyhow. The cold night air dried the perspiration that would've defeated even a good dose of powder. She pulled her hair back into a ponytail and secured it with a band she had in her pocket.

But instead of driving home, she decided to walk. It was only about eight blocks, and she needed to unwind. She wrapped her scarf around her neck and started home.

The evening was oddly silent. She'd grown used to the owl asking "whoo" and the horrible screams that would reply.

There was nothing of the sort this evening. Just a twinkling, starry night to shelter her.

As she walked in the door of her home, she took off her coat and scarf, putting it in the closet. She locked the door and came into the living room. Her father was still up.

"You okay?" she asked.

"Thief's gone, Ainsley." His voice cracked. She rushed to her father's side. The cat had been missing for several days now.

"I'm sorry, Dad. I don't know what to say."

"It's not like him to leave like this," her father said. "Maybe I ruined his whole life by getting him fixed. Maybe he's so mad at me he ran away."

"He wouldn't do that, Dad. Thief loves you."

"I know he does," her father said. "I guess when you care about someone, you try to do the right thing, and sometimes it ends up being the wrong thing."

"Animals are notoriously forgiving, you know." She smiled. Her father smiled too. "Maybe he'll come back tomorrow."

He stroked her hair and then noticed her face. "Are you okay? You look exhausted."

"I'm fine," she said, patting him on the leg. "But I'd better get upstairs and into bed. I am tired."

"Okay, sweetie. I'll see you in the morning."

She walked up the stairs, her legs sore and shaky. But there was a smile on her face. Life would be back to normal.

Except that monster wedding she had one week to plan.

## CHAPTER 38

WOLFE GROANED as the dogs barked enthusiastically on either side of his bed. The sun was clear and bright, higher in the sky than he would've thought by how tired he was feeling. He'd stayed up writing until nearly 3:00 a.m.

"What is it?" he mumbled as they barked again. Then he heard it. Knocking. He rolled out of bed, pulled a heavy sweatshirt on and made his way downstairs. When he opened the door, Ainsley stood there.

"Hi," she said. "You left the wedding in a hurry. And didn't call me last night."

"I stayed up late writing, and by the time I glanced at the clock it was way too late. How'd everything go? How'd the reception go?" He stepped aside to let her in.

"Writing?" She smiled at him.

"Yes. I've found a story I want to tell." He studied her as she walked past him and into the living room, trying to find a hint of what he saw last night.

"I'm so happy for you," she said, turning to him.

"So? What about you? How did it go last night?"

"Where did you run off to?"

"That is a story that requires a big breakfast and lots of time. Have you eaten yet?"

She shook her head.

"What's wrong? Didn't everything go okay last night?"

"It was perfect," she said. "Melb thought it was the most beautiful thing she'd ever seen. The food was amazing."

He sighed. "I'm sorry I missed it. What did Alfred think? Did he get the shots he wanted?" He didn't really want to know, but it was important to her, so he figured he'd better ask.

She took him by the arm and led him into the kitchen where they sat at the breakfast table. "I have a story for you too, but I want you to know something."

"What?"

"I'm sorry."

"For what?"

"For…being selfish. I didn't see what all this was doing to me. To us. All I could see was success."

He took her hand. "Ainsley, there's nothing wrong with having stars in your eyes. For dreaming big. For following your heart."

"But I put our relationship in jeopardy, and I'm sorry for that. I realized the only thing I want is to be your wife. I don't want the kind of lifestyle where every part of you is scrutinized and if you make a mistake the whole world knows and judges you for it."

"What are you saying?"

"I'm saying that I'm done becoming the next Martha Stewart. It's not what I want."

He frowned. "But last night…I saw you at the reception… acting…"

"Good grief, that was just an act! I was trying to act so horrible Alfred would just fire me, but instead he grew more insistent. But it didn't matter anyway, because it all worked out. It's over. Believe me, it's really over." And then she burst into tears. He quickly moved to her side and held her until she was able to talk. "Wolfe," she said, "I've really messed up. We're to be married in a week, and I don't have anything done for the wedding. And I don't think I will have anything done. I don't think I can pull it off. I've ruined our wedding day!"

"No, no, sweetheart, no…" he said, trying to comfort her. He lifted her chin. "The only thing that will ruin our wedding day is if you are not there." He wiped her tears. "Let's have a small wedding, just family

and close friends, and do it at the church with the reverend. Let's make it simple…simply about our love."

"You're not mad?"

"No, Ainsley. I love you no matter what."

Thankfully, though, he didn't have to love the woman he thought he saw at Melb's wedding!

Jack sat in his jail cell, lonely but at peace. He'd spent the last several days contemplating what he might do with his life when—if—he got out of jail, and for the first time in his life, he didn't know. He didn't have an answer. And for some odd reason, it felt good. For all his life, he'd planned ahead like every day was guaranteed to him. But last night he realized every day is a gift. Every day has its own purpose. He'd lived so far in advance of himself, afraid he wouldn't have enough money, he'd missed the very essence of life.

Keys rattling a few feet away made him look up. The sheriff was coming toward his cell. He stood up and went to the bars.

"Good morning, Jack," the sheriff said. His eyes looked tired.

"Good morning."

"You're free today."

"Free? On bail?"

"No. Just free."

"Really?

"The truth of the matter is that we don't have the money to prosecute you. So we're just going to have to let you go."

"Oh. Wow." And he had been so hard on small towns. This was actually going to work out well.

The sheriff said, "But sir, I hope you know this kind of behavior will not be tolerated in this town. Get your act together. Become a productive citizen."

"You're not making me get outta town? I thought that was the standard line for somebody like me."

The sheriff smiled. "You have a lot of misconceptions, don't you?"

"I guess so."

He unlocked the door and opened it. "Can I give you a ride home?"

"Really? Yeah…that'd be great. I was just going to ask someone if they could go by and feed my cat."

The sheriff led him outside. "You have a cat?"

"Yeah. Her name's Blot. I adopted her. But ever since I've had her, she's just gotten lazy and fat."

The sheriff smiled as they got in his car. "Cats do that sometimes. You haven't spoiled her have you?"

He laughed. "I don't think so."

A few minutes later, they arrived at Jack's house. Jack said, "Sheriff, won't you come in?" When the sheriff hesitated, he said, "Please. I just…I'd like some company. Just for a few minutes."

"Sure. Why not?"

Jack walked up the front porch stairs and the sheriff followed. As he unlocked his door, the sheriff said, "Nice cat door. Was thinking of getting one installed myself. Except my cat has gone missing now."

"Oh no. That's too bad. The one at the jail?"

"Yeah. Thief. I can't imagine where he'd be."

Jack opened the door and let the sheriff in. They walked through the house and Jack called for Blot. "Here, kitty. Here! Here, kitty!"

But there was no cat. Jack stood in the middle of the living room, perplexed. "Where could she be?"

"Maybe she went out for some food," the sheriff said.

"I left enough for five days."

And then they heard it. A faint meow. Coming from the bedroom. Jack hurried toward the sound, and the sheriff followed. He opened the closet door.

"Blot!" Surrounding the cat were seven little kittens, only a day or two old.

"Thief!" the sheriff cried, as his cat ducked under some clothes and disappeared. "Why, you scoundrel! Is this your woman?"

Thief meowed and reappeared to settle next to Blot. The sheriff said, "This must've been his last hurrah before the surgery." He looked at Thief. "So you're settling down, are you? Decided to stay with just one lady cat?"

Thief nuzzled Blot, and she meowed softly. The sheriff laughed. "Goodness, gracious me! The way things turn out sometimes! I'm glad you're okay, fellow. I've been worried about you."

Jack smiled. "Thief can stay here as long as he wants."

The sheriff stuck out his hand. "Welcome to Skary."

"Thank you, sir." He smiled, looking at the litter. "A new place to call home."

Mayor Wullisworth, in long, khaki pants, a white, button-down shirt, and a striking red and gray tie, followed Martin down the long, stale hallway of the hospital. Martin stopped outside Miss Peeple's room, glancing in the window to make sure she was still there.

"She looks bad," Martin said.

The mayor straightened up his tie. "How do I look?"

"Like the fabulous mayor of Skary that you are," Martin smiled.

"I feel good," said the mayor. "I feel strong."

"You don't even look tired, and we stayed up really late last night."

"Martin, you are quite a friend. I want you to know that. You never gave up on me or this town. You should be mayor."

"No sir. It's your calling."

Mayor Wullisworth tugged on the cuffs of his sleeves. "I think you are right, Martin. This town needs to know its roots. It needs to understand why we were founded, what our purpose was for being created. I think when they understand that, a passion will be birthed in them that will be unstoppable."

"You ready to go in there?"

"Alone, if that's okay."

"Most certainly," Martin said. "I will be in the waiting area."

Mayor Wullisworth walked into the room. It smelled septic. Miss Peeple stirred, barely opening her eyes. The mayor went over to her bedside.

"Miss Peeple, it's Mayor Wullisworth."

Her eyes flittered open, and she turned her head. "Mayor…"

He pulled over a stool and sat down beside her. "I want you to know that I will be forever indebted to you. Martin Blarty told me everything you did for this town. You risked your reputation for the good of this town. That is a tremendous sacrifice."

Missy seemed to try to speak, but then she simply watched him.

"I also understand that you spent your entire life savings for an ad trying to garner business for Skary. I can't tell you how amazed I am." He took her cold, bony hand. Tears reflected in her eyes. "Missy, I think everyone underestimated how much you love this town and why. This town saved your mother's life, and therefore gave you life. I know it is a hard thing to admit your grandmother was a prostitute, but in doing so, you have allowed this town an opportunity to find itself and to thrive." He squeezed her hand. "I believe with all my heart that this town will live, and that it will become a flourishing community again. Every town has its flaws. We certainly have our share. But we have a purpose, too. And we have that because of you."

And then Mayor Wullisworth stood and bent down, kissing Missy first on the forehead and then on the cheek. She looked up at him, tears trickling down her face. "You dog," she said in barely a whisper. "After all this time, now that I'm about to die, you decide to fall in love with me."

Mayor Wullisworth smiled. Her hand slipped from his, and he bent down one more time and kissed her forehead, smoothing out her long gray hair. A large smile formed on her lips. She looked into his eyes one last time before hers closed gently. She took a final breath and then died.

"YOU LOOK BEAUTIFUL," her father said, standing behind her and staring at her in the mirror before them.

Ainsley smoothed out the wrinkles of her slim wedding dress. The train was four feet long behind her, swirled in a perfect circle. Her veil, high on her head, fell down her back like a waterfall.

"The makeup is perfect," she told Marlee, who stood in the corner of the room doing her own makeup. "And the hair is too."

"Honey, you could be bald and barefaced, and you'd still be the prettiest woman I know," Marlee replied.

"How are you feeling?" her dad asked.

"Great, actually." She laughed. "It's nice to not have to worry about anything other than kissing the man of my dreams and saying, 'I do'!"

"Yeah, not too much can go wrong there," Marlee said. "I once was at a wedding where the bride knocked over one of the candles, and it caught the back of her dress on fire! The groom had to stomp on it to put it out."

"Won't have to worry about any of that," Ainsley said, facing the mirror. "Or the flowers wilting. Or the cake falling." She swallowed down that last bit of regret and held her chin high. "None of it matters except the man at the altar."

"Speaking of that, it's time, my child." Her father hugged her and swept his hand across her cheek.

Her heart leapt at the prospect of seeing Wolfe on their wedding day. "Let's go!"

Her father and Marlee drove her to the church, pulling the car up

right in front of the church steps. Her father got out and quickly went to the other side to help her out of the car. Marlee said, "You still don't have any idea where he's taking you on your honeymoon?"

"Not a clue!" Ainsley gushed. "He's kept it a perfect secret!"

Outside the car, the air was cool and calm. The day was brilliantly sunny despite the cold. She could even feel the sun's warm rays on her bare shoulders. Her father and Marlee helped her up the steps.

"Break a leg, kid," Marlee said, and rushed inside to find a seat. Her father took her arm and they walked to the front door together.

"This is it," she smiled.

"This is it!" her father said. "You are marrying a wonderful man today. You two will be happy beyond belief."

"Thank you, Daddy," she said, looking into his eyes. "Are you going to be okay?"

"Me?" He laughed. "Sure! Do you know how long I've been trying to get you out of the house?"

She giggled, suppressing a slight hysteria, then said, "Okay, let's go."

She and her father went through the doors. She was looking down, trying to make sure she didn't step on her dress. When she looked up, she gasped.

She could hardly believe her eyes. "Daddy...," she whispered.

"Wolfe did this," he whispered back.

Before her was the most glorious sight she'd ever seen. The church had been transformed into a heavenly scene. Candles. Flowers. Red and white petals that had been scattered all over the floor. The front of the church looked like a flower garden. Sprays of flowers, arrangements that she could hardly believe, filled every corridor of the church.

The entire crowd, everyone she'd ever wanted to come to her wedding, was turned to look at her, expectant and joyful expressions on each face. Ainsley's shaking hand was covering her mouth. She finally looked at Wolfe, who was standing up front with the reverend. He grinned at her, the twinkle in his eye saying, *This is all for you.*

The organ started, and she couldn't help the tears that fell. Her father stepped forward, and she clung to him all the way down the aisle.

When they got to the front, Reverend Peck said, "Who gives this woman to be with this man?"

"I do," her father said. He lifted her veil to kiss her and gave her hand to Wolfe. "I love you," he whispered.

Ainsley turned to Wolfe. She wanted to cry her eyes out, but the joy that bubbled up inside her seemed to dry the tears. She couldn't say thank you, but she knew Wolfe knew. He looked down at her and read everything in her mind.

Today was the best day of her whole life.

"Wolfe!" she nearly screamed.

"What do you think?" he smiled.

She could not believe what she was seeing. The Mansion Restaurant had been turned into a place she hardly recognized. Linen tablecloths covered every table. Candlelight flickered against the ceiling and walls. Soft music played in the background. Each table was set with brilliant white china. White roses were the centerpieces. She was speechless as the crowd turned to greet them.

"Is this what you dreamed your reception would be like?" he asked her.

She shook her head. "This is beyond my imagination!"

He laughed.

"How did you do this?"

"I have a lot of connections, called in a few favors. Your dad had forewarned me that you hadn't quite gotten the wedding together, so I paid some very well-known wedding planners a lot of money to make a miracle happen. I had a sneaking suspicion about it a while back, to tell you the truth, and had reserved the banquet hall just in case. But this place made more sense. It has roots. And this is the first place you ever spoke to me."

"Yeah, I remember," she laughed. "You ordered meat 'oaf.'"

"I've come a long way since then."

She turned to him and kissed him full on the lips. "You are so amazing!" Then she said, "Hey! Now do I get to know where we're going on our honeymoon?"

"Yes, now you do."

"Where?"

He smiled. "The Hamptons."

Ainsley squealed. "The Hamptons? Oh my gosh! I've always wanted to go to the Hamptons! That's perfect! A vacation to the Hamptons! Wolfe, that's so wonderful!"

"Not a vacation, sweetheart."

"Not a vacation? What do you mean?."

"I didn't buy you a vacation to the Hamptons."

"You didn't?" She frowned.

"I bought you a house in the Hamptons."

She gasped and felt dizzy. "A…a house?"

"A house. A summer home. We can go there anytime you like. Bring your dad and your brother and your friends sometimes too. You'll get to see it tomorrow."

This time she couldn't hold back her tears. She wept into the collar of his tuxedo.

"I am the happiest woman in the world."

Melb, though a little exhausted as they had driven straight through from their honeymoon at the Bass Pro Shop out east, was delighted for Ainsley and Wolfe. She and Oliver sat together with Garth, Ginger, and Butch as they all watched Ainsley and Wolfe cut their wedding cake.

"Life doesn't get any better than this, does it, dear?" Oliver said, touching her hand.

"You got that right," she said. "You know, though, there's one thing that is just eating me alive."

"What's that?" Oliver asked.

"Well, I never did bond with that owl. I tried and tried, did everything the book said, but never did. And now he seems to have disappeared."

Garth leaned in. "You're talking about that owl that was always making a racket with his who-who-ing?"

"Yes," Melb said. "He's vanished."

"No. I found the owl after your wedding, right outside the community center, in fact. Broke its wing."

"Oh no!" Melb said. "Is he going to be okay?"

"Yes. Patched up the wing, should be fine in a couple of weeks."

"Poor guy."

"Well, one thing you might want to know," Garth said. "Your guy ain't a guy."

"What?"

"That owl is female."

In rapid succession, cocked eyebrows popped up all around the table. Melb blushed. "Oh… So the 'he' is a 'she'."

Oliver laughed. "Well, I guess the mystery is solved as to why that owl never did take a liking to you."

Everyone else laughed, and Melb couldn't help but chuckle herself. "Well, it's not the mystery of the universe solved, but at least I can sleep at night!"

Alfred found Reverend Peck at a table by himself finally. How that man could draw a crowd sometimes! He was sipping some punch and eating cake when Alfred sat down next to him.

"Hi Alfred," the reverend said with a smile.

"You remember me?" Alfred asked, astonished.

"Of course. How are you?"

"I'm…I'm good. Life has thrown me some curve balls, but I'm trying to make the best of it."

"That's good to hear," the reverend said.

"But I wanted a moment to talk with you."

"Sure."

"I'm not going to confess a deep dark secret or anything like that, though I have a few more than I'd like to admit."

"It'd be fine if you did. I'm always available, Alfred."

"Um, well, thank you. But anyway, what I wanted to know is whether I could be of service to you."

"How so?"

"Well, long before I was an editor, and long before I was agent, I majored in marketing."

"No kidding?"

"I'm really quite good at it, to tell you the truth. I can sell sirloin to a vegetarian."

"Interesting."

"What I'm trying to say here is that I'd like to help you with your church. Try to get the word out about it, try to get some new bodies in the pews."

The reverend smiled. "That is so kind of you, Alfred. But I don't have the money to pay for something like that."

"Consider it a gift. Just a chance for me to do something I'm good at, give back to the community."

"The community. Your community?" the reverend asked.

Alfred smiled. "Yeah, I guess that's what I'm calling it. My community."

The reverend set down his fork and thought for a moment. "Well, Alfred, this is very interesting. Just last night I told the Lord Jesus that if He wanted anything to happen with the little church, He was going to have to make it happen, because I no longer had the strength to do anything more than stand there and preach the Word. Sounds like He was listening."

Alfred smiled a little.

"I accept your offer on one condition."

"What's that?"

"You'll be one of those in the pews."

Alfred grinned. "Yes sir."

"Then I accept."

And then Alfred went on to tell the reverend that he was sure with the right tactics, the church could grow like a weed.

The reverend had to point out that Alfred was going to have to find a new analogy.

"AND SO, WITH its prostitutes, misfits, alcoholics, and more, Skary, Indiana, became a refuge for those who had lost their way in life. They saw people for who God created them to be, not for the way life had used and abused them. In many respects, Skary didn't have a chance at ever succeeding, ever becoming a flourishing town of productive citizens. But three pastors knew that the kind of grace they were offering produced the kind of people who took a second chance and made all they could of it.

"So, on September 5, 1870, Skary, Indiana, officially became a town. And nobody hid in the shadows of the wilderness anymore. Life was built one steppingstone at a time.

"And a young woman named Clara gave birth to a little baby named Jillian. And Jillian grew up and married a man named Stewart Peeple. Together, they had two children, Sissy and Missy.

"Years later, it would be Missy Clara Peeple who would sacrifice everything near and dear to her to try to save the town that had once saved her grandmother and her mother. And on the day she was buried, a woman who was scorned and disliked most of her life, had the whole town show up at her funeral, to pay their respects to a woman hardly anyone understood, but who all now appreciated for what she gave back to the community, which was a sense of hope and purpose.

"Whatever Skary, Indiana, may be in the future, its roots will always be grounded in what it was created to be. And because of that, every person in the town found their own purpose, their own chance to make a difference, their own chance to see that love can conquer all."

Wolfe quietly closed his manuscript. The gigantic crowd that had filled the community center could hardly be heard breathing. And then they erupted into applause. People were wiping tears from their eyes and shaking each other's hands.

Ainsley bounded up onto the stage and hugged him with all her strength.

"Wolfe! That was a beautiful story!"

He smiled. After returning from their honeymoon, he'd written it in three weeks. "I wrote it with all my heart. I've never felt so passionate about writing anything in my life. It still needs some work, though."

A man walked up and stuck out his hand to Wolfe. "Sir," he said, "I think that mighta just changed my life. Me and the wife, we were planning on moving next year. Going off to a bigger place. But I think we'll stay. Heck, it's where our roots are." He smiled warmly at Wolfe. "That was the most inspirational thing I think I've ever heard."

The man walked off, and Wolfe turned to Ainsley. "Inspirational," he said quietly and smiled. "Yeah, inspirational."

Alfred Tennison stood at the back of the room, his heart in a pitter-pattered mess of emotions as he listened to his favorite author read once again. He'd never heard Wolfe read with this kind of passion and emotion. In fact, in all the years he'd known him, he thought the guy usually did quite a dull reading of his own material.

He noticed the woman next to him sniffling up a storm. What was with all the boohooing this town did? The woman glanced up at him, noticing his stares. "I'm sorry. I get emotional when I hear such inspiring stories." She held out her hand. "Hi, I'm Lois. Lois Stepaphanolopolis. Oliver's cousin."

"Oh. Um, hi. Alfred Tennison."

Lois stared at Wolfe on the platform. "Tell you what. The guy ought to be writing inspirational fiction."

"Inspirational fiction? What's that?"

"Don't you know? It's fiction with meaning and purpose. Stories that give people hope for their future. Shows people God loves 'em."

"That's interesting. I've been an agent and an editor. Maybe I'll look into it. I'm sort of out of work."

The woman laughed. "Well, everybody gets along real well in that industry, and the writers, they're divinely inspired, hearing straight from God, so they don't need any editors to tell them what to do. When you're hearing from the Good Lord, there's hardly room for a mistake, you know! In fact, I hear the writers don't even take a bit of money for what they write—they just do it out of the goodness of their hearts—so I guess they wouldn't need any sort of agent. And I think the publishers donate all their earnings to missions or something like that."

Alfred sighed. "Oh. That's too bad."

Lois moved a step closer to Alfred. "You say you're an agent?"

"Was."

"I've been looking for an agent. I'm an actress, you see. I do the role of Sandra Dee in the most unforgettable way."

I could write another entire book thanking people in my life! With the help of so many, through time, talents, and prayers, I'm able to do this wonderful thing called writing. God knows each of you and your precious hearts.

I'd like to especially thank Dudley Delffs and Don Pape, two fabulously cool people who are an encouragement to me in so many different ways. Your confidence in my work and this crazy town called Skary has done more for my belief in myself than you'll ever know! And to everyone else at WaterBrook Press who works behind the scenes to make great things happen, thank you for helping to bring *Boo Who* to life and into the hands of readers!

For Janet Kobobel Grant, my agent, thank you for your wisdom, encouragement, and guidance.

Thanks so much to Sandy, Ron and Barb, and Bill, a group of people who pray for me, for those I work with, and for those who will read this book. Even through your own trials and tribulations in your lives, you remain faithful to pray, and I'm so thankful for every word of every prayer you have spoken. And for the wise words with which you minister to me.

Pastor Paul and WCC, the Flock That Rocks—having the greatest church in the world stand beside me on this adventure is priceless. Thank you for your continued support.

Thank you Sara Lewis, my superwoman baby-sitter, who keeps the kids entertained (not easy!) while their mom works. And thanks Mom and Dad for always being available to help me with the kids. Thank you to the rest of the family who encourage me on a daily basis and are my greatest promoters!

Without my husband, Sean, none of this would be possible. It seems his greatest desire in the world is to see my dreams come true. I

am the most blessed woman in the world, and I thank you for the unbelievable sacrifice you made in order for me to write this book. May God bless you beyond measure, in ways you never imagined! And to John-Caleb and Cate, thank you dear ones for letting Mommy go to the computer for long stretches of time!

To God be the glory, and thank You Father for the opportunity to serve You through writing novels. May each reader be blessed in a unique and special way by the power of Your Spirit.

Please visit me at my Web site:
www.renegutteridge.com